A NOVEL

GOATS

Mark Jude Poirier

talk miramax books

HYPERION

NEW YORK

ISBN 0-7868-8713-3

Designed by Christine Weathersbee

FIRST EDITION

10 9 8 7 6 5 4 3 2 1

For Matt, Chris, and Greg: The Three Scumbags

Thanks to Madison Smartt Bell, who pushed me into this, and to Diana Ossana, who pulled me out.

Friends who read through this in its various states should be thanked, too. They are Ben Neihart, Elaine Lander, Karla Kuban, Malinda McCollum, and Larry McMurtry. Thanks for your patience and suggestions.

The Maytag Corporation, the Johns Hopkins University, and the James Michener Society, with their generous fellowships, allowed me time to write this.

Hilary Bass, Jin Auh, and Sarah Chalfant: thanks for your tenacity and insight.

I was fortunate to come across a book called *Goatwalking* by Jim Corbett (Viking Press, New York, 1991), which answered many questions about trekking with goats in the Sonora desert. Of course, the goat characters in this novel don't always behave like real goats—this is fiction—but Mr. Corbett's book helped me to make them a little more realistic.

GOATS

ONE

Goat Man taught Ellis how to do bongs when Ellis was eleven. At the time, Goat Man was thirty-six, a veteran pot-smoker with a chunky voice and tarry lungs. Ellis's lungs were pink and fresh back then.

They sat at a swirly glass table in the pool house, with the air conditioner blasting away the white June sun streaming through the windows. The bong they used was fashioned from a tennis ball can and some aluminum foil.

"Put your thumb over that little hole and breathe deep," Goat Man said. "If the smoke's too hot, lift your face and take in some air."

Ellis raised the homemade bong to his mouth and inhaled. Goat Man held the lighter. Ellis had wanted to use the pipe he had always watched Goat Man smoke, the long wooden one that looked like an Indian's peace pipe, but Goat Man thought Ellis's first time should be gratifying, so he explained the cooling effect of the water and rigged up the bong. The bowl glowed as Ellis filled his lungs. The ice cubes clinked and the water bubbled pleasantly. There was no need for him to lift his face; the smoke was mild and sat comfortably in his chest. No coughing or burning, and it tasted like the desert smells after it rains.

"Now keep it in there as long as you can," Goat Man said.

Ellis remembered once holding his breath for almost two minutes in his friend's pool. He had held it longer than anyone else at the birthday party—way longer.

He felt the smoke in his lungs. It occupied space, pushed up against his ribs. He imagined it seeping slowly into the crinkles of his brain. He let it out in one big rush, followed by a few mildly grating coughs. The cloud that he created was bigger than he had imagined it would be, and thicker, too. Goat Man, nodding and clapping lightly, was barely visible from behind it.

"You're a pro," Goat Man said. "An expert."

"Thanks," Ellis said.

Two hits later, Ellis's face locked into a grin. He tried to knead it down with his fingers, but his cheeks and lips were rubber—they'd snap back into the stupid smile.

"Don't fight it," Goat Man said. "You're stoned, man. You're lucky, too. Most people don't get stoned their first time. Then again, most people don't start with my special hybrid."

Goat Man lived in their pool house, a small adobe bungalow with a kitchen and fashionably crude Mexican tile throughout. He tended to the landscaping—mostly Xeriscaping, just rocks and cacti arranged into groupings here and there. He also kept the pool clear and blue, and free of waterlogged rabbits and lizards. In exchange, Ellis's languid mother Wendy gave him food, the pool house, and a meager salary. She also provided him with a place to keep his goats.

The goat pen was just a token: slabs of dry, gray wood and snatched real-estate signs haphazardly nailed together. It was at the bottom of a hill below the house, edging a sandy arroyo that rarely filled with water. The goats could jump the fence, or squeeze through holes whenever they felt like it. It wasn't often that they felt like it, though. The four of them hung out, jumped on the roof of the adjoining shack, or kneeled in the shade of the faded green palo verde trees. A few times, after a squabble or a monsoon, one or two of the goats did stray. Ellis was the one who fetched them. Goat Man couldn't be bothered; he knew they'd be home sooner or later.

Once, when Ellis was in fifth grade, as he stepped off the school bus, he spied Freida, a large doe with swollen teats—the most majestic and conceited goat of the small herd. She was standing near the street sign bleating, almost crying. When she saw Ellis, she trotted up to him, hooves clicking and crunching the gravel on the hot asphalt. She nibbled on a loose strap that hung from Ellis's backpack as he patted her plump side.

Aubrey, a sixth grader who wore a bra and had a boyfriend who drove a big truck, swaggered up to Ellis and Freida. "My mother says Goat Man knows his goats in the biblical sense," she said.

"What?" Ellis asked.

"It means he fucks them, moron."

Ellis looked up at her: bangs sprayed into a tall shield, smears of blue eyeshadow, and a thick coat of wet lip gloss. She looked like a lady, a mean lady. He punched her right in the jaw.

Freida didn't like violence. She jumped around, squealing like a baby, teats swaying, leaking drops of milk. Aubrey was on top of Ellis, digging her press-on nails into his neck and periodically slapping his face, trying to get him to admit that he, too, knew the goats in the biblical sense. Ellis watched Aubrey's nostrils flare and contract as she yelled. He felt the gravel grinding into the back of his head.

"Say it. Say 'I, Ellis Whitman, fuck goats.'" She grabbed a pointy rock and scraped it across his forehead and down his cheek.

He never said it.

• • •

"Aubrey from down the street?" Goat Man asked later.

"Yeah, her," Ellis said.

Ellis lay on the diving board while Goat Man tended to his cuts and scrapes. "This one over your eye is kind of deep. What'd she use?"

"A rock," Ellis said. "A plain old rock."

"Why didn't you kick her ass?"

"Punched her first. That's all she deserved."

"I see," Goat Man said. He broke a piece from the aloe plant near the filter pump and dripped globs of it into Ellis's wound.

"Ouch!" Ellis yelled.

"This will make it heal faster."

"It stings."

"Ignore the pain," Goat Man said.

"How?"

"Try to think of the last song you heard today." Goat Man squeezed another glob of aloe into the cut and smoothed it with his thumb. "And play it over in your head."

Ellis thought about it. He hadn't heard any songs at school. The last song he had heard must have been an advertising jingle from the twenty minutes of TV he had watched that morning during breakfast. *Ace is the place with the helpful hardware man.* "The last song I heard was from an Ace Hardware commercial," Ellis said.

"That sucks," Goat Man said, "but I'm done with your wounds."

"Thanks, Goat Man."

The cut scabbed over in the shape of the letter C. Part of Ellis's eyebrow never grew back.

TWO

On the breezy September evening preceding fourteen-year-old Ellis's departure for boarding school, Goat Man treated him to his most savory domestic. The plant was deep maroon, the color of drying blood, with a waxy shine and sticky buds that oozed when they were snipped.

Goat Man and Ellis were sprawled around the pool house, smoking from the big peace pipe. Peter Tosh wailed on the stereo: "Ketchy, ketchy, shuby, shuby . . ."

"I haven't been this high this quick since those honey blunts last summer," Ellis said. "This hybrid rules."

"Rules," Goat Man said.

After the third bowl, the room took on fiery hues for Ellis, like he was looking through a bottle of Juicy Red Hawaiian Punch with the Styrofoam label peeled off. Goat Man lounged on the Navajo rug and stared, almost hypnotized, at the ceiling fan. The fan wasn't on. Neither said anything.

Later, they wandered into the main house. They sat around the kitchen table in oversize pigskin chairs—handmade *equipales*—smoking more, and shoveling two-pound Sonoran-style burritos into their mouths, sauce dripping from their chins.

"My roommate better be cool," Ellis said.

"Might be," Goat Man said. "At least you know he's smart."

"Probably some computer hacker with bad breath."

"Maybe," Goat Man said. "Or maybe he's a rich wastoid with the best weed on the East Coast."

Ellis finished his burrito and fixed himself a bowl of vanilla ice cream topped with peanut butter chips. "I'll be farting up a storm tomorrow on the plane," he said.

"Make me one of those," Goat Man said. He pointed at the ice cream with his pipe.

Ellis took one bite and was overwhelmed by the sugar. He handed it to Goat Man. "Here," he said. "Too sweet."

"All packed?"

"Yesterday," Ellis said. "And the day before."

"I'll give you a bag of choice buds to stuff in your underwear tomorrow morning," Goat Man said, spooning ice cream into his mouth.

"You have to mail some to me, too. You promised."

"Of course," Goat Man said. "Of course."

Wendy's latest house shoes, mules with plastic daisies fastened to the tops, made slap noises on the tiles, so Ellis and Goat Man had fair warning before she appeared. This time, she poked her head through the swinging door and said, "Ooh" in a baby voice. "Ooh."

"What?" Ellis said to her.

"Just sad, that's all," she said. "My boy's leaving me tomorrow."

"It's not like I'm going to war."

"He'll live," Goat Man said. Salsa and melted ice cream clung to his scraggly beard. "And you'll still have me."

Wendy stood in the doorway, propping the door open with her foot and rocking dreamily, bumping her shoulders on either side of the jamb. "It's not too late, Ellis," she said. "They loved you at Green Fields."

In April, she and Ellis had visited the small country day school on the west side of Tucson. The school was casual and progressive—no halls, just small, white adobe buildings, outdoor lockers with no locks, and relaxed-looking students. Some sported blue or purple hair and loafed around campus barefoot. They carried fat, impressive textbooks: calculus, physics, statistics. The dirt parking lot was crowded with glossy, top-dollar European sedans parked next to junky pickups and old Volvo station wagons. Each vehicle was marked with its own collection of punk or ska band stickers.

Ellis had liked Green Fields—the art dome built by hippies in the early seventies, the library where everyone talked freely, the smell of horses and cut grass—but not enough to stay in Tucson.

Looking over the table messed with burrito plops, dope twigs, and melted ice cream, he knew he was doing the right thing by leaving.

He had gone through a stack of bills and forms with Wendy earlier that week, showing her how he was paying hundreds of dollars to the electric company in advance, and guiding her through an insurance claim with the deliberation of a patient kindergarten teacher. Money wasn't the problem—she just didn't pay bills. She never had. Ellis had taken care of them since age ten when the electricity was turned off in the middle of a 110-degree July.

If it didn't work out this year at boarding school, he could always dye his hair blue and go to Green Fields next fall.

"I'll be back at Thanksgiving," he told his mother. "Just keep an eye on the mail, so I don't come back to a stack of new problems."

"You don't get it, do you?" Wendy said. "I'll miss you." She walked over and started working Ellis's brush cut like a crystal ball. She rested her chin on his shoulder and lightly kissed his cheek.

"I get it," Ellis said, watching Goat Man slurp the melted ice cream like a child eating soup.

"I'll miss you, too," Goat Man said. "A lot."

THREE

"**M**y brother went here last year—now he goes to Yale—and he told me that a freshman visited the doctor with a sore asshole and it turned out that his roommate was knocking him out with colorform at night and butt-raping him," Barney said.

"*Chloro*form," Ellis said.

"Isn't that sick?"

"Guess so," Ellis said. "I heard that story before, though, only it was at some college in California." He traced the scar on his forehead with his thumb, thinking about the year ahead with Barney as his roommate, then began to slowly unpack his suitcases. Because of his brother, Barney seemed to feel obliged to inform Ellis about all the details of life at Gates Academy. So far, Ellis was unimpressed. Barney didn't get high, Ellis could tell.

Before Ellis had arrived, Barney had decorated the room with academic awards, science fair ribbons, and photos of his Boy Scout troop. Above the dresser on a shelf that appeared to be constructed just for it, sat an ostentatious golden trophy: *Barnabus Cannel, Churchill Jr. High Citizenship Award*. All Ellis had brought to hang on the wall was a *High Times* calendar and a Bob Marley postcard. He tacked the calendar to the inside of the closet door. September featured a photograph of three grinning Rastafarians playing in their bountiful harvest. One guy had buds the size of carrots mussed into his thick dreadlocks.

Instead of listening to Barney, Ellis peered out the window at the dense woods. He'd have to hike in there to spark up until he could figure out something better. He felt around in his suitcase for the sock where he had stashed his weed.

FOUR

"**I** can't believe someone got a ninety-seven. I got a seventy-one, a C minus. You saw me, I studied my balls off," Barney said. "Maybe you don't remember, bong boy."

"I remember your stupid-ass flash cards with all the kings' names on them," Ellis said.

"My mother's gonna kill me this weekend. I'll probably be down to a C plus in history."

"You'll live," Ellis said. Eight weeks had passed, and he was used to Barney's whining. He looked out the window at the prematurely naked woods. Hundreds of small black birds congregated on the elm closest to the dorm, refoliating it with darkness.

"What'd you get?" Barney asked.

"A ninety-seven," Ellis said. There was no use in keeping a secret from Barney; he would just snoop anyway.

"You suck," Barney said. "Fire up that bong, would you?"

"No," Ellis said. "You got a seventy-one, you don't deserve it." Ellis had only a few bowls' worth of shake anyway, and he wasn't about to let Barney cough it all away. "And I don't think I want to go to D.C." Instead of joining Barney at his home in Washington, he hoped to spend the long Columbus Day weekend sleeping and watching the antiquated TV that the dorm monitor rolled into the common room on weekends. Sycophants in the dorm hung posters in the halls: *TV Party! Every Saturday and Sunday noon till ? Movies and snacks!* Ellis was curious to see who went to these bullshit TV parties. And he kind of wanted to watch TV, anyway. He hadn't since he left Tucson, and he missed lazy, mindless afternoons when hours slipped by and disappeared into nowhere. Nothing to show for those hours. Nothing.

He needed a break from Barney and academics. He spent most of his time at Gates doing homework, or helping Barney do his.

"Just come," Barney said. "We can walk into Georgetown." Barney twirled a pencil in his fingers and looked to Ellis hopefully. "You're just gonna sit around here waiting for pot in the mail that probably won't come."

"It'll come."

"Goat Man's probably too stoned to remember."

"Shut up."

"Why do you worship him?" Barney said. "He's just some dope-smoker who walks around the desert with goats like some idiot in the Bible."

"You're such a fucking moron sometimes," Ellis said. "Why do you worship your brother, who all the seniors say was the biggest brown-noser to ever graduate from Gates?"

"At least my brother goes to Yale. All Goat Man does is get high and chase goats around."

"Just shut up. I'd like to get into how people seek enlightenment and fulfillment in different ways, but you're too fucking stupid to understand."

A few days later, when Barney said, "My mom's way less of a bitch when I have friends over," Ellis knew he should go. Ellis could tell Barney was scared of his own mother—or at least hated her. Barney never called her unless he absolutely needed money or needed to discuss travel arrangements. Ellis doubted they had spoken more than three times since school started. Barney hadn't hung any photos of her around the room. He had hung three of his brother Todd, each of which was neatly framed.

Ellis had tacked two photos of Wendy to his cork board. One was old and yellowed, and featured Wendy in her hippie days: long, straight hair and huge hoop earrings. The other was taken at Halloween when she dressed like a cowgirl in denim, gingham, and a big hat. Ellis told Barney that was how all people in Tucson dressed.

So they left Gates Wednesday night to spend the short break at Barney's mom's Watergate apartment.

Barney's mother was tranquilized but still managed to be surly. She spoke of Ellis in the third person, even when he was standing right next to her: "Tell your friend that he'll have to sleep on the pull-out sofa in the guest room. I don't want him messing up the bed." Each time she appeared, ducking in and out from the vast marble bathroom, she wore a long, shockingly white robe, high-heeled red sandals, and a turban of sorts. Barney had proudly told Ellis how she juggled doctors, tricking each of them into giving her more drugs: "Valium, Halcion, and new ones like Ambien and BuSpar."

The first afternoon, Ellis and Barney sat on her balcony, swigging her whiskey and looking into the microworld of Watergate: a round swimming pool, a tiny Safeway, a drugstore, a liquor store, a dry cleaners. No one who lived there ever had to leave the giant doughnut.

The prickly Astroturf on the balcony made Ellis's legs itch, so he got up, sat in a faded director's chair. He peered over the railing at the old, introverted snobs milling around below. "Why would your mother live here?" he asked.

"All her friends do," Barney said.

"I know it's historical and exclusive, but it kind of blows."

"I know," Barney said. He pushed his haylike bangs to the side. "As soon as her masseuse leaves, I'll get money from her, and we'll walk over to Georgetown."

Ellis took a healthy swig from the Cutty Sark. It tasted rancid, but it was starting to kick in. He was numb behind his forehead, and his face was sweating in the cool October breezes that swept up from below. He wondered if Goat Man had gotten back from his trek yet, and why he hadn't mailed the herb he had promised. He mused aloud about how nice it would be to do bong hits up on the balcony.

"We could buy some at Malcolm X Park," Barney said. "My brother bought some there once. I went with him."

The streets of Georgetown overwhelmed Ellis at first. Too crowded, like Vegas or Disneyland. They walked up Wisconsin Avenue, passing pubs, restaurants, and the same stores from every mall Ellis had ever seen. Barney's eyes were bright and his mouth agape. Ellis couldn't understand the attraction, the reputation for fun that Georgetown held among his classmates back at Gates. "Everyone is partying, and it's not even dark yet," Barney said.

"Don't use *party* as a verb," Ellis said.

"What?"

"Forget it." A turquoise-and-peach-trimmed store across the

street, Santa Fe Today, caught Ellis's eye. "We have to go there," he said.

"Why?" Barney asked.

Ellis just walked over to the store, cutting through honking traffic. They went inside and looked at all the overpriced wares from Mexico: blankets, baskets, sombreros, dried chili peppers, rustically constructed furniture.

A saleswoman wearing a starched white shirt, pressed jeans, and shined lizard-skin cowboy boots pattered over to them. "We're about to close, so if there's anything I can help you find?"

"Is Frank Whitman here?" Ellis asked.

"No, he only comes down here once a month," the woman said. "Do you want to speak to Judy? She's the manager."

"No," Ellis said. "Thanks." He and Barney left the store. A string of rusted cowbells punctuated their exit.

Even though it was the first time he had laid eyes on it, Ellis hated Santa Fe Today, his father's store. His father also owned one in Manhattan and another in Boston. He hated Judy the manager, too. His father had brought her along on a buying trip to Tucson one summer. The other managers and buyers had accompanied him as well, but Judy was the worst. Her lips were painted huge, and her poorly bleached hair never moved. She flagrantly flirted with his father, grabbing him on the knee all during lunch, and laughing like a fool. Her teeth were wide, like the goats', but outrageously white in contrast to her overly tanned skin. By the time dessert arrived—strawberries and cream—it was clear to Ellis that his father was fucking Judy. Judy fed Ellis's dad the strawberries, and Ellis's dad sucked her fingers. Ellis had wanted to tell his father to stop, to stop being such a pig, but he kept quiet and watched the other lunch guests whispering and blushing.

That lunch, two years earlier, was the last time he had seen his father. He and his mother rarely spoke of him, but when they did, his name was Fucker Frank.

"My mom bought a couch in there once. It's that couch in the living room, under the bookshelves." Barney said.

"Oh," Ellis said.

The boys walked down to M Street and took a left, pushing through throngs of shoppers and tourists. Barney had raved about a bar down there called the Charing Cross, where teenagers without I.D.s congregated.

"We'll go in separately," Barney said. "Although, maybe we should go in together. You look old enough."

Ellis did look old enough. At fourteen, he was already six feet tall, and he wore his blond hair short like most generic college guys in Georgetown. "Why don't you buy a baseball cap? It'll make you look older," Ellis told Barney.

They went inside a sporting goods store, and Barney chose a Yale cap: navy blue with a felt Y on the front. He worked the bill of his new cap, bending it until it held a well-used look. He attempted a more mature posture as they walked toward the bar, pushing out his chest and cocking his chin upward.

There was a short line of college and high-school kids outside. The talk revolved around fake I.D.s and previous times at the Charing Cross—the usual puking episodes and drunken, semi-furtive sexual encounters in the back room behind the jukebox.

"That blond chick in the front is hot," Barney whispered.

"Her boyfriend's gigantic," Ellis said. The guy had a cruel neck, and shoulders twice as broad as Barney's.

"I'll give her the eye."

"What?"

"The eye." Barney began to gaze longingly at the girl. His eyes bugged.

To Ellis, Barney looked like he was constipated. "Don't," Ellis told Barney. "You look like you're taking a dump."

Barney continued, but the girl's boyfriend, a hammerhead with a flattop and a purple Gonzaga Football jacket, noticed him before the girl did. "Got a problem?" the guy said.

"No problem," Barney told him, grinning stupidly. "She'll be mine before the night's over," he whispered to Ellis.

"What'd you say?" the football player asked, heaving toward Barney.

"Nothing."

"You said something, you little shit." He grabbed Barney by the sweater.

"I swear, I didn't say anything."

"Yes, you did, you whispered something to him." The guy looked to Ellis.

"He said he felt nauseated." Ellis told the guy. "We've been drinking Cutty Sark all day."

The girl walked back to them. "It's our turn to get in. Come on." She grabbed the football player by his jacket and tugged him toward the door. "Come on."

He released Barney and issued a warning: "I better not see your ass anymore tonight." He followed his girlfriend into the bar.

"This place sucks, anyway," Barney said, straightening his collar. "It's all high-school kids."

"You're so lucky, Barney."

"Let's go to Malcolm X Park."

"Pay the man," Barney said as he jumped out of the cab. Leaving Ellis to pay the cab fare every time was one of Barney's obnoxious attempts at urbanity. It wasn't worth the money to give Barney the satisfaction of knowing how annoying it was, so Ellis dutifully paid. From Georgetown to Malcolm X Park was only five bucks anyway.

"I'll do all the talking," Barney told Ellis as they hurried across wet grass and sparkling, glass-covered asphalt. "And try to look psycho so no one bothers you."

They walked over to a parking lot next to a spray-painted playground. "This is where my brother bought it before," Barney said. "I remember."

"Do what you have to," Ellis said.

Barney walked up to a fat man who wore a painter's cap, a green bomber jacket, and baggy jeans. The man was leaning up against a boatlike American sedan, dull white with maroon trim. Ellis could see a swarthy woman asleep in the car, her head tilted back over the front seat and her mouth open. He hoped she was only asleep.

"We need to buy," Barney told the man.

"Buy what?" the man asked, looking around.

"Pot. We need to buy pot."

"You think just because I'm black, I sell drugs?" In fact, the man was white—light brown hair poking out from under his cap, blue-gray eyes, even in the deadened light. He grabbed Barney by his sweater, the same way the football player had done earlier, and pulled him close to his face.

"No . . . I mean, no . . . I'm sorry," Barney said.

"He didn't mean anything," Ellis said. "We don't need any pot."

"You're in luck." The man grinned and released Barney. "Step into my office." He opened the back door of his car and guided Barney inside. "You, too," he said to Ellis. "Get on in."

The three of them sat in the back on a loud vinyl seat, the man between Barney and Ellis. The car smelled like the canned cherry pie filling that they sometimes slapped down on the boys' trays and called dessert back at Gates. A seat-belt buckle dug into Ellis's back, but he didn't dare squirm.

The woman woke up and turned around. "Three boys in the back. I like it," she said. Her lipstick trailed off her mouth and up her cheek on one side like half a clown's smile. "Shut that door, boy number three," she told Ellis.

"You're a stupid fuck, and you're a stupid fuck," the man said to Barney and Ellis as soon as the door slammed. The man produced a small silver gun, a lady's gun, from the pocket of his bomber jacket, and pressed it into Barney's ear. He tossed his painter's cap at the dash. "I feel like a treat," he said, leaning over Ellis to lock the door, keeping the gun in Barney's ear with his other hand. Ellis could smell the man's pine-scented cologne.

The woman in the front seat chattered and bobbed like a caged monkey. "Treat time, treat time . . ." she said.

The man began to lick Barney's ear around the barrel of the gun. He ran his tongue down Barney's neck and then up to his chin. He took off Barney's cap and fit it on his own head—backwards. Barney's face was side-pressed against the window, his eyes white and zigzagging.

Ellis's head buzzed. This was like a generic dream. Vile things were happening and Ellis's arms and legs were dead, lifeless, like bags of dirt.

"Kiss me," the man said, but Barney just whimpered and shook. "Kiss me or I'll pull it, I'll pull the trigger and send your brains to Baltimore."

"You better kiss boy number two, boy number one," the woman said. "He'll do it, he'll shoot your brains out. I seen him. He's a good kisser." She made puckering noises that were both comical and sickening. "Treat time, treat time . . ."

"Open your mouth, dumb fuck," the man said.

Barney obeyed, opening his mouth like he was at the dentist.

Ellis looked away, then stared straight ahead through the smudged, fogged windshield at a swing set bathed in yellow light from a tilted street lamp. He tried to think of all the songs he had heard that day—spastic Fishbone's "Ma and Pa" in the CD store, the New Age flutey number in Santa Fe Today. The Spanish one in the cab had been the last: "*Tócame, tócame por favor . . .*" But now all he heard were the man's kisses: wet smacks and slurps like the dubbed-in exaggerated ones on soap operas.

"Don't look, don't none of you look, or I'll do it," the man said. "I'll blow his head off."

"You boys better not look," the woman said. She playfully covered her eyes with her purse like peek-a-boo.

Ellis couldn't have looked anyway. He didn't want to see Barney's wide, desperate eyes again.

Just as the man unzipped his trousers and flopped out his dick, Ellis heard a knock on the window by his head and a woman's deep voice: "You all here to party?" When Ellis looked at her, he saw her grin, the gummy gaps, and her crazy, loose eyes. "Looking to party?" She knocked on the window harder with her palm, smudged it, and tried the door handle.

With no thought, Ellis unlocked the door, and she opened it. She leaned her head inside. Her hair, matted and dreaded, smelled like concentrated piss. "Looking to party?" she repeated.

"Get the hell out, bitch," the man yelled. He tucked the gun back into his jacket, left his dick out.

"What you doing with these boys?" she said.

Ellis pushed by her, touched her crusty sleeve, humming that dumb song from the cab: "*Tócame, tócame por favor . . .*"

Barney yelped, and Ellis turned around. "Come on, Barney."

The woman in the front seat started the car, revved the engine.

The crazy woman outside the car stepped back and slammed the door. "Motherfucking fat . . ." she mumbled.

Barney tumbled out his door, and the car squealed away.

The woman turned to Ellis. "You boys looking to party?" she asked.

"No," Ellis said. "We're not looking to party." He walked over to Barney, who was on his hands and knees, staring at the asphalt.

"You're not gonna tell anyone?" Barney said, not moving, not looking up at Ellis. "You better not."

"I won't. Why would I?" Ellis said. "I don't suppose you saw their front license plate? I looked at the back, but they didn't have one there."

"You better not tell anyone."

"I won't. I promise." Ellis said, crouching down. "Are you okay? Can you get up?" Barney didn't say anything, so Ellis continued: "I think that gun was a toy, and I think—"

"You better not tell." Barney began to spit and retch.

"Maybe she saw the license plate," Ellis said. But when he turned to look at the crazy woman, she was gone.

FIVE

Goat Man trekked mostly after dark. It was night three. One or two more to go before reaching the border. A practice run; nothing new, only it had just rained heavily for a few days, so many of the arroyos were filled, and the saturated desert flora took on brighter hues—even at night.

He wanted his three traveling goats to tame their aversion to water. Freida, a white-and-black speckled Nubian-Alpine, one of two does, was so afraid of water that she panicked at the sight of a puddle, shaking her head, jumping nervously. That would change. He'd teach her and Gigi and Lance to wade through water up to their necks. He'd show them how to swim if need be.

He could tell by the distance to the dark Chiricahua range that he and his goats were making good time—better time than the last trip. The nearly full moon, obscured only slightly by twin sketchy clouds, illuminated the landscape, but Goat Man's field of vision had diminished somewhat over the years. Religious pot smoking and squinting in the sun could do that. He'd buy new sunglasses when he returned to Tucson, and this time he wouldn't lose them like he always did.

He needed his pipe during night treks. The smoke kept the insects away. As he approached wet washes or small creeks, he thought he could actually see the bugs circumnavigating his face. The pipe, the bowl hanging about six inches in front of him, was his guide. He'd follow the orange glow to the border, and whenever he felt like he needed more guidance, he'd inhale and be reassured by the light.

The goats needed the pipe as well. If they strayed and felt like returning to Goat Man, they'd follow the rich scent back to him. Whenever Goat Man noticed one of the goats was missing, he'd smoke more vigorously and quickly suck through a generous bowl of hybrid, blowing clouds in every direction.

Goat Man drank only milk from Freida and Gigi during the trek. That was almost all he needed. He milked them both, shooting the milk into a tin cup and drinking it right then: warm and sour, but filling and salubrious. He supplemented his diet with vitamin C and minerals, tablets he kept in a small leather pouch that hung on a shoelace around his neck. He had read up on goat trekking, nutrition, what he needed to do for optimum energy and progress. Neither of the does minded the milking in the slightest; in fact, they often rubbed up against Goat Man's legs when their teats became tumid and cumbersome.

The goats didn't need water. They took all they required from the plants they constantly nibbled: filaree, patata, cat-claw, wild mustard, staghorn cholla fruit. Even during summer treks, the goats refused water. Only once, in August, when Goat Man noticed Freida's urine was as dark as coffee, did he see her drink water. She drank from an algae-laden puddle a few weeks after the final monsoon of that season.

Now Lance was distracted and nervous. He strayed, and Gigi

and Freida followed. Goat Man sucked his pipe and hummed Otis Redding's "Respect." His griff had been good that month, gooey buds with tiny red hairs that stuck when he pressed them against the windows of the pool house—plus a sweeter, thicker smoke than the previous harvest. He felt bad for not having sent it to Ellis at school, but he had no choice.

He had used a trick he learned from his cousin. He pressed fresh buds into greeting cards and ironed the cards flat. He stuffed the cards in envelopes and brought them to the print shop on Fourth Avenue to be laminated. Then he put them all in a reinforced manila envelope.

"I know you, and if you're trying to mail what I think you're trying to mail, I wouldn't," Jonathan had warned. Jonathan was the mail carrier for the neighborhood. He wore tie-dyed socks with his official-looking black walking shoes.

"What do you mean?"

"The U.S. Mail is the worst way to get it to him. Might as well just drive out to the prison and check yourself in."

"Oh," Goat Man said. "I thought after I gave the packages to you, I was home free." Jonathan had often joined Goat Man for hits of hybrid in the pool house.

"Take this back. Smoke it yourself. Ellis can get some more over Christmas." Jonathan handed the big envelope back to Goat Man. "It's almost November already. He'll be home before you know it."

Jonathan turned around at the end of the driveway. "It's legal to send mushroom spores, though—any type, I think!" he yelled. "I'm sorry, I really am."

Goat Man waved. He returned to the pool house and wrote Ellis a note:

I hope things are OK with you. Things are good here. I'm bored though. Jonathan says I shouldn't mail any hybrid but I'll think of a way or just risk it if you're desperate. Are you? Your mom seems OK. The goats are good. I miss you. See you on turkey day.

Later, Goat Man

SIX

Before he had time to find Lance and the two does, the pink morning light was creeping over the desert. Goat Man used Lance as the pack-goat. With Lance off somewhere, he had no tent to set up or any other supplies, only his pipe and a few buds. He climbed a ridge and looked around the desert. He saw a small stream gleam silver in the south. Perfect for teaching the goats about water. The early sun and the bowls of dope changed everything's color. Some of the mesquite bushes and palo verdes were actually green, and the saguaros looked lavender, velvety.

He discovered the three goats. They were kneeling on an easy-sloped hill just above a small canyon recently carved in the earth by the storms. He joined them, clearing away a few rocks and setting up his two-man tent.

The morning light pushed through the nylon, making everything inside the tent glow orange. After he unrolled his sleeping bag, Goat Man quickly fell asleep.

It was about two in the afternoon when Goat Man woke. The sun hung slightly to the west, pressing on his drowsy eyes. He packed his tent and shot milk from both Gigi and Freida into the cup. From the look of her red, flaccid teats, Lance had probably been nursing from Gigi during Goat Man's sleep. He'd have to watch for that. He attached leather leashes to the three of them, and he walked south, toward the stream.

As they approached the water, climbing over black and gray stones and kicking through knee-high saltbush, the goats began to bleat in protest. Freida started the ruckus, and the other two chimed in. When Goat Man tied Gigi and Freida to a cottonwood, they screamed.

"There's nothing to gripe about."

Goat Man and Lance trotted toward the stream.

At the edge, Goat Man took off his hiking boots and socks. Lance kept the leash taut, pulling away from the trickling stream. Goat Man waded in the cool, ankle-deep water to the middle, about five feet from the bank. He tugged the leash, but Lance wouldn't budge from his spot on a water-smoothed rock. "Come on, man." Lance wouldn't even look at Goat Man. Finally, when Goat Man fully leaned into his tug, the link attaching the leash to the collar snapped. Lance ran away, and Goat Man landed ass-first in the cold water.

Wetback. That's what they had first called him: Wetback. But he liked it. In the days of hotrods and headbands, back when women had hips, Goat Man was known as Wetback. As it became a term of endearment, his friends altered it to *WB*, then to *Web* and finally, by senior year at St. Michael's High in Spencertown, Illinois, to *Webster*. Goat Man had preferred *Wetback*.

Goat Man wasn't Mexican, Mexican-American, or Chicano. He wasn't Hispanic or even vaguely Latino. His mother was of Irish decent and his father, Italian. He did have a set of half-Mexican cousins, and in tenth grade, after spending the summer down in Texas with them—eating strange new food and picking up a little Spanish—Goat Man began to affect a Mexican accent and slick his dark hair back with pomade.

Of course, the nuns and the brothers at St. Michael's called Goat Man by his birth name—Stephen Luke Cagliano—blowing his image every morning when attendance was taken. He told people to call him Javier, and when they weren't calling him Wetback or Webster, his friends did. Javier always had the weed, and it was stupid to offend the man with the weed. Sometimes Goat Man referred to himself as "Vato Loco."

On Saturdays, Goat Man and his friends would pile into jacked-up Novas and Chargers and cruise, looking for a fox or a high, their eyes barely above the dash, ducking from cops, looking mellow. They rarely found foxes; mostly they found highs. Goat Man's cousin Jesús in El Paso kept half the teenage population of Spencertown stoned on a regular basis.

The weed arrived by mail about twice a month, always in dolls, packed inside their hollow heads. They were cheap dolls, plastic jobs from just across the border in Juárez, with blinking eyes that stuck in mid-blink. They had perfectly stoned, half-asleep expressions. Goat Man saved these doll heads. He nailed them to a tree about twenty yards into the woods behind his house, creating a hideous totem pole of cracked, plastic baby faces that became legendary among the kids in his neighborhood. Some said it was the site of an illegal abortion operation, with Goat Man performing them on anyone with thirty dollars. The other rumor spread by the local kids was that Goat Man was a leftover lunatic freak, and each doll head represented one of Charles Manson's victims.

When people bought weed from him, he made them deal in his terminology: "Vato Loco says a full baby head is one hundred, a half head, fifty, man." It was Mexican ditch weed, dry and brown like pencil-sharpener waste by the time it hit Illinois. But it was often all that was available in their corner of the Midwest.

Goat Man invested his profits in his wheels: a sky-blue AMC Pacer. He bought it his senior year, new, right off the lot. "It's all glass, man. Like a fishtank." He had it lowered, and saved for mag wheels. "Speedy Chicano" was airbrushed on the hood. He lost his virginity in the Pacer after a round of bong hits, and it was the Pacer that he drove out to the University of Arizona when he started that fall.

The Pacer finally died in 1988. Besides, it had been a joke for years, and Goat Man knew it. He bought a used Jetta then, which is what he drove for the next twelve years. The graduating sorority girl who sold him the Jetta told him it would last him forever, and so far she was right.

Goat Man had wanted to go to the University of Texas at El Paso and live with his cousins, but he wasn't admitted. The closest university to Texas that had accepted him was the University of Arizona. He figured he'd find *cholos* to hang with in Tucson, a *barrio* to call his home. Besides, Tucson wasn't too far from El Paso.

SEVEN

Goat Man dried his feet on his poncho, pulled his socks on, and wormed into his boots.

Lance wouldn't stray far, and Freida and Gigi deserved to remain tethered for a while longer. He hiked up a small mound of soft red rock, feeling the flex in his calves, and had a look around.

He gazed over a valley of sparse, sandy chaparral that edged a ranch. Too far west, he thought. He'd have to redirect and move southeasterly to avoid the ranches. He couldn't be seen, not even by hermetic ranch hands or wandering cowboys.

Freida and Gigi were angry with him when he returned to their tree. He let them scream as he untied them. None of them drifted from the afternoon shade. Goat Man fired up his pipe, and the goats nibbled at the previously unreachable shoots of weeds. This is how I was meant to travel, Goat Man thought. Lazy meandering. No plans. No agenda. He washed away the familiar burnt herbal coating in his mouth and throat with a few tin cups of Freida's milk. Lance returned before dark, lounging next to him and farting loudly every few minutes.

A priest back in Spencertown had once told Goat Man that humans required social interaction to survive. Goat Man didn't accept the priest's statement—unless his definition of social interaction included arguing with goats. He did miss Ellis, though. Especially in the afternoons when they had normally hung out together. Ellis would return from school, and sometimes they'd get high. Ellis would ask Goat Man about girls and music and drugs, and they'd talk or splash around in the pool until dinner. Every afternoon had been like that.

EIGHT

The boys sat in the computer lab, staring at empty screens. Neither of them ever got e-mail. It didn't matter, anyway. They weren't allowed to have computers in their dorm rooms, so even if someone sent them a good pornographic image, they had nowhere private where they could look at it. There was a rumor that the reason why the no-computers-in-dorm-rooms rule had been instated was that two juniors last year were running a cyber casino. Another rumor was that a former math teacher was caught by the FBI with hundreds of downloaded images of nude boys from the Netherlands. The only Internet access on campus now was in the library, where the librarian stood watch over every terminal.

"I haven't been high for twenty-seven days," Ellis whispered. "No wonder I'm doing so shitty in history."

"Eighty-six isn't shitty," Barney said. "What's your average in there now, like a ninety-five?"

"I don't know. You're the one tracking my grades."

"Told you Goat Man wouldn't send it," Barney said. "After you smoke that much weed, it has to affect your brain."

"Goat Man is one of the smartest guys I know," Ellis said. "He knows more about goats and the desert than anyone."

"And pot," Barney whispered.

"And pot," Ellis said. "He's a botanist."

"Other people here get stoned, you know."

"I know," Ellis said. "I'll sit next to Stan at dinner tonight and see what I can weasel out of him."

"He's a definite stoner," Barney said, "an addict."

"It's impossible to be addicted to pot. It's not addictive."

On Sundays and Thursdays, dinner at Gates was somewhat formal. The boys had to adhere to the dress code of the rest of the school day: a blue blazer, gray flannel trousers or khakis, a rep tie, and a white shirt. Few boys objected to the formalities of Sunday and Thursday dinners because Minnie, an attractive young woman from the town, served them on those nights. She was the youngest woman on campus, aside from Ms. Glenfield, a mustachioed geometry teacher whom the boys had dismissed as a lesbian. Three other women, all much older, all looking like mechanics in drag, served the boys as well, and arguments would ensue as to which table Minnie served last time.

Ellis was eleven for nineteen in having Minnie serve his table. He had the best record in the ninth grade. Once, she had even put her hand on Ellis's shoulder when she asked if he wanted more water. He had seen her freckled cheeks and sage green eyes up close. He knew her light brown hair smelled like strawberry candy, and that she sprinkled herself with baby powder. Her elegantly thin nose wasn't too small or generic like the ones on all Wendy's plastic-surgeried friends; its tip was adorned with a faint, shallow dimple. Her lips were full, but not fat-looking. Best was her almost-constant expression—like she was stifling a laugh, like she knew something funny or embarrassing about each boy at the table. She could give Ellis the sickeningly pleasant loopy feeling in his stomach just by setting silverware in his presence.

It had gotten to the point where four or five other freshmen followed Ellis around and sat at the table where he sat. The upperclassmen didn't seem to care as much about Minnie.

Because it was Tuesday, Ellis didn't have to worry about being tailed around the dining room by Minnie fans. On the informal days, dinner was conducted buffet-style: no servers, so Minnie stayed in the kitchen. No ties required. And the food was shittier on informal days.

Stan was sitting by himself in the corner near the condiments. His hair was as long as was legal at Gates—level with the chin. Blazing tie-dye colors peeked out from under the collar of his oxford shirt, and a leather strap with crystals and swirly ceramic beads choked his neck.

"Hey, Stan," Ellis said. He placed his tray across from Stan's and sat down. "Mind if I sit here?"

"Nope." He tucked his hair behind his ears.

"I hate this shit." Ellis poked his fork into the watery veal cutlet on his plate and held it up like a specimen. "I might give up meat altogether."

"I love meat," Stan said. "I'll eat it if you don't want it."

"Haven't you heard what they do to veal calves?"

"I don't give a shit, man," Stan said. "Cows are stupid as hell."

Ellis slapped the soggy cutlet on Stan's plate. Ellis had actually wanted it. He felt foiled when he learned Stan didn't give a shit about cows. Ellis was hungry and didn't give a shit about cows, either. Not a big shit, anyway. Stan was right, he thought, cows are stupid, much stupider than goats. He'd seen cows at the Pima County Fair. They stared stupidly and sniffed each other's butts. Now he watched as Stan shoveled gray morsels into his mouth.

"This school blows," Ellis said.

"You mean the classes? Algebra sucks," Stan said. Veal juice had puddled on his plate.

"The whole atmosphere sucks. No one here has any fun."

"I guess," Stan said, before he forked the last piece of veal into his mouth.

"I wish I knew someone who got stoned."

"I wish we were near a McDonald's," Stan said. "Bye, dude." He wiped his chin on his sleeve, picked up his tray, and walked off.

"Damn," Ellis whispered.

After dinner, Barney asked Ellis if he had had any luck with Stan. Barney sat with his feet on his desk and his hands behind his head.

"Nope. Stan's a carnivorous bastard." Ellis belly-flopped onto his bed and rolled over to face Barney. He shook off his shoes, tan bucks.

"What?"

"Forget it. Tomorrow, after your crew practice, you want to walk to Peterson's and try for beer?"

Barney swiveled around, kicking a few papers onto the floor. "That wouldn't give us much time to drink it," he said. "I don't get out of practice until after six."

"We'll drink some on the way back and finish it here after lights out. We'll get a twelver. My treat."

"Okay," Barney said. "Will you help me with this algebra again?" Barney collected the papers from the floor and opened his book. He flipped through the pages. "Completing the square is impossible."

"I gotta call my mom first," Ellis said. "I'll be back in a second."

The machine picked up, and he left a message: "Wendy, I was thinking that maybe you should mail some money to the car insurance company. Your policy is almost up and . . ."

The boathouse reeked of mildew and old canvas, but Ellis sort of liked it. The smells carried vivid memories of camping with his parents and Goat Man in an old green army tent. Around the campfire, his dad had told creepy stories of crazy men with metal hooks for hands, and baby-smothering cats that would eat their victims' little faces. Frank put his hand in front of the flashlight and cast huge shadows on the top of the tent, moaning, "The hand, the hand . . ." He used a monster voice that made Ellis laugh nervously and want to pee. Wendy yelled at Frank, "This is too much for Ellis, you bastard!" She hugged Ellis, brought his head to her shoulder, smoothed his hair.

But Ellis wasn't scared that night, sleeping between his parents with Goat Man stretched at his feet. He felt safe. He liked waking before everyone else and watching them sleep. Wendy barely moved; Frank ground his teeth and mumbled. Goat Man wheezed. Ellis could get real close to their faces, touch their noses with his, feel their breath—and they wouldn't wake up. He ran his thumb over his father's greenish whiskers—one way smooth, one way rough. He twisted Goat Man's wiry beard until Goat Man swatted at him like a fly. Then he crawled over to Wendy and traced her eyebrows. Two boomerangs, he thought, two flying boomerangs.

• • •

The freshmen crew was still out, so Ellis examined the old boats suspended from the thick roof beams. Members of crews from years past—1947 was the oldest he could find—painted their names on the undersides. Too many people were named Charles. He looked closely at all the boats for his father's name, but he couldn't find it.

The coach, a fat man with a skinny frame, steered his small metal motorboat into the house. He would putt-putt after the crew in the little boat, and berate them through a bullhorn. Ellis had seen him out there and had heard from Barney that he was mean.

"How tall are you?" he asked Ellis before he tied his boat.

"About six feet."

"What year are you?" The coach finished parking the boat, clanking it against the wood, and walked on the rotted planks over to Ellis.

"Freshman."

"Why the hell isn't your ass out on that boat?"

"I'm just here to meet Barney. He said they'd be back after six."

"That doesn't answer my question."

"I'm out of shape," Ellis said. "I hate exercise."

"You're Barney's friend. What's your name?" The coach stared at Ellis's legs.

"Ellis Whitman."

"Okay, Ellis." The coach walked out of the boathouse toward campus.

A few minutes later, the freshman crew rowed in. Barney was flushed and panting.

"Let's go," Barney said. "I'm sick of the boat and that fucking coxswain Rosenberg." He pulled on an anorak and a pair of ratty blue sweatpants over the Yale sweatshirt and cycling shorts he wore for the workout.

The rotting leaves and mud that covered the trail smelled faintly of sour milk, but Ellis didn't mind. The majority of the trip to Peterson's was on this trail, the trail that all the boys took to escape the atmosphere of Gates from time to time. The boys mostly used the trail as a place to masturbate. They'd hike out a ways, kneel behind a few trees or bushes, and whack away. The trail was littered on both sides with weathered and soiled girlie magazines. At almost any point along the way, a Gates boy could walk twenty or so feet off the trail and find a magazine intact enough to use. Once, Ellis found one from 1978. All the women in it wore blue eyeshadow. Another time, he found one that featured only fat ladies, grotesquely fat ladies with stretched nipples like slices of bologna.

Ellis took the trail to town at least twice per week, ducking behind a tree on his way. It ended at Route 22, and about a mile to the left, down a twisty road, was the small town center.

Unlike the majority of Gates boys, Ellis hardly ever went to Peterson's Market. Most afternoons in town, while Barney was at crew practice, Ellis sat on the second floor of the Burke Municipal Library with his algebra book, watching the public high-school students spill onto the white steps in front of their pillared school. There weren't many public schoolers. Ellis figured there were fewer than one hundred in the school, about one hundred fewer students than at Gates. He began recognizing the same kids, making up names and stories for each of them in his head. The girl with the red perm was a cheerleader, very popular—Sharon. She had an autistic twin at home. The twin spent all day strapped to her bed. Sharon's boyfriend—who, in Ellis's mind this week, was the thin guy with the blond hair and green sneakers—would go to pick her up for a date and hear the autistic twin's frustrated grunts. Sharon would lie and say it was her sick dog. Then she and her boyfriend, whom Ellis dubbed Noah, would have sex in Noah's car, a hotrod with a bumping stereo that blasted Puffy or some other safety hip-hop. And there was Ellis, alone in the overheated library with his equations and graphs.

"There better be someone who'll buy for us," Barney said. "Last time I was there with Douglas, it took us more than twenty minutes. One lady said she'd call the police if she saw us here again."

"We'll find someone."

Peterson's parking lot was barren, so the boys sat on an old cement drainage pipe by the woods. It was covered with graffiti: BURKE HIGH RULES, BURKE BULLDOGS #1, FIONA GIVES GOOD HEAD, DO BONGS. Ellis traced DO BONGS with his finger, until a car pulled up.

"You ask first," Barney told him.

"Wuss."

Ellis walked toward the car, a dented forest-green Volkswagen Rabbit. The woman inside was fishing in her purse. She had a cigarette in her mouth. When she stepped out of her car, Ellis cautiously approached her, dragging his feet a little, plowing them through gravel.

"Excuse me, ma'am," he said.

"Please don't call me *ma'am*." she said. "I'm barely thirty-one." She looked tired, with purple pouches under her eyes. Her shapeless brown hair draped recklessly over the left half of her face, nearly touching her burning cigarette.

"Sorry," Ellis told the woman.

"What do you want?"

"If it's not too much to ask, would you maybe purchase a twelve-pack of Budweiser for my friend and me? I mean, I'd give you the money and—"

"No problemo."

Ellis handed her a ten and grinned back toward Barney.

A few minutes later, the woman emerged from Peterson's with a bag. She pulled out the twelve-pack—cans—and handed it over to Ellis. "You and your friend go to Gates, right?"

"Yes," Ellis said, hugging the cool and heavy twelver.

"Figures," she said. She lit up a fresh cigarette. "You mind if I have one of those?"

"No. Here." Ellis ripped open the packaging and handed her a can.

"Shitty day," she said, leaning on her car, looking off into the woods. She cracked the beer and slurped the initial foam.

Barney walked up. "Hey," he said. "Thanks. I thought we'd be shoulder-tapping for an hour."

"I remember what it was like," she said. "You boys need a ride back to campus? I go by there anyway."

"We just—"

"I mean we could stop somewhere, like out near the quarry and finish this." She placed her beer on the top of her car, opened the rear door, and shoved some trash off the seat. "I got plenty of room."

"No, we can't," Barney said.

"We can't," Ellis said.

"I see." She climbed into her car and started it up. Top 40 techno-music blasted from the tinny speakers in the back. She tapped her hand on the steering wheel and nodded her head in time to the beat, staring straight ahead zombielike, not glancing at Ellis or Barney. As she drove onto Route 22, she stuck her arm out the window, and flipped them off.

Her beer had fallen from the car and was fizzing at the boys' feet.

"At least she didn't have a gun," Ellis said, kicking the can.

"Shit," Barney said. "I thought you might've gotten in there with her."

"I'm not stupid."

"I know. I just thought for a second—"

"Let's go," Ellis said. "We only have an hour and twenty minutes."

"We might have to stash some beers in my bag."

"I'll drink my six and you can drink your five," Ellis said. "The one she took was one of yours."

"You gave it to her."

"I paid for it, dork," Ellis said. "We have to work on the Latin dialogue tonight."

NINE

During that trek, Goat Man never did get the goats in the stream, or in a puddle, or in any water whatsoever, so he set up a kiddie pool in their pen at home. The pool was decorated with bug-eyed psychedelic cartoon starfish and seahorses. At first, the goats were curious about the empty plastic pool, looking closely at the seahorses and starfish, sniffing, licking. Two of them even stood in it until Lance ordered them out and took reign himself. But as soon as Goat Man dragged the garden hose down and began to fill the pool with water, all four goats ran to the other end of the pen and screamed at him. He sprayed them with the hose. They all followed Lance over the wall and took refuge down the arroyo on a rotten mattress under a rogue olive tree.

Lance had not always been the king. He had earned his place when he beat Chucky, an older buck, in a simple head-butting challenge. Chucky died a few weeks after the duel, then Lance only had to compete with Mr. T, who didn't seem to care about being king. Mr. T was a wether—a fat, wide-hipped eunuch whose demeanor was nothing like the real Mr. T's. At times, Goat Man himself was the leader of the herd. He'd lower his head in challenge, and the goats would back off. They always had. He thought he might have to usurp the position from Lance again if he didn't make any progress with the kiddie pool. First he'd try simple bribery: Corn Pops cereal. He went up to the pool house to fetch a box.

Bennet, Wendy's current boyfriend, was lying out by the pool. Wendy usually took to younger men with steady incomes, so Goat Man was surprised when he started seeing Bennet sprawled around all the time. Bennet was in his late thirties, perhaps even as old as Wendy, and he was supposedly an artist, an abstract painter. Goat Man had yet to see Bennet do any painting, though, and the guy had been lingering for almost a month. Bennet rolled over and rubbed the golden fur on his stomach when Goat Man walked through the gate.

"I thought you weren't getting back from your trek for two more days," Bennet said, squinting up at Goat Man.

"Came back early yesterday," Goat Man said.

"You were here last night?"

"Yeah, but I was dead to the world. I slept from five in the afternoon until seven this morning." That was almost the truth. The night before he had been dead to the world, but he was awakened at ten or so by squeals of delight and loud splashes from outside. He looked out his window to see Bennet and Wendy skinny dipping in the electric purple light of the pool. Bennet was diving under water, nibbling at Wendy. Wendy was calling him Mr. Sharky. "Stop, stop, Mr. Sharky! It tickles!" Her white breasts floated in front of her. Bennet finally tackled her on the wicker couch right below Goat Man's window. Earning his keep, Goat Man had thought, as Bennet rocked Wendy on the crunchy-sounding furniture.

• • •

"Where do you go on these treks?" Bennet asked, still squinting.

"I wander."

"Where?"

"All over the southern part of the state." Goat Man walked toward the pool house but stopped to straighten the cushions on the wicker couch even though they weren't askew. "I can't be specific about the location."

"Why?"

"It's my job," Goat Man said.

"No, why do you trek?"

"It's my job." He wasn't really sure why he had started to trek. To relax. To escape the city. Now it was for preparation.

Inside, his pipe lay on the glass table next to a Ziploc bag of buds. He packed a bowl, sat down on a Navajo rug, and began to toke. Once, during a Santana concert at the Pima County Fairgrounds, Goat Man had seen a man exhale smoke through his tear ducts. Goat Man tried for this. He stretched his cheeks, bugged his eyes, and popped his ears. It didn't work. It never had. The ceiling fan twirled slowly, and he watched a blade until he became dizzy. He still had to vacuum the pool and do some rock work near the driveway before he worked with the goats again.

He felt the hair on his neck—dirty and hot. Hair generated heat. And right then, Goat Man made what he felt was an important decision, a step into the future, maybe a sincere change: he'd get a real haircut, wear it like a *vato* again.

He heard three quick knocks on the door and rolled over to see Bennet standing just inside. "I've never been in here," Bennet said. He sniffed, and added, "Marijuana?"

Goat Man stood, felt the blood rush out of his head. "You get high?"

"I used to, but I've moved on."

"Too bad."

"I've never been in here," Bennet said. "Just wanted to see what it was like."

"This room, the kitchenette, the bathroom, my bedroom—that's it."

"Bigger than it looks from outside." Bennet walked to the kitchen area. He opened the refrigerator. "Nice place," he said into it.

"Yes," Goat Man said flatly. "I like it."

Bennet shut the refrigerator and faced Goat Man. "I can see why. No rent. No worries." He smiled at Goat Man, almost eerily, and shook a pebble from his sandal.

Tirso, a stout Chileno, had always trimmed Goat Man's hair. Goat Man had gotten only trims since the seventies. He kept his salt-and-pepper hair long, draping down his back or tied in a ponytail. Each time Goat Man went to Tirso's shop, which was only about twice a year, Tirso had a new assistant. Inevitably there'd be a line for Tirso, and an empty barber chair in front of the assistant. That day, Tirso had a new assistant who looked inbred—twisted nose and gray side-set eyes. He motioned quickly with scissors and a comb for Goat Man to have a seat.

"No thanks," Goat Man said, "I'm waiting for Tirso."

"Go on," Tirso said. "Give Denny a try."

What the hell, Goat Man thought. You can't screw up a crew-cut. "Okay." He climbed into Denny's seat.

"How would you like it ?" Denny asked, snipping the scissors in the air like he was warming up.

"I'll make it real easy for you," Goat Man said, undoing the rubber band which held his ponytail, and shaking out his hair.

"See those electric clippers? Use them with the half-inch attachment and run them all over my head."

"You sure?" Denny wrapped the plastic cape around Goat Man's neck. "I know how to cut hair. I can do it any way you like."

"Just leave me with a half inch, please."

"Okay."

Tirso looked over. "You sure, Goat Man?"

"I got a real job," Goat Man said. "I can't look like a scrub anymore."

"What's the job?"

"I'm working in the Biosphere," Goat Man said. "I'm helping to breed a non-eco-intrusive goat."

"You get to live in the Biosphere?" Denny asked, snapping a guard on the clippers. "No way."

"Only for a month, but I get paid real well."

"I knew all your work with goats would come to something," Tirso said.

"Here goes," Denny said. He fired up the clippers.

Goat Man watched the long hair pile up on his plastic-covered lap. Too much gray. Not even forty yet, and already half of it was gray. His father's hair had been ink black when he died at the age of seventy-two. Goat Man flicked the hair off his lap from underneath the cape. "Can you shave my mustache and beard?"

"I can just trim them and clean them up if you'd like," Denny said.

"Shave it all," Goat Man said. "I'm a scientist, not a hippie."

When it was over, Denny spun the chair around, and Goat Man saw himself in the mirror. His hair hadn't been this short since he was a kid battling lice. The freshly exposed skin of his cheeks and chin was pink and new, lighter than the rest of his face. The space between his upper lip and nose looked wider. His chin seemed smaller. He resembled his uncle Liam, who had died in Vietnam when Goat Man was young. Goat Man's mother, Liam's sister, hung a photo of Liam in the kitchen next to the eerie blinking Saint Jude picture above the phone. Goat Man had rarely looked at Liam's photo when he was a kid because it meant also looking at the Saint Jude picture: *Saint Jude, Most Holy Apostle, Pray for Us.* Still, Goat Man was sure he was the spitting image of Liam. Maybe he'd stop in at the movie theater on the way home. They had one of those coin-operated photo booths there, and a few snapshots in the mail to Illinois might make his mother happy. Maybe he'd send one to Ellis, too. Just the photo in an envelope, no note. Let him guess who it was.

Goat Man took off his shoes and socks, rolled up his pants, and stood in the middle of the kiddie pool in the pen. It was eighty degrees and sunny, warm for November, but the water in the pool was a little chilly. He shook the box of Corn Pops, and soon the four goats gathered around. At first they didn't recognize him with his hair cut. Lance and Mr. T put their heads down to challenge him, so he took out his pipe and packed a bowl.

They still kept a safe distance between themselves and the kiddie pool—about ten feet. Goat Man threw one Corn Pop toward Lance. Lance immediately grabbed it with his lips and munched it—Lance was familiar with the Corn Pops box, so there was no hesitation or sniffing. Goat Man shook the box again, and Lance took a step forward. Lance started bleating, and then the others joined in. Goat Man lit his pipe, put the box between his knees, plugged his ears with his thumbs, and began to pull through the bowl of hybrid. That just made them bleat louder. They screamed and jumped maniacally. Freida danced around like a puppet, legs lifting up jerkily, head bobbing.

He stood in the pool for over ten minutes, abiding the cacophony of goat shrieks, until Lance made his move. Goat Man had not been watching him closely, so when Lance pounced into the pool and snatched the box, Goat Man was caught off guard and fell over. He landed on his ass: wet again because of Lance. He saw Lance run down the wash with the box in his mouth. Mr. T followed him. Freida and Gigi stayed where they were, mocking Goat Man with their curious stares.

TEN

"**Y**ou got a thick letter from your dad," Barney told Ellis. Barney examined the envelope, held it up to the light. "I didn't know he lived in New York."

"I've never visited him," Ellis said.

Ellis read the letter to himself:

> *Ellis—I hope your days at Gates are as meaningful as mine were. I'd like to see you over Thanksgiving. Judy and I will be celebrating the holiday down in Georgetown at her house. You'll love D.C. Lots to do right around her neighborhood. I've enclosed bus and train tickets so you can join us. It's all very easy . . . Call me in New York.*
>
> *—Frank*

"To hell with that," Ellis said. "I don't even know his phone number in New York." He tossed the envelope onto his desk.

"What?"

"He wants me to go to Georgetown to spend Thanksgiving with him and his skanky girlfriend."

"I'll be down there," Barney said. "We can go out again."

"I'm not going down there again," Ellis said. "You can have these." Ellis flung the tickets at Barney and headed out toward the pay phone at the end of the hall.

Barney peeked his head around the doorway "Wait. You said you'd help me with algebra."

"I'll be back in a second," Ellis yelled. "Stop stressing."

Ellis hated calling long distance. It was annoying, a pain in the ass. His calling card had sixteen digits. He punched in his card numbers and then his mother's phone number. Bennet answered the phone.

"Who's this?" Ellis asked.

"Who's this?"

"Let me talk to Wendy."

"Tell me who this is."

Ellis hung up. Wrong number, he figured. He punched in the twenty-seven numbers again.

"Hello," Bennet said.

"Is this 520-555-8567?"

"Who is this?"

"Is it, or not?"

"Tell me who this is."

Ellis hung up again. This time, he realized it must be one of his mother's boyfriends. She was due for a new one. Maybe this guy is cool, Ellis thought. But he didn't feel like dealing with him right now. His mother probably wasn't home, anyway. It was only four or five in the afternoon in Tucson, so she was either on the tennis court or in her step aerobics class—unless she'd found some other way to kill her afternoons.

Barney lifted his algebra book and waved it as Ellis entered the room.

"I know," Ellis said. "Why don't you just copy my homework and ask if you have any questions." Ellis handed him the problem set from his folder, and Barney began to copy.

"You're not going all the way back to Arizona for Thanksgiving, are you?" Barney asked. "We really only have two days off."

"I know," Ellis said.

"And Christmas break is only three weeks after Thanksgiving. It'd be dumb to go all the way to Arizona."

"I know."

"My brother will be in D.C. He's really cool."

"So you've mentioned," Ellis said. "What about all the guys from other countries? What about that senior from Samoa? Where do they go for Thanksgiving?"

"They stay here and have a depressing meal with all the teachers and their grubby wives and kids," Barney said. "My brother had to do it one year when my mom was in rehab."

"Oh," Ellis said.

"Why don't you want to see your dad?"

"He sucks."

"At least he sends you letters and stuff," Barney said. "Mine's not allowed."

"Why?"

"He's not allowed."

"Why?"

"Because."

"If you don't want to say, just tell me," Ellis said.

"Okay, I won't."

"How many people have I told about the guy kissing you in the car?"

"None," Barney said. "Right?"

"Barney," Ellis said, "if you tell me not to tell, I won't tell."

"Okay," Barney said. He moved from his desk and stretched flat on his bed. He spoke to the ceiling: "My mom sucks."

"So?"

"So, when I was like seven or eight, she totally fucked over my dad and now he's not legally allowed to contact us. The school even knows."

"That sucks."

"My brother Todd tracked him down," Barney said. "He lives with a lady in Houston. I get news from Todd, but if my mother finds out, my dad's totally busted or something."

"Why?"

Barney sat up. He folded his right ear forward. "See that pink bump?" he said. "It's a burn scar."

"Nasty," Ellis said, moving toward Barney, looking closely. The scar was raised, the size of a bug. It sort of webbed the back of Barney's ear to his head.

"When I was eight, my mother made Todd and me dress up, wear ties and shit and shine our shoes and comb our hair, but she didn't tell us why. She just said, 'All the best, boys. Put forth all the best.' Then we go into the living room, and she has this slide projector and screen set up. I don't know where the hell she got them. And she's all dressed up, too, wearing a black velvet dress, and her hair's all done high on her head and she's smoking—she never smoked."

"Weird," Ellis said.

"Then she pulls the curtains shut, flicks out the light, and turns on the slide projector and says, 'Watch closely.' The first slide is of my dad on the beach. He's tan and shit, just sitting there in the sand looking out into the ocean, wearing his sunglasses. The next one shows him and another guy, a guy with a crewcut. Just hanging out on the beach."

"Yes," Ellis said.

"The next one shows them kissing, my dad's hand on the guy's stomach, and me and Todd freak. Todd calls my mom a bitch and starts crying. I turn away from the screen and stare at the smoke from my mom's cigarette swirling in the projection ray.

"Then my mother grabs my head and twists it so I have to look at the screen. She pulls my eyelids back and says, 'Look at Big Todd kiss Dennis. Look at your father kiss Dennis on Poodle Beach,' and somewhere in there she burns behind my ear with her cigarette—probably not on purpose."

"But your dad lives with a lady now?" Ellis said.

"That's what Todd says."

"My mailman Jonathan is gay," Ellis said. "His partner's name is Paul."

"So?"

Ellis looked at the letter again. Three days with Judy and Fucker Frank. Maybe Frank will be okay, he thought. "I could tell my father that we're working on a project for school, and we could hang out somewhere."

"Cool," Barney said. He went back over to his desk and flipped through papers. "What's the answer for number eight? I can't read your writing."

"The one that has x like to the tenth power times some other shit?"

"Yup."

"X," Ellis said. "It reduces to x."

Ellis walked down the hall to the pay phone and punched in all the numbers again.

"Hello," Bennet said.

"May I leave a message for Wendy?"

"Who is this?"

"Just tell her that Ellis is spending Thanksgiving with Fucker Frank and Judy. If she doesn't want me to, she knows how to contact me."

"So, this is Ell—"

"And remind her that the Volvo is supposed to be serviced this month and that I miss her, and say hello to Goat Man and tell him I thought the postcard was stupid but funny." Ellis hung up and went back to the room.

"You know, Ellis," Barney said, "Coach was asking about you again. He wants you out there on that boat."

"Not a likely scenario," Ellis said.

The bus and train rides down to Washington from Pennsylvania were the same as before—Barney pointed out obvious things like Philadelphia and Baltimore, and Ellis rolled his eyes. Barney periodically shut up and allowed Ellis to read his history text. More kings, popes, and treaties. It's all about fat guys and their stuff, Ellis thought. Once, he had tried to explain his concept of history to Barney, but Barney couldn't follow him.

"I know it's about fat guys," Barney had said, "but how do you remember which fat guy did what?"

"Easy," Ellis said. "Look at his picture in the book. Then read what he did, and look at his picture again."

"That wouldn't help me," Barney said, and he went back to his flashcards.

Graffitied telephone poles, signs, and sooty buildings flew by the train. Old factories with bashed-out windows, mattresses, junkyards crowded with stacks of flattened cars, a sign that read, BEWARE MUTE DOG. The homes built right up to the tracks, with their drooping clotheslines and muddy lawns, depressed Ellis, so he looked down at the painting of Pope Leo X in his textbook: chubby, dimpled hands, adorned with heavily jeweled rings and folded in prayer. The pope had the homely, fleshy face of an infant. Ellis imagined him taking bribes and using the money or gems to trade for food. He saw a stream of blood run down the pope's powder-white cheek as he bit into a thick, undercooked turkey leg.

"One more stop to Union Station," Barney said.

"I could hear the conductor fine," Ellis said.

Ellis didn't want to, but he needed to ask Barney where Judy's house was. He pulled the crumpled paper from his pocket and handed it to Barney.

"That's right in Georgetown. Near that CD store and that place where I bought the cap," Barney said. "We'll split a cab to the Watergate, then you can go on."

The cab stunk like cabbage farts, and the sticky backseat was riddled with black cigarette burns.

The driver looked like one of those crazed dervishes Ellis had seen on *The Moslem*, a documentary that had played repeatedly on cable over the summer. Ellis had watched the program three times, wondering each time how the whirling men kept from puking, and how the hell they derived religious satisfaction and ecstasy from their spins and chants. Ellis hated spinning around, hated being dizzy. As a little kid, he avoided the swings and the whirligig at the playground, and he had refused to go on even the most babyish carnival rides at the Pima County Fair.

Ellis couldn't abide the smell in the cab any longer, so he got out before Barney when it heaved to a stop in front of the Watergate. "Pay the man," Ellis said, before he slammed the door in Barney's face.

Barney opened the door. "Ellis, I only have a twenty."

"I got change," the cabdriver said.

Ellis sat on a cold cement bench by the lobby door, waiting for Barney. It was only noon, and because Ellis had never informed them that he was getting an earlier train, Fucker Frank and Judy weren't expecting him until two or three. He asked Barney if he could hang out for a while at his mom's place.

"Sure. She's not even home. She doesn't get back from San Francisco until tonight. My brother Todd might be home. He's cool."

"I know," Ellis said.

The boys hefted their bags, walking over the white marble floor of the lobby onto the squishy red carpet by the elevator. Two elderly women wrapped in furs were waiting for the elevator. One of them poked Ellis on the shoulder.

"You boys back from college for the holiday?" she asked, grinning. Her face held a yellowish tint and looked as if it was being pulled tight from behind.

"No ma'am, prep school," Ellis said.

"Oh? Where?"

"Gates," Barney said haughtily.

"That used to be one of the better ones," she said. Then she turned to the other woman and whispered too loudly, "Of course that's where poor Mrs. Van Leer's son went. Remember Charles? The skinny tennis player from the club?" She shot herself in the head with her gloved finger.

Figures his name was Charles, Ellis thought. For the hell of it, he might try to find Charles Van Leer's photograph in one of the old yearbooks in the library at Gates. He wondered what the depressed guy looked like. Would he see some sort of suicidal pain in the guy's face? Probably not. If painful facial expressions were any real precursors to suicide, then half of the boys at Gates would blow their heads off before Christmas break.

He had already found his father in the '63 through '66 year-books. Frank looked like a dork in his first three: thick, black-framed glasses, a blond flattop, and a dramatically forced grin. His senior picture was decent, though—he had replaced the black eyeglass frames with thin wire ones, and his hair was long enough to comb. Under his picture it read: "Crew I, II, III, IV. Williams lock."

"Hello?" Barney yelled as he opened the door. "You here, Todd?"

"Duh!" Todd shouted from the living room.

Barney and Ellis plopped their bags down in the foyer, hung their jackets in the closet, and walked across worn Indian rugs to the living room. Todd lounged on the countrified leather-and-wood couch from Santa Fe Today with a half-empty bottle of gin and some squeezed-out lime rinds cluttering the coffee table in front of him. He was watching *Home Shopping Club*, and the perky woman on the screen was peddling a limited-edition, handpainted, porcelain Eskimo doll named Misko: "Cute as a button and authentic in his little fur coat and ice boots." Ellis realized it was the first time he had watched TV since he left Tucson for Gates, and he sat down on the floor in front of the couch. He couldn't wait for Christmas break, and for the first time, he felt a physical rush of anticipation. Bongs with Goat Man, and hours in front of mean-ingless cable shows. And he could go through Wendy's bills, make sure he hadn't screwed anything up back in August.

"Hey," Todd said. "Have a seat." He sat up and patted the cushions. "You guys want a drink? There's some Sprite in the fridge you can mix it with."

"Sure," Ellis said. He sat next to Todd, feeling more at ease in the apartment this time, knowing their mother was thousands of miles away.

"By the way, this is Ellis," Barney said. Barney sat on the other side of Todd.

"So you're Barney's stoner roommate," Todd said. "That's good. He needs to loosen up." Todd looked too much like Barney: identical wide nose and full liver-lips, and the same amphibious eyes. Todd was much fatter, though, with a double chin and chubby hands like Pope Leo's.

"You can't really call me a stoner anymore," Ellis said. "It's been over forty days since I've smoked."

"Barney says there's some voodoo shepherd who lives with your mom in Arizona," Todd said.

"I didn't say that," Barney said.

"He lives in the pool house and keeps goats down in the desert. He grows the best hybrid," Ellis said. "He's a genius with plants."

The *Home Shopping Club* hostess continued to chatter loudly about Misko: "Each is signed by the artist herself and the quantities are limited to two thousand. Forget the original price of $350. Forget even $250. Misko is yours for only $199!" A blinking red box on the bottom right corner of the screen kept count of the number sold: 961, 962, 970 . . .

"For a fucking doll?" Barney said. "Change this."

"No pot up at Gates this year?" Todd asked Ellis.

"Please change this, Todd. That woman is making me sick," Barney said.

"None that I can find," Ellis said.

"Change it, Todd," Barney said. "Give me the remote." Barney lunged for it, but Todd held it away, in Ellis's face.

Todd shooed Barney with his free hand. "Isn't there a senior there named Linus?" Todd asked.

"He got kicked out in September," Ellis said. "They found his stash and a scale. He didn't talk to freshmen, anyway."

Barney got up and changed the channel with the button on the TV. He stopped on MTV, where they were playing an old Paula Abdul video. Paula was dancing enthusiastically with a cartoon cat. Todd shut her off with the remote.

"Linus was the only guy I knew when I was there," Todd said. "It was pretty dry then, too."

Ellis hoped that Todd would break out with some weed, but he didn't. He said he hadn't smoked since he was at Gates. All he did at Yale was drink, mostly gin. He had taken to skipping the tonic and drinking it straight with half a lime on the side, like tequila. He'd take a sip, then suck on the lime and wince.

"We have a lime tree in Tucson," Ellis said.

"Cool," Todd said. "Barney, get off your ass and mix Ellis a cocktail. There's Sprite in the fridge."

The boys sat in front of the TV with the sound muted, drinking gin and Sprite, and then just gin. They laughed at *Home Shopping Club* all afternoon until Barney went to the bathroom and threw up. Doll Hour ended, then came the Jewelry Box, a two-hour segment featuring faux gems. The gin made the unctuous host funny. Ellis watched how quickly the host's wet mouth moved, watched his lips stretch and mold as he disingenuously admired the twinkle of the jewels. The man's hair didn't move. It looked like fluffed spiderwebs.

About the time Barney puked, Ellis collapsed on the rug, his legs under the coffee table and his head spinning like a dervish. He shifted slightly so he could rest his cheek on the cool wood floor.

ELEVEN

Goat Man posed at the edge of the plastic kiddie pool with a Corn Pop in his hand. Every two minutes or so, he gave another Corn Pop to Lance. Lance stood in the kiddie pool with the water up past his knees, earning the Corn Pops. He would crane his neck and gently grab the Corn Pop off Goat Man's palm with his slimy, porno-pink lips. "Good Lance," Goat Man would say. "You're a good buck."

Goat Man had not convinced any of the other goats to do the same. He figured if he worked hard, Freida might come around by Christmas. After nearly twenty minutes and ten Corn Pops, Goat Man freed Lance from pool duty, dried his front and hind legs with an old blanket. He got a good whiff of Lance's stink and knew Lance had pissed himself all over his hind legs—a trick Lance sometimes did, Goat Man thought, to compensate for the removal of his stink glands.

In a while he'd have to join Wendy and Bennet for an early Thanksgiving dinner. Lately, Wendy had been driving north to Sedona for channeling workshops, hikes to vortices, and other New Age crap. Bennet fueled it, encouraging her, sometimes joining her on her trips. Goat Man was sick of listening to their rich-kid mysticism. Only yesterday, Bennet had told Goat Man he had experienced womb memories while sitting on a ledge overlooking Oak Creek Canyon, just outside of Sedona.

Wendy walked into the pool house the night before and had said, "I no longer like relating to people who don't have the common courtesy to be themselves."

"Huh?" Goat Man said.

"If you're stoned, you're not letting your spirit spill forth. It's like your spirit is sifted through a poison net."

"I get it."

He remembered the days when Wendy smoked quite a bit herself. He had met her at a friend's party back in the eighties. She was six months pregnant with Ellis at the time, already fighting bitterly with Frank. Goat Man had been sitting in a circle of grass in the backyard with four other people. His friend Shane had brought a hookah-pipe to the party, and the five of them smoked Nepalese hash through snaky tubes. Wendy walked up to the circle, swollen stomach pushing out at them, and asked if she could join.

"You sure you want to? Being pregnant and all," Shane said.

"You sound like my fucking husband," she said. She rubbed her stomach.

"I think it might harm the baby," Shane said. "This is potent hash. From Nepal."

"This is wrong," Goat Man said.

"Fuck you guys," she said. "As if I'd really take prenatal care advice from a bunch of losers."

"At least we're not pregnant," Goat Man said. His thoughts were beginning to lose their hashed numbness as he glared at Wendy. She wore an orange-and-red African top, cut-off Levi's, and clogs—an outdated look for the time, which reminded Goat Man of the girls in his high-school class. As Wendy stood arms akimbo in front of him, her stomach protruded even more, and he could see how far along she was. Goat Man imagined her nursing an infant with a joint in her mouth. "You're a killjoy," he told her. He stood and walked off toward the house.

"Fuck you, man!" She chased Goat Man, stumbling in her clogs. She jumped on his back and pulled his hair. Goat Man was frozen. He couldn't very well punch or push a pregnant woman. He just stood there and abided the attack until Frank peeled her off. Frank grabbed her under her arms from behind and dragged her away. She lost a clog in the dirt of the driveway. Her crazed screaming finally faded when Frank got her in the car.

"Killjoy," Goat Man mumbled as he rubbed his head.

A few months after that party, Goat Man saw Wendy and Frank at another one. Wendy had baby Ellis strapped to her back in a beaded leather papoose carrier. Frank apologized profusely to Goat Man. Wendy just apologized.

"I shouldn't have attacked you," she said stonily. The bags under her green eyes were as big as slugs.

"Okay," Goat Man said.

"I'm sorry I didn't stick around after I pulled her off you," Frank said. Frank had cut his hair and shaved his muttonchops since the previous party. Goat Man thought he looked like a cop.

"Okay," Goat Man said.

"Shane says you do yard work," Frank said.

"Sometimes," Goat Man said.

"Frank's useless in the yard, and I've got him," Wendy said, turning around to show him Ellis. "I used to like to dig around in the dirt, but now I've got him to feed and change all day."

Goat Man looked at baby Ellis. He was red, with no hair. His face was ugly, crunched. When Ellis moved his fingers and yawned, Goat Man flinched.

"We have an appraiser coming out to the house," Frank said, "and the yard looks like shit."

"When do you need me?" Goat Man said.

"Tomorrow," Frank and Wendy said in unison.

Goat Man shared joints with Wendy every afternoon after he had finished with the landscaping and she had put Ellis down for a nap. She'd complain about her sore breasts, how Ellis wouldn't take her nipple, how the milk pumps were sucking the life out her. They watched *As the World Turns*, Wendy obsessing on how stupid the soap opera was, complaining about the third-rate acting and maudlin music. It was during one of these smoky afternoons that Wendy suggested Goat Man move into the pool house: "It's totally empty, we never go out there, and we'd never bother you."

He moved in the following week.

Goat Man kept his promise: no weed before Thanksgiving dinner. He even put on a nerdy red-and-blue rep tie before he joined them for turkey in the dining room.

"With your tie and your haircut and clean-shaven face, I never recognize you anymore, Javier," Wendy said.

"What can I say? I'm cleaning up my act," Goat Man said.

"You look ten years younger," Bennet said. "Very *GQ*."

"Thanks." Goat Man said. "I guess."

Bennet's niece Aubrey, a slinky teenager, acted as waitress, serving everyone. Goat Man was surprised to see her at first. "You're that one, aren't you?" he asked her when she first emerged from the kitchen carrying a big ceramic bowl of stuffing.

"That one what?" she asked.

"That one who gave Ellis his scar," Goat Man said. "The one who beat the shit out of him at the bus stop years ago?"

"He punched me," she said. She flipped her hair back and grinned at Goat Man.

Hipster, Goat Man thought. She wore flared overalls and clunky green suede work boots. Her hair hung long and straight, like a seventies shampoo model. He pictured her image on a plastic bottle of cream rinse.

"I'm sure Ellis has forgiven her," Wendy said. "Besides, we already figured out that Ellis and Aubrey haven't seen each other in years. Right, Aubrey?"

"Yup," she said, still grinning at Goat Man. She sat across from him.

"Too bad Ellis isn't here," Goat Man said.

"You know where he is, don't you?" Wendy said. "He's with Fucker Frank at his slutty girlfriend's in Washington. I left a message for him to call me. He better."

"You said no more Fucker Frank talk," Bennet whined.

"Sure," she said.

"Who's Fucker Frank?" Aubrey asked.

"My ex-husband," Wendy said. "Ellis's anal-retentive asshole father." She lanced a chunk of white meat with her fork.

"Wendy, come on," Bennet said.

"Okay." She turned to Goat Man and breathed deeply. "Tell me about the next trek you're planning."

"It'll be in the same area as the last three, but this time I'll only bring Freida and Lance," he said. "I think Gigi's teats are dried for good."

"Is Lance that big male with the stubby horns?" Bennet asked. "The one with the kidney-shaped spot on his back?"

"That's him," Goat Man said.

"He sometimes comes up and sits next to me while I'm reading the paper by the pool," Bennet said. "He has bad gas."

"If goats can't fart and burp," Goat Man said, "their intestines explode."

"I doubt it," Aubrey said. She flipped her hair over her shoulder.

"I've seen it," Goat Man said. "A major mess."

Wendy turned to Goat Man and grabbed his shoulder. "I think you may be on to something with these treks, Javier. A return to the earth, a reciprocal relationship with animals, a journey of mind and body."

"Okay," Goat Man said. "Okay."

"I bet Johanna would love to hear about your treks, Javier. Wouldn't she, Bennet? She's into new forms of spirit healing," Wendy said.

"I don't know if these treks have helped heal my spirit," Goat Man said.

"They may have helped and you didn't even realize it because you're not in touch with your spirit yet," Bennet said.

"That's a good point," Wendy said. "Johanna's coming down to Tucson in three weeks to give a few workshops. You can meet her."

"That's okay," Goat Man said.

"I want to hear more about Fucker Frank," Aubrey said.

TWELVE

Ellis woke up under the coffee table in Barney's mother's living room and looked at the old clock on the mantle: 4:30 p.m. He staggered to the kitchen and called Judy's from a tiny cell phone. It was the only phone he could find.

"I lost track of time," he told his father.

"Where the hell are you?" Frank said. "We thought something horrible happened to you. Judy's been keeping the meal warm for hours. The turkey's all dried out."

Just baste it, Ellis thought. "I'm at the Watergate, at my friend's."

"What the hell are you doing there? Which building are you in? I'll meet you out front."

"The building farthest to the left, closest to the Potomac. I'll wait outside." Ellis didn't say anything to Barney or Todd. He could hear Barney in the bathroom dry-heaving, and Todd was asleep on the couch cuddling the remote.

Ellis grabbed his bag and coat and walked down to meet his father.

Frank pulled up in a Range Rover, a new, sea-foam-green one. His hair was longer than Ellis had remembered, slicked back, and he was wearing glasses similar to the nerdy ones he wore during his first few years of prep school—big, black poetry glasses. Ellis opened the passenger door and climbed in the car.

"Well," Frank said. "It's good to see you. You look tall."

"I guess I grew," Ellis said, noticing how his father sat stiffly, gripping the steering wheel. "You look different, too."

Ellis had thought this moment would be different, thought Frank might try to hug him or something. He had imagined that Frank would at least feign some sort of compassion. That last time in Tucson, it was Wendy—not Ellis—who set Frank off. She yelled at him for exposing Ellis to trash like Judy. Wendy hadn't even known the half of it. She wasn't present at the lunch where Frank and Judy pawed each other, making transparent sexual innuendoes that even twelve-year-old Ellis had understood. Wendy had only met Judy for a few seconds when Frank initially came by to pick up Ellis. When Frank dropped Ellis off three hours later, Wendy, purple with rage, opened the front door.

"It's bad enough you never see Ellis, but when you do, you bring along that slut!" Wendy said. "You're really quite disgusting."

"Why don't you go do some yoga or something," Frank said. "Better yet, call one of your charlatan shrinks, and send me the bill."

"You're some father, exposing your son to hookers."

"Judy happens to run one of my stores," Frank said. "She works. Some women today have jobs—careers, even."

"I bet she works," Wendy said. "I bet she works real hard."

"You're pathetic," Frank said. "A mess."

"See you in another three years, Frank," Wendy said. Then she turned to Ellis. "Ellis, say good-bye to your father. You probably won't see him for a while."

"Bye," Ellis said. Ellis had been standing to the side of Frank during the argument, trying to think of the last song he had heard that day.

Frank put the Range Rover in gear and maneuvered onto a busy street. Ellis felt the smooth leather of the seat, like a goat's belly. Frank was wearing cologne that smelled like limes.

"So I look different? Judy will be glad to know that. She's been working on my image. No more Brooks Brothers."

"You look tanner, too." Ellis said. "Don't I look pale?"

They pulled onto M Street, the area that Ellis already knew well. "This is the heart of Georgetown," Frank said. "Want to see my store?"

"Okay." Ellis had to piss, and the bumper-to-bumper cars on Wisconsin Avenue were ridiculous—traffic lights were meaningless to the drivers, and parking spaces lost their boundaries. He hoped he could use the bathroom in Frank's store.

Outside the Range Rover, two kids were selling Hoya sweatshirts from a cardboard box, and a woman stood on the corner balancing a two-liter jug of cola on her head. She held a cardboard sign with EMANSIPASHIN scrawled over it. Everyone else walked as if they were late for something.

But Frank only slowed down in front of Santa Fe Today; he didn't stop. "This is it," he said.

The pain in Ellis's bladder radiated into his stomach and he felt nauseated.

"I sold my other two," Frank said. "This whole Western thing is already done in Boston and New York, so I unloaded the stores. Washington is slower with the trends, so I'll keep this one going for another year."

"Oh," Ellis said. What would Judy do when he closed this

store? He didn't broach the subject. He was keeping his responses short, exhaling only through his nose, hoping to hide the gin smell he imagined was rotting in his mouth.

Judy's house was deceivingly colossal, white, with a black iron gate. The house seemed to conceal its true dimensions. From the front, it looked like all the other large Georgetown homes that Ellis had seen, but it stretched back farther than a bowling alley. Groomed hedges grew beneath its broad lower windows, and a flagstone walk neatly edged with mulch stretched from the front door to the gate. "A senator from Georgia lived in this house for ten years in the eighteen hundreds," Frank said, swinging open the squeaky gate. "Then it was Judy's grandfather's."

Judy greeted them at the front door. She wore a black turtleneck and gray pleated pants. Her hair was no longer blond, it was dark brown. This wasn't the Judy Ellis remembered, who had groped his father and had her fingers sucked at the lunch years earlier. Not the same face; not the same woman.

"Nice to finally meet you, Ellis," she said. She hugged him, squeezing his bladder, then backed off. "Been hitting the bottle today?"

Ellis cringed.

"Ellis, have you been drinking? Is that what you were doing over at the Watergate?" Frank asked, sniffing nervously.

"Yup."

"Put your bag upstairs in the first room on the left, and meet us at the table," Judy said. "You can eat away any inebriation you might have left."

Ellis frantically climbed the stairs, lugging his bag like a cadet, passing dulled oil paintings of men dressed for the hunt and women rolling hoops. The hall was a length of polished hardwood, with a thin Oriental rug that looked as if it was woven especially to meet its dimensions. The guest room was more modern: a light wooden dresser, a maroon futon, and generic Scandinavian bookshelves laden with paperbacks. He plopped his bag on the futon and hopped into the bathroom, sighing and grinning as the bowl bubbled up.

"I'm not sure I share Judy's carefree attitude about your afternoon drinking," Frank said, as Ellis sat down at the table. "Does Wendy know you drink?"

Ellis swirled his mashed potatoes into a peak and took a bite of stuffing. He could hear himself chew.

"Like the stuffing?" Judy asked him.

"Yes, ma'am," Ellis said.

"Please call me Judy."

"You're in the ninth grade, only fifteen years old. What were you drinking, anyway? And where were this kid's parents?" Frank asked.

"I'm fourteen, and we were drinking gin, Gordon's I think, Gordon's London dry gin," Ellis said. "Barney's mom was in San Francisco. He never sees his father."

Frank pushed his poetry glasses farther up his nose, excused himself, and went into the kitchen.

"We'll wander around Georgetown tomorrow and go to the Smithsonian on Saturday," Judy said. "Have you been to the Smithsonian, the air and space one?"

"No," Ellis said. He had worked his way through a small scoop of stuffing, and he took another helping. He wondered what Frank was doing in the kitchen.

"It's great," she said. "Every time I'm there, there's something new. Last time they had this Star Trek exhibit and this whole thing about the sexual overtones in the show."

"Oh."

"Frank knows you're fourteen."

"I know."

"That's how he refers to you," she said. "As his fourteen-year-old son."

"As opposed to his ten other sons of various ages?"

"He knows you're fourteen," she said. "He's not dumb."

Ellis said "I know" again. He felt like leaving. He had already screwed things up by getting drunk. Frank didn't really want him here. He wondered why Frank had invited him down.

It was just like Wendy had said over and over: "Frank's lame. Once in a while he wants to play father, but most of the time he wants to be anonymous."

THIRTEEN

"Why hasn't he called yet?" Wendy said. She was walking laps around the card table. "Javier, call Frank, will you?"

Goat Man, Bennet, and Aubrey had finished with their Thanksgiving meal and were playing Scrabble. Bennet had just put the word *fix* on a triple-word square for forty-five points. Bennet's turn followed Aubrey's. She set up Bennet for high-scoring moves.

"I'm ahead of you by sixty-one," Bennet said, "and you, Aubrey, by eighty-seven."

Goat Man wanted his pipe. He tried to ignore everyone but he couldn't.

Aubrey twisted her hair and sighed histrionically.

Wendy poked Goat Man's shoulder with a wooden spoon. "Please call there, Javier. I'll dial it for you."

"No. He'll call. He said he would, and he will," Goat Man said. Then he announced that he quit the Scrabble game.

"You can't quit," Bennet said. "We're already halfway done."

"Sorry, gotta tend to the goats," he said.

"Can I go with you?" Aubrey asked.

"They get nervous at night with strangers," he told her. "They might attack you."

"The Chupacabre's probably down there sucking all their blood right now," Aubrey said. "I saw it on the news."

"I'll take my chances," Goat Man said.

"Chupacabre," Aubrey whispered.

Goat Man sat on a musty bale of hay at the edge of the goat pen and belched. His stomach was full of Thanksgiving. He looked up at the sky, which was bruised with purple and gray clouds. As he lit his pipe and let the sweet smoke into his lungs, he tried to forget Wendy, tried to forget how intolerant and hypocritical she was becoming. He thought of Ellis and wondered how he was doing in D.C. with Frank.

He thought about the treks, the main trek in March. It would be easy by then, seamless and worry-free. Both Lance and Freida would be water-trained, and he would be so accustomed to the treks that he wouldn't screw up. He couldn't screw up.

Jesús, Goat Man's cousin from El Paso, the same guy who had packed doll heads full of dry ditch weed and mailed them off to Goat Man during his high-school years, had called him that morning. Goat Man reassured him that the main trek would go off without a hitch. But even as he said it, he felt like he was forgetting something.

Goat Man looked across the desert at his Jetta parked in the street near the wash. It sickened him. It was a mobile blight. The car, with its boxy shape, oxidized and faded maroon paint, peeling "Chicano Power" sticker, and 170,000 miles, shamed Goat Man, even in front of the goats. The goats hated riding in it. They protested loudly whenever they were forced inside it. Goat Man wanted to run through the wash, find a big stick, and beat the shit out of the Jetta, beat it until it became part of the desert like the rotted mattress or the goat pen. Instead, he smoked through another bowl and looked up toward the house at the purple reflections from the pool jiggling on the adobe walls.

He liked living in the pool house, enjoyed cleaning the pool and keeping the grounds, but he knew it wouldn't last. Wendy had become too unaccepting of his hybrid: the smoking and the growing of it. She didn't come right out and say it, but he knew she'd soon ask him to dismantle his greenhouse, take down the sodium lights, kill the plants. Bennet had something to do with it. Goat Man felt as if Bennet watched him a little too closely, lingered too much. Lurked. A lurker. Two weeks ago, he had discovered Bennet leaning up against the greenhouse, cupping his eyes with his hands, trying to see in.

"Wendy told me you grew," Bennet had said. "I just wanted to see it."

"They're just plants."

"Just curious."

"If you want some, let me know. You don't have to snoop around."

"I wasn't—"

Goat Man had already started walking away.

Goat Man's lifestyle just didn't jibe with Wendy's anymore, especially without Ellis around. She'd soon boot his ass—he could feel it. There was no way he'd quit smoking; he had already committed to a fuzzed-over, smoothed life. If she would just wait until the end of March, after he got his payment for the trek, then he'd have enough money to move out if she made him. He could move into one of the hundreds of generic singles apartment complexes that were popping up all over the city.

Lance trotted over from the wash and rubbed his slimy lips and nose on Goat Man's leg. Lance stank. Somehow he worked the remnants of stink glands. Maybe he had pissed himself again. Then Lance hurried over to the kiddie pool and jumped in with a mild splash. He started screaming at Goat Man, demanding Corn Pops.

"You finished the box this afternoon."

Lance screamed louder. Goat Man shook out his pipe, and hiked up to the pool house to get away from the ruckus.

Wendy was waiting for him by the pool, sitting on a lounge chair, sipping from a tall, blue-rimmed glass. She stirred her drink with her finger.

"You were down there a while," she said.

"I guess I lost track of time."

"Pot?" Then she sighed. "Doesn't matter. Ellis hasn't called. It's eleven in D.C. now. He's not calling tonight." She took a chug from her drink.

"He'll call tomorrow." Goat Man sat in the lounge chair next to hers, adjusted the back so he could look at the sky. A few stars.

"I just don't want Frank fucking with him. I don't want Ellis to be a Frank clone."

"He won't be."

"I don't know. After Gates, Ellis will be going to some East Coast college, then he'll be working in Boston or New York or Washington. We'll never see him." Wendy dumped the rest of her drink into the pool. It was brown and syrupy, and it hung like a squid's ink in the illuminated water.

"He'll be home in a few weeks," Goat Man said.

"I know. I'm worrying too much. Gates is a great school. I should be happy. It just feels like the beginning of the end . . ." Her voice trailed off as she turned away from Goat Man.

"Sometimes it feels like that to me, too," Goat Man whispered to himself.

FOURTEEN

Frank had some paperwork at the store to finish, so Judy and Ellis walked through Georgetown without him. They'd meet Frank for lunch at The Tombs, which Ellis knew from his previous visit to D.C.: a self-consciously preppy and beer-soaked restaurant with oars mounted on the walls. Barney had insisted they go there for hamburgers. Judy had told Ellis that The Tombs was the place where she had first gotten drunk. Ellis couldn't remember the first place where he had gotten drunk, but he figured it was probably the pool house.

The Georgetown campus was gray and gloomy in the cold November air—dark, creepy gothic buildings with gargoyles perched in front of steeples that towered up like giant gravestones into the galvanized sky. There were actual gravestones, too. They marked the eternal resting places of forlorn Jesuits and stood in crooked rows behind the freshman dorms.

The grass on the Georgetown campus was dead and frozen, the trees naked and black. A few grubby pigeons and quick, starving squirrels were the only signs of life on the holiday-deserted campus. Judy and Ellis stopped in front of a blue-black statue of John Carroll, the founder of the university. John Carroll looked grumpy—a frown or smirk, blank eyes, and a ceremonial robe.

In the ancient Healy building, they climbed endless flights of stone steps that smelled faintly of church—patchouli, holy smoke. Judy had said there was a great view from the bell tower. Their footsteps echoed in the cold, misty air. Toward the top, as Ellis began to lose his breath, he decided he didn't care about seeing the view. He'd rather be drinking gin with Barney and Todd in front of the TV at the Watergate. He'd rather be watching Doll Hour on the Home Shopping Channel.

Up there in the open air, Ellis's sweat seemed to freeze on his forehead. Judy pointed out various landmarks, including the Watergate. It was closer than Ellis had imagined; he could easily walk there if he needed to—just down and across a few streets, then along the river for a bit. Through the mild fog, they could see the Lincoln and the Washington memorials, and the imposing Kennedy Center. Ellis was winded from the climb, and a little resentful that Judy had made him do it. He'd most likely see all the monuments up close tomorrow, anyway. They'd probably tour each one of them.

Judy spotted her house, and Ellis saw her grin melt. "It's back," she said.

"What's back?"

"The suspicious truck." She cupped her gloved hands above her eyes, even though there was no glare.

"What makes it suspicious?"

"It's a jalopy, and one of my neighbors thinks the hippies that drive it sell dope to the students here."

"Looks like an old pickup truck to me," Ellis said. "Looks like every truck in Tucson."

"I'm getting a closer look," Judy said. She disappeared down the stairwell. "Hurry up, Ellis."

• • •

As soon as they walked into Judy's overheated house, she called her neighbor. The truck had moved. It was a block away, on the street behind them. The neighbor wasn't home, so Judy left a message: "The drug-dealing truck is back. Call me as soon as you get home." She hung up and looked at Ellis. "I'm going up to the attic. I'll use Frank's binoculars. Come on."

"Can I use your phone for a second?"

"Sure," she said. "I'll be up there." She marched up the stairs, repeating, "I'm gonna bust those suckers."

Judy's phone was an archaic black desk model—dial. Ellis couldn't use his card without touch-tone, so he just dialed. Bennet answered, as usual.

"May I speak to Wendy, please?" Ellis said.

"May I tell her who's calling?"

"Put her on."

"Who is this?" Bennet sounded panicked.

Ellis heard Wendy say, "Give me that, you idiot!" in the background. "Ellis?" she said into the receiver.

"Hi, Mom," he said.

"You there now? Where are you?" Wendy whispered.

"At Judy's. Is that your new boyfriend?"

"Not so new. What kind of place does the slut have?" Wendy was frantic, almost hyperventilating. Then she burped. "I'm nauseated from the double dose of sleeping pills I took last night."

"It's not the same Judy," Ellis said. "Calm down. You shouldn't take those pills."

"What's that about Judy?"

Ellis explained that it was a different Judy, that this one wasn't a skank like the other, that this one was actually educated and well mannered. "And attractive," he said.

"Attractive? What do you mean by attractive?"

"Pretty," Ellis said, but then he realized he was upsetting her, so he told her about the truck outside, how spastic Judy was when she saw it, how she was currently spying on it with binoculars.

"Sounds like something Frank would do," Wendy said. "They'll be happy and constipated together."

"Frank looks different. He says Judy's helping him with his image and he wears poetry glasses."

"Poetry glasses?"

"Yeah, thick nerd ones like Elvis Costello or Drew Carey."

"What else about Frank?"

"Hair slicked back, and longer," Ellis said. "I gotta go, Mom. I'll call you Monday night from school."

"I want more details," Wendy said, "a lot more."

He examined the portrait of Judy's grandfather that hung above the brick mantle. The plaque under the painting read HUMPHRY JAMES PERKINS III, PHILANTHROPIST. Judy had pointed it out earlier, telling Ellis that *philanthropist* was a good vocabulary word. "So is *cretin,*" Ellis had responded.

Humphry sat with his hands folded on his knee, his trusty retriever by his side. His smile was eerie—slight, perverted, like he was thinking about something really sick. Ellis imagined Humphry lecherously gazing upon little girls in a playground, or wrestling a blow-up doll, dressing in latex hotpants.

Ellis heard the rumble of the pickup truck and saw it chug past the steamed window. He went upstairs to tell Judy.

The attic was clean and empty—more polished hardwood floors and walls. It smelled faintly of pine. The only things up there were an easel with some crunched tubes of oil paint, and a half-finished painting of what looked sort of like Frank. The subject had the same poetry glasses. Judy was leaning out a window clutching the binoculars. Leaning too far, Ellis thought. It made him nervous.

"Judy," Ellis said. "The truck's gone. I just saw it drive by."

Judy pulled back in and shut the window. "It parked down the street. And don't look at that painting. It's a surprise." She ran over and stood in front of the canvas, her arms out. "Let's go downstairs. I'm sending you on a mission."

"Okay." He knew it must be Frank's portrait. He wondered if she had painted the one of Humphry, and if so, would Frank also have a pervert's smile.

Ellis's assignment was to walk by the truck and look at the driver. He was to remember every detail of the driver's face, estimate his height, look for tattoos or other distinguishing marks. As he strolled down the wet cobblestone, Ellis heard a familiar Peter Tosh song flowing from the truck: "Oh, Mama, whatcha gonna do now?"

"Hey," Ellis said to the man in the truck. The man was eating a messy submarine sandwich, bobbing his head to the bongos and bass. He was pale, with blond, ropy dreadlocks and a twisted goatee.

"Hey," Ellis repeated. "What's up?"

"Just hanging these flyers." He handed one to Ellis. "You a student here?"

"No." Ellis looked at the flyer. It advertised a D.C.-area reggae band show at the Kingston Club: Inner Circle with Emoro, Africa's most celebrated dancing Pygmy. And the Kingston Club's phone number on the bottom: 202-ONE-LOVE. "Thanks." Ellis started back toward Judy's but turned around after a few steps. "How'd you get the dreads?"

"I threw away my comb, and I wash it with castile soap."

"Maybe I'll do that this summer," Ellis said.

FIFTEEN

Goat Man woke early and started to clean the pool. There wasn't much to it, very few leaves to chase down, and the pH was perfect. The landscaping in the pool area was meticulously groomed as well, but he felt like he should look busy in case Wendy or Bennet happened to come outside. Wendy had said that she was taking the day off, giving her body and soul a rest from exercise. "We'll just lounge by the pool, especially if it's nice out," she had said. "I'll make some snacks." Goat Man kept expecting her to appear—he left a few leaves in the low end so he could vacuum them in front of her when she did appear.

It was pleasant—still too warm for late November, but he'd take it. He had waked and baked, sucked his pipe seconds after getting out of bed, so he was able to stay by the pool and pretend to clean it without becoming too bored. The fuzz in his brain made everything more interesting: the way the angle of the vacuum pole changed as it hit the water, the dancing reflections of the pool on the stucco wall, the comfort of his well-worn hiking boots. He could experience his pot better before his brain was clogged with the day's business.

Bennet strolled out to the pool area first, carrying the newspaper in his armpit and a small tray with cereal, juice, and a tube of suntan lotion. He wore green flip-flops and his skimpy, racing-red bathing suit. Goat Man had learned long ago never to trust a man wearing a slingshot for a bathing suit. Bennet gingerly placed the tray on the deck and lay down on a chaise. As he reached for his suntan oil, he knocked over his juice. The glass shattered on the hard deck, and the juice streamed in all directions.

"Damn it," Bennet said.

Goat Man laughed quietly.

"Javier, could you come over here and clean this," Bennet said. "I'll switch chairs to give you room." He stood and moved to another lounge chair near the diving board.

"Excuse me?"

"You'll need to pick up the glass shards first, then spray the juice off with a hose so it doesn't get sticky," Bennet said, opening his newspaper.

"You spilled the juice," Goat Man said. "You broke the glass."

"Yes?"

"Then get off your ass and clean up the mess. I'm busy with the pool."

"It's your job." Bennet didn't look up from behind the paper.

"Hey, buddy," Goat Man said, "fuck you."

Bennet threw the paper down, stood up, puffed out his furry chest, and marched toward Goat Man.

Bennet's right testicle peeked out of his swimsuit. It was pink against his bronzed leg. Bennet put his face up to Goat Man's and stared into Goat Man's eyes.

"You're free-balling," Goat Man said blankly.

"What?"

"One of your nuts wants out."

Bennet looked down, said "Christ," and tucked it back in. "I think you, me, and Wendy need to have a talk about your place around here."

"The pool house?" He knew what Bennet meant by *place*, but he wanted to hear him explain it. He focused again on chasing down the leaves. It was time to suck up the last few. "You want to check out the pool house again?"

"No, your job."

"Oh, that."

"It must be nice to walk around stoned all the time knowing that you don't have to do much of any work, knowing that you don't have to pay rent or worry about food."

"It is nice." Goat Man ran the vacuum over the last leaf and watched it disappear.

Wendy and Aubrey came out to the pool area, slamming the wrought-iron gate behind them. They weren't dressed for the pool. Wendy was wearing a flowing Indian-print skirt and a pink top, and Aubrey wore ripped jeans with an old KURT COBAIN R.I.P. T-shirt and green suede Adidas.

"The pool looks great, Javier," Wendy said. "You need anything at the mall?"

"Some boxer shorts, all cotton, size thirty-four/thirty-six," Goat Man said. "Nothing too fancy." He looked over at Bennet.

"Okay," she said.

"What about me?" Bennet said.

"I'll get you a new bathing suit," Wendy said.

"I thought you liked this bathing suit," he said. His nut had worked its way out again.

"It doesn't leave much to the imagination," Wendy said, "especially when your ball's hanging out."

"That is so sick," Aubrey said. "Like I really want to see your ball."

"And Bennet, clean up the juice mess before the ants come," Wendy said.

Goat Man walked down and sat in the dirt with the goats. In a few weeks, Freida and Gigi might go into heat. With the unpredictable climate, it was difficult to chart exactly when, but they had gone into heat at Christmastime before. He'd have to keep an eye on their cycles. When their hindquarters swelled, reddened, and they began to wildly flutter their tails, he'd have to sequester them—he didn't want any kids this year, at least not until after the important trek in March. And Freida had been good about staying in milk. As long as he milked her a few times a day, her milk was consistent.

He noticed that some bites had been taken out of the rim of the plastic kiddie pool. Whoever had been chewing on it would be sick. Now he'd have to hide the kiddie pool up near the house. He examined each of the goat's beards to see which had been sick. Lance's beard looked fine; so did Gigi's, but Freida's and Mr. T's were stained green from bile. Freida's even had a few dime-sized pieces of blue plastic dangling in it. Stupid goat. There was plenty of fodder and plant life for them to graze on, but they opted for plastic. He had thought for years that Freida was stupid, but this clinched it. He wished Gigi were a better milk producer.

Goat Man emptied the kiddie pool—the water was thriving with algae anyway—and rolled it up the hill toward the house, eventually leaning it against Bennet's pristine red Jeep in the garage.

Bennet was swimming laps. The juice and glass were cleaned up, but Bennet had left the hose on the deck. The metal nozzle would leave a rust stain, but Goat Man didn't bother moving it.

Inside the pool house, Goat Man rolled a fat one, lay down on the rug under the fan, and thought about how he, too, should swim laps. He used to swim laps every morning, before anyone else was up, but since Bennet had moved in, laps seemed impossible.

The fan rocked slightly on the ceiling, like it might come unattached someday and bash Goat Man's head. He'd fix it later. Now he just watched it closely, willing it to stay up there. The spinning blades tricked him into slumber before he lit his fatty.

A few hours later, a knocking awakened him. Goat Man lazed up and staggered to the door.

"We got you these," Aubrey said. She held up some baggy boxers printed with bright yellow bananas. "And these." She held up two other pairs—one with lips, the other with geckos. "I picked them out."

"I like the lizard ones." He opened the door all the way and motioned that she come in, but cringed when he realized his pipe and two bags were out on the table. The fatty was still on the floor.

Aubrey walked directly over to the table and held a bag up to the skylight. "I've never done this, but I'm dying to." She pushed her scarlet hair behind her ears and shook the dope.

"What about your uncle Bennet?"

"He's inside trying on his new swim trunks, then Wendy and him are going to some spirit workshop bullshit." She picked up Goat Man's pipe and twirled it through her fingers.

"We'll have to do a bong if it's really your first time," Goat Man said. He walked over to his closet and rummaged for a minute before he remembered that Ellis had taken the bong to Gates. He found the rigged tennis ball can behind a duffel bag, but it was missing the bowl and was rusted on the inside. "I have an idea," he said.

He went to his refrigerator, took out a half-full two-liter bottle of 7-Up and dumped the contents down the sink. "You plug the drain in the bathroom sink and empty all the ice trays into it," he instructed Aubrey. He began to saw off the bottom of the 7-Up jug with a serrated steak knife. The cutting made a heinous squealing and grating noise, but soon he was done, and he tossed the sawed-off bottom in the trash. He found his electrical tape, unscrewed the bowl from his pipe, and attached it to the top of the jug.

"Run the cold water into the ice until it almost overflows," he told Aubrey. "I'll pack us a nice bowl."

Goat Man submerged the bottle, except for the bowl on top, and tilted it sideways so water rushed in. Then he held a lighter to the packed buds and slowly pulled the bottle up. The pressure sucked the smoking bowl, and the bottle filled with thick smoke. Goat Man unwrapped the tape, pulled off the hot bowl, and covered the top of the bottle with his palm. He was careful not to let any smoke escape.

"You ready?"

Aubrey nodded with a feral look of anticipation on her face.

"Just breathe in from the top when I let my palm up. It should be nice and cool. And hold it in your lungs as long as you can."

"I'm not dumb," she said. She leaned over the sink, and Goat Man stepped aside. Holding her hair back, she inhaled the contents of the bottle without coughing. She walked over and lay on the rug in the other room. The fatty sat next to her head. Goat Man was grateful she hadn't stepped on it.

Her green sneakers moved like windshield wipers as she held her breath. After she blew it out, she grabbed the fatty and stood up. "What next?"

"You didn't burn your throat?"

"No. At first I wanted to cough, but I held it in there pretty long, didn't I?"

"We'll just smoke the joint." He pointed at it. "I got the bowl wet, anyway."

"Cool," she said. She grabbed the fatty and sat at the glass table, where Goat Man joined her.

"Your uncle's gonna kill me."

"I won't tell him. I'm not stupid."

"Good." Goat Man sparked up the fatty.

After taking a huge, almost ceremonial, hit, he passed the glowing fatty over to Aubrey. "Fat pappy," he said from his gut, still holding the hit in his lungs. "Toke the fat pappy, girlie."

She toked too vigorously and coughed, violent and thick. Goat Man, still holding the smoke in his lungs, motioned with his hand for her to try again. She did, and coughed again, but not as hard. On her third try, she didn't cough. But she blew it out before Goat Man blew out his original hit.

"I love this," she said, lying on the rug again. "Thank you so much."

"No problem." Goat Man put on a Steel Pulse CD and sat down next to Aubrey on the rug.

Aubrey began to swivel her head on the rug in time with the mellowed beat. "I love this music."

Stupid, Goat Man thought. He didn't say anything, just looked up at the fan.

"Is this Bob Marley?" she asked.

"No."

"It sounds just like Bob Marley." Her hair spilled out over the floor.

"It's not."

"My head feels ticklish inside. Like it's full of furry spiders."

She shut up and rolled prone. Her ass looked like a perfect little ski-jump. For a weak moment, Goat Man thought about lying on top of her. He brushed his boot down her back from her neck and took the jump. He stepped on her ass. "Get up," he said.

"Why?"

"Because."

She stood and looked Goat Man in the eye. "What do you do?"

"What do you mean?"

"Like what do you *do* all day?" She tucked her hair behind her ears.

"Do?"

"What do you do?"

"Landscaping," Goat Man said. "I work with the goats and clean the pool."

"All day?" Aubrey sat at the glass table again. She opened the Ziploc bag and fingered the buds. "Don't you get bored?"

"I do other stuff," Goat Man said, snatching the bag, "but I'm not at liberty to talk about it."

"I bet," she said. "Like get high all day."

"Why do you think I got my hair and beard cut off?" He sat down.

"Boredom," she said.

SIXTEEN

Ellis was crabby and didn't allow himself to be impressed by the Lincoln Memorial—too many steps, and his legs were tired from the previous day's walk through Georgetown and Northwest D.C. Frank and Judy had spent twenty minutes that morning discussing the order in which they'd visit the monuments. Frank had even turned off the stereo in the Land Rover so they could bicker without interruption. Ellis had watched them argue, listened to how they said every word diplomatically, how none of their sentences really meant anything. They should wrestle, wrestle every morning, Ellis had thought, as he sat in the comfortable backseat and watched the bustling city slide by. The winner of the wrestling match gets his or her way for the rest of the day.

Up there next to giant Lincoln, they argued about a purple-and-rust-colored sweater a man was wearing. Frank found it smart looking, but Judy decided it was clearly the most hideous garment in the history of textile. Frank asked Ellis his opinion.

"I don't give a fuck," he said.

"Ellis, that's inappropriate," Frank said.

"That's okay, Frank," Judy said. "I can see how a stranger's sweater might not be of interest to Ellis."

Ellis sighed and looked up at big white Abe. One more night, he thought, and then it's back to Gates—back to normal. Only three weeks and he'd be home in Tucson.

"Ellis, I don't understand this. You show up drunk for Thanksgiving dinner, you insult Judy and me, you walk around with a permanent pout on your face. What are you like at school?" Frank grabbed Ellis by the shoulder and turned him around.

Ellis stared impassively into Frank's poetry glasses. "I'm getting all A's except for an A minus in Latin—*Me accuso*," he said. He turned around and stared up at Abe again. Abe looked cross-eyed.

A guy in a Georgetown sweatshirt with his baby on his shoulders was posing in front of Lincoln. The baby was oblivious, casually playing with his father's hair, chewing on a few strands. The man's wife snapped a photo. When Ellis turned back to Frank and Judy, they were rubbing noses and giggling.

Later, at around five o'clock, as they sat around Judy's kitchen table playing rummy, Ellis mustered up enough gumption to ask if he could go to a CD store he had seen the day before.

"It'll be dark soon, Ellis," Judy said. "Georgetown can be dangerous."

"It's really close," Ellis said. "I'll be back in less than an hour." There was no good CD store anywhere near Gates, let alone one that also sold T-shirts and shoes. Ellis had seen a cool Wailers shirt in the window, and he wanted to give it to Goat Man for Christmas.

"I'll drive you there. We'll all go," Frank said. "Which store is it?"

"It's called Smash," Ellis said. "On M Street."

• • •

When they arrived at the store, Ellis went immediately to the reggae section, cutting through a bunch of skinheads admiring boots. He found four CDs he had wanted for a while and then moved over to the ska bin, where he found three more, including a Prince Buster's Greatest Hits that he had only heard about. He chose four T-shirts: Mighty Mighty Bosstones, the Wailers one for Goat Man, Bob Marley's *Uprising* on green, red, and yellow tie-dye, and finally, a black shirt with a big maroon BLUNT logo. The Blunt shirt was on the discount rack, only five bucks.

"Ellis, what bands do you think my nieces like?" Judy asked. "They're around your age." She looked curiously at the posters of sullen European musicians.

"Just get them Blunt shirts," Ellis said. "They're on sale."

"I've never heard of them," she said. "The last concert I went to was Billy Joel. What do I know?"

Ellis watched Frank examine some platform sneakers and thigh-high motorcycle boots.

"You're not planning on buying all that, are you?" Frank asked Ellis, motioning to the shirts and CDs Ellis held.

"Yes." Ellis dumped it all on the counter and a tragically wan, red-haired woman with a Celtic tattoo on her forearm and poetry glasses similar to Frank's started ringing it up.

Frank told her to hold on.

She looked up at him and rolled her eyes. She turned around and cranked up the volume on the stereo. The louder music was caustic: grinding, industrial, painful. Then she looked to Ellis. "You want this stuff, or not?"

"Yes," Ellis said.

"How are you paying for all this?" Frank asked. "I'm not paying for all of this."

"With this," Ellis said, snapping his MasterCard on the counter.

"Where'd you get that?" Frank asked.

"From Wendy," Ellis said.

The woman began to ring up the merchandise again.

"I didn't have a credit card until I was in business school," Frank said.

"Really?" Judy said. "I had my first when I was eighteen—Lord and Taylor."

Ellis's booty totaled over two hundred dollars, two big bags' worth. "You ready?" Ellis asked them.

"I still can't believe it," Frank said. "What a lavish life you're leading, just dropping two hundred dollars in a record store. How can Wendy afford you?"

"Her stepfather," Ellis said. "But you still have to mail her alimony?"

"Yes," Frank sighed. "Of course."

Ellis phoned Barney from the kitchen after they returned from the CD store.

"Why haven't you called?" Barney said.

"I got busted for drinking with you and Todd, and I've had to do all this stuff with Fucker Frank and Judy." He stretched the old phone cord, peeking around the kitchen door to see if either Frank or Judy was in earshot.

"Todd got pot," Barney said. "He called this guy from Yale who's also from D.C., and that guy gave him the name of another guy who told him where we should go. Guess where?"

"Malcolm X Park?"

"No. All we had to do was go to the lobby right here. A cabby sold it to us."

"You smoked any yet?"

"Yeah, last night we got baked out of our minds."

"Where was your mother?"

"In New York, and she'll be there for three more days."

"I'll be over later tonight. Save me some."

"We will."

Ellis thought about asking Fucker Frank if he could go over to Barney's to work on a project for school, but he knew Frank wasn't that dumb. He resolved to wait a good while before he'd sneak out.

The stairs were easier than he had thought—only a few minor creaks as he carefully placed his socked feet. But, as he stepped out the back door, he decided sneaking off to Barney's for the chance at smoking a little weed was stupid, mean to Frank and Judy even. Besides, he had no way of getting into the house again if he let the lock click behind him. Frank or Judy might check his room and freak out when they saw he was gone. He felt like an asshole standing out there on the steps in his socks. He bent down and pulled the doormat into the jamb so the door wouldn't lock behind him and slipped his feet into his shoes.

Ellis skulked around the house in the cold, misty night, and he looked through the den's fogged window to see Frank and Judy in the blue flickering glow of the TV. They were laughing, having a tickle fight, Judy on top of Frank, going at his stomach.

He couldn't remember ever hearing Wendy laugh like that. Especially not with Frank.

He sneaked back into the house, locked the door, and went to sleep.

• • •

Ellis called Barney the next morning.

"Where the hell were you last night?" Barney asked.

"I decided not to sneak out."

"Why?" Barney asked.

"I decided it wouldn't be worth it to get caught," Ellis said. "Frank already hates me enough."

"We saved a bunch for you," Barney said. "Come over now. My mom's still not back."

"I'll ask, but Frank will say no."

"Ask."

Frank was gone, at the store. Judy was in the kitchen, making scrambled eggs for Ellis the way he had requested: with grated cheddar sprinkled over the top before they left the pan. When Ellis walked in, she was dancing around the tiles and singing along with Cher on the radio: "Do you believe in life after love . . ."

"After breakfast, can I go over to Barney's?"

Judy clicked off the radio and turned down the stove. "Is he the one you drank gin with?"

"Yes." Ellis sat at the small kitchen table. "But the gin's gone."

"You have to promise no more drinking." She pointed at Ellis with a spatula.

"Okay."

"Frank will kill me," she said. "You know that, don't you?"

"I know," Ellis said. "Thanks."

"You better eat these eggs fast, before he calls here and wrecks your plans." She placed the steaming plate in front of Ellis.

"Thanks."

• • •

"Let me smell it," Ellis said. He put the bag up to his nose like a surgical mask, and sniffed. It smelled like pizza. He looked at it closely. There were two or three pathetic little dried buds, but the rest was spice, probably oregano. "You got taken."

"What?" Todd said. "We got totally baked from it."

"I'll pick out the real stuff," Ellis said. "The rest you can put on spaghetti." Ellis sifted through the shake, pinching out two bumble-bee-size buds. He wasn't even sure if they were weed. He held the buds up to the light and said, "Let's give these a whirl."

"That's not enough for a fat joint," Barney said.

"I brought a pipe," Ellis said.

Ellis packed the bowl with the buds, picking out a few seeds, and passed it to Todd. "You go ahead."

"We saved it for you," Barney said.

"That's cool," Ellis said. "I appreciate it and all that, but sometimes I get bad headaches from shit-shake like this."

"I'll smoke it," Todd said. "I get headaches all the time, anyway."

From the smell, Ellis could tell it was shitty pot, probably years old, never frozen for preservation, with all the flavor dried out of it. Goat Man had once told him that marijuana plants were ninety percent genetic and ten percent human intervention. Ellis told Barney and Todd that the stuff they had bought was ninety percent shit and ten percent human neglect.

SEVENTEEN

The next morning, Goat Man woke at six to swim laps. He wanted to beat Bennet to the pool. The laps would do him good. And later, he'd load the goats into the Jetta and go on another practice trek.

Steam rose from the water in the fuzzy morning light. He turned on the pool light, but the electric-purple color was too artificial, too bright, so he turned it off and dove into the dark water. The pool was refreshing as it washed away the crusty remnants of sleep. He liked the dark water. It made him feel both dead and alive.

But without his hybrid, Goat Man's brain raced—worries flushed through his mind: the main trek, Wendy's growing intolerance, stupid-ass Freida. It took him about thirty laps before he was able to calm down and relish the endorphins igniting his brain. Then he just glided through, experiencing the water, reaching for the wall, counting his breaths.

Bennet appeared and stood on the end of the diving board, tanned toes hooking over the edge. He wore his new trunks—big, boxy, and green—and crunched an apple while he watched Goat Man. Goat Man noticed him up there right away, and he continued to swim, harder.

"I didn't think you had it in you to exercise!" Bennet yelled. "You need to extend your arms more and learn to breathe on both sides!"

Goat Man heard him but pretended he didn't and kept swimming. He'd swim until it was physically impossible to swim anymore, until his body stopped working, until Bennet gave up on swimming laps himself and went back in the house.

But Bennet was more patient than Goat Man was fit, and when Goat Man's exhausted legs stopped functioning and his arms became lifeless and heavy, Bennet was ready to dive in and take reign over the pool.

Goat Man climbed out of the pool and hacked up the previous day's hybrid damage into a trimmed kumquat bush.

Bennet stood in the shallow end of the pool, stretching his neck and arms. "That's disgusting," he said. "Your lungs are begging for mercy."

"Leave me alone." Goat Man coughed a few more times, looking at the yellow-and-pink light spreading its way up into the eastern sky.

"I just remembered," Bennet said. "I'll thank you not to lean the goats' pool against my Jeep."

"You're welcome," Goat Man said.

A bemused look washed across Bennet's face. "Aubrey seems to think you're some kind of god. I told her you weren't." Bennet dove under and started his laps.

Goat Man staggered into the pool house in search of his pipe. When he found it—under some magazines on the floor in front of the couch—he lit it up and took a strong hit. He fell asleep on his couch.

• • •

He awoke a few hours later in his itchy, damp swimsuit. He felt it was time to leave; he had to go trekking. He quickly changed out of his trunks, packed up his tent and vitamins, and walked down to the goats.

They were all hanging out near the pen, Lance standing on the roof of the shack, Mr. T playfully chasing Gigi. Freida was kneeling in the corner, her eyes closed and her lips pursed in a snobby pout. Maybe she was jealous of Gigi. Maybe her own pheromonic loins had lost their luster.

Lance noticed Goat Man's packs and immediately leaped down from the roof and trotted over to him. Freida looked up but instantly resumed her haughty indifference. Goat Man took two leather leashes from the shack and hooked them up to Lance and Freida. This trek would be Freida's last chance to prove herself before Goat Man focused his energy on Gigi as his main traveling milk goat.

He led them down the wash to his Jetta. Some kid had scraped POOP into the side of the car, probably with a key.

As usual, Lance and Freida were hesitant to jump into the Jetta. Goat Man gave Lance the privilege of riding shotgun, but he still had to shove the goat's majestic ass into the car. The backseat, with all its fast-food waste, beer cans, and greasy rags, was left for Freida. She was more difficult, screaming like a baby when Goat Man began to force her in. She kicked Goat Man in the ear—a burning, swift kick that set him on his ass. "Get in there!" He tackled her, scraping his elbow on a rock, picked her up and crammed her in.

Out near I-10, he remembered that he hadn't told Wendy he was leaving, which was stupid because he wanted her to think he was more responsible. He pulled over at a 7-Eleven and used the dusty, faded pay phone. The receiver was scorching hot, baking in the sun, too hot to let it touch his face.

Bennet answered.

"Let me speak to Wendy," Goat Man said.

"May I tell her who's calling?"

"You know who this is. Let me talk to her."

"Why do you need to talk to her so badly?"

"Put her on the phone."

"Why are you so desperate?"

Goat Man hung up.

Lance was bleating loudly at a man on a motorcycle who had pulled up next to the Jetta. The man pulled off his helmet. "Those are the ugliest dogs I've ever seen," he said.

Lance wouldn't shut up.

"Thank you," Goat Man said, not in the mood.

"Just kidding," the man said. "I know they're goats."

Goat Man jumped into his smelly Jetta and backed out. In his rearview mirror, he noticed Freida chewing on a Styrofoam cup. It was almost half gone. He pulled his emergency brake, causing the car to doughnut before stopping in a cloud of dust and smoke. He yelled at Freida: "I'm completely sick of your shit!"

Freida stared at him blankly, crunching the cup, her lower jaw moving eliptically.

Lance spit a fart.

The motorcycle man rode by and waved to the goats.

EIGHTEEN

Ellis had three hours before his train departed, so he sat around the kitchen with Judy, while Frank napped upstairs.

He flipped through his history book, feigning interest in it.

Judy jabbered. "Aren't you curious to know how your father and I met?"

"I guess," Ellis said. "Yeah."

"I needed some new furnishings for my ski house in Colorado—you'll have to come out there sometime, it's in Telluride, right up against a big mountain, near Oprah's ski house—so, I went to his store . . ."

Ellis meant to remember every detail for Wendy, but he spaced out, thought about Minnie, the food server back at Gates, what her breasts might look like. Before he knew it, Judy was telling him about her second date with Frank: ice skating.

"Sounds nice," Ellis said.

"Frank's a marvelous skater. He played hockey at Gates, you know."

"I thought he only did crew."

"That was his first love, but he played hockey and basketball, too. He played basketball in college."

Ellis went upstairs to the guest room to finish packing and to actually study some history. Frank, in his robe, was emerging from Judy's room. His hair was sticking out in all directions, and his eyes were half-closed and puffy. Ellis laughed at him.

"What?" Frank said.

"Your hair."

"Oh, yeah," Frank mumbled, as he mussed Ellis's hair and continued down the stairs.

Ellis couldn't bear to open his history book. He was sick of it, sick of all his classes, so he perused the shelves of paperbacks and pulled out a dirty romance novel with a racy couple in a half-naked, passionate embrace on the cover. He immediately flipped to a sex scene: *Jack tongued her quivering loins until Samantha could take it no more. She panted madly, pinned his sinewy shoulders down to the bed, and . . .* When Ellis reshelved the last paperback he had pulled, he was amazed to see he had squandered over an hour reading stupid sex scenes. He felt like jerking off, too, but it was almost time to leave. He went into the bathroom and did it anyway, finished up in just a few minutes.

Frank and Judy drove Ellis to Union Station. The people they passed on the wet D.C. streets looked motivated and eager, as if they had places to go, even swaddled in their blandly colored rain gear. Ellis felt a bit uneasy watching these people, but he wasn't sure why. He wondered if he could ever live in a real city like D.C. Goat Man couldn't, Ellis knew.

"You don't have to come to the train," Ellis said as they pulled up in front of Union Station. "I know where it is."

"I can't really park here, anyway," Frank said.

"That's cool," Ellis said. Ellis hopped out of the car into the November drizzle. He looked over at the row of flagpoles that stood before the station, at the soggy flags from all fifty states. He couldn't find Arizona's.

Judy stepped out of the car and hugged Ellis tightly. She smelled good—like vanilla. "Bye," she said. "I loved meeting you."

"Thanks," Ellis said. "Thanks for having me."

Ellis reached into the car as Frank extended his hand across the seat.

"Bye," Ellis said. He firmly shook Frank's hand.

"Bye, Ellis."

Ellis felt like a baby, but he was a little angry that Frank didn't get out of the car to hug him. Maybe Frank was still upset about the gin incident. Maybe he didn't want to get his hair wet. Maybe this whole trip was something Judy put him up to, an obligation.

Ellis lugged his bag through the cold rain.

Ellis met Barney near the McDonald's inside Union Station. "It's over," Ellis said.

"What's over?"

"No more Fucker Frank."

"Was he an asshole?"

"Not really," Ellis said, but he wasn't sure. He had spent the last fifteen minutes wondering.

"Look what I got." Barney pulled a bottle of gin from his pack and held it up like a torch.

"Put that away," Ellis said. "Duh. We'll buy some drinks and dump it in."

The boys bought Sprites at McDonald's and dumped half of each on a wet sidewalk outside in front of the deserted Postal Museum entrance. The soda fizzed as it trickled into the street. They replaced the dumped Sprite in each of their cups with gin and walked to their train.

The only two seats together were next to a burly man with a

raised pink scar on his upper lip. As soon as Ellis sat down next to him, the man introduced himself as Quentin, from Glasgow.

"I'm Ellis from Tucson, Arizona, and this is Barney from here in D.C.," Ellis said. Quentin reeked of cigarettes.

"Arizona," Quentin said. "Like cactus and cowboys?"

Ellis could barely understand him. "Sort of."

The train started with a jerk. Ellis was looking forward to returning to Gates, returning to normal.

"So where're you boys headed?" Quentin asked.

"Back to school," Barney said.

"Great," Quentin said. "Where's your school?"

"Pennsylvania, northern Pennsylvania," Ellis said.

"Great," Quentin said. "What're you boys drinking? I can smell something."

"It's gin," Barney whispered.

"Great," Quentin said. "I never drink alone." He pulled a small tin flask from his coat pocket and toasted the boys. "To new drinking chums."

Quentin lewdly harassed any woman who was unlucky enough to walk by his seat.

"Sit on me face or I'll cry."

After he became more drunk, Quentin harassed men, too. "Hey, mate, you look like you could use a good buggering, and I've got the two lads who can give it to you," he told one.

Barney laughed loudly, clutched his gut, and keeled over, which embarrassed Ellis.

A uniformed ticket collector came by and ended it all. "The three of you will be asked to leave the train at the next stop if any of this continues," he told them.

Barney laughed harder, and Ellis socked him in the stomach.

"We'll be quiet," Quentin said.

"I'll keep him quiet," Ellis said, shoving Barney.

"You better," the attendant said. "I'm serious."

Ellis was tired anyway, and his stomach burned from the gin and Sprite. He felt a little guilty for socking Barney in the gut, especially with Barney moaning and all, but Barney had deserved it, laughing like a retard the way he did.

"You boys play rugby?" Quentin asked.

Barney looked up. "No," he moaned.

"No," Ellis said.

"Too bad," Quentin said. "I thought we might have something serious to talk about."

"Is that how you got your scar? From playing rugby?" Barney asked. "Ellis got his from a girl," he added. "His eyebrow's fucked up from a girl."

"I didn't get it from playing rugby," Quentin said, thumbing his scar, "but I got it playing a rugby game."

"What?" Barney said.

"I was playing soggy biscuit and I lost. I refused to eat the biscuit, so me mates beat the hell out of me," Quentin said. "Made me eat the biscuit, anyway—the bastards."

"What's soggy biscuit?" Barney asked.

Ellis didn't care what soggy biscuit was.

"The whole team stands around and tosses off onto a biscuit—a cookie. The last one's spunk on the biscuit, has to eat it," Quentin said. "You've never played?"

"What's spunk?" Barney asked.

"Sperm, you moron," Ellis said. "Let's change the subject."

"Gross," Barney said. "I'd rather have a scar. You could get AIDS."

Ellis brought Barney's backpack into the train's cramped restroom and refilled their saturated McDonald's cups. This time they had nothing to dilute the gin with; they'd have to drink it straight. He spilled a little as the train rattled onward. The harshness made them wince as they sipped it through plastic straws. But Ellis wanted to get drunker so he could more easily abide Barney and Quentin. After a few minutes, the bottom of Barney's paper cup collapsed, and the gin spilled onto his lap.

Ellis laughed.

"It's not funny," Barney said. His face was reddening like he might cry. He was drunk and grumpy, all set for a fit—Ellis could tell.

"I can see the wee tears in his eyes," Quentin said.

"I'm moving," Barney said. He gathered his stuff and moved to another car, dripping gin down the aisle.

Ellis fell asleep a few minutes after Barney moved. He dreamed of Judy. She was the horse, and he had to ride her to the bus stop. She was his Latin teacher, too, and school was held in the Tucson Mall, near Banana Republic. The faces were vague and colorless—except for Judy's. She asserted herself in Ellis's dream, forced him to listen to her conjugate strange new verbs that Ellis felt he should have known.

Quentin shook him awake in Philadelphia. The gin worked its ways on Ellis stronger than before. The train seemed to be spinning through the station like a fucked-up carnival ride, even though it had stopped.

"I have to get off here," Quentin said. "It was nice knowing you, Ellis. What's your last name?"

"Whitman." Ellis was still half asleep, gripping the seat.

"Great to meet you, Ellis Whitman." Quentin squeezed by Ellis. "Tell your little friend, no hard feelings, will you?"

"Sure."

NINETEEN

To punish Freida for munching the Styrofoam cup and Lance for his flatulence, Goat Man decided to drive up snowy Mount Lemmon. They'd trek down the backside toward Oracle, and camp in Charlow Gap. The goats would have a good five or six hours of snow walking. Neither of them had ever been in snow, but Goat Man thought they deserved discomfort.

The highway twisted up the mountain through four or five distinct zones of flora: from prickly pear cacti and yucca plants to ferns and towering pines. When Goat Man had first come out to Tucson for college, he and his new friends drove up the mountain almost every weekend, filling the back of the Pacer with cheap beer—Coors was still a novelty for Goat Man because he was from Illinois. Sometimes they'd eat magic mushrooms and sit on the ledges at Windy Point, laughing and arguing about what the rock formations resembled.

The goats were well behaved riding up the mountain. Freida slept, and Lance looked curiously at the changing landscape. Goat Man hadn't been on Mount Lemmon for a few years. The last time had been when he and Ellis camped in Rose Canyon. There was a lake up there, stocked with stinky, diseased trout. They were too easy to catch, apathetic fish, no challenge whatsoever. He and Ellis had caught about fifteen each, some big, but threw them all back. Many of them looked like someone else had caught them and thrown them back just minutes earlier, as if being out of the water with hooks in their mouths was nothing new, nothing to get excited about. Goat Man had wanted Ellis to experience real fishing, so the next week, they drove down to Mexico, near Guaymas, where they spent a few nights in a tent on a deserted beach and two days on a deep-sea-fishing vessel. The second day on the boat, in the pounding Mexican sun, Ellis, with his twelve-year-old stick arms, hooked a six-foot marlin. He spent two and a half hours strapped into the fishing chair, pulling in the fish, his face a rich crimson with sun damage and exertion. Goat Man and a few of the guys from the charter boat cheered him on, applied sunscreen to his arms and face, held drinks up to his mouth, until he finally reeled it all the way onto the boat. Goat Man snapped several photos of exhilarated Ellis kneeling next to his catch. Later that night, as they ate tortilla soup and fish tacos in a San Carlos restaurant, Ellis thanked Goat Man for taking him fishing, said that as he was pulling in the fish, he could think of nothing else but the fish. "I didn't worry about Wendy at home alone or think about Fucker Frank. I just thought about getting the fish."

"You think about your parents a lot?" Goat Man asked.

"Don't you?"

"My parents are different," Goat Man said. "I never had to worry about them."

"You're lucky," Ellis said. He took a bite from his messy taco, the dressing streaming off his elbow. "My arms feel like rubber," he said between chews. "I hope those pictures come out."

"They will," Goat Man said—but the pictures wouldn't come out. As they packed the car the next morning, Goat Man dropped the camera. It hit the car's bumper before it landed in the sand with the film hatch popped open.

Past the ranger station on Mount Lemmon, it no longer felt like the Sonora Desert. The air was cold and moist, full of pine that smelled almost artificial, like a clean public restroom, and there were patches of glowing snow on either side of the highway. Freida woke up and bleated loudly.

"Quiet, please," Goat Man said.

Freida bleated louder.

Goat Man looked back at her in his rearview mirror. She was sitting up on her ass, rocking her head. "Quiet down," he said.

She didn't, so he tried to drown her cries by turning on his crackly radio. The tuner was stuck on AM 1290—Christian hits: "Lord, I can see, you've come to rescue me . . ."

A few minutes later, as they approached the little ski resort, Goat Man's eyes began to burn from the familiar sharp fumes of goat urine. The seat behind him held a puddle of Freida's acrid piss. He rolled down his window and felt the icy air. It wasn't Freida's fault; she had tried to warn him. But Goat Man still hated her.

The snow was no longer patchy; it completely covered the ground. Goat Man watched people unload their colorful ski gear from their cars in the parking lot of the small resort. There was a new chair lift, and it looked like they had chopped away more of the forest to make better ski runs. He should bring Ellis up here at Christmastime, he thought.

The pavement ended, and Goat Man drove up a wet dirt road. Snow was melting in the midday sun, forming streams that dug through the road, creating nasty muck-filled potholes. The goats were quiet. Freida slept, hunched in a ball away from her piss. Lance nervously gazed at the snow.

Goat Man parked in a muddy lot near a small power station on the peak. After he opened all four car doors, neither of the goats jumped out like they usually did. Freida just glanced up briefly and resumed her slumber. Lance looked at the muddy, snowy ground and snorted. Goat Man left Lance's door open and walked around to his own. From his seat behind the wheel, he shoved Lance out into the cold air. Lance darted for a rock about twenty feet from the car, and he stood majestically upon it, assessing the mud and snow on his hooves. Freida would be tougher. He couldn't shove her from the piss-soaked seat without getting himself wet. He'd have to pull her by the collar.

She didn't budge, but she did emit a few languid bleats.

Goat Man tugged harder on her collar.

She nipped him, drawing blood from his wrist with her pinching yellow teeth.

Goat Man calmly walked over near Lance and found a stick the size of a baseball bat. He didn't believe in quirts or whips; he had never felt the need for them—until now. He swatted Freida's ass as best as he could within the confines of the car. She jumped up and over into the front seat, sitting behind the wheel. She left piss prints. He swatted her again, this time on her side. She jumped in the backseat and drooped her tail.

Goat Man stood back from the car and sucked a few cold breaths through his teeth. He wanted his pipe. He needed to smoke a bowl right then. He opened the squeaky trunk and dug through his bag. He frisked himself, checking all his pockets. No pipe, no buds. He had left them at home. He could see the pipe and bag sitting on his kitchen counter next to the toaster.

"Okay, Freida, you win. Come on, Lance, we're going home."

Lance didn't move. He stood firm on the rock.

"Please."

Lance stood firm, so Goat Man walked over and tugged his collar. He was able to drag Lance to the car and get him in the front seat. Freida was again napping in the back. Goat Man slammed all the car doors and started the Jetta. "Hold on," he said.

He got out of the car and made a big snowball, his hands turning pink and numb. He carried the muddy snowball—about the size of a pumpkin when he finished—to the car, opened the backdoor, and smashed it over Freida's head. She sneezed and shook her head, then fell back asleep. "I hate you," Goat Man said. "I really hate you."

TWENTY

By the time Ellis and Barney reached their dorm at Gates, Ellis felt hung-over with a dull headache and burning stomach. Barney was petulant, ready to bite, still upset about the problems he had on the train.

Ellis unpacked his bag and lay down on his bed. He noticed Barney stuffing his clothes into the hamper.

"You better wash the pants you spilled the gin on in the sink. I can smell them from here."

"Fuck you," Barney said. He stuffed the khakis into the plastic hamper.

"I don't want to get busted because of your stupid pants." Ellis sat up. "Wash them in the sink with shampoo."

"Suck me."

"What?" Ellis stood, surprised.

"I said suck me, asshole."

"You little fuck."

Ellis tackled Barney and punched his eye. He hurt his knuckles on Barney's forehead. They rolled into the dresser, and a few of Barney's trophies crashed to the floor.

"Hey!" Barney screamed. He tore out a bloody chunk of

Ellis's hair, about the size of a dime. Barney scrambled to his feet, one hand over his punched eye.

"You shit!" Ellis stood and shoved Barney, who stumbled backward and leaned against his desk. Ellis took the shit's citizenship trophy from its perch and hurled it at him. It hit the window, which smashed into a million dazzling triangles. But Ellis barely noticed the noise or the shards that covered the desk. He heaved the hamper at Barney.

As soon as the hamper left his grip, Ellis knew he had fucked up bad. He felt the warm blood trickle down from his scalp and soak his collar.

By this time, several boys had gathered at the door to watch the ruckus. Barney was moaning, sitting at his desk of shards with his head down. Ellis leaned over and picked up a few trophies, noticing his misty breath in the cold air pouring in through the broken window. Then someone tackled him.

It was Mr. Hopkins, the health teacher who lived at the end of the hall and acted as dorm monitor. "That's quite enough," he said, pinning Ellis's shoulders to the floor with his meaty arms. From underneath, Mr. Hopkins looked bigger than usual. Ellis didn't struggle.

"I was just picking up the trophies," Ellis said. "We already stopped."

"Calm down," Mr. Hopkins said. "You calm down, Whitman."

Barney stood, stumbled over to Ellis, and kicked him squarely in the balls.

Pain shot through Ellis's gut, raced through his whole body. He gasped and coughed, felt like he couldn't breathe.

All the while, Ellis knew stupid Mr. Hopkins didn't realize he had been kicked. He didn't notice Ellis was gagging until Benson Bruner, a chipped-toothed sophomore from a few rooms down, pushed Mr. Hopkins off and rolled limp Ellis onto his stomach. Barney squatted in the corner by his bed and cried with his head on his knees. Ellis hacked, coughed more.

Benson Bruner and Mr. Hopkins slowly ushered Ellis down the stairs and across the lawn to the infirmary. They were talking, maybe to Ellis, but Ellis couldn't hear what they were saying. A bunch of boys followed until Mr. Hopkins yelled at them to return to their rooms. He helped Ellis into a bed that smelled like mint.

"I didn't know you were kicked," Mr. Hopkins said, adjusting the pillow under Ellis's shoulders.

"Okay," Ellis mumbled.

"Sorry, guy," Mr. Hopkins said, mussing Ellis's bloody hair. He wiped his hand on his pants, and he and Benson Bruner left.

The boy in the bed next to Ellis's, Rosenberg—the coxswain from the freshman crew—stared at him. "You're so busted," he said.

"What?" Ellis looked around at the boring room: white walls, white floor, white sheets, no windows, three beds. His balls still hurt. So did his scalp, which was sticky with blood.

"You and Barney are so busted." Rosenberg grinned wildly.

"What?"

"The fight. Plus your room stinks of booze. Plus you and Barney both stink of booze. Plus the broken window."

"Plus you're an asshole." Ellis lifted the blanket and slid his hand under the elastic of his boxers. He cupped his tender balls. "How the hell do you know all this already?"

"Jason and Slake ran ahead and told me the whole thing."

"That's pathetic," Ellis said. "Why the hell are you in here, anyway?"

Rosenberg pulled back his sheet, exposing a cast that started at his foot and ran all the way up his thigh. "I broke my leg skiing over Thanksgiving. You know, Hopkins almost killed you. You were choking on your own spew and he had you pinned on your back. You could sue him and the school."

"I wasn't spewing," Ellis said. "When do I get busted?"

"I bet they're talking to Barney now."

The fat nurse walked in. She had a face like a big toe, and was well hated by the boys at Gates for her halitosis and unsympathetic ear. "I was just reading about testicular injuries," she said to Ellis. "I'm supposed to make you urinate and check for blood."

"I don't have to."

Rosenberg snickered.

"Fuck you, Rosenberg," Ellis said.

"Hey!" the nurse said. "You're in enough trouble. None of that language. Now get up and pee in this." She handed Ellis a plastic cup sealed in a plastic bag, and pointed toward the bathroom.

Ellis's piss looked fine, like the diluted apple juice in the cafeteria. The cup was warm in his hand.

"Here you go." He handed the cup to the nurse. He walked lightly back to the bed, careful not to let his balls swing or bounce. He eased into the bed and spread his legs. He wanted to strangle Barney until his fat lips turned purple and exploded. The blots of blood on the pillowcase reminded him to ask about his head.

"We'll put some ointment on that," the nurse said.

"That's it?"

"That's it." The nurse walked toward the door carrying the piss.

"Will I have a bald spot?"

"Maybe," she said, easing the door shut.

"You think my hair will grow back on this spot?" Ellis asked Rosenberg.

"Probably not," Rosenberg said. "It'll be like your fucked-up eyebrow."

About an hour later, the nurse summoned Ellis into her office. Dr. Eldridge, the headmaster, was sitting behind the nurse's cluttered desk, dressed casually in a green sweater and jeans that looked as if they'd been ironed. His eyebrows were gray, almost white, but his hair was black, too black. Ellis stared at a faded poster of a grinning chimp in a nursing uniform. It read, "Love a Nurse!" Goat Man had once said that chimpanzees were cannibals. The TV confirmed this. Ellis had seen a documentary on cable that featured chimps eating baboons, tearing off their limbs and feeding greedily on the flesh.

"Mr. Whitman, have a seat. We need to get to the bottom of this tonight so we can all get on with our lives," Dr. Eldridge said.

Ellis sat down, still gazing at the chimp nurse.

"What happened tonight?" Dr. Eldridge asked.

"Barney was being obnoxious, so I tackled him."

"And before that?"

"He was obnoxious before that."

"I mean the drinking," Dr. Eldridge said. He twirled one of the nurse's pens.

"He was obnoxious before the drinking."

"You're not funny or clever," Dr. Eldridge said. He went on to tell Ellis about the dangers of teenage drinking, about a student from Gates who had gone on to Dartmouth and died from alcohol poisoning at a frat party, about other students who had to drop out of colleges for alcohol rehabilitation. "No weekend privileges until further notice."

"I'll never drink before coming back to Gates again," Ellis said. As he spoke, he was sickened by what he was saying. He was glad no one else was around to see him being so obsequious. "I think it made Barney cranky, and that's why we fought."

Dr. Eldridge stared at Ellis, squinted. "What do you do in your spare time?"

"I don't have any spare time," Ellis said.

"What about crew? You're tall." Dr. Eldridge leaned back in his chair. "The best times of my life were spent on boats. I wasn't lucky enough to have the opportunity to row in prep school. I had to wait until college. The coach would love to have you, and we just bought three new racing shells."

"Maybe," Ellis said, "but I don't want to."

"We'll find something for you." He stood, and shook Ellis's hand. "If you ever just want to talk, come visit my office."

"Thank you, sir," Ellis said.

"Now let's give Nurse Wallace her office back. They put plastic over your window, so you can return to your room. I trust you and Barney—Mr. Cannel—I trust you and Mr. Cannel will get along fine from now on."

"We will," Ellis said. He glanced one last time at the chimpanzee. He imagined it gnawing on another chimp's arm, bright blood blooming through its white nursing uniform.

TWENTY-ONE

In the early evening, Wendy knocked twice on Goat Man's door and walked in. He was naked, kneeling on the kitchen counter, changing the bulb above the sink.

"Excuse me," he said, covering himself with a dishrag and a bag of frozen corn.

"Sorry." Wendy stepped back outside and shut the door. "There's someone I want you to meet," she yelled.

"Wait a minute." Goat Man danced around the counter into his bedroom, where he sniffed a few pairs of boxers that he had strewn over the floor. He settled on his red velour robe. Ellis had always called it a pimp robe.

As he walked back into the family room, in strolled Wendy and another woman: long black hair, flowing printed skirt, and comfortable-looking brown shoes. The strange woman gazed expectantly at Goat Man with dopey eyes. "Everyone decent in here?" she said.

"This is Johanna," Wendy said. "And Johanna, this is Javier."

"Nice to meet you," Johanna said, walking up to Goat Man. "Wendy has told me all about your treks. I'm curious to learn more."

Johanna stared at Goat Man so intently that he thought he

had something on his nose. He wiped it with the sleeve of his robe.

Wendy and Johanna sat on the couch. Goat Man took a seat across from them in a rocking chair. He played with the edge of the Navajo rug with his bare feet, hiding his toes.

"So, Javier, I'm very interested in the voice of the nomadic animal, the spirit of the animal. How would I get to know these goats?" Johanna asked. She reached over and squeezed Goat Man's knee.

"Hang out with them," Goat Man said.

"Would I need to talk to them? Pet them? Take them for walks?"

"Feed them. Feed them Corn Pops and they're your friends for life," Goat Man said. Johanna was pretty: deep brown eyes, a little dart of a nose, and full lips. She was swarthy—maybe half Hawaiian or something, Goat Man thought.

"So that's where the reciprocity of soul sharing begins?"

"I guess," Goat Man said. He watched Wendy nodding enthusiastically, clinging to every word Johanna uttered.

"May I see your goats? I mean, may I see your *friends?*" Johanna asked. She squeezed his knee again, harder. "I didn't want to imply that you owned them, like slaves or something."

"Of course not. They own me."

"May I meet them?"

"Sure," Goat Man said. "Let me just put my boots on."

The goats stirred when Goat Man, Wendy, and Johanna reached the pen and shined their flashlights on them. Lance was perched in his usual spot on the roof of the shack. Gigi sauntered up to Goat Man and stealthily began to chew the belt of his robe.

"This one here is Gigi," Goat Man said, pulling the slimy belt out of her mouth.

"She's magnificent," Johanna said. "Look at her twinkling, soulful eyes."

"They're filled with ointment," Goat Man said. "She has a little case of pinkeye."

"I never knew how blessed I was having these goats so close," Wendy said.

"Oh, you *are* blessed," Johanna said. "They're so stunning, so knowing. What's his name?" She pointed her flashlight at Lance.

"That's Lance," Goat Man said.

"He's proud," Johanna said. "Regal."

"That's what he thinks," Goat Man said.

She then pointed to Mr. T with her flashlight. He had walked over to the other end of the pen and was rubbing his withers on a an old, tilted SOLD sign. "And who's that handsome fella?"

"Mr. T," Goat Man said. "I think he's masturbating. If you wait a few minutes, he'll start to make a weird purring sound."

"I can see we've disturbed them. We should let them continue with their dreaming. Goats dream, don't they?" Johanna asked.

"I think so," Goat Man said. "They bleat in their sleep sometimes. Their flanks and rumps twitch, too."

"Javier, I'll be contacting you soon about getting to know your friends," Johanna said.

"I'll be down at the pen a lot more," Wendy added.

They walked up the narrow dirt path toward the house, Goat Man's pimp robe snagging on a few chollas. Wendy and Johanna said goodnight, as Goat Man strayed off to the pool area.

Goat Man threw the slobbery robe belt into the kitchen sink and finished changing the bulb. He looked over at the table where his pipe and buds sat, but decided not to smoke. He had already gotten stoned twice that day to make up for his unsuccessful trip to Mount Lemmon, and he planned on doing laps in the morning. He'd beat Bennet out to the pool again.

Goat Man awoke to his obnoxious alarm at six, pulled on his trunks, and went out to the pool. The deck was cold against his bare feet. The desert was alive with noise: families of quail cooing, coyotes howling like sirens in the distance. It was still dark, cloudy, and the pool water was as black as coffee. He cannonballed off the freezing diving board into the steamy water and began his laps.

In the shallow end, near the wall, Goat Man bumped into something bristly. He shrieked and took in a little water, but then decided it must be one of the rabbits from the desert that fell into the pool periodically and ended up dead in the skimmer. When he got out of the pool and tried to look at it, he could only make out the size—too big for a drowned rabbit. Maybe a coyote. He ran over to the light switch, his wet feet slapping the deck. He flicked the light on.

In the artificial purple light, he saw Mr. T's white butt bobbing in the low end.

He dove into the pool and swam over to Mr. T., but it was way too late—Mr. T was stiff and waterlogged. He lifted the heavy goat out of the water and plopped him on the deck.

Goat Man punched Mr. T on the side. He sounded hollow. The goat's black and pink lips were curled into a stiffened smile that Goat Man tried to press down. The lips were stuck that way. He threw the dead goat over his shoulders like a sack of feed and headed toward the gate.

Bennet came out of the house then, scratching his head. "Oh, my," he said.

"You can have the pool first this morning, I've got a goat to bury," Goat Man said.

"How'd he get through the fence?"

"I might have left the gate open last night."

"It's a known fact that marijuana causes people to be forgetful," Bennet said, tossing his towel on the diving board.

"It's a known fact that you're an asshole." Goat Man again dropped Mr. T onto the deck—a wet, heavy smack—and went into the pool house to get his boots.

The other goats gathered around and sniffed Mr. T, as Goat Man dug the grave in the red morning light. The dark cloud cover was dense. It might rain, so he had to make the grave deep. He dug. The loose, rocky soil was easy to break up, and he progressed quickly.

Freida nibbled some on Mr. T's collar, so Goat Man thwacked her side with his shovel. She screamed and ran off down the wash. "I'd like to toss your ass in this hole!" he yelled after her. He felt ridiculous in his wet swim trunks and boots, and he was freezing. He rolled Mr. T into the hole. The goat's stiff legs stuck up at weird, wrong angles.

Wendy walked down to him as he was shoveling the dirt over Mr. T. "Bennet told me what happened. I'm really sorry," she said, hugging herself in her thick terry robe.

"At least it wasn't Lance."

"That's not very nice."

"I'm practical when it comes to goats—not emotional."

"You must be very sad, anyway," she said. She stood behind him and massaged his cold neck. She made it difficult to pat the dirt.

"I didn't know Mr. T that well. He was always bitching at the girls, jealous of them. He never really paid much attention to me," Goat Man said.

"You're freezing," Wendy said.

"Yes," he said. "I'll miss Mr. T. He was a good-looking buck in his time."

Goat Man finished patting the dirt down, and he and Wendy walked up to the pool. Bennet wasn't out there, so Goat Man removed his boots and jumped into the warm water. He treaded water in the deep end, while Wendy lay in a lounge chair.

"Guess who called me this morning," Wendy said. She kicked off her mules.

"I have no idea."

"Dr. Eldridge from Gates."

"Who's he?" Goat Man breathed hard, huffed.

"The headmaster. Ellis did some drinking on the train back to school from his stay with Fucker Frank. Then he and his roommate got in a big fight. I have to send a check for two hundred dollars to repair a window that Ellis smashed," she said. "They couldn't get hold of Frank because he was still at his slutty girlfriend's house in Washington."

"Shit." Goat Man swam to the shallow end and crouched so just his head was above the water.

"He also told me that Ellis has the highest grades in his class. That's probably why they didn't boot him."

"I can't see Ellis in a fight like that," Goat Man said. "Is he all right?"

"He's fine. Dr. Eldridge told me to encourage him to do crew so he can get into a good college. He's only in the ninth grade, and they're already pushing college."

"He's only fourteen," Goat Man said. The water warmed him. He felt his shoulders and upper back loosen and relax. "He shouldn't have to think about that."

"In a way it's disgusting, but in another way, it's good," Wendy said.

"I guess."

"I miss Ellis more than I thought," she said. "Way more."

"How're all the bills and stuff?"

"That's not why I miss him," Wendy said. "I'm a mother and my boy is three thousand miles away. I'm missing a piece of myself."

"He'll be home before you know it."

"He won't recognize you without your beard or long hair," Wendy said. "What's gotten into you? The haircut, and now exercise."

"I thought about what you said about healthy body and soul. It made sense. I'm really cutting back on the weed, too." Before she was into all the mystical New Age crap, it had been much more difficult to bullshit her. Now it seemed too easy.

"That's good to hear," Wendy said. "You know, Johanna was quite taken with you." Wendy sat up. "She told me last night that you're the first man she's been attracted to in a while. She's mostly a lesbian."

"Oh," Goat Man said.

A thin jackrabbit hopped into the pool area. It didn't seem to notice Goat Man or Wendy in the muted morning light. It nibbled on a few shoots of weed sprouting up between the rocks near the filter, then moved casually over to Wendy's lounge chair. She shooed it away with her hand, and it spastically darted out between the posts of the wrought-iron fence.

TWENTY-TWO

Ellis and Barney didn't talk much for a few days after the fight. Neither of them apologized to the other. As final exams loomed closer, Barney resorted to obsequiousness: "I don't mind it when you play your CDs that loud . . . Your tie looks cool . . . I like ska, really . . . Goat Man seems cool . . ." Ellis knew Barney would soon ask him for help in algebra and history, and probably in Latin, too.

Each night as Barney struggled through equations and graphs, Ellis felt him getting closer to breaking down and asking for help. They were learning about functions and limits in algebra, and Ellis knew Barney was having problems. Once, Barney threw his calculator across the room. "Careful you don't break the new window," Ellis said.

A week after the fight, almost to the hour when he delivered the painful kick, Barney finally spoke directly about algebra. He was sitting at his desk twirling his pencils. Ellis was kicked back on his bed.

"What do you think of the new stuff in algebra?" Barney asked.

"Easy," Ellis said.

"I don't get it."

"Sometimes, no matter how hard a person studies, it's impossible to grasp certain concepts from certain teachers." Ellis rolled over and faced Barney. "I read that in one of those airline magazines," Ellis said. "In one of those ads for those learn-at-home deals."

"I believe it," Barney said. "I study all the time and all I ever get is B minuses, and you barely study and smoke pot all the time and get all A's." Barney pushed his chair back and turned to get a better look at Ellis. "By the way, wasn't it nice of me not to bring up your pot-smoking to Dr. Eldridge?"

"You smoked it, too, and I haven't smoked in months."

"Still, I could have shown them where you hide your bong and pipe," Barney said. Ellis kept them in his underwear drawer—he rarely bothered to cover them.

"I could make it sound like you're a junkie, Barney. All I'd have to do is tell them about Licky Face and how you jumped in his car and almost got us killed—all for the prospect of weed."

"You got in the car, too," Barney said.

"So?"

"If you told anyone, I'd tell something about you."

"Like what?"

"I guess my point is that I would never tell on you or tell anything about you unless I really had to," Barney said.

"That wasn't your point," Ellis said. "You're trying to blackmail me into helping you with algebra."

"No, I'm not. I'm just saying I would never tell anything about you—if I knew something."

Ellis didn't say anything. He had gotten three messages earlier that week to call his mother and decided now would be a good time to do it. She probably had questions about credit cards or insurance or her statements from her brokers or the water bill. It was mean to make her wait. He marked his page in his history text with a sock, and walked out of the room to the pay phone.

Bennet answered.

"May I speak to my mother please?"

"Who's calling?" Bennet asked.

"How many children does Wendy have? Put her on." He could hear Bennet breathing on the receiver, not summoning Wendy. "Put her on." He heard Bennet place the phone down and walk away. Ellis wondered what type of shoes the guy was wearing that would make such loud clunks on the tiles. Probably lizard-skin cowboy boots tipped with metal. His mother had dated men who wore shoes like that before. One guy she dated wore clogs.

"Hello," Wendy said.

"It's Ellis."

"Hey, how're the balls?" she asked.

"Eldridge called you?" Ellis traced the graffiti carved in the wall above the grubby phone: *Led Ze*.

"He's nice. Sensible. He thinks you're the greatest, wants you to join crew."

"If you're going to harass me to join, I'm hanging up."

"I want to hear how the rest of your stay with Fucker Frank and his whorish girlfriend went."

"She's not whorish," Ellis said.

"Whatever."

"The rest of the stay was kind of boring."

"Frank's boring," Wendy said. "You're not going to see them again for Christmas, are you? You can't. Please say you won't."

Ellis had moved the receiver from his chin so he could examine the gunk gathered on it. It probably had shit on it from the sixties. It probably had shit on it from Fucker Frank's school days. "I don't think Fucker Frank likes me. He thinks I'm a spoiled, drunken fifteen-year-old."

"You're fourteen," Wendy said.

"I know. He won't be inviting me to spend holidays with him anymore, especially since Eldridge probably called him, too. I'll get the usual cheapo, Frank-style gift in the mail a few days after New Year's," Ellis said. "I got Goat Man the coolest Wailers shirt for Christmas. It's an old-style tour shirt."

"He'll love it, I'm sure. I think he's depressed. He found Mr. T drowned in the pool the other day."

Ellis could hear Bennet in the background bothering Wendy to get off the phone. "I'll let you go," Ellis said. "I'll tell you more about Frank and Judy when I see you in a few weeks."

"I can't wait to see you."

"Only so you can hear about Frank and Judy."

"Not true. I miss you."

"Okay," Ellis said. "I miss you, too. Tell Goat Man I'm sorry about Mr. T and I miss him and I'll send him another postcard."

Ellis wondered how Mr. T ended up in the pool. Ellis had been the one who named Mr. T. He named him after Mr. T breakfast cereal because the goat had speckles the same size and tawny color as the puffs of oat and corn. He missed all the goats' stupid personalities, especially Freida's. He liked how Freida minded him and not Goat Man. For years, she had faithfully followed Ellis around and obeyed him. She respected him. She didn't respect Goat Man.

Once, when Ellis was in the third grade and his class was studying farms, Goat Man brought Freida in for the students to pet. Freida was still a cute, timid kid at the time. Goat Man also gave a short speech about goat husbandry. The highlight of the visit for the kids was when Freida pissed on the green rug in the reading corner. "Your dad's goat has pretty eyes," a girl in Ellis's class told him. He didn't tell her that Goat Man wasn't his father.

• • •

Barney was still struggling with the algebra problems when Ellis returned to the room. "I don't get this function stuff," he told Ellis.

"Bummer," Ellis said, sitting on his bed, removing his well-worn Adidas.

Barney didn't look up from the book. "Will you help me?" he mumbled.

Ellis heard him, but said, "What?"

Barney still didn't look up. "I can't do this. Will you help me?"

"I don't know if I can," Ellis said. He flung his shoes into the open closet. "My balls still kind of hurt. It's hard to concentrate. And this scab on my head is itchy."

"I'm sorry about that," Barney said. He sighed and looked at Ellis. "Well?"

"What?"

"Aren't you gonna apologize?"

"No," Ellis said. "You deserved everything."

"I didn't deserve to have my award thrown through the window," Barney said.

"Yes, you did. And I didn't mean for it to go through the window."

"Will you help me with this math, or what?"

"Okay," Ellis said. He pushed his chair over next to Barney's and tried to explain the basic tenets of functions and limits by using an analogy of an assembly line. "You put the number in one end and when it comes out, it's something different. And if you put a different number through the same function, the function affects it differently—sometimes."

"I don't get it," Barney said.

TWENTY-THREE

Today Goat Man's early swim was interrupted by Wendy, who threw a Styrofoam kick board at him to get his attention. It thunked him on the head.

"Ouch." Goat Man stood in the shallow end and rubbed his temple.

"Sorry," Wendy said. "I didn't feel like yelling. Ellis will be back in six days and I need your advice."

"About what?" Goat Man squatted to keep his body submerged in the warm water.

"About his Christmas present. Bennet said to get him a mountain bike. Would he use it? He's not very athletic." Wendy rubbed her sandal over a rust spot on the deck. Goat Man knew the spot remained from the time Bennet left the hose on the deck after spraying off his spilled juice.

"He might use it," Goat Man said. "If he doesn't, I will."

"What would he really want? I'll get him a bike, but I need to know what he'd really want. Can you think of anything?" She rubbed the deck harder with her leather sole, and squatted down to touch the stain. She sniffed her finger.

Goat Man was getting Ellis a bigger bong for Christmas. "Some CDs," he said to Wendy. "I'll tell you which ones he'd

[131]

want if we drive down to the reggae shop on Fourth Avenue."

"How about one-thirty or two?" Wendy said. "Bennet and I will buy the bike first." She looked relieved; her face relaxed, and she stopped bothering with the rust stain.

"I just have a little rock work I want to finish out front, but I'll be finished by one." Goat Man ducked under and resumed his swim. He had lost count when Wendy interrupted him, so he started again at one. Bennet would have to wait longer to start his own laps.

As he kicked and reached through the water, Goat Man thought about Bennet: the sneaky leech. Bennet didn't appear to be into the spiritual crap as much as Wendy, and his niece Aubrey was okay. But there was something about Bennet that Goat Man couldn't figure out, something that made Goat Man squirm whenever he was around: a barely detectable stink . . . vibes . . . a resemblance to a hated person from the past . . . body language . . . the pitch of his voice . . .

Before he knew it, he had finished his one hundred laps. As he trudged out of the pool, he saw Bennet pushing through the gate.

"Double workout today?" Bennet asked. He stretched his arm behind his back like he was trying to scratch an unreachable itch.

"Yeah," Goat Man said, toweling off.

"You're really keeping at it. I thought after that first day when I saw you cough up your lung that you'd quit." Bennet stretched his other arm in the same manner.

"Yeah," Goat Man said. He threw his towel around his neck and walked into the pool house. He spread the towel over the rocking chair and grabbed his pipe and bag.

• • •

As Goat Man finished arranging rocks around the clusters of prickly pear cacti that flanked the driveway, Wendy and Bennet pulled up in the shiny Jeep. Ellis's new mountain bike clung to the rack on the back. Goat Man looked up and waved. It was good that Wendy saw him working on the rocks. He was dirty and sweaty, looked like an actual laborer.

"Come see this bike!" Wendy yelled. She and Bennet were taking it off the rack. Goat Man walked up the gravel driveway to the garage.

"It's carbon fiber. Handmade in Colorado. The whole thing, with the shocks and all, only weighs twenty-two pounds," Bennet said. He petted the bike's seat as if it were a good dog. "Titanium components."

"Great," Goat Man said. "Ellis'll like it, I bet."

"He better," Wendy said.

"It's almost as good as mine," Bennet said, grinning. He looked up at his bike hanging from rubber-coated hooks screwed into the ceiling of the garage. It was shinier than the one they had just bought for Ellis.

Goat Man doubted that Bennet had ever used it. He had never seen him take it down from the hooks. It hung there like an expensive work of art. "You know how to ride that?" Goat Man asked.

"I haven't been out on it as much as I'd like, but once Ellis gets here, I'll have someone to go riding with," Bennet said.

Goat Man doubted that, too. Ellis would hate Bennet. He'd see through him in a second like he saw through all of Wendy's other boyfriends. Ellis had been calling her boyfriends sponges and mooches since age five. "Maybe there are trails where he can ride it in Pennsylvania," Goat Man said.

"That's true," Wendy said. "Gates is out in the sticks. Will you be ready to go to the record store in about twenty minutes?"

"Sure," Goat Man said.

The little reggae store was at the end of Fourth Avenue, near the spray-painted Value Village Thrift Center and a foam-rubber factory store. There were always transients, hippies, and punks lurking on Fourth Avenue, some of whom knew Goat Man and waved or nodded at him from flyblown shadows.

The dimly lit store reeked of incense and hemp. The record and CD bins were sloppily painted in red, green, and yellow. The owner, a light black man with thick dreadlocks, skanked around the counter to the beat of Burning Spear. When he saw Goat Man, he turned down the music and walked over. "Goat Mon, how are you? Great to see you." Goat Man knew for a fact that Reggie was from Phoenix and that his Jamaican accent was bogus. He didn't mind that Reggie had dreadlocks and considered himself a Rastafarian, but the phony accent was stupid, annoying.

"Hey, Reggie, this is Wendy," Goat Man said.

Reggie took her hand and kissed it lightly. "What a beautiful woman like you doing with a lowly goat herder like he?"

"We need to buy some CDs for my son, Ellis," Wendy said. She wiped the top of her hand on her opposite sleeve.

"You are Ellis's mother? How is the mighty blunt boy?" Reggie asked.

"Fine," Wendy said, confused.

"Never in my eyes did I see a white boy savor the pipe like him," Reggie said. "You raise him on the pipe?"

Goat Man cringed and told Reggie to shut up.

"He's at boarding school now, so he no longer *savors the*

pipe." Wendy said. "Let's get the CDs," she said to Goat Man.

"Okay," Goat Man said. He quickly found five for Ellis, while Wendy stood by the door, arms folded, nervously tapping her foot off-beat to the mellow music.

Reggie added up the cost on a small calculator. "Seventy-two," he said.

"Why no tax?" Wendy asked, walking over. She dug through her bag.

"I don't believe in it," Reggie said.

"Oh, brother," Wendy said. She counted the bills onto the counter and left the store.

"She got a bug in her ass?" Reggie asked Goat Man.

Goat Man got into Wendy's Volvo without saying anything, tried to relax in the comfortable leather seat. He knew Wendy was about to erupt, and he didn't want to be the catalyst.

"Javier," she said calmly as she weaseled into traffic, "I'm not dumb. I know Ellis used to get high with you all the time, but that *mighty blunt boy* and *savor the pipe* stuff . . . It scares me to think you brought him to Rastafarian bake-outs."

"Ellis introduced me to Reggie," Goat Man said. "He's been going to his store since sixth grade."

"Please don't tempt him with your marijuana this Christmas break."

"I won't," Goat Man said. He had never considered that he had *tempted* Ellis with his hybrid.

"I'm not sure I should have bought him these CDs." She stuck her hand in the bag and pulled one out: Jimmy Cliff's *The Harder They Come*. She tried to examine it while driving. "Actually, I don't see any pot songs on this one."

"That one is very inspirational. I'm sure you know it. It's from the movie," Goat Man said. "I think I saw it with you and Frank at the old Loft Theater when Ellis was a baby. Remember? People were lighting up right there in the theater."

"I don't remember," Wendy said.

Goat Man sang: "The harder they come, the harder they fall . . ."

"I don't remember."

Goat Man sang more: "You can get it if you really want, but you must try . . ."

Wendy turned up the warbled, New Age wind songs on her stereo.

TWENTY-FOUR

Ellis finished the two-hour algebra final in forty minutes, and he walked across the muddy quad back to his dorm. His Latin final was on Thursday—a straight translation with dictionaries allowed, followed by an inane skit that he and three other boys had already prepared. No need to study. After that, he was finished for the semester, headed home to Tucson.

He flipped on his CD player and loaded the carousel. After pressing *random*, he lounged back on his bed with his hands behind his neck. He gazed at the ceiling, at a symmetrical water spot that looked like a fat man, and sang along with the squeaky lead singer of the Selecter: "I love my collie . . ."

Ellis had two days after his Latin final before his flight to Tucson, two days of freedom, and he was already restless thinking about it.

He stood up and jogged down the hall to the pay phone. After the sixteen digits of his calling card, he punched in 202-ONE-LOVE: the Kingston Club down in D.C.

The recorded message told him that Toots and the Maytals were playing on Friday. "Amazing," he mumbled as he hung up the dirty receiver. "Amazing."

When he returned to his room, he flipped through his CDs

until he found his Toots one. He pressed *stop* on his stereo, and snatched each of the five CDs out of the carousel, Frisbeeing them onto Barney's bed. He loaded Toots and lay back as Toots's raspy, kind voice washed over him, made him feel high. He remembered when he had first heard the CD in the pool house with Goat Man. It was summer, they were packing for a camping trip to the beach in Kino Bay, Mexico. Of course, they had been smoking up. Goat Man couldn't find his flashlight. Ellis watched as Goat Man went from totally irate to mellowed calm—he had started by cursing himself and digging violently in his closet, and ended up sprawling on the rug and forgetting about looking for the flashlight. It was Toots's friendly, mollifying voice that had done it.

Ellis had to go back to D.C. to see Toots. Goat Man would kill him if he didn't. He hurried down the hall again with a note-book and pen in hand, and called to get all the necessary train and bus information.

When he returned to the room, Barney was there, red and sweaty.

"I bombed that algebra big time," he told Ellis.

"How do you know?"

"You remember the last five, those nasty word problems?"

"Yes."

"I only answered one of them," Barney said. "It was the one where he asked how many kids did Mrs. Jones have. I kept get-ting negative numbers."

"Oh," Ellis said. "Sorry."

"I'll probably be in basic math next semester with all the other morons. I'll be a year behind and I won't be able to take calculus senior year and I'll never get into a good college."

"You could go to summer school. Algebra is easier in the summer."

"I guess."

"Barney, when are you going home for break?"

"Sunday. I have crew on Friday and Saturday."

"I need you to help me out," Ellis said. "Friday morning I'm going to D.C. and I'll be back really early Saturday morning, like around six or seven. You have to cover for me."

"What? Why?" Barney said. He sat on his bed, shoving the CDs to the side, and loosened the laces on his worn bucks.

"If for some fluky reason Hopkins notices I'm gone, tell him I'm finishing a biology lab."

"I can't lie," Barney said. "Eldridge said one more slip-up and I'm out. Same with you."

"If that one chance in a million happens, and I get caught, I'll tell them that I told you I was finishing the lab," Ellis said. "It will look like it was all my fault. They couldn't blame you for anything."

"That's retarded," Barney said.

Ellis turned up his CD player, closed his eyes, and said, "Toots. I want to see Toots. He's old, you know."

Toots wailed, "Pressure drop, oh pressure . . ."

"Duh," Barney said. "You're white, rich, and groomed. What do you know about oppression?"

"Not much," Ellis said. "But I can learn."

"You're gonna spend like twenty hours on the train?"

"There's no express bus to Philly, but if I get a bus to Williamsport, I can get another to Harrisburg, and get the train to Philly. From there it's easy."

"How're you gonna pay?"

"MasterCard."

"Won't your mom see the bill, and then think you went to see your dad again?"

"Shut up," Ellis said.

"Toots's probably playing in Philly."

"How would I find out about it?"

"I don't know."

"I'm going to D.C."

"You'll get thrown out if you get caught."

"Shut up."

"And if one of those buses or trains is late," Barney said, "you're fucked."

Ellis imagined having to pack up all his stuff for good, returning to Tucson and having to tell Wendy he was booted. He imagined calling Frank and telling him. Judy might answer the phone, and he'd have to tell her, too. He'd tell her first, maybe let her tell Frank. He wondered if Green Fields Country Day School in Tucson would admit him after being expelled from Gates. They wouldn't. He'd have to go to one of the big gangbanger public schools in Tucson. He'd be crucified. Shot in the parking lot. Or Wendy would send him to another boarding school, one for fuck-ups, where he'd get ass-raped on a nightly basis.

"Okay, I'm not going," he told Barney. "You suck."

"Because I'm right?"

The Latin exam was as effortless as Ellis had expected, but there was no way Mr. Winters would raise his grade from an A— to an A. He had said Ellis's accent was off.

"How do you know my accent is off?" Ellis had asked. "There is no Latin accent."

"I studied with the masters, I know what good Latin sounds like," Mr. Winters said.

Ellis felt like asking him why someone who had studied with the masters spent his time boring a bunch of rich kids to death, but he didn't want to get worked up over his A−, considering most of the other guys had C's and D's. When Ellis handed Mr. Winters his exam, Mr. Winters told him to practice his pronunciation over the vacation. "Sure thing," Ellis said. "Every day."

"I'm getting beer," Ellis told Barney when they returned to their room. "I don't care what you say, I need to celebrate."

"You'll have to drink it by yourself," Barney said. "I plan on graduating from Gates."

"If I have to miss Toots, I can have a few beers."

The naked black trees that flanked the trail no longer provided any shade and the whole woods took on a new, open appearance. The sun was bright, but it was still cold as Ellis walked through the icy snow patches with the wind at his face. Ellis thought for a second about ducking behind a tree, finding an old magazine, and beating off, rubbing one out—he hadn't done it in four days—but it was too cold, way too cold. He'd do it in bed tonight. Barney didn't care. He didn't care when Barney did it. Sometimes they did it at the same time in their dark room, neither saying anything to the other. All the boys at Gates whacked off too much, so no one bothered to tease anyone about it. Whenever a fresh magazine appeared in the woods, the boys told each other where to find it. Because the Gates boys weren't allowed to have computers in their rooms, they didn't have access to the fresh cyberporn most had at home. There was a mood of group deprivation that bred a camaraderie, a code: share the porn.

About halfway to Peterson's, Rosenberg hobbled out on his crutches from behind a tree. "Hey, Whitman," Rosenberg said. "Where you headed?"

"Beer run," Ellis said. "Don't tell anyone or I'll kill you."

"You're restricted for the rest of the year, right?"

"Just until after spring break," Ellis said. "I think."

"You got time for this?" Rosenberg produced a fat blunt from his wool pea coat.

"That's a big one," Ellis said.

"It's authentic," Rosenberg said. "I even dipped it in Schlitz last night. A real ghetto blunt."

"I didn't know you got high."

"My dad lives in Maui, how could I not get high?" Rosenberg grinned and lit it up. By the way he inhaled and handled the burning blunt, Ellis could tell he was a veteran.

Ellis took it, sniffed the sweet, glowing end, and toked deeply. He took such a powerful hit that the burning end flared up. It burned right, not like the dried shit-shake that Barney and Todd had wasted their money on in D.C. Ellis loved watching the smoke puff from his mouth. In the cold, it looked thick and mighty. Like Goat Man's.

A few minutes after Ellis's third deep hit, the weed imposed itself—a tingling in the forehead, a weighing down of the limbs, a dopey, agreeable mood. Good, Ellis thought, leaning against a tree. He never knew Rosenberg was so cool. Rosenberg looked like the kid on the cover of *Great Expectations:* big, soulful eyes, rosy cheeks, baggy pants, and that ancient pea coat. Ellis was supposed to read *Great Expectations* next semester. Barney had read it in eighth grade and complained that it sucked.

The boys didn't say anything, they just enjoyed the cannabis, passing it back and forth, nodding their heads in the sweet clouds of the other, laughing stupidly. Ellis spaced getting beer, wondered for a second why he had walked into the woods in the first place. He thought about Tucson, about sitting in the sun by the pool, hiking with the goats in the Santa Catalina Mountains, eating real Mexican food with Goat Man somewhere on South Sixth Avenue.

"I wish I knew you got stoned earlier," Ellis said to Rosenberg.

"I thought you might be a stoner."

"Why?"

"You get good grades and you're not really a dork," Rosenberg said. "Plus, you have more reggae CDs than anyone."

"I ran out of weed like three months ago," Ellis said. "I almost forgot how nice it was to get really high. This weed is really good."

A while later, when the blunt got too short to handle, Ellis leaned back against the tree trunk, feeling the ridges in the frozen bark with the back of his head. He concentrated on the cold air. He thought of the summer days in Tucson when it was almost too hot to leave the house, when Wendy would go into the garage, start the car, and run its air conditioning for ten minutes before she got in. The pool wasn't refreshing after July, too warm, like a bath, and because of the intense sun, Goat Man had to keep the chlorine level high, almost toxic. Even the birds flew around the desert with their beaks open, like they were dumbfounded and beaten by the heat. Now, Ellis sucked the cold air through his teeth and tried to convince himself that it was refreshing, like a new stick of gum. He had to get moving—he couldn't just stand there in the woods with Rosenberg, but he felt like staying put and dreaming.

"Mr. Whitman and Mr. Rosenberg, is that reefer I smell?"

Ellis had heard the voice, but it didn't register at first. For a second, he had thought it was Rosenberg, until he looked up and saw the coach jogging toward them, wearing an ugly Day-Glo orange track suit.

Neither Ellis nor Rosenberg could say anything. Ellis figured the semester at Gates wasn't a complete waste of time or money, he'd get credit for his classes, and they'd probably count them all in the public school in Tucson or at a boarding school for delinquents. Or maybe Green Fields would still take him—he'd beg. Blue-haired and barefoot would be a nice change from Gates.

"Well?" Coach said.

"Yes," Rosenberg said. "It's pot. Mine. Ellis didn't have any."

"Yes, I did," Ellis said.

"Mr. Rosenberg, you limp along, I'll catch up with you later. I want to talk to Mr. Whitman here—alone," Coach said.

"Okay," Rosenberg said. His crutches crunched the snow as he hobbled down the trail toward campus. He looked back over his shoulder at Ellis. "Sorry," he said.

"It's cool," Ellis said.

The coach's breath smelled of coffee and plaque, and Ellis winced slightly when the coach got in his face and began to talk. "It's not cool. Didn't you and Mr. Cannel get into some sort of trouble a few weeks ago?"

"Yes."

"This would just about get you booted for sure, wouldn't it?"

Ellis noticed thick, twisty hairs sprouting from the coach's nose. "Probably," he said.

"I'll tell you what. I'll see you at practice this afternoon. On the boat, if the water's not too icy." The coach put his hand on Ellis's shoulder. "I might forget I saw you here in the woods today."

Ellis stood there and stared at the trees in front of him. The leafless branches were like black scribbles against the bright sky.

"I'll see your ass out on that boat this afternoon," Coach said. "Understand?"

Ellis said, "I'll be there."

"Good. And no more smoking. Save your lungs for the boat." The coach slowly jogged off toward Peterson's.

Ellis would be joining Barney for all those practices, waking up at five in the morning, pulling for hours on the rowing machines in the stinky gym, paddling on the freezing lake, running laps around the track. He'd puke for sure. He couldn't remember the last time he had run a lap.

There was too much ice, so the crew lined up at the track. The boys were shivering in their workout clothes as the coach lectured: "I don't want any of you getting fat over Christmas. No Twinkies, no Big Macs, no Dairy Queen." A few of the boys emitted obligatory guffaws. Ellis didn't. He just rolled his eyes and then focused on the coach's protruding gut. He pictured him in front of the Playboy Channel with a Hostess Pudding Pie in one hand and a Bud Light in the other. Why the hell had he been jogging on the Beat-Off Trail, anyway? Fat pervert.

The coach continued: "We have a new member of the crew, I'm sure you all know him, it's Ellis Whitman. Ellis, how tall are you? Six-one, six-two?" Ellis shrugged. He didn't know. The last time he had checked, he was six feet, but that was in the beginning of the summer, seven months ago.

"I want four miles slow," the coach yelled. "Then we'll jog over to the gym for the ergometers."

The boys began to run. They formed a big clump, and before the first bend of the track, Ellis found himself behind everyone else. They all seemed so fast. One problem was Ellis's footwear: he had old Stan Smith Adidas that he had taken from Goat Man's closet. They were made for tennis, not running, and the soles and support were worn. Plus, he was utterly out of shape. He was winded almost instantly, and before he finished the first lap, only one-sixteenth of what he had to run, a searing U-shaped stitch enveloped his gut. He thought he should catch up to Barney and stay close behind him. He could concentrate on the back of Barney's head and try to forget the cramp. He'd go on automatic pilot, dream about the Toots and the Maytals concert he'd miss, and before he knew it, he'd be on lap sixteen, ready to sprint ahead of Barney during the last stretch.

When he tried to pick up his pace, the cramp dug deeper. A few strides later, it won, and Ellis keeled over. He collapsed on the hard, frozen field, clutching his gut and panting. He had not even completed two laps, a measly half-mile.

"What're you doing?" Coach said. He squatted over Ellis. Ellis could barely see the coach's face—his belly blocked it.

"I can't," Ellis said.

"You better," Coach said.

"I can't. I'll die."

"Get up."

Ellis tried to get up, but the cramp made him wince and hunch over.

"Even I can run four miles, and I'm fat." Coach said. "Take deeper breaths and rub the area of the stitch—hard."

Ellis started jogging again. The cramp concentrated on his right side, crawled up his ribs, until he stopped again, and dry-heaved. A few boys stopped to see if he was okay, but the coach yelled at them to continue running. The coach trotted over to Ellis and patted his back until he stopped gagging.

"Okay?" Coach said. "We have a lot of work to do. Maybe you'll do better on the machines."

Ellis tried to spit out a glob of something from his lungs or stomach. It hung from his chin and dribbled down his sweat-shirt.

TWENTY-FIVE

Goat Man wondered what Lance's problem was. Lance always had to be king, and he fought hard for the honor. Because of his status, he could mate with any of the does. But he didn't. He never did. As far as Goat Man knew, Lance was still a virgin, maybe even gay—although he had never seen him do anything with Mr. T.

Goat Man was pretty sure that Gigi was in heat. Lance could mate with her, and bring her into lactation, but Goat Man didn't want another kid yet. Gigi hadn't been a good milk goat in a few years, anyway. Last year, Goat Man induced lactation in her, and milked her every twelve hours, but her supply weakened and disappeared in just a few weeks. He could skip a milking with Freida, or milk her three times a day, and she'd always produce.

Ellis was flying home tomorrow, and Goat Man had spent the day trimming oleander bushes, cleaning the pool, and painting the door of the pool house. He told the goats about his productive day, but they didn't care. Wendy and Bennet were up in Sedona for some spiritual healing, returning in the morning; Goat Man had the place to himself. He had already swum, so he went inside the main house to see if there was anything good on cable TV.

Goat Man always felt weird going into the main house when Wendy was gone, like the furniture and personal effects were those of a stranger, like he was an intruder—but she had cable in there, and a perpetually stocked refrigerator. He plopped in front of the big TV, lit up his pipe, and started channel surfing. He settled on *Cops* and watched three husky mustachioed officers frisk a suspected crack dealer as her baby screeched in the background. One of the cops picked up the baby, its face pixellated, while the other two cuffed the woman and stuffed her into the squad car. The fattest cop spoke to the camera: "It's always not good when there's kids involved, especially babies." 'Tard, Goat Man thought. As he changed the channels, the phone rang in the kitchen.

"Hello," Goat Man said.

"Hey, baby," the caller whispered. It was an older woman's voice. Raspy. As raspy as his own. "Can you talk?"

"What?" Goat Man said.

"Can you come over?"

"You've got the wrong number." He hung up on her.

He looked back at the photographs on the wall above the TV: mostly Ellis, although Goat Man and Wendy had sneaked into a few. So had Fucker Frank. There was one of Fucker Frank with Ellis on his shoulders at the Pima County Fair. An overlit corn dog stand glowed in the background. Ellis was about four, still probably fond of Frank. Goat Man had gone to the fair with them, they all had looked at show goats, and Goat Man met the man from whom he eventually bought Lance. Frank and Wendy fought loudly during a 4-H presentation, shooting insults at one another, disregarding the teenagers showing their prized livestock in the ring in front of them. Wendy and Frank were finally asked to leave when Wendy socked Frank in the face and young

Ellis started to bawl. She refused to ride in the car with Frank and she left with a skinny cowboy in his dusty pickup truck. She didn't come home for three days, and when she did, she said she was taking Ellis to live in Wyoming with the cowboy. "Go ahead," Frank said. She left with Ellis and returned an hour later. That night, Goat Man heard Wendy and Frank playing around in the pool, laughing and splashing. That's how it had worked— major fight, lovey-dovey, major fight, lovey-dovey—until Frank finally moved to New York. Back then, Goat Man had fantasized about taking Ellis away from his parents, moving to California or Oregon and raising Ellis right. After Frank left, though, Goat Man figured things would calm down, and they did.

There was only nonalcoholic beer in the refrigerator, probably Bennet's, so Goat Man looked out in the garage for some other beer. Wendy and Bennet had taken Bennet's pristine Jeep to Sedona, so Wendy's Volvo sat by itself in the garage. As soon as he saw the car, Goat Man went back into the house to get the keys. She left them in an old tin camp cup by the phone; she always did.

Goat Man rarely took Wendy's car, but tonight he felt like going to the Silver Nugget, a bar on dumpy First Avenue that he had frequented periodically since he initially moved to Tucson.

Before he hopped in the Volvo, he molded his short hair with water, shaved, and put on one of Bennet's madras shirts. The shirt was a little too big, but he thought he actually looked good for a change—healthy and confident in the rearview mirror. He flipped on the stereo in the car and played with the bass and treble settings. He picked up Wendy's cell phone from its cradle but realized he had no one to call.

• • •

The bartender—Stanley—was a big guy, a muscle head, with flaming red hair and a beard. Tonight he wore a red-and-white Santa hat. When Goat Man sat down at the bar, Stanley asked for his I.D.

"You kidding? It's me—Javier," Goat Man said.

"Christ, man. I didn't recognize you without your beard, and most of your hair is gone. You look like a fucking frat boy," Stanley said.

"Thanks, I guess. Start me off with a double of Teacher's, no ice."

"Sure." He poured the whiskey. "What've you been doing other than grooming?"

"The same old stuff."

"Goats?"

"Goats," Goat Man said.

"I saw on CNN that they're using goats to clear brush in Laguna Beach in California, to keep the brush from catching on fire like it did a few years ago."

"I actually spearheaded that."

"No shit?" Stanley said.

"It took a while to convince them, but I knew goats would be perfect."

"I always thought you'd find something good with those goats."

Stanley poured drinks for a few guys at the end of the bar, and a young woman sauntered over from the jukebox. She had already sat down next to Goat Man before he realized it was Aubrey.

"I hope you like Johnny Cash," she said.

"What the hell are you doing here?"

"I said I hope you like Johnny Cash because I just loaded the jukebox with seven Johnny Cash songs." She was done up in a tight rib-knit sweater, frayed jeans, and clogs. Her style recalled to Goat Man the style of the girls from his high-school years.

"Johnny Cash is my muse," Goat Man said.

Aubrey laughed. She was drunk. Her eyes looked loose, like they might fall out of her head. Goat Man wondered why a high-school girl like Aubrey, who obviously had a well-done bogus I.D., would go to a bar like the Silver Nugget. She'd be more comfortable at O'Malley's or any of the other generic college bars in town. The Silver Nugget didn't have much to offer an aspiring sorority girl like Aubrey. It was a spacious horseshoe-shaped bar with a few old pool tables, faded posters of eighties beer girls, a big jar of pickled eggs behind the bar.

"Stanley," she called, "set this fellow Johnny Cash fan up with another of whatever he's having." She turned to Goat Man. "I'm happy you're here." She tossed her hair over her shoulder. She wore dangling silver earrings that looked like fish skeletons.

"Me, too," Goat Man said. "Thanks for the drink."

"So what do you do all day besides get high and play with your goats?" Aubrey asked.

"Lots of things. What do you do?"

"Go to school."

"What else?"

"Lots of things," she said. She laughed again.

Goat Man quickly chugged his drink and ordered them both Coors. Aubrey sang along enthusiastically to "I Walk the Line," and asked Goat Man to dance. She looked like she was about to laugh, her lips mashing together.

"To Johnny Cash?" he asked.

"Come on," she said. She tugged him off his stool by his belt loop, and wrapped herself around him. They swayed, but not really to the Johnny Cash record. Goat Man rested his chin on her head and breathed in the scent of her hair. Even in the smoky bar, he could smell the honeysuckle. When she started nibbling his ear, making the back of his neck tingle, he thought, This is too easy.

As he opened the door of the Volvo for her, he smiled, thinking of his rotting Jetta. As soon as he sat down behind the wheel, she started on his ear again and unzipped his fly. He kissed her neck, but retreated and asked if she had any condoms.

"No," she said. She slid her hand through his fly and under the lizard-print boxers that she and Wendy had bought for him.

This is too easy, he thought.

This might be wrong.

"Let's go back up to Wendy's," he said. He turned the key and started the car. She kept her hand where it was until they pulled into traffic on First Avenue. Then she eased her hand out and gingerly zipped his fly.

"Fine," she said. She played with the stereo.

Aubrey waited in the pool house while Goat Man rifled through Wendy's medicine cabinet for condoms. All he found were ribbed ones. He also found a bottle of Prozac, prescription made out to Bennet.

When he returned to the pool house Aubrey was sitting at his glass table, naked, smoking his pipe. "I hope you don't mind," she rasped, holding in a hit.

This is too easy.

This might be wrong.

He joined her at the table, hitting his pipe himself.

They ended up on the rug under the ceiling fan, Goat Man

nearly losing it as Aubrey put the condom on him. It was over in just a few minutes.

"That was fast," Aubrey said. "I barely got comfortable."

"Sorry," Goat Man said.

They lay on their backs and stared at the fan while they shared another bowl. Goat Man played with Aubrey's breasts, cupping them like little mounds of beach sand.

Aubrey sighed and rolled her eyes. "What time is it?" she asked, sitting up.

"I don't know," he said. "Real late."

"Can you walk me home?" she asked.

"Just down the road?"

"Yup," she said. "I have an algebra exam tomorrow."

Goat Man felt like a lecher. He felt it in his stomach immediately—a guilty knot. He jumped up and jogged over to the couch, stepping on the slimy condom. It stuck to his foot. He peeled off the condom, threw it behind the couch, and pulled on his jeans. "You have an algebra exam?"

"Yes. But I studied," she said. She stood up and stretched, reaching her arms over her head, aiming her breasts at him.

"Shit," he said. "What grade are you in?"

"I'm a senior," she said. "Class treasurer and first-squad cheer-leader."

"How the hell did you get into the Silver Nugget, anyway?" Goat Man scanned the room for his boots.

"Stanley never cards me."

"Let's not tell anyone about this," Goat Man said. "Especially not Bennet." He began to lace his boots—tightly. His hands shook, which made tying the knots difficult.

"There's not much to tell," she said. "Is it true about you and your goats?" She grabbed her jeans, shook them out.

"What?"

"About you knowing your goats in the biblical sense?"

"I admit I hang out with goats too much, but I do not, nor have I ever known any of them in the biblical sense." Goat Man sighed. "Hurry up and get dressed, I'm walking you home now."

"I was just wondering," Aubrey said. "God."

"No problem," Goat Man said. His voice quavered a bit. "Did Bennet tell you that shit about me and my goats?"

"No," Aubrey said. "My mom told me a long time ago."

"It's definitely not true," he said. "I hate my goats."

TWENTY-SIX

Ellis's flight to Tucson was typical: an old man who smelled like minty turds in the next seat, a bitchy overworked stewardess, and a two-hour layover in Houston.

He had expected that Goat Man, or at least Wendy, would be there to greet him at the airport, but as he emerged from the jetway, he couldn't spot either of them. A few cowboys, geriatric couples in windbreakers, and jumpy families greeting their loved ones clogged Ellis's way. He hefted his backpack toward the baggage claim area. His legs still ached from the two crew workouts—the ice had never receded, so the boys only had to run laps and use the rowing machines. Near the security checks, Ellis bumped into a blond man with big Popeye forearms.

"Excuse me," Ellis said.

The man didn't say anything. He stood firm and stared at Ellis.

Ellis walked around the man and sat on the edge of the baggage carousel, a little worried that his ass would get pinched by the conveyer belt once it started to move, but too tired to budge. The Popeye-armed man had walked over and was staring at him again. Ellis tried to ignore him, but every time he looked up, the man's eyes were locked to his. When the conveyer started, and luggage began to tumble down the metal chute, Ellis stood and waited for his bags.

He grabbed his first bag, a blue duffel, and plopped it at his feet. As he watched for his brown suitcase, he felt something brush his leg. He looked down, and saw the blond man's furry arm reaching for the handle of his duffel.

"What the hell?" Ellis said.

"Sorry," the man said. He stood up. "You Ellis?"

"Why?" Ellis said, lifting his duffel away from the man.

"Are you Ellis?"

"Leave me alone," Ellis said, backing away.

"I'm not a pervert," the man said. "I'm Bennet."

"Why didn't you say something to begin with?"

"I wasn't sure it was you. I was trying to read the tag on your bag," Bennet said. He extended his hand to Ellis.

"You could've just asked instead of stalking me," Ellis said. He shook Bennet's hand. Bennet had a killer grip. "Where's my mom?"

"We drove down from Sedona this morning and she felt carsick. She's been in bed all day,"

"So why didn't Goat Man come?"

"Probably too stoned," Bennet said.

"I doubt it," Ellis said.

"Once we get the rest of your luggage, we'll hop in my Jeep. It's red."

"So?" Ellis said. If Goat Man and Wendy were busy, they could have told him to take a cab. In D.C., he had become a pro at taking cabs. He had never taken one in Tucson, though. It seemed no one ever took cabs in Tucson.

• • •

As they drove down Kino Expressway, Ellis noticed how open the land was—he could see lights for miles in all directions, and the sky was clear enough that he could make out Mars, or whatever planet glows in the west. Venus, maybe. It was warm, about sixty-five degrees, and with the top down, the Jeep ride was pleasant. Ellis was relieved that riding with the top off made conversation impossible.

When they pulled up the gravel driveway, Bennet asked if everything looked the same.

"Yes," Ellis said. "All the same."

Ellis climbed the tile steps to his room and dropped his cumbersome bags on his bed. Bennet hadn't offered to help because when he got out of the Jeep, he noticed a small white scratch on the hood and stayed in the garage to buff it. In the middle of Ellis's bedroom was an exercise bench with giant resistant rubber bands and awkward, torturous-looking arm and leg attachments. Ellis walked down the hall to Wendy's room.

She was lying in the middle of her boxy Scandinavian bed on a mountain of pillows. A wet cloth was draped over her face. When Ellis said "Mom," she twitched and pulled the cloth from her face.

"Ellis, you scared the hell out of me. My head hurts. Come give me a hug and tell me about your trip." Her voice was scratchy. She lay there feebly, not motioning to him at all.

Ellis leaned over and hugged her. She smelled like vitamins. "My flights were fine. What's that stupid exercise thing doing in my room?"

"That's Bennet's." She spread the cloth over her face again.

"Why's it in my room?"

"He had it on the porch, but it got all covered in spiderwebs," she said from behind the wet cloth.

"He'll move it out of my room then?"

"We'll see. He likes to pump up on it."

"Gross."

"I'll have him get it out of there tomorrow," Wendy said. "And his other stuff, too."

"What other stuff?" Ellis peeled the cloth off his mother's face.

"Just clothes. Give that back!" She snatched the cloth from Ellis and spread it on her face. "Sometimes he likes to sleep in there, and some of his clothes are in your dresser. Just the bottom drawers." She sighed, then moaned. "I want to hear more about Judy and Frank tomorrow when this migraine passes."

"What the hell?" Ellis stomped down the hall back to his room. He pulled open the drawers and started throwing Bennet's clothes in the hall. He paused when he came upon Bennet's racing-red bikini swimsuit. He held it up and away from himself as if it were toxic, and he flicked it into the hall with the rest of Bennet's clothes. He then went down to the kitchen, ignoring Bennet in the den. He took out a plastic trash bag from under the sink and marched back up the stairs, again passing Bennet without a word. He stuffed the clothes in the bag and deposited the bundle on the foot of Wendy's bed. She didn't stir.

Ellis went back down to the den and found Bennet where he had seen him before: sitting in a chair watching CNN with his mouth agape.

"Bennet, when do you plan on using the exercise machine?" Ellis asked.

"I use it every other morning at around nine after I swim," Bennet said.

"You might want to move it out of my room. I'll be sleeping as much as possible between now and January fifteenth."

Bennet looked puzzled, and then he grinned. "You can use it if you want."

"I don't," Ellis said. "I want it gone by tomorrow night." He started to walk into the kitchen.

"You're starting to chap my hide," Bennet mumbled.

Ellis heard him but ignored the remark. He found the makings of a turkey sandwich in the refrigerator, and he started to assemble one to take out to the pool house and split with Goat Man. The vitamins and weird herbs in the fridge reminded him of Wendy upstairs suffering through her migraine. He went back up to ask her if she needed anything, but she was snoring lightly when he walked into her room.

TWENTY-SEVEN

Goat Man knew Ellis was due home, might already be home, but he didn't want to go to the main house and disturb everyone. Ellis would come out to the pool house as soon as he could break away from Wendy, who was probably quizzing him about Frank.

Goat Man scraped sticky resin from his pipe with a small metal pick. He wiped it on a sheet of rolling paper, smearing the paper with the brown substance. He hadn't smoked all day, not even after his swim or after his chores. He had spent twenty minutes in the humid greenhouse, selecting the five best buds—gooey, with slight ruby-colored fur. His plants in the greenhouse were beautiful and bountiful, mostly generous females. Down next to the wash, he had cultivated more plants, but their bud yields weren't as great. Too many male plants, and he suspected the goats nibbled on them.

After he finished cleaning out his pipe, Goat Man turned up his CD player—Sun Ra—and danced around stupidly on the Navajo rug, lifting his knees and arms in kung-fu poses.

He didn't hear when Ellis knocked, and he was surprised to see him standing in the doorway with a fat sandwich on a plate. Goat Man turned down Sun Ra and said, "Hey."

"For when we get the munchies," Ellis said, holding up the plate.

"Great," Goat Man said. "You look taller."

"You don't look like Goat Man anymore. Where's all your hair? And your beard?" Ellis walked up to Goat Man and mussed his short hair.

"I was going to send you a picture," he said. "I get it cut every month now. You look pale." He put his arm around Ellis's shoulder and squeezed.

"I am pale. I'm psyched to be home." Ellis sat down at the table and watched closely as Goat Man loaded a bowl. "After you cut me off, I only got to smoke twice. Once, shit weed, and the other time sweet stuff from Maui."

"I've cut way back. I'm swimming laps again." Goat Man passed the pipe to Ellis and held the lighter as Ellis toked. "Bennet's a pool hog. That's why I'm swimming again. You met him yet?"

Ellis passed the smoking pipe to Goat Man and let the smoke leak from his nostrils. "He's an asshole," he said. "He picked me up at the airport. I can't even call here without him answering the phone and screwing things up."

Goat Man held in his hit, thought of all the stupid Bennet-moments that he had abided over the last few months. He laughed and lost his hit just as he remembered the time Bennet accused him of stealing his precious rag-wool socks from the wrought-iron gate where he had hung them to dry. "Why would I steal your socks? I have plenty," Goat Man had said. "Drugs make people do strange things," Bennet said. A few weeks later, Goat Man saw Lance and Mr. T playing tug-o-war with one of the socks.

"I would have picked you up at the airport," Goat Man told Ellis. "You're right, Bennet is an asshole."

"He's like all her others," Ellis said. He took another hit.

"I'm not sure about Bennet," Goat Man said. "He's gotten her into all that mystical crystal stuff. They go up to Sedona a lot."

Ellis blew out his hit and passed the pipe back to Goat Man for repacking. "It's cashed," he said. "That Thomas guy got her into roller-blading, and now he's gone. Remember how she used to wear that Spandex shit all the time?"

"Bennet's different," Goat Man said. "Sneaky."

"He'll be gone before I go back to Gates." Ellis picked at the marijuana on the table. "Savory. Why'd you cut back?"

"Long story," Goat Man said. He didn't want to tell Ellis how he thought Wendy was about to kick him out. "I like swimming."

"Guess what I'm stuck doing at Gates," Ellis said.

"What?" Goat Man handed Ellis the loaded pipe.

"Crew." Ellis lit the bowl and inhaled, tracing the flame over the whole load.

"Rowing?"

Ellis nodded in slow motion. He thought about the laps the coach had made him run even after he had nearly passed out from the cramp. He saw the hairs in the coach's flaring nostrils as he warned him about returning to Gates out of shape: "By April, I want you to kiss all the freshmen good-bye, and I want you on the varsity boat."

In the morning, Ellis would run through the arroyo to the trails in Ventana Canyon. The next morning he'd run a little farther, and the next, farther, until he worked up to three miles a day. Barney had told him that the first week was the hardest, but from then on, running was great, almost like getting stoned. Ellis doubted it, but he didn't want to cramp up again on the track. He passed the pipe to Goat Man and blew out his hit. "Enough for me," he said.

"One more for me," Goat Man said. His cheeks imploded and his chest swelled as he hit the pipe. He held it in his lungs and watched as Ellis removed the Sun Ra disc from the stereo and replaced it with Toots and the Maytals. Soon they were both bobbing their heads and humming to the music: "Country roads, take me home . . ." He blew out the hit and tapped the burning buds into a Silver Nugget ashtray. He licked his thumb and smothered the last glowing bits of cannabis.

"Let's eat this." Ellis took a bite of the turkey sandwich and slid the plate across the table to Goat Man. "You couldn't figure out how to send me dope?"

"I had the best way. I laminated greeting cards packed with flattened buds, but Jonathan told me not to risk it."

"He's a worry wart."

"I guess I am, too," Goat Man said. "I thought you were coming home for Thanksgiving, and when you didn't, I figured it was only a few more weeks until Christmas break."

"This almost makes up for it." Ellis held up a bud, waved it in front of Goat Man's face.

"I have some weird news," Goat Man said.

"What?"

"There's something else about Bennet."

"What?" Ellis said.

"He's someone's uncle," Goat Man said.

"Whose?"

"Aubrey's," Goat Man said.

"Aubrey?"

"That girl who beat the shit out of you in grade school."

Ellis traced his scar with his index finger. "I know who she is," he said. "She's evil."

"She's not evil," Goat Man said. He hadn't anticipated that

Ellis's presence would add another layer of guilt, but it did. He remembered tending to Ellis's wounds after Aubrey beat him up, and he knew Ellis hated her, but more important, he didn't want Ellis to think he was a perverted old man. A lecher. A pedophile. He thought of telling Ellis right then, but he couldn't.

"Well," Ellis said, "I missed you a lot."

"Me, too."

TWENTY-EIGHT

Ellis forgot it was Christmas morning until he was well into his run, past the old horse hitches and through the sandiest part of the wash where the rocks were loose and the foliage sparse. He remembered Wendy saying something about opening gifts at nine, but he was enjoying himself, breathing deeply, pushing. It was easy to forget he was running and ignore the pain in his legs and gut because of the canyon: towering, sheer walls of red and gray rock. The steep mountains looked as if they were reaching into the sky, like they could fold down on Ellis at any moment. He wanted to walk, not because he was tired or in pain, but because he wanted to take in the scenery slowly. Maybe Wendy or Goat Man would hike up the canyon with him later on. He knew it was corny, but he loved the mountains. He didn't know how much he had missed them, and he felt lucky and humbled to be spending Christmas morning in their shadows.

Ellis had finished his Christmas shopping two nights before in the mall with Goat Man. Neither of them could figure out what to buy Bennet.

"Goggles?" Ellis had asked Goat Man in the sporting goods store.

"He probably has two pairs of the best—one to actually use while swimming and the other to keep perfect in the box they came in. Let's get him one of these." Goat Man held a small box. On the front of the box was a muscular, greased-up man with a weight hanging from a strap that wrapped around his head. It read, *Neck Exerciser for Power and Bulk.*

"That looks painful," Ellis said. "How much is it?"

"Only sixteen bucks."

"Let's get it."

At a discount store, they also bought him a three-dollar bottle of Fresh Man Cologne.

Barney was half-right: the jogging was getting easier—but Ellis wondered if it was because of the scenery. He felt the ganja in his lungs when he ran. A burning cough would sometimes crawl up his windpipe and snag in his throat, and he'd taste the pot. Sometimes when he burped, he tasted pot, too. He figured that when he returned to Gates and stopped smoking altogether, running and working out would be twice as easy.

When he reached the first waterfall, Ellis turned around and started back down the trail, going so fast over the rocks, he thought he was losing control. This felt good, like his feet moved by themselves, placed themselves in the right places, kept rolling, made him leap when he should leap, cut to the side when he should cut to the side.

In the autumn, before he had left for Gates, the only thing out near the canyon was the resort, which, except for the patches of nuclear-green golf course, blended well with the Sonora Desert. Now, in all directions, was a vast sea of red roofs from the sprawl of tract homes that had sprouted up in the last few months. All those years, when his mother had asked him what he wanted for Christmas, he should have said land.

Ellis stopped at the goat pen before he went up to the house. Freida was asleep and didn't budge when he petted her back, but Lance jumped down from the roof of the shed and greeted him with a friendly head nudge. "Hey, Stinky, you're the only stud now that Mr. T's gone," he told Lance. The goat tried to chew on the hem of Ellis's shorts, until Ellis swatted him away.

Bennet was swimming laps when Ellis walked by the pool. Bennet was always swimming laps when Ellis returned from his runs. Ellis thought it might be nice to return from a run and splash into the heated pool, but he couldn't with Bennet in there every morning. One of these days, he'd time it just right with Goat Man so that he'd return from his run just as Goat Man finished his laps. Then he'd jump in the pool and make Bennet wait while he splashed around. Ellis watched Bennet in the pool that morning: he skillfully carved the water with no splashes, elegantly performed flip-turns, but he still looked like a lubberly polar bear in a zoo moat, displacing the water over the edges of the pool.

Ellis knocked on Goat Man's door, opening it. "Merry Christmas," he said.

Goat Man was stretched on the rug, gazing up at the slow fan. "Is it time to open the gifts yet?"

"I just got back, and Bennet's still in the pool, so probably not."

"Let me find your real present," Goat Man said. "For reasons that will become obvious, I can't give it to you in front of your mother." He dug through the closet and pulled out a two-foot, blue glass bong. "When I bought this last week, I didn't know you were cutting back and doing all this running. I hope you'll still be able to use it."

"Thanks, Goat Man. Let's try it now." Ellis grabbed it and held it up to the skylight. The morning sun cast blue refractions down his face. He unscrewed the bowl, and whistled through it. "Need a screen."

"Here." Goat Man flicked a little round screen from the table toward Ellis. It landed under the couch.

Ellis got down on his hands and knees and peeked under the couch. "What's this?" He grabbed something, then flung it away. It was the used condom. "Gross!" Ellis rushed into the bathroom and scrubbed his hands under hot water. "That's fucking sick!"

"Sorry." Goat Man went over to the kitchen and returned with a sheet of paper towel. He scooped up the condom with the paper towel, and retrieved the screen as he repeated his apology to Ellis.

Ellis emerged from the bathroom. "You get the screen in the bowl yet?"

"I'll pack it up now." Goat Man crammed the screen into the bowl and packed it with a few little buds. "Sorry about the rubber. I spaced it out."

"So," Ellis asked, "who is she?" He sat down at the table with Goat Man.

"Someone I met at the Silver Nugget," Goat Man said. He quickly put his mouth to the top of the bong and lit the bowl. "We forgot the water." They both laughed and Goat Man took a hit anyway.

Someone knocked on the door.

"Damn," Ellis said. "Turn the fan on high and press out the bowl."

"Hold on!" Goat Man yelled at the door. He fanned the air in front of the bong as he walked it into his bedroom.

"Remember when we could sit out on the diving board without any fear?" Ellis said to him.

Ellis opened the door. Bennet stood in front of him in his swim trunks, dripping. He sniffed. "We're opening gifts in ten minutes as soon as I dry off and change. You think you and Javier will be coherent enough to join us?"

"No, man. I could barely make it to the door," Ellis said. "Goat Man's still in his room sniffing glue and twitching."

"I'll see you in the living room in ten minutes," Bennet said.

Wendy had pulled the puffed-out leather loveseat and recliner over near the Christmas tree. Bennet was stretched in the recliner when Goat Man and Ellis walked in. Wendy was shaking one of her gifts.

"We're here, I'm stinky from my run, so let's get this show on the road," Ellis said. He sat on the floor while Wendy and Goat Man took the loveseat. Ellis picked up one of the gifts and read the card apathetically: "'To Wendy, love Bennet.' It's heavy."

"You'll have to open that one in private," Bennet said. He sat up and snatched the box away from Ellis. He placed it on the floor next to his chair.

"Okay, next. 'To Javier, love Wendy. Enjoy, live, and free yourself,'" Ellis read.

"I hope this changes your life like it did mine," Wendy said.

Goat Man carefully unwrapped the package, folding the green-and-red tartan paper into a neat little bundle. It was a book, *Chemical Free Feeling*, written by a swami guy with a purple turban who put his own grinning self on the cover. "Thanks," Goat Man said. "I'll give it a read."

"Maybe Ellis should read it, too," Bennet said.

"Maybe you should shut the hell up," Ellis said to Bennet.

"Ellis, don't be rude on Christmas," Wendy said, her eyes widening. "Now let's have the next gift."

They finished opening the gifts in fewer than twenty minutes. Each time Bennet and Wendy opened one from the other, they'd kiss.

Goat Man pulled the WAILERS T-shirt over the ragged BUFFET BAR AND CROCKPOT '88 one he was wearing, and thanked Ellis profusely. Ellis pretended to love the Arizona geology book he received from Goat Man—he knew it was partially a ruse, a show for Wendy and Bennet, but it was actually cool-looking with its photos of Canyon de Chelly and the Chiricahuas—places where he and Goat Man had hiked and camped.

When Ellis thought there were finally no more gifts, Wendy stood up and said, "Ellis, wait here. I'll be right back with your big present." She disappeared into the storage room. Ellis had already unwrapped quite a booty: several CDs, piles of clothes from Abercrombie and Summit Hut, a snowboard, books. Wendy emerged pushing his new mountain bike.

"Shit," he said. "Thanks, Mom." He looked at the bike: it was about the right size, and had all kinds of confusing components. "I hope I can figure it out," he said. "The last bike I had was that BMX one without any gears."

"Bennet will help you," Wendy said. "He has his own mountain bike."

"We can go riding tomorrow," Bennet said, rubbing his hands together. "I got a book that shows all the trails in southern Arizona."

"Great," Ellis said. He posed a smile.

"We have brunch reservations at La Paloma in forty-five minutes, so we should get ready," Wendy said. "Ellis, run up and take your shower."

After a fatiguing brunch, during which Bennet had recounted his college football years in excruciating detail, Wendy insisted they sit around the kitchen table and play Scrabble.

Whenever Ellis got up, Wendy would ask him where he was going. The third time she asked, Ellis said, "I'm going to take a piss. Should I do it in a cup so you can screen it for drugs?"

Bennet's turn came after Goat Man's, so Goat Man, instead of concentrating on maximizing his own score, spent his turns blocking Bennet from any high-scoring plays. Bennet was in last place, with fifty fewer points than Goat Man, who was in third. Ellis played the word *hookah* on a double-word square for thirty-two points.

"That's a foreign word," Bennet said. "You can't play that."

"What?" Ellis said.

"Foreign word," Bennet said.

"I'll get the dictionary, the *English* dictionary, if you want to challenge me," Ellis said. "You want to challenge me?"

"Fine," Bennet said.

"Don't," Wendy said to Bennet. "You'll lose your turn."

"Challenge or not?" Ellis asked.

"Challenge," Bennet said.

Ellis flipped through the dictionary. "Hookah," he read, "Noun. An Eastern smoking pipe designed with a long tube passing through an urn of water that cools the smoke as it draws through."

"Still a foreign word," Bennet said.

"But it's in an English dictionary the same way the words *chauffeur* and *liverwurst* are," Goat Man said.

"You lose your turn, honey," Wendy told Bennet.

"If you're ganging up on me, I'm not playing anymore." Bennet threw his tiles into the box, went over to the fridge, and cracked a Diet Coke. He stomped up the stairs.

Ellis laughed. So did Goat Man.

"You two are cruel," Wendy said.

"We waited until he was out of the room before we laughed at him," Ellis said.

"All Bennet wants is to fit in, and you two shut him out."

"*Hookah* is a word," Ellis said. "He didn't have to quit. Have you ever smoked from a hookah, Mom?"

"That's not important," Wendy said.

"I bet you did smoke from a hookah. You and all your hippie friends," Ellis said. He looked over to Goat Man. "Did she?"

Goat Man wanted to tell Ellis about the party when he first met Wendy, when she was pregnant with him, but when he saw Wendy's ashen face, he said, "I don't know." It was true, he didn't know if she had ever gotten high from a hookah pipe, but he did know that she had wanted to at that party. She was ready to soak her brain in Nepalese hash even with Ellis in her womb. Now she was giving away books about chemical-free lifestyles, and living with a man who owned a jumbo bottle of Prozac.

"Ellis, you know Frank and I used to use drugs recreationally, but it's not something I'm proud of, or would advocate," Wendy said. She glared at Goat Man expectantly. He didn't say anything, just stared at all the words spelled out on the Scrabble board. "Ellis," she continued, "I'm serious about this. I would really like it if you promised me you wouldn't smoke pot anymore."

"What?" Ellis said. "That's dumb."

"We'll type up a contract on the computer. Bennet and I do it all the time. Just yesterday, I signed one saying I wouldn't call him stupid anymore," Wendy said. "What do you think of the idea, Javier?"

"You shouldn't call Bennet stupid."

"No, I mean about Ellis not smoking anymore."

"I better go tend to the goats," he said. He stood up. "I need to milk Freida before she bursts."

"This concerns you," she said. She grabbed Goat Man's shoulder and pushed him back into his chair. "You're older than Ellis, more set in your ways. Although I'd really like it if you got rid of all your plants and stopped smoking, I feel like I can only help guide your spirit. Ellis, I feel like I'm responsible for cultivating your spirit, defining your spiritual boundaries."

"What?" Ellis said.

Goat Man stared at the Scrabble board again. He noticed *weird* was spelled incorrectly: w-i-e-r-d. He had built the word *index* off the i, onto a double word square, so he didn't say anything.

"I just don't want you limiting yourself to a cloud of marijuana," Wendy told Ellis. "Think of expansion."

"Stupid," Ellis said. "Are you in a cult with Bennet?"

"Of course not. I don't think it's strange for a mother to want the best for her son," Wendy said.

"Last summer, right before I left for Gates, you sat out by the pool with us and smoked," Ellis said. "The night before I left for Gates, you saw us smoking at the kitchen table, and you didn't say anything."

"I've grown away from that," she said. "I want you to grow away from it."

"This is really stupid," Ellis said. He stood up and walked toward the sliding glass door. "I can't smoke it at school, anyway. I'm on crew."

"My friend and teacher Johanna will be here tomorrow," Wendy said. "I want you to talk with her, Ellis."

Ellis slammed the door loud enough to cause both Wendy and Goat Man to flinch. Goat Man looked up at Wendy. She stared at him. Her lower lip was trembling. She scared him, so he stood, gently, and slunk out the door.

Goat Man met Ellis down by the pen. It was around six, the sun was sinking in a fiery sky behind the bowl of city lights. Ellis was petting Freida. She was cooing, making sickening gurgling noises.

"I can't stand Freida," Goat Man said.

"How long has Bennet been here?" Ellis asked.

"Long."

Ellis stopped petting Freida and stared at the horizon. The westernmost Catalina Mountains were black and jagged against the sky. "Can we go on a trek before I go back to school?"

"How about Molino Basin to Tanque Verde Falls? We could do it in two or three days," Goat Man suggested. He hadn't planned on any trek with Ellis, but he felt sorry for him. "This time you try Freida's milk. No packing food."

"Okay. When?"

"We can leave Tuesday, if it's all right with Wendy," Goat Man said. "That reminds me, I have to milk Freida."

"I saw Lance sucking on her teats. He had milk in his beard."

"Weird," Goat Man said. "You want to go up and give that new bong of yours a proper initiation?"

"I have to run farther tomorrow, so let's wait until tomorrow afternoon. What time do you finish your laps in the morning?"

"Seven or so," Goat Man said.

"Tomorrow I'll beat Bennet to the pool. Right after you finish your laps, I'll jump in and swim some to make him wait and piss him off," Ellis said.

"That's why I started swimming again in the first place," Goat Man said.

TWENTY-NINE

The next morning, Ellis did jump in the pool right after Goat Man finished his laps. He treaded water for a few minutes before Bennet appeared in his trunks with a towel around his neck.

"How much longer will you be?" Bennet asked.

"I'm supposed to tread for thirty minutes and I've only been in here for five," Ellis said. Bennet looked at his digital watch. This might be a mistake, Ellis thought. If Bennet waited by the pool, he would actually have to tread for twenty-five more minutes. He was already winded from the run, and he had a stitch digging into his side. Bennet took a seat on the diving board, aiming his face eastward at the sun. Ellis thought: Please go away, please go away, please go away.

Bennet kept trying to make conversation with Ellis. "Are all the students at Gates really smart?" he asked.

"Nah," Ellis said.

"Your mother says you're the smartest freshman."

"Uf," Ellis grunted. He tried hard to ignore Bennet. He stared at a bird entering a saguaro cactus through a hole near the top. He thought that he should know the name of the bird, he thought he should know the names of other birds. He tallied the number of desert birds he could name: cactus wren, roadrunner, quail. Quail was too general. There were quail all over the world. The quail in the desert must have a special name.

"Is crew fun? I'd be good at it. There's nowhere in Tucson where you can row, probably no sculls in the whole state. Are you going to stay back East this summer to train?"

Ellis heard him, but didn't say anything.

"Huh?" Bennet said. "You staying in the East this summer to train?"

Ellis dared to look at Bennet, who was looking at his watch.

"I remember football camp when I was your age. From age fifteen to twenty-three, I spent my summers in football camps. I had some of my best times in football camps. That was before I got in touch with my spirit . . ."

Ellis tuned out and concentrated on staying afloat. He thought about Frank. He should tell Frank he was rowing for Gates. Frank would like that. He'd probably be getting a late Christmas gift from Frank and Judy in the next few days, so he could mention crew in the thank-you note. He had actually managed to mail Frank's gift on time for Christmas. It was a sweater—puke green, but natty. The gift was sort of an experiment. He imagined both Frank and Judy would like it even though he thought it was the ugliest color he had ever seen knitted into the shape of a sweater. It looked like something that someone with big black poetry glasses might wear, though. Frank would love it.

To hell with this, Ellis thought. He swam to the shallow end and staggered up the steps. He shook his head like a dog, then jumped on his left foot to get the water out of his ear.

"Looking good," Bennet said, "but you were only in there nine minutes, not thirty."

There were no towels hanging on the gate, and he didn't

want to ask Bennet for his, so Ellis walked across the deck to the pool house and knocked. He tried to open the door, but it was locked.

"Yeah?" Goat Man said.

"I need a towel. Open up," Ellis said. He could see steam rising from his arms. He heard Bennet splash into the pool behind him.

Goat Man opened the door with a towel in hand. He handed it to Ellis. "Let's fire up that bong later," Goat Man said.

"Want to go down to Reggie's first? I haven't seen him since summer." Ellis said. "We'll take my mother's car."

"Okay."

"I'll run in and get dressed and eat something and be ready to go."

"It's not even eight yet," Goat Man said. "Reggie doesn't open his shop until around eleven."

Ellis killed time in front of the TV. First he watched flamboyant New York club kids in their makeup and bizarre outfits parade across the stage on a trashy talk show. The stupefied audience couldn't grasp the meaning behind the kids. Ellis couldn't either, nor did he want to. Ellis was particularly disgusted by Richie Rich, a kid with canary yellow hair, a ruffled shirt, and a huge lollipop that he licked suggestively as the audience members asked him questions. "It's all about glamour," Richie Rich said as he batted his false lashes. Ellis changed the channels and settled on a PBS documentary about salamanders dying out because of acid rain. At ten thirty, he walked out to the pool house with a mild headache.

Ellis pushed open the door and saw a familiar woman sitting

at the table sucking his new Christmas bong. "Hey," Ellis said, "where's Goat Man?"

She blew out her hit in a thin stream. "Hi, Ellis. Remember me?"

He traced the scar on his forehead. Aubrey. "Hi," he said. "That's my bong. Where's Goat Man?"

"He's in there getting dressed," she said. "Sit down. Let's get high as balls."

"No, thanks," Ellis said. "We're about to go somewhere."

Goat Man emerged from his bedroom, buttoning his worn denim shirt. "Is it ten thirty already?" he asked. He looked at Aubrey. "Sorry, Aubrey, we gotta go."

"That's okay," she said. She walked over to Goat Man, put one hand up under his shirt, and the other on his ass. She pulled him close and kissed his ear. "See you." She strutted out.

"Aubrey?" Ellis asked after she left. He bit his lower lip.

"I know," Goat Man said. He could see Ellis was bummed and disgusted.

"You could go to jail for that. She's too young." He didn't look at Goat Man; he looked at the rug.

"She's a senior—eighteen."

"When I was in fifth grade, she was in sixth," Ellis said. "The oldest she could be is sixteen."

"I ran into her at the Silver Nugget the other night."

"She kicked my ass more than once, you know, and now she's using my bong." Ellis thought of the new Aubrey, with her sway and curves, her flirty laugh. She had changed a lot since the days when she was scraping rocks across his forehead at the bus stop. She no longer had that hillbilly air about her. He could see how Goat Man might be into her. Still, this was wrong and kind of sickening. "You're old enough to be her dad."

"No more," Goat Man said. "I promise." Goat Man imagined what Aubrey's father might look like: no neck, military flat-top hair, squished boxer's nose. Bennet, but bigger, smarter, and meaner. He was probably a cop or a karate instructor or a body builder. Actually, if he lived up in their neighborhood, he couldn't be any of those. He was probably a lawyer. "No more."

"Sure."

"Seriously. No more. I think she just likes my hybrid."

"Sure," Ellis repeated.

Before either of them was satisfied with the discussion of Aubrey, Wendy and Johanna walked into the pool house without knocking. "Ellis, this is Johanna," Wendy said.

"Hi," Ellis said. He looked at Johanna's freakishly long hair. It hung past her waist. He wondered if she had constant headaches because of it. He looked at her brown nipples through her flimsy silk blouse. They pointed sideways, toward her elbows. Then he caught himself staring, and he looked at her face again.

"Hello, Ellis," Johanna said. "I can't wait to get to know you better. Are you coming to any of our workshops while you're home?"

"Probably not," Ellis said.

"He might," Wendy said.

"We're having an open forum on Tuesday night," Johanna said. "Both you and Javier are welcome to come."

"We're going on a trek Tuesday," Ellis said. "Sorry."

"Exciting," Johanna said. "With the goats?"

"You can't be going on Tuesday," Wendy whined. She slapped her shoe on the tile.

"We are," Ellis said.

"Nice bong," Wendy said. She looked to Goat Man. "I guess you haven't read that book I gave you yet."

"Not yet," Goat Man said.

Bennet walked into the pool house. "Ellis, there's a strange Scottish man at the front door who insists he knows you. He has luggage."

"What?" Ellis said. "Who?"

"He says his name's Quentin," Bennet said.

"He's here?"

"On the front stoop," Bennet said. "I wouldn't let him in. He smells like a brewery."

"Who is he, Ellis?" Wendy asked.

"He's a guy I met on a train."

"Odd," Johanna said.

When Ellis opened the front door, Quentin was leaning over, testing a prickly pear cactus pad with a stick, the way someone might poke an injured wild animal to see if it's still alive.

"Quentin, what are you doing here?" Ellis asked. The whole crowd—Wendy, Goat Man, Bennet, and Johanna—stood behind Ellis in the front hall and gawked.

"You told me to drop in if I was ever in Arizona," Quentin said. "It's not inconvenient? I can take me bag and get an hotel." Quentin squinted at them all.

"No, no, come in and meet everyone," Ellis said.

Ellis introduced Quentin to everyone. Quentin kissed Wendy's and Johanna's hands. Johanna pulled her hand away from Quentin's lingering lips. Quentin would sleep in Ellis's room. Ellis would sleep on the couch in the pool house. When Quentin excused himself to use the bathroom, Wendy pinned Ellis against the wall in the foyer.

"What the hell do think you're doing letting this drunk into our house?" she whispered loudly. Her eyes were moist, her lower lip trembled.

"What was I supposed to do?" Ellis said. "He's from Scotland. He's only staying two nights. I told him that I'm leaving for the trek on Tuesday."

"I don't like this, Ellis. I wanted both you and Javier at Johanna's workshop on Tuesday. What are we supposed to do with this Quentin for two days? What does he eat?" Wendy held her chest, began to breathe quickly.

"Mellow out," Ellis said. "Jesus. There's a Scottish man staying with us for two days. Don't blow a clot."

"There's just too much going on right now," Wendy said.

Ellis agreed with Wendy, there was too much going on right now.

Wendy's right eye twitched and her lip continued to quiver. She stomped upstairs.

Johanna followed her, chanting, "Redirect. Redirect, sister . . ."

Ellis showed Quentin to a lounge chair by the pool, excused himself, and walked down the hill to sit with the goats.

THIRTY

Wendy had given Goat Man a hundred-dollar bill and the keys to her Volvo and told him, "Get Quentin out of my house for as long as possible." Goat Man figured it was the least he could do for Wendy—and Ellis. Ellis didn't need Wendy on his back. So he took the hundred dollars and loaded Quentin into the car.

Goat Man had planned on getting Quentin drunk quickly and sending him off to bed quietly, but it didn't work. After about twenty minutes at the Nugget, Quentin had swallowed the mescal worm and patted the asses of three women, the third of whom shoved him and yelled, "Fuck you, asshole!"

"Most Scots think American beer is piss water," Quentin bellowed, "I just think it's piss. Coors is piss." He pushed a bottle off the bar. Miraculously it didn't smash, but it clanked around on the cement floor before rolling under a table. Three grim cowboys stood and surrounded Quentin. Two were taller than him.

"What was that you were saying about American beers?" one of the cowboys said. He had a waxed mustache and dead, silver eyes.

"He didn't mean anything," Goat Man said.

Quentin faked a hick accent as best as a Scot could. "Where's Jethro? Where's the ceee-ment pond?"

Goat Man didn't want to fight. He hadn't fought in years. He always lost because every fight situation he had been in was like the one he was in now: he was outnumbered, and defending someone who didn't deserve to be defended. Goat Man motioned to the mustached cowboy. "He's retarded," he whispered to him. "He doesn't know what he's saying."

"You'll keep him quiet?" the cowboy asked.

"I will," Goat Man said.

The cowboy tipped his ARIZONA FEEDS cap skeptically and told his friends to back off. With his Cro-Magnon forehead and close-set eyes, Quentin did look sort of retarded.

Stanley, the bartender, walked over. "Get him out of here now," he said to Goat Man.

"What's all this about?" Quentin asked. "Set me up with another nip of the worm stuff."

"We gotta go," Goat Man said, pushing Quentin toward the door. "I'll take you to another place with cheaper beer and better company."

"I was just making friends with some real live cowboys," Quentin said.

Goat Man was amazed that Quentin didn't put up more of a stink about leaving; he complied, saluting the cowboys as he left.

After a strip club and two more bars, Goat Man was exhausted. Quentin wasn't. No matter how much Quentin danced, or how much alcohol Quentin consumed, or how many times Quentin *whoop*ed it up, Quentin didn't seem to tire. At last call,

Goat Man pulled Quentin away from three women and convinced him that going to a party at an apartment complex in Marana was a bad idea. "Marana's too far," Goat Man said, "and besides, I have some weed."

Leaning against Wendy's car in the dirt parking lot of the Bay Horse Tavern, Goat Man lit up the only bowl he had brought along. A truck with women leaning from its windows screeched out onto Grant Road. The women synchronously yelled, "Bye, Quentin!" Quentin waved and blew kisses.

Goat Man allowed Quentin to smoke through most of the bowl, hoping it would have soporific effects. It didn't. Instead, Quentin began to philosophize.

"You know," Quentin said, "people are the same everywhere. Those cowboys might as well be shepherds in Stirling, and those women I met might as well be waitresses in Glasgow."

Goat Man wished he would just shut up.

After the bars, they arrived home to find that there was nowhere to continue the debauchery—Ellis was asleep on the couch in the pool house, and the main house with Wendy, Bennet, and maybe Johanna, was out of the question. Goat Man ended up giving Quentin Ellis's new bong and a bag of hybrid. They sat out by the pool for a while, Quentin sucking vigorously on the bubbling bong, until Goat Man could tolerate him no longer. Quentin's deep laugh echoed off the stucco walls. Goat Man hoped Wendy wouldn't wake up. At three o'clock, when Goat Man finally walked inside to go to sleep, he left Quentin sitting on the diving board, humming a Hank Williams song.

• • •

Ellis and Goat Man were awakened by Jonathan the mailman. He pounded on the door of the pool house until Ellis got up and let him in.

"Hi, Ellis," Jonathan said. "How's school?"

"Hi," Ellis said. "School's okay."

"You look pale."

"I feel pale," Ellis said. "I'm tired."

"There's a naked guy with a bong and an erection asleep on your front steps," Jonathan said. "Here's a package for you—from Frank."

"What the hell?" Goat Man said, emerging from his room in his pimp robe.

"There's a big guy, naked, asleep out front," Jonathan said. "I figured I should tell you before I bothered Wendy, so I came back here. It's a nice bong he's clutching."

"Shit," Goat Man said. He thumbed the crust from his eyes, pulled his hiking boots over his bare feet, and the three of them walked around to the front of the house.

It was nine thirty. Bennet had already done his laps, and his Jeep and Wendy's Volvo were both gone. Goat Man knew neither of them had seen Quentin. If they had, he would have heard about it already.

"Did you guys use my bong last night?" Ellis asked Goat Man as they approached the front. "What did you do?" Ellis noticed Quentin's shirt hanging from the arm of a saguaro, and then he saw Quentin: a big, pink lump sprawled on the front steps. "Gross."

"We went out drinking and then came back here for hybrid," Goat Man said. "Is he dead?" He shoved Quentin's beefy leg with his boot. His foot left a white impression in Quentin's pink thigh.

"I heard him cough," Jonathan said. "Here's the rest of your mail." He handed Ellis the envelopes and waved good-bye. "Javier, you owe me for this one," he yelled from the bottom of the driveway. "And Ellis, get some sun."

Neither Ellis nor Goat Man could look directly at Quentin, a wasted mound of flesh. Neither of them knew how to go about waking or moving him—he was draped awkwardly over the steps, his neck crunched. "We could get the wheelbarrow and roll him into the shallow end of the pool," Ellis suggested.

"Too heavy," Goat Man said. "Go get a blanket for him, it's cold this morning." Goat Man adjusted his own robe.

Just then, Quentin moaned and shot a solid stream of piss into the air. It arched and almost hit Ellis on the shoulder, but Ellis was quick and jumped out of the way.

"His bladder still works," Goat Man said.

"Sick." Ellis leaned down and gingerly peeled Quentin's fingers from the bong. "I'll take this," he said, grabbing the bong. He sat down on the steps next to the nude man and opened the package from Frank. It was a sweater, bile green, not much unlike the one he had sent to Frank, and some hiking boots—leather, made in Italy. The card said that Judy had sneaked peeks into his shoes while he was visiting during Thanksgiving in order to get the right size.

"Nice boots," Goat Man said. He whistled like a construction worker.

"I can use them tomorrow, break them in," Ellis said. "I don't know about this sweater, though." He held it up by the shoulders. "It looks pretty Frankish."

"Ugly," Goat Man said, "but expensive. That cashmere?"

"That's what the label says. Is there a Sulka store in Tucson?"

"I doubt it."

"I'll return it if I ever see one," Ellis said. "I'd probably get fifty bucks for it."

"More," Goat Man said. "Much more." He nudged Quentin's leg again. "What're we going to do with him?"

"I don't know," Ellis said. "I don't want to look at him anymore."

THIRTY-ONE

Tuesday morning, both Ellis and Goat Man got up at six. Goat Man swam his laps, while Ellis jogged through Ventana Canyon.

They had prodded Quentin off the front steps the morning before by spraying him with the hose just before Wendy arrived home from the supermarket. Quentin spent the rest of the day and night up in Ellis's room, sleeping off his hangover. His hangover had been a relief for everyone, especially Goat Man, who had dreaded a repeat of the night before.

When Ellis returned from his run that morning, Goat Man was just getting out of the pool. "You better hop in if you don't want Bennet to get it," Goat Man said, toweling off. Steam rose from his hair and shoulders.

"I'm saving my energy for the trek," Ellis said. "How's the Jetta?"

"It still runs," Goat Man said. "But last time I took the goats out, Freida pissed all over the backseat. Be ready to leave in an hour."

"Okay."

Wendy and Quentin were sitting at the kitchen table eating huevos rancheros.

"... after I met the friendly cowboys, we went to another pub and I met two friendly women," Quentin was telling Wendy. "I don't know why I was so fatigued."

"I can't imagine," Wendy said. "Ellis, sit down with us and have some breakfast."

"I gotta take a shower and get ready to go," he told her. He sprinted upstairs and bumped into swim-ready Bennet in the hall.

"Not so fast," he told Ellis. "What's the rush?"

"Move," Ellis said.

"What's the rush?"

"Move, please," Ellis said. "I need to get ready to leave."

"Your mother was planning on you and Javier coming to the spirit workshop tonight. She's disappointed."

"Oh," Ellis said. "Move."

"When are you returning?"

"Thursday or Friday. Move."

"Wendy's leaving for the Earth Women retreat on Wednesday morning. You won't see her until Monday."

"What's your point?" Ellis asked.

"I just thought you might want to go to this workshop tonight and make her happy. Postpone your trek one day. What's the big deal?"

"Move."

Bennet stepped aside and let him pass.

Goat Man remembered his pipe and buds, packed enough for the trek. He loaded his backpack with other necessities as well: two pairs of woolen socks, thermal underwear, a snakebite kit, and his tin cup. He needed to get the goats ready—just Freida and Lance—so he walked down to the pen with the leashes.

Lance was kneeling up on the roof of the shack, but Freida was nowhere in sight.

Ellis jogged down to the pen wearing his new hiking boots and his backpack. "Where's Freida?"

"Probably off eating trash."

"Freida!" Ellis called.

A few seconds later, Freida bounded out from behind thick mesquite with half of one of Bennet's rag wool socks in her mouth. She ran up to Ellis, and he petted her.

The goats behaved well—Freida even jumped in the stinky Jetta as soon as Ellis told her to do so, and forty minutes later they were in the bright sun, on the Arizona Trail, zigzagging through beaver-tail cacti and yucca, up the southern face of Molino Basin. The goats raced ahead. It was Lance's favorite kind of hike: all uphill with boulders small enough to jump on.

At the top of the southern face, Goat Man and Ellis stopped and greeted the goats, who were loyally waiting for them.

Ellis sat on a rock. "This was dumb," he said, untying his new hiking boots. "I should have worn my old ones."

"We should have smothered them in Vaseline last night. They'd be nice and soft if we had," Goat Man said. "They'll break in soon."

"I hope so." Ellis stared south at the dark, rolling Rincon range while he kneaded his sore feet. "I'm sort of hungry. Come here, Freida."

She obeyed and walked over to Ellis. He reached into his pack for his tin cup and began to milk her. He squeezed a bit too hard and Freida screamed. "Sorry," he said, "just a little more."

Lance trotted over and smeared his forehead against Ellis's leg, giving Ellis the stink. "He reeks. I thought you had his stink glands removed."

"I did," Goat Man said, "but maybe they didn't get them all." Goat Man had watched the procedure as it was performed on young Lance. He had seen the yellow glands behind Lance's horn buds. Ugly things, each one the size of a match head, clumped together like grapes. The veterinarian cauterized the cell masses. The stench in the vet's office was unbearable. It smelled like urine and musk. "He's been doing that lately."

Ellis grimaced with each sip of Freida's warm, watery milk. He had forgotten how vile it was, and with the Lance stink burning his nostrils, it was twice as disgusting. He couldn't possibly survive more than a few hours if Freida's milk was all he had. He'd have to convince Goat Man to show him which plants he could eat. He knew what Goat Man would say when he asked about the plants: "Did you ever read those books I gave you?" Then Ellis would have to say that he hadn't read the books yet, and Goat Man would say, "I gave them to you five or six years ago." Goat Man would eventually acquiesce and find some bitter leaves or flowers or sticks for Ellis to eat. That's how it had worked before. Ellis decided to hold out until the next morning before he asked Goat Man about the plants.

"Lace up those boots, and let's haul ass," Goat Man said. "I want to make it past that ranch before it's dark."

"Okay." Ellis began to relace his boots. He flinched a few times at the soreness.

"Ellis," Goat Man said, "any girls around Gates?"

"Duh. It's a boys' school," Ellis said. "We do have plenty of porno. The woods is full of it."

"How handy," Goat Man said. "So to speak."

"There's one food server, Minnie, and she's served my table more than any other," Ellis said. "No matter which table I sit at, it seems like she goes out of her way to serve it. She's amazing." He finished tying his boots and stood up. He noticed for the first time that he was taller than Goat Man—he stared straight into his forehead.

"Must be tough with no girls around."

"It is," Ellis said.

"So you can see why I might have gotten together with Aubrey?"

"I don't care," Ellis said quickly. "Really. I wouldn't care if you kept screwing around with her." He did care, though. He was angry and jealous, but he wasn't quite sure why.

"Nothing more's gonna happen. I promise."

"Don't worry about it," Ellis said. He watched a spastic zebra-tailed lizard do push-ups in the sun on a pointed rock.

"Okay," Goat Man said. "You know, if we stay up on this ridge and walk north, I think we'll get to some really nice pools. We can camp there and you can wash off Lance's stink."

"Which trail?"

"No trail," Goat Man said.

They walked along the windy ridge, over rocks and through abrasive brush—amoles, shin-daggers. The goats sped ahead through the chaparral, but with his torturous new hiking boots, Ellis lagged. Goat Man thought some hybrid might help Ellis forget the boots, so he lit up his pipe.

"Thanks," Ellis said. He took a deep hit and stepped over a blackened, necrotic saguaro teeming with fruit flies. He handed the pipe back to Goat Man and kept hiking. As soon as he blew out the hit, Goat Man handed the pipe back to him for another. This continued until they reached an egg-shaped boulder that jutted over a deep, narrow canyon.

Ellis sat on the boulder and looked at the waterfalls and pools below. The noise from the falls was hypnotic, and after he shook the pack off his back, he lay on the smooth, cool rock and experienced the numbness and funniness of the pot. Goat Man stretched beside him.

"Goat Man," Ellis asked, "is it the pot that makes me feel so happy or am I just happy because the pot makes me feel so good?"

"Huh?"

"Does the pot make me happy or am I happy because the pot makes me feel so good?"

"I'm not following."

"Forget it," Ellis said. He pinched his rubber cheeks and stretched them out like bubble gum. They didn't feel like his own; they felt like someone else's, like someone had somehow covered his with theirs. He stared at the sky. The clouds looked as though they had been combed.

Goat Man watched Lance and Freida standing on a taller rock that balanced on the edge of the canyon. Both goats peered down at the water. Goat Man fantasized about running up to Freida and pushing her over. She'd kick and bleat as she fell, and she'd make a formidable splash as she hit the pool forty feet below.

Ellis and Goat Man relaxed up there for a while longer, appreciating the view, gazing into the canyon, until Goat Man suddenly stood and brushed off his ass. "Let's hike down to the pools before it gets dark."

"Okay," Ellis said. "You gonna swim?"

"Might," Goat Man said. "If there's still some sun for me to dry in, I might."

They scrambled down the side of the canyon, turned over rocks, stomped dry brush weeds, scraped their ankles and knees, before they reached the pool.

After pitching Goat Man's orange tent in the dirt next to a deep swimming hole, Ellis took off his boots. He dangled his blistered feet into the cold water and enjoyed the last half hour of warm daylight. He massaged wet sand on his thigh where Lance had rubbed his stink.

Goat Man swam in the dark, numbing water, floated on his back like a sea otter. Tiny fish nipped at his ass, reminding him where he was.

"This is perfect," Ellis said. He knew Goat Man couldn't hear him, but he repeated it. He thought of the frozen Gates campus, the tests he'd have next semester, the grueling crew workouts, the crappy food. He looked up the side of the canyon at the cacti and bushes. A few dark birds looped around the purpling sky.

Goat Man climbed out of the pool at the other end and lay in the sun on a warmed rock. He was hungry, but he knew Freida wouldn't come down near the water. If he wanted milk, he'd have to climb up to where she and Lance were perched. Maybe Ellis would. "Ellis," he called, "how about hiking up to Freida and filling my cup?"

"I'm not putting on my boots until I have to." Ellis turned and called Freida.

"She's not gonna come," Goat Man said. He walked gingerly around the pool toward Ellis, being careful not to step on anything sharp with his bare feet. "Lance might come down near the water if I had Corn Pops, but Freida won't."

Ellis shouted up to Freida, and she bleated rudely in response. He called again. She stood and started down toward the water, hopping skillfully from rock to rock, making clicking skid noises with her hooves.

Goat Man squatted next to Ellis and cupped his hands above

his eyes as he watched Freida descend the side of the canyon. She kicked up a little dust, flattened a few gray salt bushes.

Ellis's calls echoed up the canyon, and Freida continued down until she was standing between them. "Naked men shouldn't squat," Ellis told Goat Man. "Not near me, anyway. I'm not milking her for you until you get dressed."

"I can't believe it," Goat Man said. "I can't believe she came down." He dried himself with his poncho and pulled on his grubby shorts. There was Freida, only steps away from the deep pool, and only ten or fifteen yards from a crushing waterfall.

"What's the big deal?" Ellis said as he started to milk her, careful not to let his fingertips touch the teat. He applied pressure with his first finger to hold the milk in the teat, and then with the second, third, and fourth fingers to work the milk out. When the milk flow slowed, he gently massaged Freida's pink udder until the flow picked up and he was able to force it out with his finger technique. He filled Goat Man's cup to the brim.

"When's your spring break?" Goat Man asked.

"At the end of March," Ellis said. "Why?"

"Just wondering. Ellis, do you think you could convince Freida to step in the water?"

"Why?"

"On some of my longer treks, I've had to cross rivers and running washes and none of the goats will do it. I have to bribe Lance with Corn Pops just to get him to stand in the kiddie pool."

Ellis hobbled over to where the pool was shallow. He stepped in. The bottom was sandy, soft on his feet with silt and algae. He turned to Freida and called her. "Come here!" He clapped his hands. She stared at him and bleated, shook her withers, but finally acquiesced when Ellis changed the tone of his voice to disappointment.

First, she stood at the edge of the pool and tested the water with her nose. After sneezing and shaking her head, she put her front hooves in the water. Finally, she put her hind hooves in—past her dewclaws—and stood calmly, while Ellis scratched her head and patted her side. "I'm the goat master," Ellis declared.

"You are," Goat Man said, amazed.

THIRTY-TWO

It was impossible for Ellis and Goat Man to sleep. The goats bleated and kicked around all night; they were used to trekking at night, so they were restless. There was nothing Goat Man and Ellis could do to quiet them. Freida even walked down to the tent at one point and began to chew on the zipper.

In the morning, there was no hiding from the sun, but neither Goat Man nor Ellis wanted to get out of their sleeping bags.

"I hate Freida," Goat Man mumbled. "And Lance."

"I think I may have gotten an hour of sleep." Ellis's eyes burned and his head ached, but he knew he was awake for good. His bladder was about to burst, so he unzipped his sleeping bag and tried to stand. His feet were trashed: dappled with pink blister clusters and purple smears of bruises. Three of his toenails were black, like he had dropped a brick on them.

"What's the problem?" Goat Man asked.

"My feet." He sat back down on his sleeping bag and stuck his feet in Goat Man's face. "Look."

"They smell like cheese. Put on your thick socks."

Ellis limped out of the tent into the cold morning. He pissed right next to the tent because his feet hurt too much to walk any farther. Steam rose from the silvery brittle bush he doused.

"Hey," Goat Man said. "You're practically pissing in my face."

"Sorry." He aimed his stream farther away from the tent and shot it as hard as possible without adjusting his tender feet. He hit a little cholla cactus, drenched it. He nearly fell back inside the dew-covered tent when he finished.

"Let me see those feet again," Goat Man said, sitting up. He opened the tent flap, letting the yellow morning light spill in.

Ellis rested on his butt and stuck his feet in Goat Man's face again. "I don't know how they got all bruised."

"They're fucked," Goat Man said. "Crawl out there and soak them in the water. I can fix those black toenails with a hot needle at home. That's just blood built up. When the swelling goes down, put your socks and boots back on, and we'll head back."

"I'll never make it."

"We've actually doubled back a bit. We're closer to the car than you think," Goat Man said. He knew they weren't close to the car, probably a three-hour hike.

"I hope so." Ellis gathered his boots and limped outside to soak his feet in the cold swimming hole.

Goat Man packed everything in no time and pulled out his camera from his sack. "Ellis, smile," he said. He clicked a shot of Ellis with his feet in the water. "Now a picture of your feet, a close-up."

"I just want to leave," Ellis said. "This is going to ruin my crew training."

"You can still swim. Swim in the morning. Set Bennet back another hour every morning until you leave."

"He'll love that," Ellis said. "I'm only here for about a week more."

Goat Man handed him his poncho to dry his feet.

"You know, Bennet's proof that Wendy's more screwed up than she's ever been," Ellis said.

"You think so?"

"Yes." Ellis winced as he pulled on his socks and pushed his feet into his boots. "I'm beginning to see Frank's side."

"What do you mean?"

"I mean, I'm beginning to see why Frank moved back East."

"That's good," Goat Man said. "I guess."

"Let's haul," Ellis said. He laced up his boots and tried to ignore the pain.

For over an hour, they had been hiking down a canyon clogged with bull-size granite boulders. The goats loved it. They jumped all over the place. Ellis hated it. His feet killed. The pain shot up his legs. Toward the end, on a smoother trail, Goat Man suggested Ellis take off his boots. He let him ride piggy back.

They had attached Goat Man's pack to Freida with their belts. She protested, kicked up on her hocks, and tried to bite Goat Man as he strapped it on, but Ellis yelled at her, and she stopped fussing about it. Lance looked curiously at Freida. He had a pack of his own, but he had never seen another goat with one. Freida could carry packs and produce milk, while Lance only carried packs. Maybe Lance was obsolete, Goat Man thought. The next female he bought he would train to carry packs right away: a lactating cargo goat.

"Thanks for carrying me," Ellis said. "I won't forget it."

"No problem." Goat Man trudged ahead. He knew Ellis would do the same for him.

Goat Man rested every five minutes or so. He had to. Ellis was a big kid, over six feet, and heavier than he had thought.

Lance hopped directly into the backseat as soon as Goat Man opened the door, but Freida wouldn't budge until Ellis told her to get in. It amazed Goat Man. Even when he hadn't hated Freida, back when he was nice to her and thought she was his prize goat, he hadn't gotten half as much respect as Ellis did. She sat still in the backseat as Ellis pulled burrs from her tassels. She didn't try to nip him.

As they approached Tucson city limits, they passed a hitch-hiker carrying a ripped cardboard sign that read, I-10 WEST.

"Should I pick him up? He can sit in the back with the goats," Goat Man said.

"Don't."

"I was kidding," Goat Man said.

"Don't ever pick up hitchhikers."

"I used to hitchhike all over. In college, I went all the way from Tucson to Seattle."

"I would never hitchhike. No way," Ellis said. "You never got picked up by a psycho or a pervert?"

"No. A few weirdos, but never a psycho or a pervert," Goat Man said. "One guy who picked me up was a wig salesman."

"You're lucky," Ellis said. He stared out the smudged window into the white, blinding sun. "You know what I've learned?" he continued. "I've learned that no matter what sort of sick perverted thing you can think of, someone out there does it." Ellis looked around the interior and fished through grubby coins in the ashtray. "See this nickel? I bet there's a guy out there who sticks nickels up his butt to get off. I bet there's a guy out there that walks around parking lots at night looking specifically for old Jettas to whack off on."

"I doubt that about Jettas," Goat Man said.

"My roommate, Barney, he's kind of stupid, and he got us stuck in a car with a pervert and a crazy woman. The guy kissed and licked Barney and pulled out his dick." Ellis said. "He had a gun pointed at Barney."

"Shit," Goat Man said. "In Pennsylvania?" He turned sharply up Sabino Canyon Road past two new subdivisions. The goats slid across the seat and bleated.

"In D.C.," Ellis said. "Barney made me promise not to call the cops. Don't tell Wendy."

"I won't," Goat Man said. "You know, not everyone's a pervert, not everyone's into weird shit." He clicked on the fuzzy radio, and clicked it off. "But you're lucky to be alive."

Goat Man pulled the Jetta to the edge of the arroyo and let the goats out. They bolted through the sand and dried shrubs toward their pen. Goat Man could see the blubber jiggling up and over Freida's hips. She was almost as fat as Lance.

This arroyo was where Goat Man usually parked his ugly Jetta, but with Ellis being lame, he pulled out of the sand and drove back down the road and up the driveway. There was a giant blue Cadillac in the driveway, something from the early eighties. Bennet's Jeep was parked next to it. Goat Man parked behind it.

"He must have a friend over," Ellis said.

"Another crystal-packing spirit chaser," Goat Man said.

"My mom's not back yet. We're alone with Bennet."

"Neat."

Goat Man carried Ellis into the house through the garage door. He plopped him on the couch in front of the TV and handed him the remote. "I'll go out to the pool house and get stuff for your feet."

Goat Man stepped out the sliding glass door, but stopped when he saw Bennet, sitting on the edge of the pool with his legs dangling into the shallow end. Bennet wore his red slingshot bathing suit, was leaning back, soaking in the afternoon sun. An unbelievably tanned older man with skin like gravy stood in the shallow end, his face at Bennet's crotch. "Yikes," Goat Man whispered to himself. The man hopped up on the edge of the pool next to Bennet, and they began to kiss, the man kneading Bennet's thigh.

Goat Man stepped back inside, carefully slid open the kitchen window, and banged a few pans. He dropped a big skillet into the sink, and soon Bennet was at the sliding door with a towel around his waist. "I thought you weren't getting back for a few more days," he said.

"Ellis trashed his feet," Goat Man said. "We had to come back early."

"Oh," Bennet said. "That's too bad."

"Whose car is that in the driveway?"

"My friend's," Bennet said. "I was just teaching him to swim."

Goat Man peered out the kitchen window towards the pool. "Oh, there he is. What's his name?"

"Why?"

"Just wondering," Goat Man said. "Looks a little like my grandfather."

"Gerald."

"I need some stuff for Ellis's feet," Goat Man said. "It's in the pool house." He eased by Bennet.

Gerald was treading water. He was older than Goat Man had thought—worn, ravaged by the sun, liver spots splattered all over like brown paint. He wondered how much Bennet got per hour. He deserved a lot.

"Hello," Gerald said.

"Hello. How are the swimming lessons?"

"Super."

"Super." Goat Man unlocked the pool house and went into the bathroom to find bandages and salves for Ellis's feet. Bennet met him as he was coming out.

"Wendy's not too fond of Gerald," he told Goat Man. "I'd appreciate it if you didn't tell her he was here."

"Gerald seems like a nice enough old fart."

"Just don't tell her."

"No problem." He walked into the house and tended to Ellis's feet.

THIRTY-THREE

Ellis's feet healed pretty well after a few days of TV-watching
and bong-hitting, and a visit to a podiatrist who told him to do
exactly what Goat Man had told him to do: soak them, keep
them elevated, watch the blisters for infection. He started to
swim on Saturday, beating Bennet to the pool as planned. By
Monday he was running again, this time into the national wilder-
ness area on the trails farther into Ventana Canyon where the
mountains were steeper and the foliage thinned out. He jogged
up switchbacks, past pools and waterfalls, to the top of a peak
overgrown with spiky agaves. He breathed deeply and smoothed
his burning legs. He was light-headed, but in a good way, and
looking at the trail twisting up the mountainside and through the
canyon, he was proud of himself.

As he came upon the swimming pool, Ellis saw Bennet sitting
on the diving board, waiting for Goat Man to finish his laps.

"I beat you today," Bennet told Ellis. "You'll have to wait for
me."

"I wasn't going to swim this morning, anyway," Ellis lied.
"My ear hurts."

"Good then," Bennet said. "You want to try out your new mountain bike later? I know some good trails out past Pima College."

It would make Wendy happy, Ellis thought, and he was still a little stony from his run, so he said, "Sure."

"Great," Bennet said. "I'll swim for an hour, and then we'll go. Aubrey might come over later. You remember Aubrey, don't you?"

"Sure do," Ellis said.

Goat Man climbed out of the pool, and Bennet dove in. Ellis followed Goat Man into the pool house, placing each of his steps on Goat Man's wet footprints.

He yelled to Goat Man through his bedroom door as Goat Man changed out of his swim trunks. "I'm going mountain biking with Bennet later."

"Neat," Goat Man said.

"And Aubrey is coming over later today."

Goat Man emerged from his bedroom, wearing Levi's and a blue flannel shirt, tucked in. "Oh."

Bennet's Spandex biking shorts were emblazoned in Day-Glo orange with the name of the company that manufactured his bike. He had a matching cycling shirt and helmet. Ellis wore a ratty FISHBONE T-shirt and khakis he had cut off at the knees. He was trying to fit his new bike onto the rack on the back of Bennet's Jeep.

"Let me do that," Bennet said. He tried to pull the bike away from Ellis, but Ellis didn't yield.

"I'll do it," Ellis said. He lifted his bike and slid it onto the rack. A pedal hit the Jeep's bumper.

"Careful," Bennet said.

"It's a mountain bike, not a prom dress."

"It's not the bike I'm worried about; it's the Jeep. You just took a chunk out of the bumper." Bennet kneeled and spit-shined the damage Ellis couldn't see.

"Move," Ellis said. "I need to lift yours on." He slid Bennet's bike onto the rack, and Bennet flinched. "Let's go."

The trails beyond Starr Pass were pretty fun—rocky and challenging, lined with cacti. Bennet was slow, tense, and a little shaky. There were many riders out that day, clogging the trails, ripping up the red dirt and speeding by, hopping rocks. Bennet tried to talk to each of them about their bikes. One guy showed slight interest in Bennet's bike while they rested at a fork in the trail. "It's been pretty good to me," Bennet told the guy, "I'm thinking about upgrading in the spring to the lighter one they're coming out with. It's carbon fiber tubing with titanium lugs. Of course, mine has the lightest components. It weighs in at . . ." The guy finally managed to weasel away and ride off. Bennet sat there in the dirt with Ellis, swigging Gatorade from his squeeze bottle.

"Let's go down there," Ellis said. He pointed to a narrow canyon that spilled into an open range behind the jagged mountains.

"Too technical."

"No, it's not," Ellis said. "I've seen three guys go down it since we stopped here."

"Believe me," Bennet said. "It's too much for you to handle at this point. I've done it."

"I have a helmet." Ellis rode off, crunching through the loose gravel, toward the little canyon.

"Wait," Bennet said, but Ellis was flying, pumping his pedals, bumping down the trail.

It was kind of tough, steep and rocky, but Ellis liked it. It was like riding down a flight of stairs, only if he crashed, he stood a good chance of landing in a cactus. He concentrated on the trail, looked for rocks and plants to dodge, thought of nothing else. His hands and wrists ached from the jarring as he reached the bottom, a loose arroyo congested with red boulders and hairy jumping chollas. He followed the bike tracks to a steep, packed trail of smoothed roller-coaster bumps. Each of the steep descents gave him that elevator-down rush in his stomach. When he finally skidded to a halt at the end—a sprawling trailer village—he relished the rattle in his brain and the burn in his calves. He straddled his bike and looked back for Bennet.

Bennet appeared a few minutes later, pushing his bike down the trail. He had a cut on his cheek. "I got a flat and spilled!"

"Cool," Ellis yelled.

"Not cool!" Bennet shouted. "It'll take me an hour to change this damn tube."

Two guys stopped and helped Bennet repair his flat. It was clear that Bennet didn't know what he was doing; he couldn't even get the tire off the rim. He jammed his fingers and cursed loudly several times before the two guys showed up.

Wendy jumped on Bennet and kissed him when he and Ellis walked into the kitchen after their ride. "I missed you so much in Sedona," she said. "Let me kiss your boo-boo." Then she bit his ear.

Ellis rolled his eyes and started upstairs for a shower.

"Hold on, Ellis," Wendy said. "How was your trek with Javier?"

"I trashed my feet and we had to come back early," Ellis said.

He sat on a tile step midway up the stairs, picked a burr from his sock. "They're still pretty blistered, but most have popped."

"How'd you do that?" Wendy released Bennet from her hug, and walked toward the stairs.

"I wore my new hiking boots and they weren't broken in."

"Figures Frank would give you shoddy boots," she said. "Let me see your feet."

"They're fine now, and the boots Frank gave me are almost the best you can buy," Ellis said.

"They are," Bennet said. "I might buy some for myself if we go down to Havasupi this spring."

"Frank should have warned you about breaking them in," Wendy said. "How about after Aubrey gets here we go out to dinner?"

Ellis pictured another plate of bland grain and sprouts, the food he was given the last time they had gone out for a meal. In the two weeks Ellis had been home, Wendy had gone from eating turkey and ham on Christmas, to soy milk and tofu. "Vegetarian again?" Ellis asked.

"I'll call the Greenery." Wendy clapped her hands twice and shoved Bennet out of the way.

"How about El Charro?" Ellis suggested. "You could eat a bean burrito or something."

"Do they use lard in their beans?" Wendy asked.

"I doubt it," Ellis said.

They were seated outside on the patio next to the adjoining cantina: Bar ¡Toma! Three mariachis in white, pleated guayabera shirts and tight black pants sang sweetly about love and promises. One played a small concertina. The others played guitars. A drunk man sporting a souvenir sombrero was dancing by himself near the fountain, smoking a fat cigar that smelled like cinnamon. To Ellis, the man looked sad, especially when he sat down on the edge of the fountain and wiped the sweat from his forehead.

A busboy arrived, handed out menus, and began to fill their water glasses.

"I wish that slob would put out his cigar," Aubrey said, pointing.

"*El Charro* means *the cigar*," Ellis said. "They sell them here. You were the one who asked if we could sit outside."

"I didn't know we'd have to breathe in all his crap."

"I like the smell," Ellis said. "In fact, I might buy a few cigars for Frank."

Wendy hailed a waitress. "Do you use lard in your beans?" She asked. "If you do, they're not really vegetarian."

"Canola oil," the waitress said. She grinned tightly.

Soon, they all ordered, except for Aubrey, who was lost, staring at Goat Man, gazing at him through big black-framed spectacles that rested on the tip of her nose. Ellis thought her glasses resembled Frank's poetry glasses, and he told Wendy.

"Frank wore ones like that when I first met him," Wendy said. "Back when they were only worn by nerds."

Aubrey turned to Wendy. "Fucker Frank?" she asked. "You never told me the story of Fucker Frank."

Ellis sighed.

"Well," Wendy said, "if you want to know about Fucker Frank, you'll have to talk to Ellis. He knows more than anyone at this point."

"Um," the waitress said, staring at Aubrey.

"Sorry," Aubrey said. "Just a green corn tamale or something." She turned to Ellis. "So why is Frank a fucker?" She took off her poetry glasses, placed them on the empty plate in front of her. To Ellis, Aubrey's smeared blue makeup made her look dead, like a zombie.

"Aubrey," Bennet said. "Come on."

"Just curious," Aubrey said. She picked up her glasses and slid them back on her face, sticking her pinkie finger out, featuring herself, posing as she did it.

"He's not really a fucker," Ellis said.

"That's a laugh," Wendy said. She blew the bangs out of her eyes and tapped her nails on the glass-topped table.

"Calm down," Bennet told Wendy. "Redirect. Redirect the energy."

"Let's all mellow," Goat Man said.

"No," Wendy said. "I want to hear why Ellis is suddenly best friends with Frank."

"I never said I was best friends with him, all I said was that he isn't really a fucker. And I don't think strangers should be referring to him as 'Fucker Frank.'" Ellis glared at Aubrey, who was now pretending to be interested in her empty plate.

"Aubrey's not a stranger," Wendy said. "She has every right to know the hell that Frank put me through."

"That's retarded," Ellis said. "Tell Aubrey about the hell you put Frank through."

Goat Man peeked over at Wendy and winced when he saw she was flushed and trembling. Bennet was patting her head and massaging her neck, but it was all in vain. She shrieked like a cornered javelina, threw her fork to the ground, and stood. She plowed through the mariachis as she stomped across the patio toward the parking lot.

Bennet looked over at Ellis and broke the silence. "Good job," he said.

"Shut up," Ellis said. He glared again at Aubrey. Dumb poetry glasses. Dumb makeup.

"Are we still eating here? Or can we stop at Taco Bell on the way home?" Aubrey asked Bennet. Then she looked over at Goat Man and smacked her overglossed lips.

Ellis watched the sad man toss his burning cigar in the fountain. Because Wendy had caused the mariachis to stop playing, Ellis could hear the cigar fizz.

THIRTY-FOUR

Ellis hitched up his baggy shorts and sat on the barber chair. Tirso wrapped the plastic cape around his neck. The traffic on Campbell Avenue outside created a strobe effect with the imposing afternoon sun. Ellis squinted until Tirso spun the chair away from the window.

"How are things in Ohio?" Tirso asked. Tirso ran water over a comb and began to go at Ellis's hair.

"Pennsylvania," Ellis said. "I like it."

"What do you think of the new Javier?"

"I barely recognized him without his hair and beard," Ellis said.

"And his whole goat enterprise is working out nicely." Tirso clicked on the electric clippers. They hummed as they bit through Ellis's hair.

"What goat enterprise?"

"That business with the Biosphere."

"What?"

Tirso turned off the clippers. "He's breeding goats that don't mess with the ecosystem. He works in the Biosphere."

"Is that what he said?"

"Yes."

"Oh," Ellis said. He didn't want to hear more of the lie.

"He's modest," Tirso said.

Ellis and Wendy barely spoke for the rest of Ellis's winter break. The longest conversation they had was about his airline reservations. He left his new bong with Goat Man, telling him to keep it going until March, when he'd return for spring break. Ellis was glad to be heading back to Gates—even with the running and swimming and the beautiful weather, he had been bored in Tucson toward the end of his stay. He had found himself in front of the TV too often, watching videos and loud, trashy talk shows, thinking about how disappointing everyone was. He had even missed Barney. As disgusting a realization as it was, he missed Barney. He had found himself carrying on complete conversations with Barney in his head, dumb arguments about turning out the light or losing a favorite pen.

When Ellis opened the door to his dorm room the afternoon he arrived back at Gates, Barney was asleep, balled in the fetal position on top of his comforter. The room smelled as if it had been cleaned over the break—no more foot odor, just artificial flowers. He walked over to the new window, knocked on it, and looked out at the gray woods. He dropped his suitcase on his bed. Barney stirred, so he spoke to him. "Hey, Barney, how was your break?"

"Hey, Ellis," Barney said. "My break sucked after my grades arrived. I got a C minus in history and all the rest B minuses." He sat up in his bed and yawned.

"At least you got a B minus in algebra. That's good. I didn't get my grades yet." Ellis began to unpack.

"Who pays your tuition? Your mom or your dad?"

"I think Frank does."

"Then Frank gets your report card," Barney said. His face was pink and creased from the seams in his bedding. He looked like a big baby as he yawned.

"Oh."

"Ready for more crew?" Barney asked.

"I am. I ran and swam almost every day."

"We're gonna have the best freshman boat this year," Barney said. "Rosenberg gets his cast off in a few weeks."

"Coach said if I got in shape, he'd put me on the varsity boat because of my height."

Barney didn't say anything for a few seconds. Ellis heard him sucking breaths through his teeth. Finally, he said, "Those guys will eat you alive. Half of them are trying to get on Ivy boats. They're serious."

"I know," Ellis said. "Coach probably won't put me on their boat."

"There's no way you could party if you were on the varsity boat. There's no way you could party at all."

"Don't use *party* as a verb," Ellis said.

Minnie served Ellis's table that night—roasted turkey, mashed potatoes, peas. She even broke protocol and asked him how his break was. "Great," he said. As soon as Minnie walked away, five or six boys congratulated him.

Rosenberg yelled "Stud!" too loudly and knocked over the gravy boat when he went to pat Ellis on the shoulder. The gravy streamed in all directions, but most flowed toward Barney and splattered on his lap.

"Damn!" Barney whined. "You're a fucking spaz, Rosenberg."

"Fuck you, Barney," Rosenberg sat up, dabbed at the gravy puddle on the table with his napkin.

"You guys are pathetic," Ellis said.

Dr. Eldridge approached the table. "Mr. Whitman, what's all the hubbub?" Eldridge looked different—tanned, but in a shiny way that made his eyebrows almost disappear in the gloss.

"Nothing really," Ellis said. "Mr. Rosenberg accidentally spilled the gravy."

"On my lap," Barney whined. He stood to show off the mess.

"Go clean yourself up, Mr. Cannel," Eldridge said. "Mr. Whitman will bring a plate to you after dinner."

"Thank you, sir," Barney said. He pushed in his chair, and walked off, daubing at his crotch with a napkin, eliciting laughs from the other boys.

"Everyone wouldn't be congratulating you if it were nothing," Dr. Eldridge said to Ellis. "Now what's all the commotion about?"

"The server, she asked me how my vacation was. That's all." Ellis stared at his plate.

"Okay." Dr. Eldridge walked back to his table.

Later, when Ellis brought Barney a covered plate of food, Barney said, "Shit, he hates you, man." Barney sat at his neat desk and examined the dinner.

"Who hates me?" Ellis tossed his jacket on his bed.

"Eldridge."

"He loves me."

"Why?" Barney played with the gray peas on his plate. He arranged them into a triangle.

"If Frank pays the tuition bills on time, Eldridge loves me."

• • •

"Listen up," Coach said. "I know you're all out of shape from eggnog and fruitcake, but I want you to pull ten thousand in under fifty minutes. I'll be watching your form, straightening you out."

Ellis had stupidly sat at the rower with the squeaky flywheel. The high-pitched sound annoyed him, made his dentalwork tingle. He had never pulled ten thousand meters before, had no idea how long it was or how long it would take. He tried to pace himself with Barney, who was on the machine to his right, but he lost it. Each time he looked down at the digital monitor, he saw how little progress he had made, and he became more frustrated with the squeak of the wheel.

It seemed like he was in the seven-thousand range for an eternity. Coach came over to him and told him to pull harder and keep his back straight.

Suddenly, Barney stood up from his rower, wiped his palms on his shorts, and said, "Done."

"Good, Mr. Cannel," Coach said.

Ellis looked down at the monitor: 8878. He pulled harder. He had been rowing for almost forty-five minutes. He was dizzy, light-headed. His forearms ached to the bone. He made a concerted effort to space out, forget the monitor, but he kept glancing at it. The squeak of the wheel became louder. Soon, he was the last one rowing, and he still had more than five hundred meters to pull. Stuck in the musky, overheated gym. Coach stood in front of him, arms akimbo, shaking his head.

Ellis finally finished. He wiped his palms on his shirt and looked at Coach. "What?"

"With legs like yours, I just thought you'd be the first one off," Coach said. "Quadzilla."

"That's the first time I've ever done ten thousand," Ellis said. His legs felt like gelatin, like they had been newly attached to his body. He could barely stand.

"We'll see how you do tomorrow morning with the run."

"We'll see," Ellis said.

Ellis finished dead last in the three-mile run the next morning.

At dinner that Thursday, Minnie didn't serve Ellis's table. She didn't even look over. On Sunday, the same thing happened. "You've lost it," Barney said later on in their room. "She's sweet on someone else."

"Go to hell," Ellis said. "Eldridge probably yelled at her."

THIRTY-FIVE

Goat Man dreamed Freida had captured him. She had big, pink human hands instead of hooves, and she was strangling him as she greedily licked the salty sweat from his brow. He tried to shove her off, but she was too heavy and too crafty. She'd pin him down and nip him with her golden teeth. He was relieved when the alarm sounded and saved him from his nightmare. He tottered to the bathroom in the morning's half light, took a piss, stepped into his trunks, walked outside, and dove into the warm pool.

He couldn't wipe the grotesque images of Freida from his mind, and he lost count of his laps. He'd wait for Bennet to show up, then he'd swim ten more.

Lately, Bennet had been obsequious to Goat Man. Goat Man never let Bennet know that he saw him whoring himself to Gerald.

"Javier," Bennet had said the morning before, "I have a refrigerator full of high-energy sports bars and drinks inside, and you know you're welcome to them. You can use my Soloflex whenever you want to pump up."

"Thanks," Goat Man had said. "I might just take you up on that." He had already gone into the fridge and snatched an energy bar two weeks earlier. It had tasted like dirt.

As he continued with his laps, he wondered how he might use the Bennet-as-bisexual-gigolo-to-rich-old-snowbirds information to his advantage. This made him forget the Freida dream, and his swimming became more relaxed and efficient: He breathed on either side every third stroke, he scooped his arms deeper and pulled harder. When he saw Bennet sitting on the diving board, he got out and walked toward the pool house.

"I didn't mean to drive you from the pool," Bennet said.

"Don't worry about it."

He had let the pool house regress into a dump—dirty clothes and crusty dishes everywhere. He'd clean today, after he took a shower and ate breakfast. Ellis's bong, sitting on the edge of the glass table, was a possibility as well.

A while later, Aubrey knocked and walked in. Goat Man stood in front of his stove, naked, preparing hash browns. A plate of scrambled eggs and salsa sat on the table next to the latest issue of *Goat Breeder*.

"Hey," Goat Man said, "let me get some shorts on."

"Why?"

"Because."

"Because, why?" She lumbered closer. The platforms she wore made her walk like a drunk.

"Why aren't you at school, anyway?" He wrapped a red canvas KISS THE COOK apron around his waist. "Bennet's right outside."

"He didn't see me. I'm ditching school today." She slid her hand up under the apron, flopped his dick with her fingers. "Let's get high and fool around."

He pushed her back. "We can't. We really can't anymore."

"Because of Ellis? Because I used to kick his ass? He's a conceited prick."

"No, he's not, and you're too young." Goat Man pushed her

away harder than he had meant. She nearly fell, stumbling in her platforms.

"Too late!" Aubrey's face flushed red. She stomped out, slamming the door hard enough to knock Ellis's bong off the table. It shattered on the Mexican tiles.

"Sadness," Goat Man mumbled. He turned off the stove.

And as Goat Man was bending over, picking up the shards, Wendy and Johanna walked in.

"Nice view," Johanna said. "Your little friend certainly ran out in a huff."

"What's up with Aubrey?" Wendy asked.

"Oh." Goat Man stood and rubbed his temples. "I'm really having a bad day. Can you leave me alone for maybe thirty minutes? Let me clean this up and eat my breakfast?"

"Okay," Wendy said. She tugged on Johanna's embroidered skirt. "But we'll be back for our goat-trekking lesson."

"What?" Goat Man said. He held several bong shards in his palm.

"You promised," Johanna said.

"Okay, whatever you say. Just give me thirty minutes, please."

"No problem," Johanna said. She elegantly spun around so her skirt floated a little, and she walked out with Wendy.

Goat Man started on the broken bong mess again, trying to recall when he had promised goat-trekking lessons—whatever they were—to Wendy and Johanna.

The sunlight on Goat Man's arms and face felt good in the cool morning. Mist rose from the arroyo. Ghostly wisps floated from clusters of cactus. Wendy and Johanna were both petting Gigi when Goat Man arrived at the pen.

"She's a goddess," Johanna said.

"So much wisdom," Wendy said.

"Her teats are dry," Goat Man said. "Useless."

"I wouldn't say that. Look at her soulful eyes," Johanna said. "And her hooves, they've seen many miles."

"Look at her asshole," Goat Man said. "She's all clogged up. Been eating trash again."

A corner of a red-and-orange cellophane Doritos wrapper hung from Gigi's crusted-over butt. Burrs and twigs also stuck to the mess—she had been dragging her ass in the dirt for relief.

"Oh, my God," Wendy said.

"In order to trek with goats, you have to get them in tip-top shape," Goat Man said. "Go get a wet rag and I'll have you clean her up," he told Wendy.

She shook her head. "I can't," she said. "I get squeamish about stuff like that. I used to make you or Frank change Ellis's diapers. Remember?"

"I'll do it," Johanna said. She quickly hitched up her skirt and jogged up the trail to the house.

"Get a little bucket of warm water, too," Goat Man yelled after her.

Gigi went through the trash-eating constipation-plug routine about three times a year. Goat Man hated cleaning her up, but he hated seeing her drag her ass around even more. Goat ass-dragging was a pathetic sight: the way their hind legs splayed awkwardly, and that humiliated look on their faces. He'd have Johanna do it all, tell her it was a good way to bond with the goats, then he'd administer some liquid paraffin, which Gigi usually drank without protest.

After the clean-up, they could take Gigi and Lance on the leashes and walk down the arroyo. He'd show Johanna and

Wendy how Lance liked to jump up on things and they'd say it was part of his strong spirit. Maybe he'd have Wendy and Johanna clean out the pen, rake the jelly-bean-sized turds into little heaps, and wash the fodder bins. He kicked the dirt and watched Lance up on the roof of the shed. Lance stared vacantly into the desert and chewed loudly, working his jaw in circles.

"Javier," Wendy said.

"Yes." Goat Man had forgotten she was standing next to him.

"Be objective, okay?" she said. "Do you think Ellis was out of line at the restaurant a few weeks ago? Be honest."

"I think maybe there was some miscommunication."

"I was thinking that, too," she said, a little too excitedly. "I want him to tell me exactly what his relationship with Frank is. I want him to be honest."

"Seems reasonable."

"I just want to know where I stand. I want to know what type of venom Fucker Frank is injecting into him." She rubbed her hands together. Her rings clicked.

"Seems reasonable."

"You really think so?"

"Sure," he lied.

"I'm gonna ask Johanna to help me through this one. I feel like I'm squandering all this energy that could be used on other things."

"You could be," Goat Man said. He wished Johanna would hurry up and return to the pen with the wash rag and bucket. Gigi looked around nervously. Bleated twice, twitched her withers. Goat Man suspected she might try to run away and drag her ass in private.

"What was Aubrey doing in the pool house earlier, anyway?" Wendy asked.

"She just wanted to hang out and talk about Ellis."

"I thought maybe you'd been getting her high. Bennet would be furious. Aubrey's the only one in his family that he gets along with."

"Oh."

"He's overprotective of her. She's the only one in his whole family who's not in a twelve-step program."

Goat Man watched Johanna slog down the trail with a few rags draped on her shoulders. The water sloshed over the edges of the bucket. "Bennet had to set me up with just the right bucket and washcloth," she said. "He's great. So helpful."

"He is," Goat Man said. "Wendy, you hold Gigi, and Johanna, you go at it."

THIRTY-SIX

Melted snow had refrozen and made the trail a crackled, slippery mess. It was still fun, though. Ellis's bike had arrived the day before via UPS. Bennet had packed it well—it was unscathed and easy to reassemble. Ellis had looked forward to the ride the whole time he pulled on the rowing machine during practice earlier that day. He was no longer the slowest on the machines or on the track, but Barney still beat him at both, and that bugged him.

He pedaled harder, through the slush and black mud. The afternoon sun filtered through naked trees, blinding him with flashes. His thighs and calves burned. When he saw Rosenberg out on the trail, he was relieved; he had an excuse to slow.

"Hey," Ellis said.

"Hey," Rosenberg said. "You know if there are any new magazines out here?"

"Someone said that junior with the blond afro brought back a whole stack from Europe, nasty ones, but I haven't seen them."

"Been smoking up?"

"I can't," Ellis said. "Crew."

"I can't, either. I ran out already," Rosenberg said. "When my leg's healed, can I try your bike?" Rosenberg was down to a small ankle cast, small enough that he no longer used crutches—he hobbled.

"Sure," Ellis said. "*Adios.*"

As the trail approached Route 22, it sloped steeply downward and sharply curved around a dilapidated stone wall that dated back to the 1700s. The wall served as one of the main hiding places for *Hustler*s, *Playboy*s, and *Penthouse*s. The magazines were tucked and crammed into crevices all along the wall like mail. Ellis whizzed by the wall and felt the weightlessness in his stomach as the trail dropped like a roller coaster.

At the bottom of the hill, right near the street, his right foot slipped out of the toe-clip as he tried to hop a log, and he toppled, grinding himself into the ground. His mouth filled with freezing dirt and pebbles. His face dragged against the frozen earth. The sticky warm blood coursed down Ellis's face and neck. He watched it dribble into the dirt and ice: bright, thick.

A car drove by, and another. The third pulled into the dirty snow and gravel of the shoulder.

"It's him." The woman's voice was strangely familiar, but Ellis couldn't see. His eyes were stinging with blood.

"I know him, too," another said. "How do you know him?"

"Hey," the first woman said, "do you remember me?"

Ellis felt her foot poking his rib. He rolled over and squinted up at her. It was the woman who had bought beer for him and Barney in the fall. Standing next to her was Minnie. Ellis grunted, "Uh-yup," and spit out a few pebbles, hoping they weren't teeth.

"Oh shit. Look at his face," Minnie said.

"How're your teeth?" the other woman said.

Ellis sat up in the dirt and brushed himself off. His limbs were fine, but his forehead still bled cinematically. "Okay," he told the woman.

"Fiona, open the hatch and we'll toss his bike in." Minnie walked over to Ellis and lifted him up under his arm.

He could smell her hair, that honeysuckle shampoo.

"You need stitches," she said.

Fiona looked like a Fiona: hair clamped up like a lap dog's, big lipstick, tired eyes. She still owed him the change for the twelve-pack. He limped over to her car, and Minnie opened the door for him. Trash covered the backseat—beer cans, fashion magazines, a white high-heeled shoe—so she shoved it all to the floor to make room for him.

On the way to the emergency room in Monroe, the neighboring town, Ellis held the sleeve of his fleece pullover to his face. Fiona kept trying to make conversation even though she was driving.

"Funny," she said. "Last time you wouldn't get in my car."

"Uh huh," Ellis said.

"Was that the first time out on your bike?" Fiona asked.

"Shut up, Fiona," Minnie said. "His head's still bleeding."

Fiona whispered loudly to Minnie: "I'm trying to keep him from slipping into shock. You're supposed to keep him talking. I saw it on *Rescue 911*."

"So what's your name, anyway?" Minnie asked Ellis.

He mumbled it.

"Allen?" Minnie asked.

"No. Ellis." He accentuated the *s*.

"I'm Minnie, and this is Fiona."

I know, he thought. His head tingled and burned, and the metallic taste of blood nauseated him.

There was no one else in the emergency room, but it still took a while before Ellis was stitched up, because of some insurance hassles. Fiona called Gates and told the office what had happened, while Minnie helped Ellis deal with the crabby insurance woman. "He goes to Gates for Christ's sake. His parents can pay the bill," Minnie said. "This is stupid." The woman still had to call Wendy because Ellis was a minor. Of course, Bennet answered. Ellis could hear the insurance woman arguing with him: "I can only release that information to his mother," the woman repeated to Bennet three times. "No, Frank did not put me up to this. I don't know any Franks." After she eventually spoke to Wendy and got the proper authorization, she hung up and told Ellis that the man who had answered the phone had real problems. Finally Ellis was guided to a back room behind a curtain, where a nurse checked his neck and gave him a tiny shot of anesthetic in his forehead.

A doctor, a young guy with an unkempt beard and thick eyebrows, came in and looked at Ellis's face. "Ugly," he said. "I'm Doctor Wilson."

"Ellis Whitman," Ellis said.

"Your face should be numb in a few minutes, but I'm going to start cleaning out your wounds now." He started to lift up the little flaps of skin and pick the gravel out with tweezers and rolled-up gauze. Each time the doctor touched Ellis's face, tiny bursts of pain burned through his head. But soon the anesthetic took effect, and it didn't hurt; Ellis's face felt like it was asleep and chubby.

"My roommate in college went to Gates," Dr. Wilson said. "I've been out to the campus a few times. It's nice. You boys have it made." Ellis saw that he was starting to stitch—black thread. "I'll give you about six over your cheek and then I'll do your head. You already had a scar on your forehead?"

"Yes," Ellis said. He thought of Aubrey. He wondered if she and Goat Man were still screwing around.

"Well," Dr. Wilson said, "I'll make it look like nothing happened. Your scars from today will be tiny. You need a helmet."

"I had a helmet, but my mother's stupid boyfriend forgot to pack it with the bike."

"You're the one who rode it without a helmet."

Ellis thanked Fiona profusely when she dropped him off at Gates that night. His face was still numb, so he drooled and sort of stammered as he stood outside her car with his bike.

"No problem," she said. "And if you need me to buy beer for you again or anything else, just talk to Minnie at dinner."

"Bye, Ellis," Minnie said. She got out of the car and kissed him on the forehead away from his wounds. "Take care."

"Bye." Ellis grinned hard enough to feel his stitches. He walked around his dorm and locked up his bike on an old, rusted rack under a yellow floodlight. He rushed up to his room, taking the stairs three steps at a time.

"What the hell happened to you?" Barney asked, looking up from his history text.

"I fell off my bike," Ellis said. "Guess who drove me to the emergency room."

"Shit. Did you get stitches?" Barney walked over to Ellis and examined his face. "Peel off the Band-Aids so I can see."

"I'm not supposed to change them until tomorrow," Ellis said. "Guess who drove me to the emergency room."

"Eldridge?"

"Nope."

"Coach?"

"Nope."

"Who?"

"That lady who bought beer for us that day—and Minnie," Ellis said. "They're best friends."

"Where'd you wipe out?"

"Right where the trail meets Route Twenty-two, I hit a log and lost it. I went to the emergency room with Minnie."

"Shit. I bet Coach will still make you run and pull," Barney said.

"Nope. Doctor's orders. No strenuous exercise for five days." Ellis wrung his hands and grinned.

"Why? It's your face, not your legs."

"I don't know, but I got it in writing," Ellis said. "I also got these." He tossed a bottle of Percocet onto his desk. He noticed a letter propped up next to his books. From Frank. "This come today?" he asked.

"Yeah."

In the letter, Frank told Ellis that he'd be up to Gates for an alumni day at the end of the month. He also thanked him for the sweater. *Even Judy liked it*, he wrote, *and you know how finicky she is.*

"My father's coming in a few weeks."

"Fucker Frank?"

"I don't call him that anymore," Ellis said. He struggled with the top of the Percocet, rattling the pills.

"What do you call him now?"

"Just Frank." Ellis swallowed two of the tiny white tablets and waited for the warm glaze to form on his brain.

THIRTY-SEVEN

Goat Man could hear the shouting all the way from the pool house, but he couldn't make out what Wendy was saying, so he opened his door and tried to discern a few words. No luck, just more maniacal shrieks. He moved closer to the house, squatting under the balcony of Wendy's bedroom in the dry weeds he should have plucked months ago.

"I'm not stupid!" she yelled. "Your Jeep is full of gray hairs!"

Goat Man couldn't quite hear what Bennet said, but it was something about trust.

"Liar! When was the last time?" she ranted. "That's it. I can't do it anymore. I'm stronger than that. I want you out of here!"

Finally, Goat Man thought. He listened for Bennet's response but didn't hear anything. He pulled up a few mighty weeds, tossed them into the desert, and tiptoed back around the wall to the pool house. He lay on the freshly vacuumed rug.

Bennet threw open the door to the pool house. The knob stuck into the wall. A white puff of powder from the plaster hung in the air around it. "You told her!" he yelled. "You told her, you sneaky wetback!" Bennet was purple and trembling. He kicked over the glass table, shattering it on the tiled floor, and he heaved the meaty oak-and-glass stereo cabinet over on top of Goat Man.

Goat Man tried to crawl out from under the rubble, but his stereo receiver was digging into his neck and something else had pinned his leg. He could barely see from behind the CDs and old magazines on his face. Bennet stood over him, held the rocking chair above his head. He bashed it twice on the pile before it cracked into pieces. Goat Man's back felt wet and syrupy. He couldn't stop his eyes from rolling back into his head.

He opened his eyes a few minutes later, still trapped under the mess. He groaned. He closed his eyes again in case Bennet was still lurking, but he heard nothing. He tried to shove the cabinet off his chest, but when he moved, even slightly, something poked deeper into his back. "Shit," he mumbled.

"Oh God!" Wendy screamed. "That bastard."

"I'm under here," Goat Man grunted.

"Oh God," she repeated. "He's gone. Bennet's gone." She lifted the receiver from Goat Man's neck. "Don't worry." She pushed the heavy cabinet off, and cringed when she saw the blood. "Don't move. Don't move."

"Something's jabbing me," Goat Man said, wriggling. "Something's digging into my back." He rolled over, but whatever it was still stuck in his back.

"It's your pipe! Your old pipe is stuck in your back, and you're bleeding," Wendy said. She bit her lower lip and sucked it in. "And you have a big red bump on your forehead."

"Ow." Goat Man sat up and pushed a few CDs and tapes off his lap. He tried to look at his back, wrenching his neck, but he couldn't see the pipe. "How the hell is my pipe stabbing me?"

"The part you stick in your mouth is sort of jabbed through your shirt," Wendy said. She was pale but moving like she was about to burst into a frenzy. "I'm calling 911."

"Pull the pipe out!"

She leaned down and gingerly peeled his T-shirt up, wincing at the blood. "I can't," she whined. "It's in far."

"Pull it out!"

She looked closer at the bloody pipe. "It's in real far," she said.

"Pull it out," he said, "or I will."

She pulled it out and Goat Man fell over in pain. She chucked the pipe against the wall and darted into the main house, leaving Goat Man on the floor in the rubble, moaning.

He looked around and assessed the damage. The receiver was pretty much intact, but the CD player was cracked, wires exposed.

Wendy ran back into the pool house. "Okay, I called," she said. "I'm driving you to Kino."

Goat Man looked up at her. "You can't just patch it up?"

"I don't know," she said. She helped him to his feet. "Even if I did, you need stitches and you need to have that bump on your head checked."

Goat Man had to ride in the backseat of the Volvo, doggy-style on his hands and knees. Bright blood dripped from his hip onto the leather interior.

Wendy mumbled all the way to Kino Hospital: "I'm strong. I have what it takes for interpersonal connections. I'm strong. I have what it takes for interpersonal connections . . ."

The whole procedure at Kino Hospital was quicker than both Wendy and Goat Man had expected. He was stitched up and sent on his way in less than an hour.

During the drive home, Wendy mumbled more, but she did clearly say, "Both you and Ellis got stitched this week."

"Why didn't you tell me Ellis got stitches?" Goat Man said. "What happened to him? Did he get in another fight?"

"No," Wendy said blankly. "He fell off his bike."

Wendy's face bunched up, and she began to cry. She pulled her Volvo over in the dirt shoulder of the road because she started bawling so violently.

"My back doesn't hurt that much," Goat Man said, "and I'm sure Ellis is okay."

"That's not it!" she screamed.

Goat Man thought she should probably sign on with a good shrink. He leaned forward, looked out the window at the desert, the saguaros, and appreciated the inchoate codeine high oozing through his skull. "Want me to drive?" Goat Man asked.

She sobbed and nodded.

The codeine was definitely kicking in, but it was too late. He got out and walked around the car. Wendy hopped over the stick shift into the passenger seat.

"I have an idea," Goat Man said. "Let's drive up A Mountain and clear our heads."

Wendy said nothing. Her face was buried in her lap as if she were preparing for a plane crash.

They were nowhere near A Mountain. Goat Man was getting higher, drowsy, and his back began to hurt again. He'd have to drive hanging over the wheel like an old-timer with bad glasses.

They cruised through the *barrio*, past taco shacks and indecipherable graffiti, into South Tucson. If Wendy kicked him out, he thought he might move into one of these neighborhoods for a while. All the tiny adobe houses had character, they belonged in the desert, and there wasn't a 7-Eleven in sight, only small family-owned businesses. He liked how people drove slowly here. They drove like they enjoyed the ride, no stress. Goat Man turned up Grande Avenue, took a right on Congress, and finally a left up A Mountain. Wendy had sat up. She was vacantly staring out her window at the black volcanic rocks.

They parked at the top, facing east toward the city. A teenage couple in an El Camino looked up from their heated love and glared over at Wendy and Goat Man. The girl began to apply makeup, using her boyfriend's rearview mirror.

"We ruined their moment," Wendy whispered, sniffing. "Why'd you park so close to them?"

"I didn't know," Goat Man said. He looked northeast toward the Catalinas, tried to see the stoplight at Sunrise and Kolb, the closest stoplight to their home. He couldn't make it out.

Wendy got out of the Volvo, leaned against the back bumper, and stared at the sunset. Goat Man joined her, although he couldn't lean because of his pipe wound. The western sky was smudged in oranges and reds, melting and dripping into one another. A big cloud loomed on the horizon like a pirate ship.

"Bennet's a whore," Wendy said. Her voice was raw. "He fucks old men and women for money. Old snowbirds from Michigan and New York."

"Sorry."

"Why?"

"I'm sorry he upset you," Goat Man said.

Wendy sprawled back on the car, leaning her head on the rear window. "I'm a moron," she sighed.

"You can't help who you fall for."

"I could use better judgment."

"At least you fall for people," Goat Man said. He wondered if he ever had.

THIRTY-EIGHT

Ellis had just finished his run when he spotted Frank talking to Dr. Eldridge near the entrance to the dorm. He watched them from behind a tree. They were laughing. Ellis saw Eldridge point up to his and Barney's window and laugh. Frank and Eldridge finally shook hands, and Eldridge walked off. Ellis jogged up to his father.

"Hey, Frank," Ellis said.

"Hey, Ellis. What are these?" He touched the pink scars on Ellis's face.

"I fell off my bike. I got stitches."

"What bike?"

"Wendy got me a cool mountain bike for Christmas. Her dumb-ass boyfriend forgot to mail me my helmet."

"Dr. Eldridge tells me you're doing crew." Frank smiled, stepped back a little, and looked Ellis up and down.

"Yup."

"Great," Frank said. "You'll be great. How tall are you now?"

"About six feet."

"Crew is ninety percent genetics."

"I'm freezing," Ellis said. "I have to change out of these."

"You hungry?"

"Always," Ellis said.

"Get your roommate and we'll go somewhere better than the dining hall." Frank jingled his keys in the pocket of his corduroys.

"Come up," Ellis said. "Come see my room. I have to take a shower. It'll only take a minute."

Barney wasn't up there when Ellis opened the door to his room. He was probably already in the shower. "This is it," Ellis said. "Welcome to my humble commode."

"Abode," Frank said.

"I know," Ellis said. "It was a joke."

Frank looked around.

"Have a seat. Read this." Ellis threw Frank his Latin book.

"I always hated Latin," Frank said. He sat down on Barney's bed. "Sadly enough, I was president of the Latin club when I was here. No one else would do it."

"The guy who's president now wears black nail polish," Ellis said. "I think he's the only member of the club." He dug through his dresser, gathering everything he needed for his shower. "I'll be back in a second."

Ellis passed Barney in the hall. Barney wore only a towel. "My dad's in there," Ellis told him. "Don't say anything stupid or incriminating, or I'll kill you."

"I'm not dumb," Barney said.

Ellis showered and dressed quickly. He didn't trust Barney alone with Frank. He imagined him addressing Frank as "Fucker Frank" or boring him with stories of Todd at Yale.

When Ellis returned to the room, Barney was giving Frank a tour of his awards. "This one," Barney said as he held up his citizenship trophy, "I got last year. It's dented because Ellis threw it out the window."

"I used to fight with my roommates," Frank said.

"Barney and I don't fight anymore," Ellis said. "Unless he's being an ass."

"Ellis gets touchy whenever my awards are mentioned," Barney said, "because he doesn't have any."

"Where do you boys want to eat?" Frank asked. He stood up and rubbed his hands together.

They both shrugged.

Ellis laced up his old rubber-soled hunting boots, his only shoes that weren't muddy. "Somewhere where we don't need a tie," Ellis said.

"How about that inn on Route Twenty-two? Is that still there?" Frank asked.

"Yes," Barney said. "I went there last spring when my brother graduated."

The Merryman Inn was a white farmhouse with a red barn and spirited horses penned out front. The dining room's capacity was under twenty, but the food bordered on gourmet. It was owned by an ancient couple. The wife, Betty Merryman, recognized Ellis and Barney as Gates boys right away. "I'll fatten you right up," she said. "If the food's not better than what they serve you at the school, it's free." She grinned too hard, exposing large spaces between the corners of her mouth and her gums. "Tonight we've made beef medallions with rosemary sauce, served with rice and a salad, or we have Moroccan beef with spicy couscous. The Moroccan's a bit hotter."

"Exotic for Pennsylvania," Frank said. "I'll have the Moroccan."

"I'll have the other, please," Ellis said.

"Me, too," Barney said. "I've been to Morocco. Todd got butt worms from the water."

After Barney excused himself to go to the rest room, Frank leaned over like he was about to tell Ellis a secret. "Barney seems nervous."

"I guess," Ellis said. He looked around the room at the other diners, mostly older couples talking softly. When he looked at Frank, he saw that Frank was doing the same thing, scanning the room.

"Did Wendy always overreact to things?" Ellis asked.

"Why?"

"I was just wondering," Ellis said. "She's pretty weird now. She's into crystals and freaks out a lot."

"When I first met her, she was into the Grateful Dead and freaked out a lot," Frank said.

Barney returned to the table. He had wet and styled his hair in the bathroom. The part on the left side of his head was exact. Ellis had never seen his hair like that.

"Mr. Whitman, where'd you go to college?" Barney asked Frank as he sat back down.

"Williams for undergraduate and Wharton for business school," Frank said. "Why?"

"I was just wondering," Barney said.

"Why the hell do you care?" Ellis asked.

"I was just wondering," Barney said. "God."

"If Ellis wants, he can be the fifth generation of Whitmans at Williams," Frank said.

"Let's change the topic," Ellis said.

Betty arrived with the steaming food. Over dinner, Frank asked the boys about life at Gates, often harking back to his own days there. The most subversive act Frank admitted to was sneaking a beer in his dorm after graduation dinner. "I was years older than you boys and that was my first beer."

"I bet," Ellis said.

"I don't know why we're talking about beer," Frank said. "You boys are in training."

"That's what I've been telling Ellis," Barney said. Rosemary sauce dripped from his lips and spotted his un-ironed white oxford shirt.

"Shut up," Ellis said.

"I talked to Dr. Eldridge about the problems you had in November. It sounds like things are back to normal," Frank said. "How're your classes this semester? All A's again?"

"I never got to see my first-semester report card," Ellis said.

"You got all A's," Frank said.

"But an A minus in Latin, right?" Barney said.

"No, just a plain A in Latin," Frank said. "No minus attached."

Barney dipped his napkin into his water and dabbed the rosemary sauce on his shirt. "Excuse me," he said. He pushed his chair back from the table and marched again to the bathroom.

"He's usually not this bad," Ellis said. "Really."

"He's pretty wound up," Frank said. "That's sad."

Frank shadowed Ellis the next day, attending each of Ellis's classes. Ellis's teachers raved about him and Frank beamed. It wasn't actually that embarrassing for Ellis, because there were other parents and alumni on campus that week, and Frank was infinitely cooler than most of the them. Not as supplicating. Not as stuffy. The Gates boys liked it when alumni were present; it meant the food in the dining hall would be ten times more palatable, and the teachers would ask obvious questions to make everyone look brilliant.

The coach decided to let the boys off easy that day—they'd pull ten thousand, untimed. Frank sat in a chair in front of Ellis, while Ellis pulled on the rowing machine.

"You should've seen the rowing machines we used to use," Frank said. "They were from the Marquis de Sade's dungeon of torture."

"Who's Marquis de Sade?" Ellis asked. The flywheel hummed and sent cool breezes to Ellis's face.

"A freak," Frank said. "Wrote about torturing people."

"Oh," Ellis said. "These are pretty good except for that loud one on the end."

"I should order one of these for the Telluride house," Frank said, "and get back into shape. You know, you should spend the summer up in Telluride. The mountains there are huge, and you could ride your bike all day."

"Uh-huh," Ellis said. He started to become winded. His thighs began to burn.

"Judy and I are driving across the country to Telluride, and we could pick you up here first," Frank said. "Or we could pick you up in Tucson."

"Uh-huh."

"There are music festivals, film festivals, helicopter skiing. There are lots of kids your age up there in the summer. You could get a job, get some experience."

"Maybe I could go up there for a while," Ellis said between pulls. "Except, I wouldn't get to spend much time with Goat Man."

"Just something for you to think about. How about dinner tonight?" Frank looked around the gym, down the row of rowers, and whispered, "Without Barney."

"Barney's not that bad," Ellis said. "Besides, I have a history quiz tomorrow and a problem set due in algebra, so we should just eat here." Ellis looked down at the monitor. He needed to row harder.

Minnie served Ellis and Frank's table.

"She's cute," Frank said after Minnie poured their water. "The women who served us when I was at Gates barely qualified as women—mustaches and beefy arms."

"Minnie's the only pretty one," Ellis said. "She and her friend are the ones who found me when I crashed my bike. They took me all the way to the emergency room in Monroe."

"I'll make sure to thank her," Frank said.

Rosenberg leaned across the table. "Don't be so modest, Ellis." He turned to Frank. "Everyone knows that Minnie likes Ellis."

"Shut up," Ellis told Rosenberg. "Rosenberg's imagination gets the best of him sometimes, especially when girls are involved. The closest he's ever gotten to the real thing is the scratch-and-sniff centerfold in last month's *Hustler.*"

"That was two months ago," Rosenberg said.

"Three," Barney said. "It was the December issue."

"That's disgusting," Frank said.

Ellis couldn't help but think about Minnie. He constantly did, especially since the day she and Fiona found him crashed on the side of the road. He never used magazines in the woods anymore; he didn't have to. He imagined marrying her, taking her to Arizona when he finished at Gates. She couldn't be that much older, maybe five or ten years—closer to five. Not that her age really mattered. The woman could be older than the man.

Wendy's boyfriends before Bennet had always been much younger, and Judy might be older than Frank.

Dumb, he knew. It was dumb to think this way. He wasted too much time thinking this way.

Early the next morning, Frank stopped in Ellis's Latin class to say good-bye before he left for New York. The boys were practicing skits in groups of three. One of the boys was a shopkeeper, and the other two had to come into the shop and ask for cheese, milk, and bread. Mr. Winters walked around the room repeating, "I want passion, passion, men."

"Now you can see the crap I have to endure in the name of education," Ellis whispered to Frank. Ellis played the shopkeeper in his group. "When I'm in Vatican City, I'll know how to passionately tell the natives that the cheese is in the back."

"You'll live. I did." Frank sat down and watched the boys for a few minutes before he took Ellis into the hall. "See you in Telluride this summer—I hope," Frank said. "Please think about it." He extended his hand to Ellis.

"Maybe," Ellis said, gripping his father's hand.

THIRTY-NINE

February had been a perfect month in Tucson: seventy-five degrees, sunny every day, and no more Bennet. Goat Man busied himself fixing up the pool house, repairing the damage and installing new kitchen faucets. Since Bennet had left, Wendy had taken to buying things for the house. She decided her stove was too techno, so she and Goat Man spent a week in antiques and thrift stores looking for the perfect old stove. They never found it, but Wendy did buy an old toaster: rounded chrome, early sixties Space Age. She found a blender from the same era and a waffle maker. She decided TV was evil, canceled cable, and gave the big TV to Goat Man to use in the pool house. He ordered cable service out there. Most eerie to Goat Man were the old photos of Frank she dug out of dusty boxes in the garage and had framed. She hung them all over the house, even in the bathrooms and the kitchen. There must have been thirty or forty of them, most from when Frank was a pseudohippie with longish hair and a wide leather watchband. Goat Man thought about writing to Ellis, informing him that Bennet was gone and that Wendy was pretty unstable, but Ellis would be home for spring break in a few weeks, anyway, and he didn't want to worry him.

Goat Man stared across the pen at Freida. She looked cross-eyed, stoned. Maybe she and Gigi had been nibbling on the few pot plants he had growing down in the wash. Every February or March he'd see a few goats down near the plants, not whole-heartedly eating them, only nibbling, playing. Freida and Lance were his only options for the trek. Gigi hadn't started lactating again, hadn't even gone into heat. Goat Man could have inserted a caponizing hormone pellet in the loose skin of Gigi's shoulder to bring her into milk—a guy from England had shown him how to do it years ago when he was still an agriculture student at the U of A—but he didn't. He hated making that incision in the goat's skin. That's why he had only done it once. Gigi would never stay in milk, anyway. Not with a pellet, not even if she gave birth. He'd convince Ellis to come along on the trek, and Ellis would keep Freida in line. Freida's milk never failed. He figured that if everything went as planned, the trek would only take two or three days at the most. Ellis had two weeks off for spring break; with weekends, he had sixteen days. That would be plenty of time.

Goat Man's cousin Jesús had called earlier in the month. He had wanted exact dates from Goat Man.

"I'll be down there by the twenty-fifth, maybe as early as the twenty-fourth," Goat Man had told him.

"You have to be more exact," his cousin told him.

"With goats, I can't be more exact, and without goats, I couldn't do it."

"I don't know how my people will like it."

"Oh, well," Goat Man said.

"Oh, well," his cousin had repeated. "They'll have to like it, I guess."

Out by the pen, Goat Man sat on a sun-cracked plastic milk crate and thought about the trek. He knew the land well, spent much of the fall and summer down there, had all sorts of topo-graphical maps, copies of ranchers' land deeds, trail guides. He threw a small rock at Freida. She bleated but didn't move. She hadn't budged since he finished milking her ten minutes earlier.

There was a note taped to the door of the pool house when Goat Man walked up from the pen. He thought it was another one of Wendy's requests to comb the thrift stores for sixties appliances, but the note wasn't from Wendy:

> *Just stopped by to see if you wanted to party. You owe*
> *me. Hugs and Kisses, Aubrey.*

Her handwriting was like a fifth grader's—bubbly, cutesy.

Goat Man went inside, and, as was usually the case ever since Wendy gave it to him, he flicked on the TV. He plopped on the couch. He could only find talk shows and loud, sensational news programs, so he clicked it off. He sat up and felt his hair.

Tirso was shaving an old guy with a straight razor. The old guy's darting, nervous eyes looked jaundiced next to the white shaving foam.

Goat Man took a seat and asked Tirso where Denny was.

"Denny doesn't work here anymore," he told Goat Man.

"Why not?"

"You were his only regular," Tirso said. "He cut hair like a blind man."

"He always gave me good cuts." Goat Man picked up an old *Playboy* but put it down. The white afternoon sun was pouring through the dusty window, making him squint. He stood and closed the blinds before picking up the magazine again.

Twenty minutes later, when he finally sat on the barber chair,

Goat Man said, "Just snap on that half-inch guard and run the clippers all over my head."

"You know, Javier, haircuts here are six dollars, and you probably leave a tip," Tirso said as he shook out the plastic cape. "You can run over to Wal-Mart and buy your own set of clippers with all the attachments for eighteen bucks. You could do it yourself." He wrapped the cape around Goat Man and secured it at the neck.

"Next month."

"Procrastination makes the world go around," Tirso said.

"Yes, it does," Goat Man said.

"Any new projects with the goats?"

"I'm training a few to work with the blind, like seeing eye dogs," Goat Man said. "Goats are way smarter than dogs."

"Ellis was in here over the holidays, and he hadn't heard about what you did with the goats in California." Tirso combed through Goat Man's short hair. "The brushfire prevention project. He hadn't heard about the Biosphere project, either."

"I don't like to brag," Goat Man said.

"I see." Tirso turned on the clippers and went to work on Goat Man's head.

On the way home from Tirso's, Goat Man braved the traffic on Speedway Boulevard and turned his junky Jetta into the parking lot of the Summit Hut, a large outdoor-gear store that sat in a faded strip mall next to Carpet Giant. Summit Hut sold the sunglasses he wanted, the glasses he convinced himself he needed for the trek.

"They block one-hundred percent of the UV," the earthy saleswoman said, "and they're perfect for the desert because they filter the light and make your sense of depth crisper." She handed the glasses to Goat Man. "And they're twenty percent off this week."

He adjusted them on his nose and looked out the huge windows in the front of the store. The lenses did make everything sharper. He looked at the cars in the lot. While the colors were dulled, the glasses heightened the contrast between light and shadow. Goat Man felt a tap on his shoulder. "I'll take them," he said, turning around.

But it wasn't the saleswoman tapping him; it was Bennet. "How's life in the pool house?" Bennet said impassively.

"Fine," Goat Man said. He wasn't startled, only a little confused. Bennet was out of context.

"Too bad," Bennet said. He walked off, out of the store toward his Jeep.

Goat Man watched the old woman waiting in the Jeep pick her teeth with a matchbook, check herself in the rearview mirror before Bennet hopped in.

FORTY

For the first time at Gates, Ellis was stressed about his classes. Midterm examinations were approaching, and he had slacked a little since Christmas—mostly because crew was so time-consuming and made him tired all the time.

After crew practice on the afternoon before his history midterm, he jogged back to his room to read his history text, a text written for college students: *A History of Western Society*. Four chapters had been assigned sometime in early February, but each time Ellis had tried to crack the book he was distracted and put it off. He knew Barney had read the entire assignment, even outlined the chapters, so when Barney returned to the room, he asked him if he could look at his notes.

"I spent two weeks of study halls making those notes."

"Give me a break," Ellis said. "Think of all the times I helped you."

"This is different," Barney said.

"No, it's not."

"Yes, it is."

"You selfish fuck," Ellis said. He slammed his book shut. "Good luck with algebra. I'm not helping you anymore."

Ellis stomped down the hall and took a shower. Then, skipping dinner, he sequestered himself with the book in the small brick study room in the basement of his dormitory. It was freezing down there, but he read through the dense chapters. He could predict that the essay questions would be something about Absolutism, the reforms of Peter the Great, the Enlightenment. His history teacher, Mr. Bell, always went for something broad enough that even the dimmest students (like Barney) could scrawl something down for credit. The definitions, however, would be killer. As Ellis read, he had marked things that might show up, but when he finished the assignment he had marked at least one hundred terms: Baroque, Karlsruhe, Copernicus . . . The only parts of the dry chapters Ellis remembered without any concerted effort were the paintings. Rubens's *The Education of Marie* became a permanent image in his brain: three chubby naked women, one holding her crotch—Marie de' Medici's muses; an older woman, a guy with a bass violin, and Marie herself, trying to study.

He looked at the industrial clock in the study room: forty minutes until lights out. His original plan was to study the terms for the remaining forty minutes, go back upstairs and wait for Hopkins to make his rounds, and then sneak back down to the dank little room. He was motivated almost solely by the prospect that Barney might actually score better than him on the midterm.

When his forty minutes were up, he returned to his room, but he decided he had studied enough.

"Where were you?" Barney asked. "Were you getting high?"

"None of your business. Shut off the light." Ellis pulled on his pajama bottoms.

Barney flicked out the light. The moon shone through the window, vaguely illuminating the room in muted blues. "I don't think you should be doing bongs while you're in training," Barney whispered from across the room.

"Thanks for the tip," Ellis said.

"Really," Barney said. "You'd be jeopardizing the whole crew, not just yourself."

"I'll take that into consideration. Now let me sleep."

"Did you even read the chapters?" Barney asked.

"No, they looked boring," Ellis said. "I used the pages to roll big blunts."

"Bell said half the test would be from the book," Barney said. Ellis could see him in the moonlight, grinding his head into his elbow.

"I guess I can't go to Harvard," Ellis said.

"You can look at my outline if you want," Barney said. "I have a flashlight."

"It's a little late for you to offer," Ellis said. "Did you suddenly realize you'll fail algebra without my help?"

"No, I just felt a little bad, I guess."

"You should," Ellis said. "You would've flunked last semester if it hadn't been for me."

"Sorry," Barney said. Ellis could hear that Barney was upset. His voice was cracking more than usual, and it held a higher pitch. His breathing was labored.

"I think part of this boarding-school experience is learning who your friends really are," Ellis said.

Barney didn't respond.

Ellis awoke early the next morning—at five—without the help of his alarm clock. He cracked the history text and started memorizing the terms. They weren't sticking, and his head was buzzing. Plus, he was starving, and Barney kept making wet chewing noises in his sleep. Ellis coughed loudly, on purpose, to wake Barney, but Barney just continued with the noises. The clock radio above Barney's bed flashed an emergency red 5:21. They'd ordinarily be waking for crew, but morning practices were canceled because of midterms. Ellis had two and a half hours until breakfast, so he dressed quickly, stepping into a pair of loose khakis and pulling on a T-shirt. He grabbed his fleece on the way out, slamming the door hard, hoping to wake Barney. He headed back down to the cold study dungeon in the basement.

The Arctic temperature in the study room sent Ellis back into a slumber almost immediately after he sat down at the desk. He put his face in his arms and began to dream he was chasing Freida through the quad at Gates. She had shown up in Latin class and pissed on the floor. Ellis woke up with his cheek in a small puddle of freezing drool on the desk. It was 8:20, he was late for breakfast, and he had only thirty minutes before the bell rang for history. He opened his book again.

The history test was more difficult than he had expected. The essay questions were demanding, unprecedented ones about women during the Enlightenment and the inner workings of royal cities. Ellis only knew four of the six identifications well enough to write more than a few sentences. He figured the best he could get was a B- or a C+. He'd get A's on all the other tests and papers in history, probably still end up with an A in the course, but he was upset, knowing that Barney probably did pretty well.

Ellis only had the easy algebra midterm left to contend with, and it wasn't until the next morning. Not that he needed to study for it, anyway. Then it was back home to Tucson for spring break: two weeks of sun and rest. It was just a warmup for summer, when he'd experience the same for three months.

He fantasized about the summer all through his afternoon classes. Tucson would be scorching, ablaze in unrelenting white sunlight, but Ellis would float in the pool on his inflatable lounge chair and hit his bong. He'd walk from the thickly air-conditioned house to the pool—he'd never really experience the heat, just the citywide laziness that it induced. He'd rent videos. He'd call for pizza or Mexican food every afternoon. He'd sit on the roof of the pool house at night and look at the swirl of stars with his telescope. He'd bring an ice- and beer-filled cooler up there and catch a calm, happy buzz. He'd sleep in until noon. He and Goat Man would smoke out for two months until August, when he'd have to get in shape for crew again. Maybe he'd go up to Telluride for August. Frank and Judy would make him stop hitting the bong, and the altitude would be great for training.

Barney sat at the rowing machine next to Ellis's that afternoon during practice. As they pulled on the machines and sweated all over themselves, Barney kept asking Ellis about the history midterm: "What did you think of that one essay question about women?"

Ellis rolled his eyes.

"If I hadn't've had a copy of last year's test, I probably would have just left the essay questions blank," Barney said.

Ellis pulled harder with his arms and pushed harder with his legs. He worked with such force that the machine slid a few inches on the floor of the gym with every stroke. He kept going.

His legs and arms burned, and his stomach knotted in cramping pain. But he kept going. At 9992 he yelped, pulled one last time, and watched the display turn over at 10,000. He got up and told Barney to fuck off. The coach heard and told Ellis to watch it.

"Watch what?" Ellis huffed.

"Your language, mister," Coach said.

"I finished first today." Ellis was gasping.

"So?" Coach said.

"Just seeing if you noticed," Ellis said.

"Do it again," Coach said. "I want another ten thousand."

"Yeah, right."

"I'm serious."

"Why?" Ellis asked. He looked over at Barney, who was grinning madly.

"You've been acting a little too big for your britches," Coach said. "You're still at Gates because I took pity on you."

"Well," Ellis said, "I've been thinking about that. There's a statute of limitations on things like turning me in."

"What are you talking about?"

"Go ahead and tell Eldridge you caught me and Rosenberg smoking up," Ellis said. He was still breathing hard, even harder with the slight fear that crept up his throat. "And don't forget to explain why it took you three months to tell." Ellis walked out of the gym, his sneakers squeaking on the shellacked floor.

He didn't shower after his workout; he just pulled his fleece over his sweaty T-shirt and hopped on his bike, no helmet. He tore down the snowy trail, pumped his legs, left a muddy stripe in his wake. His ears froze, turned maroon and ached, but he didn't care. The fresh air felt good. Telling off Coach felt good. He didn't stop for magazines, just plowed through to Route 22. He took the last corner carefully, steering the bike around the last log, and pedaled off toward Peterson's and the library.

He rode into the Peterson's parking lot and felt the pocket of his sweatpants for money. Two bucks and some change. He leaned his bike up against a 30 MINUTE PARKING ONLY sign and went in to buy a Gatorade.

Minnie stood by the counter, her arms around the waists of two seniors, her hands on their asses. One of the seniors was Jeff Eagleton, a conceited asshole whose father was a race-car driver or something. The other guy was Steve somebody who rowed on the varsity boat. They were buying a case of Rolling Rock.

"Hey, Ellis," Minnie said. She smiled.

"Hey," he mumbled, looking down at his muddy sweatpants.

"Ellis, heard about your stitches," Steve said.

"That was a while ago."

"You didn't see us here," Minnie said. "Okay?"

"Sure," Ellis said, confused.

Jeff Eagleton paid for the beer, and the three of them left. Minnie turned around at the door and waved to Ellis like a little girl, with just her fingers.

Ellis went to the back of the store and pulled out a cold Gatorade. The Peterson behind the counter asked Ellis if he knew Minnie.

"Yeah," Ellis said. "Why?"

"Just wondering," the Peterson said. "Eighty-seven for the Gatorade."

Ellis walked outside, chugged his Gatorade, and tossed the bottle. A burly guy in a satin Budweiser jacket walked toward him as he wheeled his bike a little and hopped on.

"Get off the bike, fag," the guy said. His hair was short on the sides and spiked on the top, but long and curly in the back. Ellis had called the style an ape-drape, but since coming to Gates he had learned other terms for it: Detroit-cut, two-haircuts, wrestling-fan, dyke-spike, hockey-cut, good-in-the-back, achy-breaky, mullet.

"What?" Ellis said.

The guy shoved Ellis down into the slushy, filthy asphalt. "I said, get off the bike, fag." He pulled a screwdriver from his back pocket and held it to Ellis's neck. The guy's breath smelled like eggs. His teeth were bright yellow. "Gates puss." He jumped on the bike and rode quickly down Route 22. The bike looked too small for the man—he looked like a clown.

Ellis sat there, his butt wet and cold, his hands stinging. He was confused, wondering how the hell the trashy asshole was riding away on his bike.

Ellis was wearing his running shoes and had to walk the muddy, snowy trail with frozen feet. But his feet didn't matter. Neither did his stupid bike, or the fucker who took it.

He passed a few guys on the trail. One of them told him that there was a new *Playboy* about ten yards into the woods, "The Women of the Ivy League." Ellis didn't care. He could only think of Minnie at the counter with those senior assholes.

He stood under the shower for a few minutes, watching the mud swirl down the drain. His ears and feet ached and tingled back to life. Then he went back to his room to get dressed for dinner.

Barney was studying for the algebra midterm, sitting at his desk, tugging on his bangs like he was trying to pull the answers out of his head. "You got mud all over the floor," he told Ellis.

"Yes," Ellis said blankly.

"That's it? *Yes?*" Barney closed his book.

"Yes," Ellis said. "Yes."

"I cleaned it up."

"Okay," Ellis said.

"Are you high?"

"No," Ellis said. He sat down on his bed and stared out the window at the trail he had walked. "I got bike-jacked at Peterson's."

"What?"

"A redneck stole my bike. He held a screwdriver to my face."

"You call the police?"

"Not yet," Ellis said. "I saw Minnie at Peterson's with two seniors. That Steve guy on the crew and Jeff Eagleshit."

"You should call the police," Barney said. "You should tell Hopkins."

"Her hair looked dirty."

"How much was that bike worth? Maybe it's covered on your mom's insurance. My brother's computer was stolen, and it was covered," Barney said. "He had to pay a deductible, though."

"She was squeezing their asses right there at the counter," Ellis said. He lay down on his stomach and buried his face in his pillow. His wet hair was cold, and his arms smelled like soap. He didn't care that his towel had slipped and Barney could see his bare ass.

"You know, Rosenberg swears she's a hooker," Barney said. "And I believe it."

"What would Rosenberg know?" Ellis said into his pillow. "He's an asshole."

"He said that she charges one hundred bones, and most of the seniors have paid it. Some guys have used her five or six times."

"I doubt it," Ellis said.

"Think about it," Barney said. "Why else would someone as hot as her work as a waitress at a boarding school? She needs money."

"Then how come she hasn't propositioned me? I was with her for hours when I got my stitches."

"Maybe she respects you," Barney said.

"Why haven't we heard about her earlier?" Ellis asked.

"The seniors probably want to keep her to themselves," Barney said. "I hardly ever see any seniors on the Beat-Off Trail. Do you?"

"No," Ellis said. "What about Todd? Why didn't he tell you about Minnie?"

"Maybe she wasn't here last year."

Ellis stood up and began to dress, sniffing a pair of khakis that sat in a lump on the lid of the hamper. "These mine or yours?"

"Yours. You need to call the police about your bike. We only have ten minutes before dinner."

"I'll deal with it when I get home on Saturday," Ellis said, pulling on the pants. "Bennet will be pissed."

"I have to spend two weeks sitting in the Watergate," Barney complained.

"I have to spend two weeks floating in the pool and getting a tan," Ellis said.

"Go to hell," Barney said. "Call the police. You'll need a police report for the insurance."

"I will," Ellis said.

Ellis didn't call the police. After dinner, he walked across the crispy frozen grass of the commons to the library. He knew exactly where to find all the old yearbooks after having looked up Frank's pictures so many times. He pulled out last year's and flipped through it. The front page was a dedication to Charles

Van Leer: 1982–1999. Ellis remembered the old women in the elevator in the Watergate, how they gossiped about Charles Van Leer killing himself. Seeing Charles Van Leer's photo, his dorky smile and super-combed hair, Ellis wanted to go back there and smack the old women's plastic-surgery-tight faces.

He flipped to the faculty and staff pages. There was Minnie, standing next to four other hair-netted women. Minnie's last name was Dragoon. Someone had circled Minnie's smiling face with blue marker. Next to the circle they scrawled, *blowjobs 25, fucks 50.*

Ellis looked around the library: a few guys were reading magazines in the corner, but otherwise it was deserted. He slowly and quietly tore the page from the yearbook and crumpled it into a tight ball.

He tossed it in the trash on the way out.

FORTY-ONE

Goat Man walked to the greenhouse brandishing a small pair of clippers for precise snips. He had planned on cutting some choice buds for the trek, enough for him and Ellis, but when he opened the door, he was hit with a waft of eye-burning fumes. The greenhouse smelled like a giant urinal puck. Pots were all over the floor, plants cut up, and empty cans and buckets of pool chemicals were smashed on the shelves. Whoever had done it was thorough. No plant escaped destruction. Most were doused in chlorine or mercuric acid—yellowed and withered, stinky and toxic-smelling.

Goat Man couldn't abide the noxious odor. It burned his eyes and throat. He jumped out and slammed the door behind him. The entire structure rattled. He squatted down and drew circles in the dirt with the broken padlock.

Freida walked up and stared stupidly at him. She looked cross-eyed.

"Go away," he said.

She stared and chewed on something. He noticed her ugly pink lips—like bubble gum.

"Go away," he repeated. "Go eat some trash."

She snorted and sprayed Goat Man with flecks of spittle and snot.

"Then I'll leave."

He walked into the pool house and looked in the freezer to see what he had for weed. Barely a few bowls' worth.

He walked down the wash to the place where he grew a few plants. Goat man noticed javelina tracks in the sand. They were daintier than goat tracks, smaller steps, smaller hooves. He wondered how the goats would react to javelina; he was surprised he had never seen it happen. No buds on the marijuana plants. Maybe the goats or javelina or jackrabbits had chewed them off, or they had never grown. He had been neglecting the arroyo plants because his greenhouse hybrid had been so tasty this year.

Goat Man hadn't bought pot from anyone in ages. He had always grown plenty of his own bounty. He wasn't even sure what it cost anymore.

He called Reggie: "It's Javier."

"Javier, where you been?"

"Around," Goat Man said.

"Not around here. We got new Two-Tone box sets. Best of British ska. You like the Two-Tone sound?"

"Ellis does. I'll tell him," Goat Man said. "Look, you know where I can score some ganja?"

"You? What happened, mon?"

"I had some problems in the greenhouse," Goat Man said. "Everything's gone."

"Busted?"

"No, someone trashed it all."

"Tragedy. You come down here tomorrow. Me set you up good."

"Great," Goat Man said. "I'll bring Ellis."

"Him home?"

"*He* flies in this afternoon for spring break."

Goat Man dug under his sink for a plastic trash bag. He went out to the pungent greenhouse and started picking up the empty pool chemical containers. He'd have to drive over to the pool supply store and buy more chemicals, hundreds' of dollars worth. He'd have to explain it all to Wendy, somehow.

He could only stay inside the greenhouse for a few moments before he had to get fresh air and wipe his burning eyes. He tried not to think about all the dead hybrid, all the wasted buds, all the times he wouldn't get high.

After he gathered the chemical containers, he dragged the hoses down from the garage. He screwed them all together and attached the whole line to the nozzle near the pool. He blasted the inside of the greenhouse, spraying all the plants and pots into one corner, diluting the puddles of noxious chemicals. The jet of water rattled the greenhouse walls. He drenched himself, too, and kept spraying long after the chemical stink had disappeared—he wanted to dilute the chemicals as much as possible before they drained into the desert and poisoned the plants there. He left the door open when he was finished, and he calmly rolled up the hose. It was almost time to fetch Ellis at the airport.

Wendy had told Goat Man to wake her from her afternoon nap at two thirty; Ellis's flight was scheduled to arrive at three fifteen. When Goat Man went into the main house, he saw Wendy on the kitchen floor, stretched out on the tiles, rolling around.

"I like the sound of my body," she told Goat Man.

"Interesting," he said.

"Get down here and roll. Listen to your body." She continued to roll from her stomach to her back. "The tiles are cool, solid, permanent."

"Good," Goat Man said. He couldn't hear her body. "We have to go get Ellis."

"You're no fun," she said. She stood and smoothed her skirt. "I haven't spoken to Ellis since he was home for Christmas. Didn't even call him about his stitches. He doesn't know Bennet's gone unless you told him."

"I didn't tell him," Goat Man said. "But Bennet might've been here recently."

"What do you mean?"

"Someone killed all my plants with the pool chemicals. The greenhouse smells like a toxic dump—or, it did before I cleaned it."

"I'm calling the police," she said. She walked over to the phone and picked up the receiver.

"What are you going to tell them? 'Someone destroyed my marijuana plants'?" Goat Man said.

On the way to the airport, Wendy chattered nervously about Ellis, telling Goat Man that certain interpersonal rifts can never be mended. Johanna had told her that sometimes mothers and sons, even though they share the same blood, are as cosmically distant as two strangers on different continents. "Should I accept that?" she asked Goat Man, as she swerved blindly into the right lane on Kino Expressway.

"I don't see why a mother and a son need to be concerned with relating cosmically," Goat Man said. "Why not just relate on a mother-son level."

"Like?"

"Like ask him about school, about girls. Ask him if he's eating enough. Ask him about his birthday next week. And you could ask him about his stitches and apologize for not calling him." Goat Man watched in the rearview mirror as the angry bread truck driver whom Wendy had cut off flipped her the bird.

"I should be really mainstream?"

"Sure."

"It's all so easy for you," Wendy said. "You know Ellis better than anyone."

"I guess," Goat Man said again. He looked out the window at the sun-faded warehouses and crowded tract homes. "You were supposed to turn back there."

"I bet there are really good junk stores in this part of town," Wendy said. "Keep your eyes peeled."

"You were supposed to turn back there."

Ellis's flight was twenty minutes late, so Wendy called Johanna from a pay phone, and Goat Man went to the small video arcade on the second floor of the airport.

The arcade was miserable. No new games since the early eighties, the latest being Pac Man, which was missing the red ball on the end of its joystick. There was a super-archaic game called Dog Patch. The object of Dog Patch was to shoot feuding hillbillies. The hillbillies were nothing more than square blips that flashed across the green-and-white screen. The gun on Dog Patch was sticky.

Goat Man settled on a classic: Asteroids. He had once been an expert at Asteroids—one quarter would last him thirty or forty minutes. Ellis was a toddler then, and Asteroids was already passé by five or six years, but Goat Man used to push Ellis in his stroller two miles down the curvy foothills streets to the 7-Eleven where they had two machines in the back, neither of which was ever plugged in. He'd buy a Slurpee for baby Ellis and play for hours.

At the airport that day, Goat Man didn't earn a single bonus ship on Asteroids. The thrust button would jam, either making his ship fly uncontrollably into asteroids, or else making it sit helplessly as it was shot by obnoxious, beeping flying saucers. He squandered six quarters in the machine before it was time to meet Ellis at the gate.

Wendy was already by the gate, sitting in an orange vinyl chair with her eyes closed. Her lips were moving like she was reciting a mantra. Goat Man didn't bother her. He sat down next to a woman with sun-weathered skin and straw hair. Her two little girls were engaged in a tug-of-war with a Barbie doll. When the head popped off, the smaller of the two fell backward and bashed her head on an armrest. The girl's shrieking sent Goat Man to a seat across the terminal, even though passengers from Ellis's flight had begun to emerge from the jetway.

Goat Man watched as people greeted one another. A fat man with a purple Colorado Rockies T-shirt hugged the two little girls and their mother. The Barbie decapitator finally settled down when the fat guy, probably her father, pulled out a stick of gum for her.

Ellis emerged. He had a brown stain on the front of his white oxford. He carried his fleece pullover and pack. He looked dazed. It was good to see him.

"What did you spill?" Goat Man asked Ellis.

"I didn't," Ellis said. "The stewardess dumped a Coke on me. She gave me a dry-cleaning voucher."

"Bad flight?"

"Sort of. There was some turbulence from Denver to here. Two people near me puked. I almost did. It was fucking disgusting. Now I'm starving."

"Well, hello." Goat Man put his arm around Ellis's shoulder and squeezed him.

"Hello, Goat Man." They began to move away from the crowd, Ellis glad to be walking through the Tucson airport with Goat Man.

"Maybe we can stop somewhere for food on the way home if Wendy's up for it," Goat Man said.

"She's here?"

"Over there." Goat Man pointed at her. Her eyes were still closed, and she was still moving her lips, but now she was rocking.

"Is she sick?" Ellis asked. He hated to see his mother like this. There was clearly something wrong with her mind. He felt the nerves start in his stomach.

"I don't think so," Goat Man said.

"Well," Ellis said, "I'd rather you and Wendy be here to pick me up than that fucking asshole Bennet."

"Your language has gone to hell."

Wendy didn't want to stop for food. She told Ellis that she'd make him any meal he wanted at home. "You guys get the table ready," she said, as they walked into the house, "and I'll head out to the supermarket. What do you want, Ellis?"

Ellis stared at all the old photos of Frank hanging on the walls. Creepy, like Wendy was a stalker or something. He placed his bags on the tiles at the base of the stairs, and said, "Pasta with pesto sauce would be good."

While Wendy went to the supermarket, he and Goat Man walked out to the pool house, where Ellis changed into one of Goat Man's T-shirts.

"How about one welcome-home bowl," Ellis said. "Where's my bong?"

"It broke," Goat Man said. "I'm sorry. I haven't replaced it yet."

"Bummer," Ellis said. "We can just use your pipe, then." Ellis was pacing, venting nervous energy.

"I've just been rolling lately," Goat Man said, staring into the glass tabletop.

"Okay, let's roll a blunt."

"I only have enough for one," Goat Man said sheepishly.

"We can pick more."

"No, we can't."

"Why?" Ellis asked.

"It's gone," Goat Man said.

"You smoked it all?"

"I didn't smoke it all. Bennet or somebody went into the greenhouse and trashed all the plants."

"Where is that asshole, anyway?" Ellis asked. He sat at the table across from Goat Man and made handprints on the glass.

"Gone," Goat Man said. "Wendy finally kicked him out."

"Maybe she's more sane than I thought," Ellis said. "That explains the weird Frank gallery in the house." He sat on the floor and looked around. "All this stuff is new. When did you get the new stereo?"

"A while back," Goat Man said.

"Nice," Ellis said. He stood up and loaded a Peter Tosh CD. Bongos and bass guitar poured from the speakers and filled the room like a substance, and for a few minutes neither Ellis nor Goat Man said a word.

Ellis broke the silence: "Would it kill you to send me a letter or call me more?"

"I'm bad at that."

"Me, too," Ellis said.

"Sorry."

"Every time I come home, there are more surprises," Ellis said. "Wendy's just as bad as you about not keeping in touch."

"Sorry."

"What about that blunt?"

"You want to smoke it or should we save it? It's up to you."

"Can't we just buy some until your plants grow?"

"We'll have to go to Reggie's tomorrow."

"Fine," Ellis said, bobbing his head to the music. "Go ahead and roll it."

The joint burned quickly, and neither of them got very high. It just made Ellis hungrier and Goat Man drowsier. They lay on the rug listening to the music. Goat Man's favorite Peter Tosh lyrics made him happy: *Birds eat it . . . Goats love to play with it.* They do, Goat Man thought, goats love to play with it.

Goat Man asked Ellis if he had brought his hiking boots home from Gates. He had.

"Why?" Ellis asked. He rolled over and faced Goat Man. The rug was prickling him a bit, and, for the first time, he noticed wrinkles sprouting from the corners of Goat Man's eyes.

"You want to go on a real trek?"

"Where to?" Ellis sat up.

"We start down near Douglas, in Mexico, in Agua Prieta, really," Goat Man said, looking straight up at the fan. "We trek out of town, east across some Mexican ranchland, and then north across the border into American ranchland."

"Cool," Ellis said.

"Supposed to be pretty, with amazing rock spires and canyons. We cross the border about ten miles east of Douglas. Total desert until we get to an old ranch road that takes us back into Douglas."

"Cool," Ellis said.

"We'll have to lie to Wendy," Goat Man said. "No one can know where we're going."

"Why?"

"We'll chart the whole thing tomorrow after we visit Reggie."

"Why can't anyone know?" Ellis asked.

"I'll explain it to you tomorrow."

Wendy served dinner wearing a canvas apron that had DON'T BLAME ME, I JUST COOKED IT! silk-screened on the front in purple. The spaghetti she prepared was over-boiled mush. The pesto was store-bought and tasted like the plastic canister it came in. Both Ellis and Goat Man pretended it was the best spaghetti they had ever eaten, smiling and *mmm*ing. Ellis wished they had an undiscriminating dog he could feed it to under the table. He and Goat Man ate it all. They were afraid not to—Wendy was like a time bomb, grinning hard and breathing audibly through her teeth.

"How's the crew training?" Goat Man asked Ellis after the meal.

Wendy brought over three bowls of ice cream.

"It's a lot of work," Ellis said, "but we have a really good freshmen crew. We'll haul ass when we finally get on the water this spring."

"I hope it's not too much for you, Ellis," Wendy said. "I hope you don't feel like you have to do it just because Frank did."

"That's not why I'm doing it," Ellis said, mashing his ice cream with his spoon.

"What are you going to do to stay in shape while you're home?" Goat Man asked. He kicked Ellis under the table.

"I don't know," Ellis said. He looked at Goat Man confusedly.

"I was thinking we could go on a trek," Goat Man said. He took a quick bite of his ice cream.

"I'd love to," Ellis said, too enthusiastically.

"How about the backside of Mount Lemmon?" Goat Man suggested. "We could take it slow and camp for five days or so."

"Wait a minute," Wendy said. "I was hoping to spend time with Ellis. Quality time." She glared at Goat Man. "We talked about this, Javier."

"I'm here for fifteen days," Ellis said.

"But it's your birthday next week. I had something planned," Wendy whined. She banged her spoon on the table. Droplets of melted ice cream clung to her long bangs.

"We'll be back by the thirtieth, right?" Ellis asked.

"With a few days to spare," Goat Man said.

"Perfect," Ellis said.

"Not perfect," Wendy said. Ellis could hear a choke in her voice. She was about to cry, staring into her dessert bowl.

Ellis rolled his eyes. "What now?" he asked.

"Nothing," Wendy said. She sniffed. "Nothing."

"What?" Ellis said.

"Nothing. It's just that, well, with Bennet gone and you guys gone, and Johanna's going to New Mexico, I'll be alone," she said. "And you didn't even notice my toaster."

"What the hell?" Ellis said. "It's an awesome toaster."

"That doesn't help," Wendy said. "Not one bit." She dabbed her moist eyes with a napkin.

"We won't be gone for that long," Ellis said.

"Why is Johanna going to New Mexico?" Goat Man asked.

"Shut up, you," she snapped at Goat Man. She wiped her face with her napkin again and sniffed.

• • •

After dinner that night, Ellis sorted through the pile of bills in the kitchen drawer. Wendy hadn't paid any of them since Christmas, and he wondered how they still had electricity and water. He prepared seventeen checks for Wendy to sign, and he applied stamps and return address labels to all the envelopes. When he finished, he went out to the garage and snagged a bottle of gin from Wendy's hiding place next to the tool cabinet. Ellis blew the dust off and brought it out to the pool house.

"Gin," Goat Man said. "It's not my drink."

"We'll do it Todd-style," Ellis said. "Wait a second." He plopped the bottle of gin on the couch and ran outside. He returned a minute later with four small limes picked from the tree near the pool. "From the cocktail tree." He held them up like they were bounty from the gods.

"We need tonic," Goat Man said.

"Just swig from the bottle and suck on a lime."

"That's what you do with tequila."

"It works with gin, too," Ellis said. He sat at the table and peeled the lime like an orange and ripped it apart into sections.

"Now watch," Ellis said. He took a generous gulp of gin and followed it by chewing frantically on the lime. It burned his throat, stripped it. He tried hard to think of something else so he wouldn't gag in front of Goat Man.

"That's sick," Goat Man said. "Really sick." He went to his refrigerator and pulled out three cans of soda: ginger ale, 7-Up, Diet Mr. Pibb. "We'll save the Mr. Pibb for last." He made himself a cocktail with the ginger ale.

Ellis continued with the macho swigging and lime-sucking. Even when the gin became unbelievably raspy, he drank on. The room tilted and fixed itself over and over. He thought about

Minnie, about the defaced yearbook photo, about her behavior at Peterson's Market.

Goat Man watched, savored his second cocktail. "Ellis, man, mellow out," he said. "You're drinking like a man who just lost his best friend."

"She's a whore," Ellis slurred. "A hillbilly whore."

"Wendy's not that bad."

"Not Wendy, you moron." Ellis calmly proceeded to the bathroom, using the back of the couch for support. He reached the toilet just as the vomit raced up his throat.

Goat Man knew he should go in there and make sure Ellis was all right, but he didn't. As long as he could hear him gagging and coughing, he was okay. Ellis deserved to puke—anyone who drank like that wanted to puke. Ellis had to learn his limits. Goat Man stood and put the gin in the refrigerator and tossed the remaining limes. He didn't want Ellis to get any dumb ideas about drinking more after he finished vomiting. Ellis stopped making noises in the bathroom, so Goat Man called to him, "You okay in there?"

"I'll be a while," Ellis said.

"Okay," Goat Man said. He flicked on the TV and watched the scrambled porno station. Once in a while he could make out a nipple, but mostly all he saw were waves of fleshtones. He heard everything, though: squeals, labored breathing, slurping noises. It got boring fast. Cheap reruns and dating shows dominated the other channels. But he continued to flip through the channels until someone knocked on the door. He hoped it wasn't Wendy.

Aubrey stood in the doorway with her arms folded. Her hair was braided, balled up on either side of her head Princess Leia–style. "I checked it out," she said flatly. "It's called statutory rape."

"And?" Goat Man said.

"And you're a statutory rapist!" she yelled.

"See you," he said, as he shut the door.

Aubrey stopped the door with her sneaker like a salesman. "I'm not as dumb as you think," she said. "I'm not just some dumb girl."

"What are you, Aubrey?"

"I'm smarter than you think."

"Okay, you're a genius, now leave," Goat Man said.

"I got the locks off the greenhouse," she said, "and I told Bennet how you got me high and raped me." She glared at Goat Man, waiting for a response.

He could see she was trying to get him worked up, so he remained calm. "I was bummed about the destruction of my plants," he said. "I thought someone else did it. I don't think I deserved it."

Aubrey muscled her way past Goat Man and sat on the couch. "You're right," she said. "You deserve a lot worse."

"What's your problem, anyway?"

"I'm not the one with the problem, you child molester."

"I'm sorry about what happened. Please leave."

"I'm not done, goat fucker." Aubrey stood and walked over to the kitchen.

"Get out, please," Goat Man said, still calm.

Aubrey picked up a glass from the counter and chucked it at Goat Man. It hit the TV and shattered. The contrast knob fell off the TV, but the screen was left intact.

"What is it with people in your family destroying my stuff?" Goat Man said, picking the knob from the broken glass on the floor. "Just get out, please."

Aubrey jumped at Goat Man, attacking his face with her

nails. He pushed her off a little too hard, and he heard her skull thunk on the Mexican tiles. He was drunker than he had thought, and he almost fell over on top of her.

Ellis staggered in from the bathroom. At first, the scene didn't register completely in his brain: Aubrey on the floor, holding her head, and Goat Man standing above her.

"What the hell?" Ellis said, looking at the blood tracing down Goat Man's cheek. "She's psycho."

Aubrey sat up and punched Goat Man in the balls before she calmly stood and walked out.

Goat Man couldn't speak.

"Barney kicked me in the balls once," Ellis told Goat Man. "Just remember, it'll pass. It'll pass, I swear." He wet a wash cloth. He squeezed it out and put it on Goat Man's forehead. "It will pass."

"I hate this," Goat Man mumbled.

"I hate Aubrey," Ellis said.

FORTY-TWO

When Ellis and Goat Man went to Fourth Avenue the next day, Reggie's store was dark.

"It's noon," Goat Man said. "Why is he closed?"

"That's retarded," Ellis said.

They walked to the Dairy Queen across the street. Goat Man limped like a rodeo cowboy because of Aubrey's punch. They ordered large vanillas in cups, and they sat at a sticky cement table in front. Ellis needed the ice cream to ease his stomach—it felt like the gin had peeled away the lining and allowed the flow of acid up his throat. The sun on his face felt good; it helped calm his stomach somehow.

"Did you know that this is closer in chemical composition to Vaseline than it is to rea' ice cream?" Ellis said, swirling his treat with a plastic spoon. "It's a petroleum distillate."

"I doubt it," Goat Man said.

"It's true," Ellis said. "Barney's brother told me."

"How would he know?" Goat Man continued to spoon the stuff into his mouth.

"He goes to Yale," Ellis said.

"Big shit."

"There's Reggie." Ellis pointed across the street to where Reggie was loading boxes into an old oxidized brown van.

They tossed their ice-cream cups and walked over to Reggie, Goat Man crippling behind Ellis.

"What's the deal?" Goat Man asked.

"I need to get out of this town," Reggie said with his legitimate Phoenix nonaccent. "Hi, Ellis."

"Hi," Ellis said. "You're closing for good?"

"I'm outta here," he said.

"Wait," Goat Man said. "What about what we talked about yesterday?"

"That was yesterday," Reggie said. "Shit's gone down and I'm outta here."

"Can you still set me up?" Goat Man asked.

Reggie looked around, up and down the block and behind him. "I'm being watched, man. I can't get into this shit with you now." He walked back into his store for another box of CDs.

Goat Man blocked him on his way back out of the shop. "After all the times I set you up with my hybrid? After all the CDs I bought from you at rip-off prices, you can't set me up?"

"No, man, I can't. Now move," Reggie said. He pushed Goat Man out of his way with the box he was carrying. "Sorry, man. Sorry for you, Ellis. How's that boarding school treating you?"

"Fine," Ellis said, "but dry. No weed."

"Sorry, man," Reggie said.

Wendy left for New Mexico with Johanna. She tagged a note for Ellis to the refrigerator with a ceramic cactus magnet: *Ellis, I'll be back before you and Goat Man. Give me a hint about what you want for your birthday. Love, Wendy.* Ellis wrote on the bottom of the note, *land*. Later, he asked Goat Man how much a good chunk of land would cost.

"No idea," Goat Man said. "Probably a lot in this area."

"It's worth it. Don't you think?"

"I guess it's a good investment."

"I'd never sell it," Ellis said.

"Oh," Goat Man said.

He and Ellis spent Saturday afternoon driving around town, buying supplies for their trek. Ellis convinced Goat Man to let him buy freeze-dried food, enough for just him, enough to last a week.

"If you want to lug it, you're more than welcome to bring it," Goat Man said. "No fires at night. You might have to crunch that stuff dry."

"Why no fires?" Ellis asked.

"I'll explain it later," Goat Man said.

Ellis was sick of the stupid intrigue. He was still hungover, with a pasty mouth and a burning stomach.

Ellis bought a new pack and some other things: a tiny flashlight, a snakebite kit, and powerful sunscreen.

Goat Man bought only a strap for his sunglasses.

FORTY-THREE

Sunday morning, they loaded the Jetta with their packs and provisions. Following Ellis's orders, Freida and Lance jumped in the backseat without any protest.

Soon they were speeding down I-10, the Jetta's engine humming and clanking irregularly. They traveled east toward New Mexico, with the crackling radio stuck on an AM country station: ". . . but he takes care of things . . ."

"How can this guy get away with rhyming *things* with *thing?*" Ellis asked. "Every song mentions trucks or love." Goat Man finger-tapped the steering wheel to the simple beat, ignored Ellis's commentary.

It was hot for March—eighty-eight degrees. With two panting goats and a broken air conditioner, the Jetta became a rank oven, and remained one even after Ellis rolled down his window. Goat Man squinted as he drove into the sun. He had forgotten his sunglasses, left them by the toaster.

They exited to Route 80 at Benson, a small town of Mormons and tourist trappers who snared people en route to Tombstone. Route 80 cut directly through Benson, and as they slowly passed a Safeway and smaller, more rustic stores, Ellis turned down the radio. "Tell me the deal," he said to Goat Man.

"What deal?" Goat Man's left arm was tired. His shoulder ached. The Jetta's alignment was off and pulled to the right—automatic lane change, he called it.

"This trek."

"Oh, " Goat Man said. He snapped off the radio. It emitted one last dense buzz through the speaker in the dash, then fizzled. "We're on a mission of philanthropy."

"And?"

"We're picking up a woman in Agua Prieta," Goat Man said. "She'll be trekking back with us."

Lance sputtered a loose fart, and Freida bleated. Both goats rustled.

"Did you hear that?" Ellis said. "You smell that?" He hung his head out the window like a dog and breathed in the fresh air. When he pulled his head back inside the car, his blond hair stood up like Don King's. He pressed it down. "What's the big deal about picking up this lady?" He tried to roll his window back up so he could better hear Goat Man, but the knob snapped off, and he banged his knuckles on the glove compartment. "Ow!"

"She's a political refugee of some sort, from Nicaragua. She's not even supposed to be in Mexico, let alone the U.S."

"Why can't she just hop the fence near McDonald's in Nogales like all the other illegal aliens?"

"If she's caught on the Mexico side, she might be killed, and if she's caught on the U.S. side, she'll be jailed and extradited," Goat Man said.

"How do you know?"

"My cousin told me."

"How does he know?" Ellis asked.

"He knows."

"So what do we do with her when we get her to Tucson?"

"Bring her to Skate Country," Goat Man said. "And if we do it, they'll give me four thousand bucks."

"Skate Country? That's a weird place to bring a political refugee."

"Good a place as any," Goat Man said. "A guy in Tucson helps the refugees move farther north into Nevada and Utah."

"The whole thing sounds dumb," Ellis said. "How much do you get paid again?"

"Four thousand."

"Just to walk through the desert with a refugee?"

"It's quite a trek," Goat Man said. "Desolate."

"You said it was beautiful."

"It's beautifully desolate."

They drove through St. David and over rolling, sandy foothills, past a dilapidated water-slide park and a few pecan farms.

As they approached Tombstone, signs for Boot Hill and the OK Corral crowded the highway. Then they chugged over the brown Mule Mountains, through the dark Mule Pass Tunnel, and into Bisbee, an old copper-mining town inhabited by hippies and misfit artists. The rickety candy-colored buildings in the historic section of town clung precariously to steep mountain faces.

"I'm hungry," Ellis said. "Let's pull in somewhere."

"Bisbee's a rip-off," Goat Man said. "We're on a trek, we can't eat at a restaurant."

"We're not on a trek until we start walking," Ellis said. "I'll pay. I want a hamburger. It'll be the last good food I'll have for a while."

Goat Man turned his Jetta onto a main street flanked with antiques stores and cafés. The jammed buildings looked like the ones from old Western movies. A few glossy sedans were parked in front of the Copper Queen Hotel, and young people wearing sunglasses and neatly-pressed casual clothes milled around out front. The street wound up a steep hill into a crack in the mountains.

"I doubt we'll find a hamburger for under ten bucks," Goat Man said.

They chose a small restaurant next to the Bisbee Mining and Historical Museum: Ye Olde Miner's Diner. They tied the goats to a green fence in front of the museum and sat at a table next to the window so they could keep an eye on them.

Average-size hamburgers were six dollars, and Ellis ate a huge one smothered in onions with a side of fries. Goat Man ordered two baked potatoes for a carbohydrate load. He told Ellis to eat half of one of the potatoes.

"I don't feel like a potato," Ellis said.

"You just had fries."

"I like fries better."

"Don't complain that you're tired when we're out stomping through the desert."

"I'm in good shape now," Ellis said. "From crew."

Outside, two ratty-haired hippie girls were lavishing the goats with attention, petting them and feeding them pulled-up weeds. The goats greedily munched and ignored the petting. After a few minutes, one of the girls emitted an audible screech, and both girls ran away. Goat Man speculated from inside the diner that Lance must have farted.

From Bisbee, they drove by mile-deep mining pits and ravaged mountainsides that had been stripped of their copper. They continued driving south for another forty minutes, until they reached Douglas. A K-Mart and a Safeway and many colorful fast-food huts edged the street like any street in Tucson. But in the historical district, closer to the Mexican border, most of the business establishments were run-down, in need of paint. Many displayed plastic Asian crap: toys, umbrellas, lawn furniture—all in offensive fluorescent colors. From the slow-moving Jetta, Ellis saw mannequins with snapped-off hands standing in store windows and modeling pantsuits and tight-fitting jeans. Some of the business signs were written in Spanish, including one for a huge discount store called El de Todo.

"What does 'El de Todo' mean?" Ellis asked.

"I don't know."

"I thought your Spanish was good."

"I'm trying to find a good place to park—I can't think of translating right now."

They drove through the neighborhoods near the border for a while. Even though it was cooler in Douglas, the white-hot sun was still annoying, blasting their faces every time they faced west, making Goat Man curse about forgetting his sunglasses. He thought about buying another pair there in Douglas, but he figured a cheap pair would probably damage his eyes.

Most of the houses in town were painted-over adobe or brick: sun-faded, single-floor boxes with dirt lawns encircled in chain link. More than a few of the houses still displayed glittery Christmas decorations and lights in their dried trees and brown shrubs. A dingy plastic Santa lay forlornly in one yard.

"I know there's a good lot around here somewhere," Goat Man said. They crept along the main drag again, behind a rickety pickup truck overloaded with bottles and cans.

"What's it called?" Ellis said.

"It doesn't have a name; it's just a lot."

"Then we can't ask for directions."

"No," Goat Man said, "we can't, but I think this is it." Goat Man pulled into a dirt area in front of a large adobe building.

They parked between a pile of construction debris and a toppled CARPET WAREHOUSE sign. The closest business establishment was a convenience mart about two blocks away, next to the border crossing station. There were a few shacks near the lot, but they looked abandoned.

"If they tow it," Goat Man said, "we'll get it when we cross back."

"There aren't any no-parking signs," Ellis said, snapping off his seat belt, eager to get outside and stretch.

Goat Man and Ellis unloaded the goats and gear in the oppressive afternoon sun. They didn't bother attaching Lance's pack; Goat Man carried it. Ellis carried his own. After they leashed the goats, they walked along a dusty sidewalk toward the border. A hot wind from the west blew up the dust from the lot, and particles of sand pelted their exposed arms and legs.

"Once we get across the border, we're looking for a big bar called Super Puerco, near a park and a church," Goat Man said.

"Cool," Ellis said.

"My cousin Jesús should be there."

"I'm going to try to stop saying *cool* on this trek," Ellis said. "If you hear me say it, punch me."

"Why?"

"To get me to stop saying it."

"Why stop saying it?" Goat Man asked.

"It makes me sound like a teenager."

"You are a teenager," Goat Man said. He noticed a group of women near the border. Each was loaded down with shopping bags. The women were laughing, pointing at the goats.

"I know," Ellis said, "but I don't have to speak like one."

"Why not?"

"It sounds vulgar. Vulgar in the common, pedestrian sense, not vulgar in the obscene sense."

"I knew what you meant," Goat Man said. "I still don't understand why you're trying to quit talking like a teenager."

"I don't want to be vulgar," Ellis said.

"I think Gates might be rubbing off on you. Next thing you know, you'll refuse to hang out with me because I'm Mexican."

"You're not really Mexican," Ellis said. "Wendy told me."

"What does she know?" Goat Man said.

"Why do you want to be Mexican?"

Goat Man stopped and stared at Ellis. "Let me do all the talking if someone talks to us as we cross the border."

"What'll you tell them about the goats?"

"That Lance is a stud, and he's going to mate with a nanny in Agua Prieta."

"You know how to say that in Spanish?" Ellis asked.

"No one is going to hassle us," Goat Man said.

FORTY-FOUR

The border crossing was unmanned. A desk sat under a rusted tin ramada. Papers were weighted with rocks to the desk, but there were no officials in sight. An empty office chair baked in the low afternoon sun about twenty feet from the desk, in a bare dirt lot.

"That was easy," Ellis said, as they walked by a large barber shop with four vacant chairs. The goats paused and peeked into the shop. An old man yelled and shook a broom at them.

A little farther down the block, Ellis and Goat Man were met with cold stares from soldiers who looked to be about Ellis's age. Each carried a machine gun and had tucked his trousers into his tall black boots.

Agua Prieta's main drag was lined with bars, bakeries, and shops that sold sombreros, tequila, and other tourist goods. The buildings were old adobe or brick; many were crumbling. Most looked like they were once painted in brilliant, gaudy colors, but the relentless sun had leeched their brightness and left them looking overexposed and tired.

The goats behaved, pausing only when they found something to eat on the sidewalk, like a bread crust or an ice-cream wrapper. In front of a little graveyard, Freida paused and began to nibble at the dry weeds sprouting desperately in front of a wooden cross. Goat Man and Ellis let the goats nibble.

Ellis looked closely at the crosses that marked the graves. Many had photos of babies or soldiers tacked to them. Some were adorned with plastic flowers and prayer cards. Spent votive candles littered the whole graveyard. Ellis could smell the perfumed wax.

When he was younger, maybe six, en route to Puerto Peñasco with Goat Man, Ellis kicked a roadside cross out of the dirt when Goat Man pulled over to piss. Ellis still remembered how Goat Man trembled in terror when he saw him holding up the cross. He gingerly helped Ellis put it back in the ground and mumbled a series of prayers.

"Let's go to Puerto Peñasco this summer," Ellis said now, squatting to pet Freida, who was still busy munching dry weeds at the base of a cross.

"Every time we go, it gets worse," Goat Man said. "All that trailer trash."

"Let's go somewhere cooler," Ellis said. "Somewhere farther south, like San Carlos."

Goat Man punched Ellis in the biceps—kind of hard.

"What the hell?" Ellis said, rubbing his arm.

"You used a variant of 'cool,'" Goat Man said.

"But you said it was okay for me to say 'cool' because I'm a teenager."

"It sounds vulgar," Goat Man said. "Not vulgar in the obscene sense, but vulgar in the common, pedestrian, prosaic sense."

"Don't punch me anymore."

"Cool," Goat Man said.

After the goats ate for a few minutes, the group continued walking up the main drag. The sun was finally sinking, and in the flaring pink horizon, they could see a carnival on the outskirts of town: a Ferris wheel of some sort, tents, a few other midway rides. Goat Man hoped Ellis wouldn't ask to go, but he did.

"We haven't even found the bar yet," Goat Man said. "You've been to a hundred carnivals."

"Not a dangerous Mexican carnival," Ellis said.

"What makes you think it's more dangerous than the ones at home?"

"They don't have any regulations down here."

"Why would you think that?"

"Because all the bureaucrats down here are crooked," Ellis said. "I know about *la mordida*."

"Just to prove to you that there are regulations down here," Goat Man said, "we can go check it out."

The only car parked near the carnival was a chicken truck. The chickens inside clucked and rustled. The goats bleated wildly at the chickens. Freida kicked around in the dirt, pulling her leash taut, straining Ellis's punched arm. Goat Man gave Lance a little freedom, and Lance head-butted the chicken truck's rear tire.

"They have the Zipper here," Ellis said. "It's illegal in nine states. I saw a report about it on *20-20*."

"Which one's the Zipper?"

"That one." Ellis pointed to the ride.

Even though it wasn't moving, it looked torturous. Goat Man could see what it did to riders—it flung them upside-down and whirled them backward seventy or eighty feet in the air. The glittery sign next to it read EL MESCLADOR.

"I'm not going on that," Goat Man said, but Ellis had already handed him Freida's leash and taken off.

Goat Man tied the goat leashes to the chain-link fence that surrounded a huge, rank Dumpster.

The carnival was nearly deserted, but the few workers who were there seemed busy. One guy was winding a power cord, a few others were carrying boxes between attractions. There was no one riding the Zipper; it was still. Goat Man assumed the carnival wasn't yet open for business.

Ellis stood next to the Zipper, trying to communicate in a mixture of Spanish, Latin, and English with the operator, a skinny guy with purple gums and a disproportionately large forehead.

"What are you trying to prove?" Goat Man said to Ellis.

"He says he'll start it for a buck," Ellis said. "You ready?"

"I'm not going on," Goat Man said. "There's a reason it's illegal in nine states."

"Wuss." Ellis handed the guy a dollar, took off his pack, gave it to Goat Man, and loaded himself into the caged seat.

The deformed man clanked the cage door shut and shoved a pin through the greasy latch.

The ride started with a fierce screech and a series of piston hisses. Soon Ellis was tossed and spun in all directions. Goat Man could only stand to watch a few rotations before he became dizzy, so he walked off toward a brightly painted trailer. A wooden sign hung loosely over the door with wire: CASA DE ENANOS. He knew he shouldn't, but he paid the woman at the door a buck, and walked in, lugging both packs.

Casa de Enanos smelled like piss, like goat piss. The first exhibit was a series of ceramic midgets and dwarfs displayed in a setting of Astroturf and plastic bushes. Each statue was about three feet tall, with eyes that were too realistic, moist looking. Most had a finger or two missing. For some reason, a pink ceramic E.T. was among the dwarfs, peeking from behind a bush. The whole scene was infused in cheap red light. "What the hell?" Goat Man said to no one, and he followed a painted arrow on the floor down a hall.

Ellis lost count after ten. The Zipper had gone through its cycle of whipping him backward and upside-down at least ten times. His neck was wrenched, his head bashed, and his stomach spun. Each time his cage swung upright, he looked down and tried to make out the carny and Goat Man, but he couldn't spot either. The dim lights from other rides whizzed by, then the sky, then the ground. Soon, everything smeared and ran together in a messy swirl. Ellis started to yell: "Okay, already! Let me off! Stop this . . ."

Goat Man walked down a narrow hall lined with yellowed black-and-white photos of Chito, a Mexican midget wrestler from the sixties. He had trouble squeezing through the hall with both packs. He had never heard of this Chito, and he'd had a period in college when he followed Mexican wrestling religiously—he had even gone to a few matches down in Nogales. One small glass case mounted on the wall held Chito's tiny wrestling mask—red vinyl, with yellow fringe and sequin-lined holes for his eyes and mouth.

Goat Man squeezed into the final section. Here, behind smudged glass, was a small room with a little velvet couch, a little rocking chair, a little table, and a little bed. A slick-haired midget man was asleep in the bed, drooling profusely. He was pale and looked dead, like he had been stored in formaldehyde. When Goat Man dropped Ellis's pack and cupped his hands over his eyes to get a better look, the midget rustled in his bed and farted loudly. Goat Man walked out of the exhibit and into the carnival.

It had gotten darker since he had entered Casa de Enanos. The colored lights of the midway twinkled weakly. He walked past a few bright food and game booths, looking for Ellis, making his way toward the goats in the lot.

The goats were asleep. Lance rested his head on Freida's back. Ellis wasn't there.

Goat Man looked back at the rides. The Zipper was the only ride not illuminated with pulsing colored lights, but it was the only ride moving, churning violently in the sky. He jogged toward it, carrying the backpacks by their straps like suitcases.

Ellis was still on the Zipper, locked in. His cage spun wildly. There was no carny in sight, so Goat Man dropped the packs, ran up the platform, and pulled back on a huge lever. The lever was wrapped in electrical tape, and stuck a little before it clicked into place. The ride jerked and squealed to a halt, but Ellis's cage was up top. He was upside-down. His cage still rocked and clinked.

"What the hell!" Ellis yelled. "It's about time. Let me down."

"Ellis, it's me," Goat Man yelled.

"I threw up," Ellis said.

"I'll have you down in a second." Goat Man looked around for a carny, but there still weren't any in sight. "I'll start it up again," he said.

"Wait!" Ellis cried.

"What?"

"Do you know how?"

"There's really only this lever."

"Okay."

Goat Man pushed the lever forward and the ride jerked into action with a blaring hiss. He stopped it when Ellis's seat was about six feet from the operating platform. "It's tough to time it just right," Goat Man said. "This thing's huge."

"I think there's something wrong with me," Ellis said. "It feels like I'm still spinning."

Goat Man could smell the puke from where he stood on the

platform; some of it dripped from Ellis's cage. "I'll have you out in a second," he told him. He jumped up and hung from Ellis's cage, but the ride wouldn't budge. At least the pin holding the cage shut was in reach. "I'm gonna pull the pin out, so hang on, and don't fall."

Before Ellis could respond, Goat Man pulled the dirty pin. The cage swung open and nearly bashed Goat Man in the head. Ellis toppled out and knocked Goat Man on his ass.

"You okay?" Goat Man asked, as he stood up. "Even in this shitty light, you look pale."

"I think there's something really wrong with me," Ellis said again. He wasn't moving from his crumpled position on the platform. "I can't see right, and it feels like I'm still spinning."

"Let's go."

"You need to help me up."

Goat Man lifted him from under his shoulders, but Ellis just fell loose; his joints buckled. He lifted Ellis again, and had him wrap his arm around his shoulder. Ellis reeked. Goat Man tried to ignore the sour stench, but it was overwhelming. As he helped Ellis stagger through the midway, Goat Man felt his own stomach churning, a wave of nausea rising from deep in his gut.

When they reached the goats, Goat Man gently let Ellis down. "We'll just hang out for a minute," he told Ellis. "You need some water?"

"Not yet," Ellis said. "I still can't see right."

"I think you need to sit still for a while."

"There's something really wrong with me."

"Don't say that," Goat Man said. "You'll be fine. Stay put."

The goats stirred, and Freida began to scream. She was sick of being tied up. Goat Man untied them, and they trotted off about ten yards to nose through a toppled trash can. Goat Man could hear them crunch through plastic and paper, but he didn't have the energy to care.

"Why would he do that?" Ellis asked.

"Who?"

"The guy running the ride," Ellis said. "Why'd he leave me on there like that? I could've died."

"Maybe he forgot," Goat Man said. "People forget."

"No one's that dumb." Ellis closed his eyes and pressed his temples. He saw the sickening smudge of lights and colors spinning and blending.

"Once I forgot a girlfriend when me and a bunch of my friends went camping," Goat Man said. "We camped in Moab right near the Colorado River, and we left her there. I didn't realize she wasn't in the van until we got to Flagstaff."

"What happened?"

"We figured she probably hitched a ride back to Tucson, so we just kept going," Goat Man said.

"That's shitty," Ellis said. "That's mean."

"I was on mushrooms the whole time."

"That's still mean." Ellis sat up. His right boot was splashed with pink vomit. He rubbed it off with the sole of his other boot.

"She knew the score when she got into a van full of stoners," Goat Man said.

"You guys could've turned around," Ellis said. "I wouldn't even ditch Barney, and sometimes I hate him."

"It was different back then," Goat Man said. "Besides, I saw her at a party that summer and she shacked up with the guy who gave her a ride."

Goat Man looked toward the goats. They were still noisily picking through the trash. He opened his pack and pulled out his canteen. He unscrewed the cap and handed it to Ellis.

"Thanks." Ellis took a swig. "I need to take a shower."

"I told you we shouldn't stop here," Goat Man said.

"You also said that Mexican carnivals have regulations."

"The same thing could've happened in the U.S.," Goat Man said. "Look at all the oil spills and train wrecks that are caused by human error."

"I've never heard of a person getting stuck on the Zipper," Ellis said. He stood and began to assess his sullied clothes.

"I saw a kid almost die on a Ferris wheel," Goat Man said. "On *Rescue 911*."

"You watch that?"

"I was changing the channel."

Ellis cleaned up as best as he could in the dirt parking lot. He used the rest of the water from the canteen to wash, and he changed out of his clothes. No one else was in the lot, anyway. He put the sullied clothes in a plastic bag he had dug from the same trash the goats had been picking through. All the colored carnival lights were glowing and strobing, but no one else pulled into the parking lot while they were there. Ellis figured that all the people in Agua Prieta knew the carnival sucked, so they avoided it. He still felt wrong from the ride. If he turned his head too quickly, he lost his balance. His brain buzzed, his mouth tasted like acid, and his neck and back were sore.

FORTY-FIVE

The rich smell of burning creosote and grilling meats filled the night air in Agua Prieta. Loud vendors sold bacon-wrapped hot dogs from smoky booths, and groups of Mexican teenagers in shined shoes and pressed jeans hurried down the cracked sidewalks. Ellis wondered about the teenagers, what it would be like to live here, where they all went for fun.

"Up there," Goat Man said. He pointed down a narrow street to El Super Puerco bar. The lighted sign depicted a nude woman riding a cartoon pig.

"Looks nice," Ellis said. "Classy."

They walked up to the place and tied the goats to a signpost. They kicked away the trash within the goats' reach. Ellis kicked a one-armed doll. It emitted a creepy baby squeak.

"Maybe you better wait out here with the goats, while I go in and find Jesús," Goat Man said.

"No way," Ellis said. "I've been in worse places."

"Like where?"

"Like in D.C.," Ellis said.

"I bet you weren't covered in puke," Goat Man said.

"I washed it off pretty good. Do I still stink?" Ellis sniffed.

"Not really," Goat Man lied. "Not that I can tell."

They pushed through a plywood door into the cantina. Blaring disco music blasted them, and a topless woman with tired, pendulous breasts greeted them. She ran her fingers through Ellis's hair and grabbed at his crotch. "What's your name?" she asked dutifully. "Five dollars."

"My name is Barney," Ellis yelled over the music. "I have no money."

"*No gracias,*" Goat Man said. He gently pulled her off Ellis.

She walked away into the crowd near the stage, and Ellis straightened his dirty hair.

"She was cute," Goat Man said.

"Shut up," Ellis said. "Let's find Jesús quick."

"He might not be here yet," Goat Man said. "We're early."

They walked across the cement floor, pushing through American and Mexican cowboys, whores, and sloppy drunks. The bored-looking woman dancing on stage was badly bruised; dark purple marks stretched down her neck onto her breasts. She was older, plump, and her tight, sequined G-string looked as if it cut into her doughy flesh. Men stuffed dollar bills under the G-string's elastic, and the stripper allowed them to kiss her injured breasts.

"That's sad," Ellis said.

"What?" Goat Man yelled over the music.

"That's sad."

"What's sad?"

"That stripper looks like someone beat her up."

Goat Man spotted Jesús in the corner. He sat at a little round table. A bug-repellent candle burned in the center. The candle cast an eerie blue halo. Jesús was fatter than Goat Man had remembered, but with his smooth face, he still looked eighteen. Seated at the table with him were two topless women.

One smoked aggressively, while the other tongued Jesús's ear. The smoker looked twelve. She had large eyes adorned with oversize fake lashes, and small breasts stiff and knobby with puberty. Goat Man walked up to the table and knocked on it for attention.

"Get the hell out of here," Jesús said.

"What?" Goat Man said.

"Get out of my face. I paid for both of them," Jesús said.

"It's me," Goat Man said. "Javier."

Jesús shooed the whore off his ear and stood, extending his hand to Goat Man. "Where the hell's your beard? Your hair? Welcome to Agua Prieta," he said. He hugged Goat Man across the small table. The younger prostitute pushed the candle out of the way so it didn't burn Jesús's untucked shirt.

"Thanks, man," Goat Man said. "How's Juana and the baby?" He glanced down at the prostitutes. They giggled between themselves, made kissy faces toward Ellis.

Jesús looked at Goat Man skeptically. "They're at home, of course."

"We're hoping to move on as soon as possible, so if you could bring the woman to us, we can get the terms settled."

"Who's *we?*" Jesús asked.

"Ellis and me," Goat Man said. He stepped to the side and let Ellis approach the table.

"Who's he?" Jesús asked.

"Ellis," Ellis said, extending his hand to Jesús.

"He's good with goats," Goat Man said. "The son of the woman whose pool house I live in."

"Oh, the pothead kid," Jesús said, shaking Ellis's hand. "Welcome to El Super Puerco. Want a girl?"

"I'd like a shower," Ellis said.

"Girls here will do that. There's one who does it on stage," Jesús said.

"No, I mean, I want to take a shower and clean up."

"Oh."

Jesús left the two prostitutes at the table and showed Goat Man and Ellis through the crowd and to a back hall. A bloated woman with black stringy hair sat at the entrance to the hall. Swarms of moths bombarded the cracked light fixture above her. A room with a bathroom went for three dollars per hour, or twelve dollars per night. It was quieter in the hall. Hardly any residue from the throbbing disco made it back there.

"I just want to get the woman and leave," Goat Man told Jesús. "Maybe get some food for Ellis."

"You're going to want a room. You're a day early; she's not here yet. She's coming in from Janos tomorrow," Jesús said, picking at the gold-flecked wallpaper peeling from the wall.

"When tomorrow?" Goat Man asked.

"Tomorrow morning, I guess," Jesús said. "Give Lulu the twelve bucks and she'll show you up to your room."

"What about the goats?" Ellis asked. He batted at the moths in front of his face.

"Shit," Goat Man said. "I hope no one ran off with them."

They paid Lulu the twelve dollars, and she led them up black stairs to their room. *"No culeros,"* she said outside the door. She wagged the key in front of Goat Man's face. *"No culeros."*

"She thinks you're fags," Jesús said.

"Tell her we're not," Ellis said. "Why are we staying in this shithole?"

"Fuck her," Goat Man said. "Give us the key." He grabbed it from the woman's moist, dimpled fingers.

The room was cramped and dank. It stank of old beer. No

desk, no night table, no dresser, just a clouded mirror on the ceiling above the two small beds.

"I'll go tie the goats somewhere safer," Goat Man told Ellis, as he dropped his pack on a bed. "Why don't you get cleaned up."

"I don't know if that's possible here," Ellis said. "We're really staying here?"

"It's not that bad," Jesús said. "Cheaper than most motels in this town."

Goat Man and Jesús left, leaving Ellis alone in the room. He dropped his own pack on the cracked tiled floor and sighed before he lay on the bed.

Ellis leaned his head back and looked at himself up in the mirror. He looked pale. He felt the same way he'd felt when Barney climbed into the pervert's car in D.C. last fall, like it was wrong to be here, not safe. He felt the nervous tingling in his stomach. His head still hurt from the Zipper. The sheets smelled like pesticide.

Ellis was baffled by the shower. It was standard-size, with grimy white tiles and a plastic curtain, but the shower head was at waist-level. He thought it must be for midgets, as he kneeled down and turned it on. He could feel the grit washing out of his hair, and saw the brown stuff trailing down the drain. Even though the room was too warm, the hot water felt right, cleansing in an otherwise polluted atmosphere. When he stood to adjust the curtain, he learned why the shower head was mounted so low—it shot directly at his dick.

No one had stolen or harmed the goats. As Goat Man and Jesús approached them, Freida walked right up and began to chew on Jesús's shoelace. Her leash had come untied, and

Goat Man was thankful that she hadn't wandered off. Lance kneeled on the dusty street, his eyes closed, but Goat Man knew he was still awake. He knew Lance could only sleep if he was on top of something—anything, as long as it was up off the ground.

"So these are the goats that'll get you through the desert," Jesús said. "This one's pretty." He patted Freida's side.

"They'll get me through the desert," Goat Man said. "Do you know where I can score some pot?"

"You need pot?"

"My greenhouse was trashed. My whole harvest is gone."

"Shit," Jesús said.

"So?"

"I can get you some easy," Jesús said.

"Tonight?"

Jesús noticed what Freida was doing. "This goat's eating my shoe," he said, shaking his foot.

"Then move. Can you get me some tonight?"

"Where are you gonna put these goats for the night?"

"You tell me," Goat Man said.

"Can't you just lock them in your car?"

"Back across the border? They'd scream. They'd scream like hell. They sound like people when they scream." Goat Man looked around at all the trash, at the people staggering in and out of the brothel. The goats shouldn't be here, he thought. Neither should Ellis.

"We'll tie them around back," Jesús said. "If anyone fucks with them, you'll hear it from your room. I'm just down the hall from you. I'll hear it, too."

"I bet," Goat Man said. He untied Lance's leash and led the goats behind the building to an alley. Jesús stood clear of Freida.

In the thin light emanating from the naked-lady-riding-the-pig sign, the alley was noticeably cleaner than the street. Almost all of the trash was confined to the Dumpster.

But Freida managed to find a dirty Pamper. She grabbed it like a prize and pulled away from Lance, who immediately looked interested. Goat Man kicked it out of her mouth, and she screamed loudly.

"She does sound like a person," Jesús said.

"I hope this is the only night they'll have to spend back here," Goat Man said, as he tied their leashes to a pipe that jutted from the side of the building. "You think the woman'll be here tomorrow?"

Jesús didn't respond. He walked around to the other side of the Dumpster.

"Will she?" Goat Man said, louder.

"There's been a change in plans," Jesús said from behind the Dumpster.

He walked around to Goat Man and shook his head dramatically, like he was really sorry. A strand of his slicked hair fell in his eyes. He slid his hands into the back pockets of his Wranglers. "I tried calling you, but there was no answer. She's not coming at all."

"What?"

"I'm sorry."

Goat Man stared at Freida; even in the dim light of the alley he could see her wet lips. He took a deep breath. "I want you to get me some pot tonight. Ellis and me will smoke a few bowls, and go to sleep. We'll leave in the morning. Can you handle that? Can you handle getting me some pot?"

"Sure. Look, I have another deal for you. It'll earn you a lot more money."

"I'm not about to prepare for another trek if you're the one organizing it," Goat Man said. "You've really fucked me over here." He squatted and scratched Lance under his chin. Lance rolled his eyes and smacked his lips in ecstasy.

"You don't have to prepare for another trek," Jesús said. "Just bring some packages back to Tucson for me. Take the same route you already planned. The packages aren't even that big. The goats could carry them."

Goat Man felt like the bad guy on *Starsky and Hutch*, or *Kojak*. Any minute a cop with a huge, puffy afro, muttonchops, and a really wide belt would pop out from behind the Dumpster and yell, "Freeze, Turkey!"

"What kind of drugs?" Goat Man asked.

"Blow," Jesús said. "It's all paid for, man. You're only dealing with me here. I'll give you *six* thousand if you can get it back to Tucson. We're not dealing with anyone else. No payoffs to anyone. None of that bullshit."

Six thousand would buy Goat Man a car—something not half as disgusting as his Jetta. Six thousand would allow him to trek a lot more. Six thousand would help rebuild the greenhouse. "There was never a refugee, was there?" Goat Man said.

"It doesn't matter," Jesús said.

"It *does* matter." Goat Man continued to scratch Lance's chin. He patted his side and pulled a burr from his brisket. "You can't tell Ellis," he insisted.

"Fine," Jesús said.

"We're leaving tomorrow morning."

"Good," Jesús said. "I'll get you some pot tonight."

"There was never a refugee," Goat Man said. He patted Lance a few more times. "Good goat."

• • •

Goat Man found Ellis in the bed closest to the window, staring at the mirror on the ceiling. Ellis didn't turn his head when he walked in.

"I got us some pot," Goat Man said. "Enough for about a week, and it's not that bad. It's pretty skunky."

"I think there are fleas in these beds," Ellis said. "Or lice. Or chiggers."

"Look," Goat Man said, holding up the bag of pot.

"I don't want any," Ellis said. "I want to get out of here."

"We'll just smoke a bowl." Goat Man pulled his pipe out of his bag.

"No," Ellis said.

"What's your problem?"

"You said this was a nice town with canyons and spires," Ellis said. "It's a dump, and this motel is disgusting."

Goat Man sat on the other bed and lit the bowl. He blew a huge hit toward Ellis. "You're a brat," he said.

"I'm a brat because I think this shithole's a shithole?" Ellis said, turning toward Goat Man.

"If things don't work out perfectly, you complain and whine like a baby." Goat Man took another hit and held it in.

"You're right," Ellis said. "I should be downstairs gazing at that bruised stripper. I should take advantage of all the wonderful opportunities here."

Goat Man didn't say anything. He just held in the hit.

"Thanks for bringing me here," Ellis said. "This is a really nice whorehouse."

Goat Man allowed the smoke to leak from his nostrils as he glared up at Ellis's reflection in the mirror. "We're leaving tomorrow morning," he said, "and we don't have to trek with the woman."

"Good. Then we can just drive back in your shitty car."

"No," Goat Man said. "We're trekking."

Ellis sat up in the bed. "That's stupid. Why can't we just walk across the border to the car?" He picked a bug off his neck, looked at it, and flicked it away.

"We can't," Goat Man said.

"That's a good reason."

"We probably can't get the goats back into Arizona," Goat Man said. "They have to be quarantined or something."

"I could walk across the border by myself," Ellis said.

"You could," Goat Man said. "Then you could wait for me in Douglas for a few days."

"I could call Wendy."

"Go ahead."

"Where the hell is that Nicaraguan woman, anyway?" Ellis said.

"She got to Tucson some other way."

"You're not gonna get any money," Ellis said. "That blows."

"I know."

"Then why do you want to trek? That's stupid."

"Shut up," Goat Man said. "Money is not my driving force."

"You're responsible for me," Ellis said. "You already screwed up by leaving me on the Zipper and making me stay at this shit-hole."

"You're a brat." Goat Man toked again, cashing the bowl, blowing out the ashy hit quickly. "And you can do whatever the hell you want. I'm trekking in the morning." He got up from the bed and dumped the ashes from the pipe into the shower. He leaned his head out of the bathroom. "You're the one who wanted to ride the Zipper so bad."

"I didn't think you'd walk off and leave me at the mercy of that freak carnival worker."

"Shut up," Goat Man said. "You're being retarded. I'm going out for a while." He pulled his poncho out of his bag and slammed the door as he left. He came back a second later to get his pipe and the pot. "And you still smell like barf," he told Ellis. He slammed the door again.

FORTY-SIX

Ellis woke before Goat Man. He hadn't slept well—El Super Puerco had become louder as the night dragged on. He spent the night trying to ignore music from the disco and carnal grunts and moans from the next room. He had wanted to wrap the pillow around his head, but it was too hot, and he was afraid he might get lice. When the noise simmered down around four, Ellis could hear Goat Man making gurgling breathing sounds similar to the ones Barney sometimes made.

That morning, Ellis was still dizzy, and starving, so he walked through the narrow streets of Agua Prieta in search of basic food. Goat Man was asleep, so Ellis left his pack in the room to let him know he hadn't left for good.

The streets held the smell of baking bread and pastries, and in the daylight he could see the mountains to the east. The air was cool, and the sky was as blue as ice.

Ellis bought some peanut butter and Bimbo bread at a small market buzzing with metallic flies. The squint-faced clerk acted as if she was doing him a favor by accepting his U.S. ten-dollar bill, and she handed him a wad of worn Mexican bills as change.

He squatted on the sidewalk outside the store, spread the

peanut butter on the bread with his fingers, and rabidly ate through two sandwiches. The salty-sweet peanut butter helped ease his vague nausea.

On his way back to El Super Puerco bar, he stopped at a bakery and bought a sweet roll and small bottle of orange juice. The roll was light and flaky, and tasted of almonds and lemon. He bought another, for Goat Man.

Ellis walked through a park and wondered why all the trees were whitewashed. The white trees matched a statue of Guadalupe and a cracking gazebo, but that couldn't be why they were painted. He continued through the sunlit streets of Agua Prieta, until he returned to the brothel, to the alley where the goats were tied. Freida was happy to see him, bleating and fluttering her tail excitedly. So was Lance. Ellis felt bad that they had to spend the night in the dirty alley. He was glad they were still there.

"We're leaving today," he told them. "We're out of this shithole." He fed them the rest of the loaf of bread, slice by slice. He spread the peanut butter on the brick wall with his fingers and let the goats lick at it.

Goat Man was awake and washing up when Ellis walked into the room. Ellis placed the sweet roll on Goat Man's bed and hastily packed all of his stuff. He threw the clothes he had soiled at the carnival out the window at the goats. His pants hit Freida, and she bleated. "Just don't eat them!" he yelled down to her.

"What'd you do that for?" Goat Man asked. He had nicked his chin shaving, and blood ran down his neck.

"What?"

"Why'd you throw your clothes out the window?"

"I don't want to lug a bunch of stinky clothes around the desert," Ellis said. "Duh."

"Duh. You could've washed them in the shower last night and let them dry," Goat Man said.

"Duh. Why'd you shave if we're hiking through the desert for two days?"

Goat Man didn't know why he had shaved. He probably shouldn't have. He probably shouldn't have even brought a razor. "I don't know," he told Ellis.

"When are we leaving this shitty town?"

"Five minutes," Goat Man said. "What made you decide to trek?"

Ellis didn't really know, but he said, "I bought a good roll at a bakery, and those little mountains to the northeast look kind of cool."

"Those are the Pedregosa Mountains," Goat Man said. "And notice that I didn't hit you? You said 'cool' again."

"Thanks. I bought a roll for you. It's on your bed."

Goat Man finished packing up his stuff and loaded a bowl of pot. He sat on his bed and lit up. After he took a few deep hits, he held the smoking pipe toward Ellis. Ellis just looked at it.

Goat Man let out his hit. "What's your problem?"

"I thought we were leaving," Ellis said. "You said five minutes seven minutes ago."

"Let's just finish this bowl," Goat Man said. He lay back on the bed and began to scratch his stomach. He felt small, itchy welts. Maybe Ellis was right about the bugs.

"You can finish the bowl," Ellis said. "I'll get the goats ready." Ellis slammed the door as he left.

"Brat," Goat Man said. He finished the bowl and felt better, less angry with Ellis, more enthusiastic about finally starting a real trek. He munched the roll quickly and tossed the paper bag into the bathroom. He figured they'd hike about ten miles out-side the town and rest until nightfall. He got up and looked out the window at Ellis and the goats. It was a nice day: blue sky with a few clouds, and not too hot yet.

Goat Man hoped Jesús was in his room and that he had packed the cocaine well.

FORTY-SEVEN

They walked through shallow buckbrush and pricker bushes for an hour or so before Ellis began to complain. "You said there were spires and canyons down here. All I see is dirt and tumble-weeds." He leaned down and ran his hands over his ankles, plucking thorns and burrs from his socks. Sweat dripped into his eyes.

"Jesús told me about the spires and canyons. We'll eventually get to some nicer stuff," Goat Man said.

"Jesús is real reliable," Ellis said. "Great cousin."

In a few hours, the landscape did become more interesting, like a Dr. Seuss scene. Mounds of gnarled gray rocks and spiky yucca plants began to dominate. The yuccas were so thick in one area, it became difficult for Ellis and Goat Man to avoid getting jabbed by the daggerlike fronds. No matter how carefully Ellis placed his steps, the fronds poked him, punctured his legs, and he'd curse. Goat Man cursed a few times, too. The goats avoided the plants by walking south for a few minutes and catching up with Ellis and Goat Man on the other side of the patch.

They walked eastward through drying riverbeds, following

the dark smears of iron in the white sand. Small pools of stagnant green water teemed with tadpoles and squiggling mosquito larvae. Ellis saw a fat-ass chuckwalla lizard lope through the loose earth and plant himself on the side of a mud puddle. He didn't bother pointing out the big lizard to Goat Man; they hadn't spoken for over an hour. But Ellis finished the last few drops from his canteen, so he'd have to speak to Goat Man soon.

The goats remained close. Lance never wandered ahead, and he only climbed a few of the rocks. Most of the time, Freida walked right next to Ellis. When she did move ahead, she'd periodically pause and check with nervous eyes to see if Ellis was still coming.

"Is there any good water out here?" Ellis finally asked Goat Man, as they stopped to set up the tent for the day.

"Not unless it rains," Goat Man said. He also sat in the dirt. "Have another shot of Freida's milk."

"It gets grosser every time." Ellis sat in the dirt, took off his boots, and kneaded his calves. His toes were striped with mud. They smelled like a dirty refrigerator.

"You could have filled your canteen with bottled water in Agua Prieta."

"You could have reminded me," Ellis said. "I'd rather drink one of those algae puddles than drink more of Freida's milk."

"Suit yourself," Goat Man said, "but don't bother me when you start spraying diarrhea." He was about ready to smack Ellis. He was sick of his brattiness. He'd light a bowl and mellow out after they got the tent up. He'd forget he was trekking with Ellis, and he'd sleep.

"Why didn't you tell me to bring more water?" Ellis pushed.

"Why did you come on this trek?"

"I thought it would be fun. You said it would be fun."

Goat Man ignored him and sucked a few deep breaths through his nostrils. My pipe. I want my pipe now. He felt around in his pockets until he found it in his shirt. He patted it for reassurance.

"Why didn't you tell me it was going to suck this bad?" Ellis said.

"It doesn't suck," Goat Man said. "It's beautiful out here, and if you can't see that, you're pathetic."

Ellis sighed.

Goat Man whistled as he stood up and undid the straps that held the pack to Lance's back. He pulled out the tent. He didn't bother to ask Ellis for help; he just set it up himself and continued whistling until the orange tent was up. He crawled into the tent and unrolled his sleeping bag. "Tie the goats to a tree with shade," he told Ellis.

Ellis peeked his head into the tent. "Why don't you?" he said. "I already have my boots off."

"Tie the goats to a tree with shade," Goat Man repeated.

"In case you haven't noticed, there aren't any trees out here."

"Figure something out. You're smart," Goat Man said. He draped a T-shirt across his eyes and tuned out. He thought about high school, when he was Ellis's age, cruising the streets, buzzed and happy.

Goat Man was sitting up and had a tasty bowl burning when Ellis returned to the tent. He no longer wanted to throttle Ellis. "Please smoke some of this," he told Ellis, holding the pipe out. "It's pretty good."

Ellis didn't say anything; he just took the pipe and smoked it until it was cashed. Ellis fell asleep clenching the warm pipe in his fist.

FORTY-EIGHT

When Ellis woke up at dusk, he knew that he had to eat something real or he'd pass out. Goat Man was snoring lightly, smiling in his sleep. Ellis decided he'd try not to complain anymore once Goat Man woke up. He'd apologize. He should have brought more water, and it wasn't Goat Man's fault that he hadn't. He should have stocked up that morning when he bought the bread and the sweet rolls.

For now, Ellis would heat up some of the freeze-dried food he had brought along. He'd prepare the wild rice mix with a few squirts of Freida's milk. He looked around the tent for Goat Man's lighter so he could make a little campfire, but the lighter was nowhere in sight. It was probably in Goat Man's pocket. As the sun was setting, it was becoming difficult to see. He dug through his own pack for matches, but couldn't find any. He did find his pan. As he rummaged though Goat Man's pack, he felt something weird, like packed meat.

Cheater, Ellis thought when he pulled out the first package. Goat Man had brought food. He pulled out three more packages, each the size of a sandwich, but heavier, and wrapped in brown paper. He stacked them up in a neat pile on the tent floor and began to open the top one.

When Ellis saw the plastic-wrapped whiteness, he realized what it was.

He rewrapped it as well as he could and stuffed all the packages back in the pack.

He was surprised to see Goat Man staring at him in the dwindling light.

"Do you always rifle through my stuff while I sleep?" Goat Man said coolly.

"I was looking for a lighter or matches so I could cook my rice."

"I said no fires. You want us to get caught?"

"Definitely not," Ellis said. He looked at Goat Man's pack. "Especially now that you're smuggling drugs."

Goat Man sat up and scratched his head. His eyes were puffy with sleep. "I thought we were coming down here to get that woman," he said. "I didn't plan this."

Ellis backed away a little bit, leaned against the side of the tent. "Yeah, right," he said.

"It's true."

"If you really believe that Jesús ever had anything like that set up, you're stupid as hell."

"I'm trying to figure out if it's Gates that's made you such a little shit, or if you would have turned into one anyway," Goat Man said. He pulled his pack close to his chest.

"I was going to apologize for being such a whiner; I was going to be a totally good trekker."

"By building a campfire and getting us busted?"

"I didn't know we were carrying cocaine or whatever that is," Ellis said, running his thumb over his brow scar. "And I forgot about no fires—I'm starving. Besides, if you're so worried about being seen, why the hell do you have an orange tent?"

"I thought I could trust you. You're a little shit, you know that?"

Ellis started bunching his sleeping bag into its tiny sack. "That means a lot coming from a drug smuggler," Ellis said. "And I'm taller than you."

"I meant *self-righteous* little shit."

"I meant *stupid* drug smuggler."

"The thing that really bugs me," Goat Man said, "is that you have no concept of anything. You think you're worldly, but you're not even close."

"And you've developed some sort of amazing worldview by smoking pot and hanging out with goats? You have to lie to make yourself interesting—even to your barber." Ellis crawled out of the tent. He sat in the dirt and put his socks and boots back on. He wanted the trek to be over. He'd go back to Gates, study hard and row for the last two months, then he'd spend the summer in Telluride with Frank and Judy. To hell with Goat Man. Let him spend the summer alone in boiling Tucson.

He looked over at Lance and Freida, whom he had halfheart-edly leashed to a creosote bush. Both were awake, standing peacefully, sniffing each other's butts. A few gambol quail scooted by Lance's legs, cooing nervously. Lance didn't acknowl-edge them, but Freida looked down at them and hissed.

Ellis followed ten or so paces behind Goat Man. Goat Man sucked his pipe, and Ellis enjoyed its aroma in the cool night air. He didn't ask for any. They hadn't spoken since they argued back at the tent; they had just trekked on through the evening with the goats close by. Ellis had finished off four cups of Freida's milk since he woke up, but he was still starving, fantasizing about

Taco Bell and Dairy Queen. He cursed Goat Man under his breath every few minutes. He could be home, eating pizza in front of MTV.

The terrain at night seemed different in the moonlight—rounded hills, broader arroyos, and rocks that looked like spongy velvet furniture. Lance liked the rocks. They were small enough to jump up on, and big enough so he still looked cool on top of them. Ellis was amazed at Lance's dexterity. Even though he was burdened with the pack, Lance sprang around like a gymnast.

Goat Man kept a close watch on Lance. He was carrying expensive cargo. He didn't want to leash him, though. If he acted casual, so would Lance. This was like any other trek. There'd be no problems. Lance was a good goat, a consistently good goat.

They hiked along a sandy arroyo for a few miles and crossed under two slack barbed-wire fences. Ellis held the wire up for the goats each time, as Goat Man forged ahead with his pipe in his mouth.

"We're stopping here," Goat Man said as he hopped over a dead saguaro. The remains of the cactus were bleached by the sun, clearly visible in the moonlight. Most of the meaty parts had rotted off, exposing the white, woody skeleton.

"There are swarms of flies in dead cacti," Ellis said.

"What's your point?" Goat Man said. Ellis was right, but this one was too dead for flies.

"Never mind."

Ellis didn't bother complaining anymore. He was trapped. He'd diligently help set up camp. He'd do whatever Goat Man said. Goat Man was stoned and stubborn. Ellis could have kept walking, they had only been at it for three or four hours since napping. He imagined that it wasn't even midnight yet, and after having slept through the afternoon, he was still full of energy.

They set up the tent quickly, and Goat Man settled inside it, as Ellis pulled out his freeze-dried food and sat on a rock. Ellis crunched through a whole packet of dried turkey dinner, felt its hyper-salty presence expanding in his stomach. Lance and Freida came over to see what he was eating. He offered small chunks to each of them. Freida spit hers out and shuddered. Lance just sniffed his and tried to kick it away with his hoof. Ellis was still hungry, but not enough to rip open the beef stroganoff.

FORTY-NINE

Goat Man shook Ellis, but Ellis had been awake for a while, bunching himself into the bottom of his sleeping bag where it was warm.

"It's raining," Goat Man said. "It's raining hard. Wake up."

"Duh," Ellis said, sticking his head out into the cool, moist air. Between the rain slapping the tent, and the goats screaming, there was no way he could have still been asleep. It had actually been the smell of damp creosote that woke him. He loved the smell, savored it. It recalled to him the summer monsoon season in Tucson, when the rain brought relief from the 110-degree heat and filled the arroyos with water. "What time is it, anyway?" he asked Goat Man.

"I don't know."

Ellis sat up. His mouth was dry and raw from crunching down the freeze-dried food before going to sleep. "What do we do with the goats?"

"Load them up and haul ass," Goat Man said.

"In this rain?"

"We'll leave them on their leashes," Goat Man said. "This is real trekking."

"This is stupid."

"You brought the right clothes, didn't you?" Goat Man asked.

"Yes," Ellis said, but he wanted to sink back into his warm sleeping bag.

By the time Goat Man and Ellis finished wadding up the wet tent and cramming it into a pack, the goats' voices had become hoarse from screaming. Lance had stopped screaming altogether. Ellis shined the flashlight on him. He was kneeling in a mud puddle, his hooves splayed oddly, defeated, his eyelids drooping.

"Won't the cocaine get wrecked if it gets wet?" Ellis asked Goat Man.

"It's sealed pretty good," Goat Man said. "But you know that."

"Knowing Jesús, he probably fucked it up," Ellis said.

"You don't know him."

"I'm glad I don't know him," Ellis said. "His whores were like in fifth grade." He walked over to the goats and turned back to Goat Man. "Maybe that sort of thing runs in your family."

With the hood of his parka pulled over his ball cap, it was tough for Ellis to see through the rain. Whenever the wind picked up, the cold rain pelted his face and dripped down his neck under his parka. The goats walked with their heads down.

When lightning struck, the landscape lit up for a second and looked like a cheapo sixties sci-fi movie set. The yuccas and cacti flashed saturated greens, and the wet sand shone, a blinding white—like snow. Otherwise it was dark.

Ellis held the goat leashes, stumbling slowly behind Goat Man's flashlight through the sloppy, drenched desert. The fronds of the yucca still managed to jab his legs, even through his rain pants. The goats tugged hard whenever the thunder cracked, and soon Ellis's arms were sore, his hands cold and aching.

"Can't we just head north now?" Ellis yelled to Goat Man through the pounding rain.

"Not yet," Goat Man said. "We're still too close to Douglas."

"How can you tell?"

"The mountains."

The rain had mellowed some by the time they reached the edge of a gushing arroyo. Goat Man shined his flashlight across the water, which was a shade lighter than chocolate milk. About forty feet of humming rapids separated the group from the other side.

"Now what?" Ellis asked. Somehow the cold had sneaked through the Gortex of his parka, and his underwear was wet and bunching up. It itched.

"We'll walk east along it," Goat Man said, "until we find a place to cross, and then we'll find the old ranching road."

"I'm freezing," Ellis said.

"Sorry," Goat Man said. He was. "Want me to take the leashes for a while?"

"I got them," Ellis said. "I feel bad for the goats. They're both freaked out."

They trudged east, but there was nowhere to cross. The wash became somewhat narrower, but the rapids grew more pronounced, white-capped. The rain had picked up again, and Ellis was fatigued from shivering. He was sick of pushing through wet chaparral and feeling the suck of mud on his boots.

When Lance stopped cold and sat in the muck, so did Ellis. Freida hunched her back and drooped her tail before she sat.

"What the hell?" Goat Man said, shining the light on Ellis. "Get up. All of you, get up."

"No," Ellis said.

"The rain's gonna stop, and it'll be light soon."

"My butt's all wet," Ellis said.

"You're sitting in a puddle."

"It was wet before. My whole body's wet. My jaw aches from shivering, and my feet are blistering up, and my arms are aching, and I can't feel my fingers."

"I said I would take the leashes."

"I still can't move," Ellis said. "Neither can Lance or Freida."

Goat Man dug around in his pocket. He pulled out his pipe and lighter and huddled down next to Ellis. Soon the bowl was glowing orange. He cupped his hand over it and motioned to Ellis.

Ellis wanted the warm smoke in his lungs, and he took the pipe. He wasn't as careful as Goat Man, and after the second hit, the bowl fizzed in the rain. But he had managed to get some into his lungs. He held the smoke there, concentrated on it. He hated to blow it out. It warmed him from the inside.

"Now let's move," Goat Man said.

Ellis ignored Goat Man and tried to spark up the bowl again.

"I'm serious," Goat Man said. He grabbed Lance's leash and tugged him to his feet. Lance sat back in the mud. "Forget the bowl. Let's go."

"Can't you just wait?"

"You're the biggest baby," Goat Man said. "You get a little wet, and your whole world falls apart."

"You're an asshole," Ellis said from down in the mud. "Who made you my boss?"

"Get up."

"I'll get up when I'm ready," Ellis said.

"Get up!" Goat Man said. "Get your ass up!" He kicked Ellis in the thigh—not hard, because his boot hit the mud first.

"Hey!" Ellis said. He stood quickly and shoved Goat Man. "If you want to go, just go. Leave me here with the goats."

"You're a spoiled brat," Goat Man said before he shoved Ellis back, hard. The end of the flashlight smacked Ellis's chin, made his teeth clank.

Ellis toppled over Lance, who sprang up and tangled his hoof in a leash. Lance tripped and grunted. He sprang up again, shook his head and withers, and ran directly into the gushing arroyo. He produced a formidable splash before being carried down the wash by the rapids.

Freida screamed.

"Damn," Goat Man said before he dropped his flashlight and jumped into the rapids after Lance.

Ellis was bewildered by the whole scene. He ran alongside the foamy wash, but with the bushes and trees and loose earth and darkness, his attempt to follow was pathetic. The only things he caught sight of floating down the wash were a few branches, but he couldn't be sure in the darkness. No Goat Man or Lance.

As he continued his vain attempt to spot Goat Man in the water, rushing through the dark, wet desert, Ellis tried to think of the last song he had heard. A disco song from El Super Puerco bar. The singer sounded like a baby: *Uppy, uppy, I want uppy. Uppy, uppy, quiero uppy* . . . The bushes and the mud finally became too much for Ellis to contend with, so he sat and looked at the sky, trying to figure out what to do next.

At least it had stopped raining and the sky was clearing in the east.

FIFTY

The sun was barely up but already making Ellis squint. He sat on the edge of the wash, watching the rapids diminish, petting Freida, who had been silent since her scream. He had hiked back to retrieve his pack and the pipe from the site of the skirmish, and he found Freida, sitting dutifully where he had left her, next to the flashlight. He knew he needed to cross the wash and walk north to find the old ranching road, but he didn't have it in him to move just yet. He just sat, overwhelmed, and drew smile faces in the cool mud with his thumb. He wished he were back at Gates, in his dorm room, arguing with Barney about algebra or crew. He wondered if he was still in Mexico, or if one of the barbed-wire fences they had crawled under marked the border. He was starving again, and cold, and the scrapes from branches and pokes from the agaves stung his arms and legs. He stood and stretched his arms over his head and jogged in place for a minute to perk up, but his wet, gritty underwear was bunched in his butt, and his boots made a sloshing noise with every step, so it was difficult to muster the motivation to move on. He sat back down, closed his eyes, and faced the morning sun. Its warmth felt good.

Ellis pictured Goat Man's wide, roaming eyes in the murky

wash; his mouth open, his blue tongue hanging out. His lungs and sinuses burned as he took in more and more water. With one final jerk, Goat Man's mouth closed, and his eyes stopped looking.

Ellis imagined Goat Man's funeral. There was Wendy, rubbing a crystal, her face ruddy and swollen from crying. No one else was in attendance. The obituary would be short: *Javier trekked with goats and enjoyed marijuana.* Ellis would make sure the obituary was longer. He would make sure that it said Goat Man was an animal behavior expert . . . a University of Arizona graduate . . . a swimmer . . . a landscape architect . . . a botanist. It was the least he could do for Goat Man, whose bloated body was probably being eaten by vultures and mangy coyotes on the side of the wash somewhere.

Ellis wondered how he and Goat Man got to arguing and shoving like they had. They had never even come close to fighting like that before.

He was a brat like Goat Man had said. He was sure of it. And now Goat Man might be dead.

Ellis said, "Goat Man" out loud. He said it again. Then he said, "Javier." His voice sounded funny, deeper and rumbly, like he needed to pop his ears. He spoke again: "Stupid pothead." Freida bleated lightly.

Ellis began to scream, but he stopped after a few seconds. He sounded stupid. Wendy used to stand on the back porch in loose linen clothes and scream at the desert. She had told Ellis it was part of her therapy, and he was welcome to join her. Sometimes she screamed "Frank!" but most of the time it was just plain screams. Once, she did it when Ellis had a friend over. Ellis lied to his friend, saying his mother had had her tonsils taken out, and the screaming was part of her rehabilitation. Ellis didn't think his friend bought it, but the kid never mentioned Wendy's scream therapy in school.

Ellis knew he had to cross the arroyo, and it looked easy enough since the rapids had shrunk. As stupid as he knew it was, he was afraid that as he trudged through the turbid brown water, he might step on Goat Man or Lance. The water looked rotten, septic, like it was teeming with all the shit from Agua Prieta—which he knew was impossible, since it was flowing *toward* Agua Prieta. He thought for a moment that he detected the sickeningly sweet stench of carrion and became dizzy, felt like he did when Goat Man saved him from the Zipper.

He leaned on Freida, hugging her plumpness. Her bristly fur felt good on the side of his face.

FIFTY-ONE

The dirt road was closer than Ellis had imagined, but he had no way of knowing how far he was from Douglas or any other town, or if this was the ranchers' road Goat Man had mentioned. He kept trudging west, gazing across the dirt road into the desert, hoping to see Goat Man or Lance appear from behind a bush or rock. Freida seemed to be doing the same thing, pausing every so often and looking behind.

The mud on his legs was beginning to dry, and his butt cheeks were itching bad. He was hungrier, and the few faded wrappers and cans that littered the side of the road reminded him that he hadn't eaten anything good for a long time. No Snickers, no Gatorade, no Doritos, no McDonald's, no Skittles. The sweet roll he devoured on the sidewalk in Agua Prieta was good. He couldn't remember if that was yesterday or the day before.

His legs and back were aching and sore, and the western horizon offered no relief—no sign of Douglas. The warm sun did feel pleasant on his neck, and the desert air was fragrant with creosote and sage. Goat Man was right, it was beautiful out here. The Pedregosa Mountains looked like giant brown animals in recline.

An hour or so later, Ellis heard the rumbling crunch of a car from behind. He felt the noise in his stomach. He pulled Freida by her collar to the side of the road and waited for the approaching car. It was a blue sport utility vehicle, and the guy driving it looked pretty normal when he pulled over and stopped alongside Ellis and Freida. He had a round face with gray hair, and a white, neatly trimmed beard—a Kenny Rogers clone with a red, bulbous nose. He wore a straw cowboy hat and a denim shirt.

The guy leaned across the passenger seat and popped open the door. "You look like hell," he told Ellis. "I'll open the back and we'll put your goat in there."

"Thanks," Ellis said, walking Freida around back.

The man opened the door for Freida, and Ellis lifted her in. As the man shut the back door, fear bloomed through Ellis's gut. But Ellis walked around to the passenger seat and climbed in anyway. He knew he had no choice. He stared through the windshield and thought about getting into the car at Malcolm X Park—the way Barney's eyes had looked, the way the car had smelled like pie-filling, the way the crazy woman in the front seat had laughed. The scene returned to him with a vile carnal immediacy. He gripped the dashboard with both hands.

"You going to shut the door?" the Kenny Rogers clone asked him. "You look like you're preparing for a crash."

"Oh," Ellis said. "Sorry." He slammed the door and tugged the seat belt over his shoulder. It did feel good to be off his feet. Ellis's eyes locked on an opened package of Peanut M & M's baking in the sun on the dashboard.

"Where to?" The man asked.

"How far is Douglas?"

"Four or five miles. This road only goes to Douglas."

"Okay."

Ellis continued to eye the M & M's. The man laid on the gas. Two M & M's slid out of the wrapper with the acceleration. The candies vibrated on the dash, teasing Ellis.

"Caught in last night's rain?"

"Yes," Ellis said.

"I thought you were another Mexican," the man said. "I almost kept driving, then I saw your hair was blond, and your backpack looked expensive."

"You would have left me out here if I had darker hair and a cheaper backpack?"

"Yup," the man said, "and I would have called the Border Patrol as soon as I got into Douglas."

Ellis gripped the dash again as they splashed through a shallow arroyo. He looked for Goat Man in the brown water, but saw nothing.

Freida bleated loudly.

"You mind?" the man asked, as he clicked on the radio. An annoying Shania Twain song blared from the back speakers, and Ellis sighed loudly.

The man turned it down. "They call me Red."

"You don't have red hair," Ellis said.

"I know. I got the name from my nose."

"Oh," Ellis said. "My name is Barney." He squirmed around a bit, tried to flex his buttocks in such a way as to scratch the itches. It didn't work, so he sat up a little, sneaking an unsatisfying butt-scratch with his thumb.

He heard Freida crunching on something, and he turned around to see her happily devouring a newspaper. He undid his seat belt and ripped the paper from Freida's mouth.

"I had a goat once," Red said. "He ate an entire tennis racquet one night. The strings and all."

"I think Freida here ate one of my sweaters once," Ellis said, "but I'm not positive."

Ellis opened the crumpled newspaper to reveal its title: *Pleasure Guide, Where Swingers Connect.* Pages of personal ads, a few, like the one at the top, included lewd photos. *BiWM looking to explore with healthy, open-mined couples in the Phoenix area . . . My name is Lucy. I've got charm, I've got class, I even like it up the ass . . . BiF looking to party with others . . .* Ellis stopped reading when he saw Red nervously glancing over at him.

"That ain't mine, Barney," Red said. "I mean, it is, but I didn't get it for what it's for. I mean—"

"No problem," Ellis said. No one is normal, he thought.

"The guy at the 7-Eleven saves them for me at the end of the month."

"No problem," Ellis repeated.

"For my pigeons. Nineteen pigeons. I got bird cages. See, I got a whole stack of *Pleasure Guides* in the back, all from this month. And I also got other papers. Not sex ones." Red awkwardly grabbed at papers on the seat behind him, shoving Ellis's pack out of the way, steering with his left hand and trying not to swerve.

"No problem." Ellis believed him; he refocused on the M & M's.

The red M & M was gone from the dash. His eyes moved frantically over the seat and floor until he spotted it next to his dirty boot. He schemed to bend down and pretend to tie his boot so he could grab the candy, but he realized how stupid he was being. "May I have some of those M & M's?"

"They're from yesterday," Red said. "You can have them all if they ain't melted."

Ellis dumped the M & M's into his mouth and chewed. He breathed deeply through his nose as he experienced the rush of chocolate and peanuts. Soon he was swirling his tongue around the corners of his teeth, probing for the last bits. Then he remembered Freida and felt bad for eating them all.

"I never even look at those newspapers," Red said. "They make me depressed."

So they drove on toward Douglas, over small hills and through more trickling arroyos. Ellis watched the wooden fence posts and yucca plants speed by and spill out of the rearview mirror. He kept expecting to see Goat Man on the side of the road with his thumb out, trusty Lance by his side.

Red never asked Ellis to explain why he was out in the middle of the desert with a goat.

FIFTY-TWO

Red dropped Ellis off in downtown Douglas, not too far from the dirt lot where Goat Man had parked the Jetta. At first, Ellis was unsure that it was the right lot, but then he saw the toppled CARPET WAREHOUSE sign. The Jetta was gone. He stood in the lot for a few minutes, trying to decide what to do. He thought about going across the border into Agua Prieta again, and looking for Jesús, but he didn't know if Jesús would still be there, and he didn't want to go back into El Super Puerco bar. He decided to walk to the convenience store next to the crossing station and call the Douglas police.

"I'm wondering where my car would be if it was towed," Ellis asked the woman on the phone.

"It depends," she said. "Was the car parked on private land, or on city land?"

"I'm not sure," Ellis said. "It's just a dirt lot in front of an old carpet warehouse, near the border crossing." He shooed Freida from chewing on his pack.

"On the east side of the street?"

"Yes," Ellis said.

"We wouldn't tow from there," she said. "How long was it there?"

Ellis had to think about that. It seemed like a week or two had passed since they pulled into Douglas, but it had only been two nights. "Two days, I guess."

"You want to report it stolen?"

"No one would steal it," Ellis said. He pulled his bunched underwear out of his butt, and scratched dried mud off his chin. "You didn't find any dead guys floating in the wash, did you?"

"Excuse me?"

Ellis hung up and walked back to the main strip.

He rushed into a five-and-dime after tying Freida to a parking meter, and he bought as much junk food as he could carry to the counter: a tube of Pringles, a box of Fiddle Faddle, a two-liter bottle of Mountain Dew, a Snickers, and a big bag of Doritos. He sat on the warm sidewalk in front of the store, the broken-armed mannequins standing behind him. He devoured his food, pausing every minute or so to throw Freida a chip or some popcorn. He didn't notice the stares from people strolling by, stepping over his extended legs, as he crammed the food into his mouth and talked to Freida.

FIFTY-THREE

Barney didn't believe Ellis.

"Like twenty?" Barney said. "I doubt it."

"Maybe more than twenty," Ellis said. "Everywhere I looked, there were more tits in my face."

"I doubt it. You can make up all kinds of shit, because you know I'll never go to Mexico." Barney flicked out the light and rolled over.

"Most were ugly and sad-looking," Ellis said. "The dancer on stage was all bruised."

"I'm tired," Barney said. "I want to get some sleep now."

"You're just pissed because you had a boring spring break in miserable D.C."

"It wasn't boring," Barney said. "I got into the Charing Cross one night with Todd's fake I.D., and I met two girls from Madeira."

"And?"

"And what?"

"And did you score?" Ellis asked.

"Not really," Barney mumbled.

"Then why are you bragging about meeting them?"

"I'm not bragging," Barney said. "I'm just mentioning it."

"Meeting—maybe not really even meeting—two girls from Madeira was the highlight of your vacation? That's pathetic."

"It wasn't the highlight," Barney said.

"What was?" Ellis asked. He didn't really care, but he was still on Arizona time and wasn't at all sleepy.

"The highlight was finding out that my grandfather went to Tufts."

"So? Big deal."

"Maybe I can get in there," Barney said.

"You have three more years before you have to worry," Ellis said.

"Really only two years," Barney said. "This time two years from now, we'll have already taken the SATs, and we'll be planning which college applications to fill out."

"I'm going to do early decision so I only have to fill one out," Ellis said.

"What makes you so sure you'll get in somewhere early decision?"

"I will," Ellis said.

"This is just another example of how conceited you are," Barney said.

"I'd rather be conceited than a nervous wreck."

He heard Barney rustle and sigh.

Ellis was unable to sleep. Goat Man had never resurfaced. Ellis hated it; he hated not knowing where Goat Man was and why Goat Man hadn't waited for him Douglas. He wasn't even positive that Goat Man was still alive. Someone could have stolen the Jetta for a joyride. The police had never even come over to the house in Tucson. No one cared that Goat Man was missing.

Wendy didn't. When Ellis told her the whole story of the trek the afternoon she returned from the New Mexico spirit camp, she said impassively that Goat Man would be home soon enough, and she asked Ellis how he had gotten back from Douglas.

"In a van," Ellis had said. "The Butterfield Coach. It was twenty-four dollars, and I had to sit next to a woman who smelled like onions and had a chicken in a cage on her lap."

"They let Freida on the van?"

"They charged me twelve extra dollars, that's why it was twenty-four."

Ellis and Wendy were stretched on the chaise longues out by the pool, absorbing the afternoon sun, sipping raspberry iced tea from tall blue glasses. A light breeze kicked up every once in a while, cooling Ellis's sunburned arms and legs.

"The workshops in New Mexico weren't any good, but I met a shaman," Wendy said.

"Aren't you even the slightest bit concerned about Goat Man?" Ellis asked. "Or Lance? That wash was gushing."

"Goat Man can swim," Wendy said. She twirled the ice in her glass with her fingers. "I don't need to worry about them."

"I worry about you a lot," Ellis said, turning in his chaise to face his mother. "You seem weird sometimes—like now."

"I'm fine," she said.

"You don't seem fine."

"Since I kicked Bennet out, I'm fine," Wendy said. She took a long sip of tea and cleared her throat. "I should worry about you, Ellis."

"You don't worry about me, do you?"

"I know you're at Gates. I know you're smart. You make pretty good decisions. You don't leave me anything to worry about."

"I got bike-jacked at Gates."

"Call the insurance tomorrow."

"Do you ever just think about me?" Ellis asked.

"Of course," Wendy said. "All the time."

"Really?"

"Of course I think about you. I'm your mother."

"You are my mother."

They stayed outside in the cooling air until the sun began to sink behind the craggy black mountains, and the last light of the day stretched their shadows across the pool.

The alarm didn't penetrate Ellis's slumber. He awoke to Barney shaking him. "Come on," Barney whined, "we have to be on the boat in ten minutes."

"No." He had been up most of the night with nervous heartburn, worrying about Goat Man, wondering if he should have called the police.

"Come on."

Ellis pulled his pillow over his face.

"Suit yourself," Barney said. "Coach is gonna be pissed."

"That fat pig," Ellis grumbled.

He fell back asleep and dreamed about the trek. Goat Man was trying to convince him to ride the Zipper, which was much taller and a lot faster, with Minnie, who happened to be down in Agua Prieta. This time, he awoke to Coach shoving him.

"Get up," Coach said. "All the others are out running laps." He wrenched Ellis's shoulder.

"What the hell?" Ellis said. "What are you doing in here?"

The coach had gotten a haircut over spring break—an angular flattop. Coach shook his finger at Ellis. "We'll all be on the boats in five minutes. Your ass better be there."

"Haven't you ever heard of jet lag?" Ellis said, sitting up, rubbing his eyes.

"Five minutes," Coach said.

"No."

"What?"

"No," Ellis repeated.

"That's it," Coach said. "You're off the crew."

"Tragic," Ellis said.

Coach walked out. He slammed the door and it bounced back open. Ellis staggered over and shut it lightly. He lay back down but knew he wouldn't be able to sleep.

He pulled on some sweats over bike shorts and a T-shirt. He dug through his luggage for his running shoes and sat on the floor as he laced them up.

The air was thick and hot, sultry, and the ground was spongy from the melted snow. It was unseasonably warm for early April in Pennsylvania, and Ellis could smell the wet earth as he trotted nervously toward the boathouse.

The boys were loading themselves onto the shell, Rosenberg sitting in his position on the stern, gripping the rudder, testing his cox box with some Beastie Boys lyrics. His nasal voice echoed though the old boathouse: "Intergalactic planetary . . ."

Ellis walked up to Coach and tapped his squishy shoulder. "Can I talk to you for a second?"

"What now?"

"I'm sorry," Ellis said. "I was still asleep back there." He took a deep breath to combat the tightness he was feeling in his throat. "I didn't know what I was saying."

"I knew what I was saying," Coach said. "I kicked your butt off the crew." He turned around and faced his boys. "Cannel, I want you at the bow. Dorst, you're three, not four."

"I'm sorry," Ellis said, louder. Ellis had been promised the bow before spring break—a reward for cutting his erg time by twelve minutes, for improving more than anyone on the crew.

Coach faced Ellis again. "You know how many times in the fourteen years I've been coaching that I've gotten rowers out of bed?"

"No."

"Today was the first time."

"Sorry," Ellis said. "Really. I have jet lag."

"So does everyone else," Coach said flatly, "and they all managed to get their butts out of bed and down here."

"I really want to get on that boat," Ellis said, his voice cracking.

Tears began coursing down Ellis's cheeks. He wiped them away, surprised at their presence, and sniffed. He bowed his head, looked at his grubby running shoes.

"I don't have time to argue," Coach said. He turned back to the crew. "Rosenberg, I need you on your toes today. No messing up . . ."

Ellis began to walk across the rotten planks, out of the boathouse and into the lemony morning sun, until he heard Coach yelling his name.

"Whitman! Whitman, where're you going? Get back here, Whitman!"

Ellis took his place at the bow, laced his socked feet into the built-in shoes, and soon the shell was gliding over the lake. Coach chugged next to the crew in his little boat, and screamed at the boys about technique: "Whitman, watch your recovery! You're moving to the catch too quick! Dorst! Dorst! What the hell are you doing!? Work the spoon! Cannel, perfect! Perfect! Whitman, you watch Cannel's stroke! Dorst! Are you retarded?!"

After Coach putted back to the boathouse and let the crew row without comment, their synch felt better, but still not perfect.

Rosenberg transformed as coxswain. Ellis noticed the intense concentration on his face, was surprised at the serious tone of his voice as he yelled into the cox box.

The boat sped through dense clouds of mist. Ellis would peek over Barney's shoulder and marvel at the thickness of the mist, how he didn't notice it until they had passed through. The slight spray kicking up at the bow was cold on Ellis's arms and legs, but he liked it; it reminded him of where he was, what he was doing.

Barney's technique was flawless; his strokes were smooth and seemingly effortless. To Ellis, he looked like the guy they had seen in the training video: catch, drive, finish, recovery. The other rowers' blades shifted and jerked in the water, but not Barney's.

Ellis himself was having problems staying in synch with Barney's perfect stroke. Rosenberg spotted this and yelled into his cox box, "Ellis, you're washing out! Keep it in there just a second longer at the finish! Good! Good!" The forced concentration was relaxing for Ellis. He only thought about his stroke, worked on getting into a comfortable groove. He couldn't think about Goat Man or the trek.

After showering, Ellis walked across the Commons toward the dining hall, and he noticed Fiona's Volkswagen parked near the administration building. Minnie was about to get into it, but when she saw Ellis, she looked around cautiously and ran over to him.

"Hey," she said.

"Why are you here so early?" Ellis asked her.

She wore green Bermuda shorts, a thin T-shirt, and thongs. "Picking up my pathetic check," she said, waving it.

"Good." Ellis started to walk away.

"Wait," she said. "I was thinking." She put her finger in her mouth, like she was scraping something off a molar. Her hair was infused with morning light, lit in fiery shades of red and auburn Ellis had never noticed before.

"What?" he said.

"If you wanted to meet me off campus like you saw me with those other guys, you could." She fanned herself with her paycheck and pushed her shoulders back.

"I don't think so," Ellis said.

"I guess that's why God gave you hands," Minnie said, giggling. "If you change your mind . . ." She tucked her paycheck in her back pocket.

"I won't," Ellis said.

"Your loss," Minnie said. "I thought you were cooler."

"I thought you were, too."

"You can't even see the scars from your stitches," she said.

"I got tan again in Arizona."

"Bye bye," she said, and she jogged back to the car, thongs slapping her heels.

He hadn't even eaten breakfast yet, and he had been kicked off crew, allowed to join again, rowed on the lake for the first time, and ended his crush on Minnie. Now he could concentrate on schoolwork—his own and Barney's—right away. He was planning on spending at least an hour each day helping Barney through the last few weeks. Barney hadn't asked, but Ellis knew it would take an hour each night, maybe even more as the algebra exam approached.

He just wished he would hear about Goat Man so he could seriously concentrate.

"I quit," Ellis said to Barney across the breakfast table. "That's it."

"You're stupid," Barney said, pouring syrup over his pancakes. "And lucky."

"Coach is cooler than I thought," Ellis said.

"He is cool."

"We have a good crew," Ellis said. "Rosenberg's a good coxswain."

"All midgets are."

"I felt a little dizzy after the workout, though," Ellis said. "Like I was still on the boat."

"That'll go away," Barney said knowingly. "It gets better the more times you're on the water. You have to watch the guy in front of you—me—and don't look at the water."

"Did I tell you about getting stuck on the Zipper? That carnival ride?"

"Is this another one of your Mexico stories?" Barney said, blotting his syrupy lips with a napkin. "Because if it is, I don't want to hear it."

"Fine," Ellis said, about to take a big bite of pancakes. He paused with the fork in front of his mouth and said, "Then I won't invite you to where I was going to invite you to."

"What?"

Ellis chewed. "Never mind," he finally said.

"What?" Barney asked. "Come on."

"No. Forget it."

"Come on," Barney pleaded.

Ellis just chewed his pancakes and grinned.

"Fine," Barney said, "then I won't tell you what Rosenberg told me about Minnie this morning before practice."

Ellis swallowed. "What?"

"You tell me first," Barney said.

"I just wanted to know if you wanted to come visit me in Telluride this summer."

"Where's that?" Barney asked.

"In Colorado. In the mountains somewhere. High elevation for training."

"That sounds cool," Barney said. "With Goat Man?"

"No," Ellis said. "Frank and Judy."

"What's Goat Man doing this summer?"

"I don't know," Ellis said. He didn't know. He wished he did know. "Same old shit. What did Rosenberg say about Minnie?"

"He swears this is true, and you can ask him in Latin if you don't believe me," Barney said. "Minnie really *is* a prostitute. Two seniors have videotapes of themselves doing her and he's seen them."

"I doubt it," Ellis said, even though he knew that a few depraved seniors might have actually made sex tapes with her, and if any freshman was privy to the tapes, it was Rosenberg.

"You doubt what?"

"I doubt she's a prostitute, and I doubt they have tapes, and I doubt Rosenberg saw them."

"Why would you doubt it?" Barney asked.

"I know her," Ellis said. "She took me to the hospital when I needed stitches."

"Who says prostitutes can't take injured people to the hospital?"

"Not all the rumors here are facts," Ellis said. "Remember how everyone said Mr. Thompson was gay, and then we find out he's married with four kids."

"I think Minnie's a slut," Barney said. "Just like the hillbilly slut that lived across the lake at Rosenberg's camp. He knows about prostitutes."

"Then how come Todd didn't tell you about her? He was here last year, and so was she," Ellis said.

"Maybe he did her, and he's embarrassed," Barney said.

That made sense to Ellis, and he didn't argue any further. He had to think about school. He took another bite of his pancakes.

Ellis and Barney fell into a comfortable routine: after they finished with crew in the afternoons, they would do algebra for an hour until dinner. Ellis was amazed at the concepts Barney didn't know, and they worked problems from all the way back in the first few chapters.

Ellis called Wendy every evening, but she hadn't heard from Goat Man. "What bills came in the mail today?" he'd ask her. She'd tell him, and he'd tell her if they needed immediate attention.

Crew and tutoring Barney every afternoon kept Ellis's mind off Goat Man for a time each day. Without Minnie to think about, Ellis knew he could finish the year strong in all his classes. He couldn't believe he was almost finished with one-fourth of high school.

• • •

After dinner, Barney walked into the room with a small box under his arm and a letter in his hand.

"What's that?" Ellis asked, pointing to the box.

"It's for you," Barney said. "You also got a letter from Frank." He tossed them both at Ellis.

The box was postmarked in El Paso, but had no return address. Ellis frantically undid the tape and brown paper, and found an ugly doll head in a Ziploc bag. On the doll's forehead, *Tucson in ten days* was scrawled in thin black marker. Ellis took the head out of the bag and stuck his fingers up inside it. Sure enough, it was there—a good amount, enough to get high a few times.

"What the hell?" Barney asked.

"It's a doll head," Ellis said.

"Who mailed it to you?"

Ellis tossed the head to Barney. "Look inside," he said.

"He finally mailed you some," Barney said, sticking his fingers in the neck hole.

"Give it back," Ellis said. "I'm putting it up here." Ellis placed the head on top of Barney's citizenship trophy. It sat nicely in the cup, only its chin was hidden behind the faux-brass brim. Ellis looked up at the doll head. One eye was closed, the other wide open, like half the doll was startled.

"You want to get high tonight?" Barney asked.

"I thought we were in training," Ellis said.

"So that pot's just going to sit there?"

"It's nice to know I have it," Ellis said.

"You should sell it."

"I have to call Wendy," Ellis said. "I'll be back in a few minutes." Ellis left the room, but stuck his head back in. "Don't touch the doll head."

FIFTY-FOUR

Goat Man germinated the seeds on damp paper towel and transferred the tiny curling sprouts to Dixie Cups of soil. He had over thirty of these cups with plants—his greenhouse was back on its way. For now, as he waited for his plants to mature, he bought his pot from a teenager named Malissa who hung out in the parking lot of a tire store on Stone Avenue. He had learned about Malissa from Jonathan the mailman.

Malissa parked her Chevy Nova in the shadow of the giant, fiberglass Paul Bunyan who towered over the intersection at Stone and Glenn and advertised the tire store. Goat Man always knew where to find her.

She scooted over to the passenger side and rolled down her window. He stood outside her car, blocking the window so no one would see what they were up to. The weed she sold had been pretty good—once it had even been sticky.

She was stone-faced, with tar-black hair and glossed lips. She wore cleavage-revealing shirts and hot pants.

"You smoke a lot," she told Goat Man.

"In a few months I won't be needing any," he said. "My plants will be ready for harvest."

"You smoke all you buy?"

"Yes," Goat Man said.

"Shit," she whispered.

"I'll need more this time," he told her. "My friend's coming back to town on Saturday." It was too hot to do anything but smoke pot, and Goat Man knew Ellis would be joining him out in the pool house on a daily basis.

"I got it." She kept the weed in a metal Care Bears lunch box. When she reached in the backseat for it, Goat Man noticed a geometry textbook and a catcher's mitt on the floor back there.

"How old are you?" Goat Man asked her.

"Fourteen." She picked through the buds with the lunch box on her lap.

"You play softball?"

"Second base."

"And you drive?"

"Yup."

"And you sell pot?"

"Duh," she said, as she stuffed fat buds into a Ziploc bag. She didn't bother weighing it. "Eighty dollars, please."

"I'm glad you play softball." Goat Man felt crummy as he handed her the cash. "Now get home and do your geometry homework."

"You're weird," Malissa said. She slid over to the driver's side after she tossed the bag at Goat Man, and started her car.

Since returning from the hell-trek and Texas, Goat Man had been driving Wendy's Volvo. His Jetta had finally died somewhere outside of Las Cruces—329,000 miles on the old car. Wendy rarely left the house, and when she did, she took Goat

Man along. Goat Man noticed that Johanna no longer visited, and Wendy stopped talking about her. He didn't ask Wendy what had happened; he was just glad she seemed finished with all the New Age spiritual crap. The photos of Frank were still up, though, and more than a few times he had caught Wendy clutching one against her chest.

"I still hate Fucker Frank," she told him once when he walked in on her. "This is just my way of controlling him." She squeezed the photo harder into her chest, standing in the square of sun pouring through the skylight in the ceiling of the kitchen.

"I see," Goat Man said, even though he didn't.

"All the photos of him remind me every hour of the day that the beast still lurks."

"Huh?" Goat Man said.

"Plus, I think he was handsome back then." She turned the photo around to Goat Man. Frank sported a dark turtleneck sweater, and had fluffy muttonchop sideburns. "I have a right to surround myself with handsome things."

"You do," Goat Man agreed. "You have every right."

"I do," she said.

Lately, she had been treading water in the pool until all hours—Goat Man once woke up and saw her out there at three A.M. She'd also started to wear clothes that looked as if they were designed for babies or old ladies: big sweatshirts with teddy bears handpainted on them, and sneakers, Keds canvas ones in pink, white, and powder blue—a few pairs with stitched-on sequins.

After parking Wendy's Volvo in the garage as quietly as possible, Goat Man tiptoed through the main house, hoping he'd make it through without Wendy seeing him. He had the bag he had just purchased from Malissa stuck inside the waist of his Levi's with his shirt tucked over it. Wendy caught him as he slid open the glass door to the pool area.

"Hi," she said. Her eyes looked sunken. She had applied too much blue eyeshadow.

"Hi," Goat Man said, stepping out. He wanted to get down to the pen, chat with Gigi and Freida, and smoke a bowl before it got too dark.

"You want to go out for burritos?" she asked. "My treat."

"Everything's your treat," Goat Man said.

"I know," she said. "So how about it?"

"Can you give me an hour?"

"No," she said. "I can't give you an hour. I'm hungry now." She stomped upstairs. "You're unreasonable!" she yelled down.

Goat Man had to stay on Wendy's good side. Jesús hadn't been very understanding when Goat Man told him what had happened to the drugs. He hadn't been very sympathetic about Lance's death, either. Since Goat Man had virtually no income, and he spent what he did have on pot, there was no way he could afford to move out of the pool house. He called upstairs to Wendy, but she didn't answer.

Earlier that week, Wendy had taken him out to lunch at El Charro. They sat inside, in a dining room decorated with old promotional calendars from the restaurant. Wendy began to bad-mouth Frank soon after the waitress took their orders. For a few minutes, Goat Man agreed, saying, "Ellis has changed quite a bit since going to Gates. He's more like Frank."

"You think so?"

"Of course," Goat Man said. "He's repeating Frank's life at Gates."

"And that Judy is such a whore. Do I want Ellis exposed to that trash? No way. And Ellis . . ."

Goat Man spaced out, no longer heard Wendy, no longer cared what she had to say about Frank or Judy. He thought about the summer with Ellis, how maybe Ellis would mellow out and be himself again. They'd hike and make road trips to Mexico, or maybe to the Grand Canyon.

Wendy grabbed Goat Man's wrist. "Have you heard anything I've said?" she asked.

"I was thinking," Goat Man said. "Sorry."

"You should be checked for attention deficit disorder," she said. "Ritalin would help you concentrate."

Now Goat Man thought about going up to Wendy's room and apologizing, but he chickened out. He didn't want to upset her further. He went outside instead.

There was a note attached to the door of the pool house:

> *Goat Man,*
> *In case you were wondering, I'm fine. You probably*
> *weren't wondering —Aubrey*
>
> *P.S. You left the greenhouse unlocked. I could have*
> *destroyed all your new plants, but I didn't. I'm a*
> *nice person.*

Real nice, Goat Man thought. He crumpled the note into a tight ball and tossed it up on the roof.

He pinched out a bowl's worth and put the remaining weed in the freezer. There'd be plenty for Ellis when he got home on Saturday. Plenty all summer. Tucson was teeming with the stuff;

there was a full-fledged price war going on—at least that's what Jonathan had said.

Goat Man wanted to find another dealer. Now that he knew Malissa was only fourteen, it made the whole prospect of buying from her depressing, and buying pot shouldn't be depressing.

At least she played softball and did her math homework.

FIFTY-FIVE

Ellis watched all the strip malls and convenience stores fly by. He hated this part of Tucson, the center of town, Speedway Boulevard. He had heard from someone that *Newsweek* deemed Speedway Boulevard the ugliest street in America. He believed it. He was glad to be in Tucson, though, glad to be sitting in his mother's Volvo with Goat Man driving. He wanted to tell Goat Man how happy he was to see him again, but even at the airport he was reluctant—maybe because neither of them had mentioned the fight they had had before Lance jumped in the arroyo. Neither of them had apologized.

"Can we stop at home before we go out there?" Ellis asked. "I want to change into shorts and drop off my luggage and say hello to Wendy."

"Sure," Goat Man said. "I just thought you'd be psyched to see your land."

"I am," Ellis said. "I've just been stuck on the plane and I feel kind of gross."

When Goat Man pulled up the gravel driveway, both he and Ellis groaned at the sight of Bennet's red Jeep, glistening in the afternoon sun.

"I thought he was gone," Ellis said.

Mark Jude Poirier

"Me, too," Goat Man said. "I'll wait in the car while you run in."

"You sure you can't help me with my bags?"

"I will later," Goat Man said, "when we get back from look-ing at your land. I don't want to see Bennet. Hurry up."

Ellis took one of his bags from the back seat and went inside. Goat Man turned up the air conditioner and the stereo. He closed his eyes, letting the cool air and the music rush over him. It was one of Ellis's ska CDs, Bim-Skala-Bim: ". . . down at Jah Laundromat today . . ."

A few minutes later, he was startled by a pounding on the windshield. It was Bennet, and he was yelling something.

He lowered the volume and opened the window.

"I'm glad you're here," Bennet said. "I have a few things I'd like to discuss."

"Sorry," Goat Man said, "not interested."

Bennet reached inside the car and grabbed the collar of Goat Man's T-shirt. "I could break your fucking neck," he said, lean-ing into Goat Man's face. "And no one would care."

"I would," Goat Man said.

Bennet pulled Goat Man's collar tighter, making it hard for Goat Man to breathe.

"I see you're driving her car now," Bennet said. "Must be nice, you fucking leech."

"Let go," Goat Man rasped. He grabbed Bennet's wrist and pulled, but Bennet didn't let up. When he tried to move across the stick shift to the passenger seat, Bennet gripped his throat directly and squeezed hard. With his right hand, Goat Man felt for the window button and pressed it to go up. It stopped and hummed loudly when it hit Bennet's arm. Bennet laughed.

When Ellis came out of the house and saw what was happening, he picked up a rock from the landscaping and yelled at Bennet: "Let go of him or I'll smash your windshield!"

Bennet released Goat Man and turned to Ellis. "If you so much as touch my car, I'll kick your ass," he said.

"Just leave," Ellis said. "Wendy doesn't want you here. No one wants you here."

"You're all fucking crazy anyway," Bennet said. Then he jumped in his Jeep and sped down the driveway, kicking up dust and gravel.

Ellis looked over his plot of land. It was picturesque, dense with saguaros and reddish rocks, three acres tucked between two adobe homes and bordering National Forest land in the Catalina Mountains. Goat Man noticed there were no washes running through the plot, which meant he couldn't grow anything out there, but he thought it was beautiful anyway. He had helped Wendy pick it out while Ellis was still back at Gates taking his final exams. At the time, desert wildflowers in brilliant bursts of orange and yellow dotted the land. Goat Man and Wendy had spent a week riding around with real-estate agents, none of whom could understand why anyone would want a prime piece of property just to let it sit there.

Wendy had been too tired to go to the airport and too tired to come out and see the land with Ellis—just hours before Ellis's flight was to arrive, she had told Goat Man that she had chronic fatigue syndrome. She was sure of it. She had read an article about it in *Cosmopolitan* that morning, and she had every symptom it mentioned: swollen glands, hair loss, lethargy . . .

"I'm sure the doctors will know what to do, and you'll be your old self again in no time," Goat Man told her.

"There's nothing they can do!" she yelled. "There's absolutely nothing they can do!" Her lips quivered.

"Get some rest," he told her. "I'll fetch Ellis at the airport."

"Thank you, Javier. I do appreciate all your help, I really do," she said, and then she yawned.

"I appreciate all your help. You took good care of Gigi and Freida while I was away." She *had* taken good care of the goats, even milked Freida enough to keep her lactating. The pen had been raked of turds before Goat Man returned, and the goats looked well fed and content.

"Want to go to the swapmeet later with Ellis?" she asked hopefully.

"Maybe," Goat Man said. "If Ellis wants to."

Now he looked over the land with Ellis, hoping Ellis would approve of it. "They'll never be a 7-Eleven out here," Goat Man said.

"This is perfect," Ellis said. "Sometimes I forget how cool Wendy can be."

"I helped pick it out."

"Thanks, Goat Man," Ellis said.

"The house on your right is owned by a surgeon, and the house on your left is owned by Canadians who are only there four weeks out of the year," Goat Man said. "Nothing more will ever be built here unless the Forest Service sells some of their land."

"It even smells good out here," Ellis said, inhaling deeply.

Goat Man pulled his pipe from his jeans pocket and shook

the burnt crud out of the bowl. He packed it with fresh stuff and held it out to Ellis.

"No, thanks," Ellis said.

"We have plenty. We don't have to ration. Jonathan set me up. We have as much as we want all summer."

"I was thinking of maybe going to Telluride with Frank and Judy this summer," Ellis said, looking down at his feet. "They'll be here to pick me up in a few weeks."

Goat Man watched a small wren perch on the top of a saguaro and peck at a rotten flower. The bird found something tasty in the remains of the blossom. It dug around frantically, shaking its rear feathers.

"You should go," Goat Man told Ellis. "That'll be good for you." He packed the bowl with his thumb and lit it up.

That's not what you're supposed to say, Ellis thought.